THE FIRST RULE OF SWIMMING

ALSO BY COURTNEY ANGELA BRKIC

Stillness: And Other Stories
The Stone Fields

THE
FIRST RULE
OF SWIMMING

A Novel

COURTNEY ANGELA BRKIC

Little, Brown and Company

New York   Boston   London

Copyright © 2013 by Courtney Angela Brkic

Little, Brown and Company
Hachette Book Group
237 Park Avenue, New York, NY 10017
littlebrown.com

First Edition: May 2013

Little, Brown and Company is a division of Hachette Book Group, Inc. The Little, Brown name and logo are trademarks of Hachette Book Group, Inc.

The publisher is not responsible for websites (or their content) that are not owned by the publisher.

The Hachette Speakers Bureau provides a wide range of authors for speaking events. To find out more, go to hachettespeakersbureau.com or call (866) 376-6591.

ISBN 978-0-316-21738-5
Library of Congress Control Number 2013931144

10 9 8 7 6 5 4 3 2 1

RRD-C

Printed in the United States of America

For Oliver and Phil

Stay. The sun in foreign skies
will not warm you as this one does.
Mouthfuls of bread are bitter there,
where you are alone and without your brothers.
                    —*Aleksa Šantić*

THE FIRST RULE OF SWIMMING

PROLOGUE

Rosmarina Island, 1982

The letter was written in a girlish hand, the purple letters drifting across the sky blue background of the stationery. It had
been folded twice, and at the bottom, beside the picture of a rainbow, the sender had written both the Croatian and American
versions of her name—*Katarina/Katherine*—as if to make sure
that her younger cousin would not confuse her with another. Or
to demonstrate, from the very outset of their correspondence, the
advantage of being two people instead of one.

Magdalena had never seen handwriting like her cousin's. In the
island school, pupils were instructed to make their letters slant to
the right, not fill the page like soap bubbles. There was something
foreign about the rainbow stationery, as well, and the way it had
been engraved with her cousin's American name and Pittsburgh
address. Although Magdalena was only eight, she immediately dis-
trusted the feminine loops, the tiny hearts that dotted every *i* and *j*.

The envelope, in a matching shade of blue, had appeared in
their mailbox that morning, covered with foreign stamps. It had
been clumsily opened and resealed, and a fingerprint too large for
a ten-year-old girl's had been left in the yellow glue, prompting
Magdalena's grandfather to set his mouth in a worried line.

"They'll open anything," she overheard him tell her grandmother. "Even a child's letter."

It was a surprise to learn that the envelope was addressed to her. Not to her grandparents, nor to her younger sister, Jadranka. It was addressed to Magdalena Babić of Rosmarina Island, and it was the first time that she had received any letter, let alone one from so far away.

I am your cousin! it proclaimed, even as Jadranka whined to be allowed to read it as well. *Do you remember me?*

In fact, Magdalena could recall nothing at all about the older girl with the light brown hair, the one who had cast her arm around Magdalena's shoulder in the photograph that sat in her grandmother's vitrine. Katarina's family had left when Magdalena was only two, a shadowy period that she tried hard to recall. But she was never sure if the faces she sometimes pictured were real or simply her imagination.

"You cried for days after she left," her grandmother told her.

You used to carry a little stuffed lamb, the letter informed her.

It was unsettling to be told these things. To have a virtual stranger remember her before she could remember herself, and she turned the letter over to her grandfather without a word.

He read it intently, like a man decoding a foreign alphabet, and when he looked up, his expression was bemused. "Six years of silence and all we hear about is cats," he told Magdalena in a tone approaching wonder. "But not a word about your uncle."

Marin Morić, his only son, had left the island with Katarina's family, and Magdalena imagined the four of them living together in America today.

But when Magdalena's grandfather explained that Katarina's mother was his younger sister—which made the letter writer his niece—Magdalena frowned. "Does that make Katarina my aunt?" she wanted to know, prompting a laugh from her grandfather, who saw that she was displeased by such generational superiority.

"No," he assured her. "More like your cousin once removed."

The family tree did not particularly interest Magdalena. "Why did they go away?" she demanded instead. It was a question that had not previously occurred to her.

His eyes dropped to the letter as if it contained the answer to her question. *I am in the fourth grade,* her cousin had written in stilted Croatian. *We go to the Church of St. Nicholas. My parents own a tailoring shop.*

It was only then that Magdalena heard her grandmother, furiously scrubbing something at the kitchen sink. Her grandfather, too, seemed to grow aware of the sound in that moment, and he looked past Magdalena to study his wife's hunched back. "They couldn't live here anymore," he answered shortly. "Especially your uncle."

Magdalena had not yet reached the age of fitting such puzzle pieces together, although she understood that her grandparents avoided certain people in the village—*informers,* her grandmother sometimes said in a venomous whisper. But she could not fathom why anybody would want to leave Rosmarina.

She was about to ask more on the matter when he put up his hand, telling her more gruffly than was his custom, "Take your sister outside to play."

At her grandparents' encouragement, she wrote back to her cousin. She told her about the island school, how she and Jadranka went swimming when the weather was warm. She told her about their dog—the way Roki churned her legs in sleep as if she were running—and playing in the abandoned houses beneath the Peak. She knew that Katarina's father had also been a fisherman, and so she asked what kind of boat he had in America.

For Valentine's Day, Katarina sent her response on a construction paper heart. This envelope, too, had been opened and resealed, and her grandfather turned it over in his weathered hands. A pink heart had been glued to a larger red heart, and he carefully peeled the two apart. But his face fell when he found nothing inside. "I thought there might be something else," he told her with a sheepish smile.

The idea of a secret message intrigued Magdalena, and she studied the two hearts, attempting to decipher a pattern in the dried glue. There were two dots and a curve, but these merely formed a smiling face.

"Why doesn't my uncle write to us?" she demanded.

"Writing would just cause trouble," her grandfather told her. "It's different with your cousin because she's a child."

Magdalena did not understand the nature of this trouble, and in truth, her uncle was just another photograph to her. A one-dimensional young man, he stood on the top shelf of her grandmother's vitrine. Since her correspondence with Katarina, even her American cousin had taken on more life than that smiling man. Katarina's favorite color was purple and she rode a silver bike, but Magdalena's uncle remained as remote and unknowable as the faces that appeared on postal stamps.

Still, it seemed strange for her cousin not to mention him. "Maybe he's a tailor like Katarina's father," Magdalena suggested.

Her grandfather blinked hard at this. "Perhaps," he told her.

For several days Magdalena considered the matter, deciding finally that it was unfair for her American cousin to have both her own father as well as Magdalena's uncle. "My uncle should come back for a visit," she suggested hopefully. Her mother, after all, worked in Split but came back to the island once or twice a year.

"No," her grandfather told her. "There's nothing left for him here."

Magdalena was stung by this observation, but she forgot it with his next words: "Your mother considered taking you and going with them. But she decided against it in the end."

This news shocked Magdalena, and for an instant she allowed herself to imagine a world without Rosmarina, without the fruit from her fig trees or the fish from her shallows. The island was as much a part of her as her name or her straight, black hair, but she pictured herself living in Pittsburgh and riding a silver bike like Katarina. The last detail had made her envious, an emotion that now seemed traitorous. "I'm glad," she told him so forcefully that he smiled.

"I'm glad, too," he told her, although there was something strange about the way he said this.

The next day he told Magdalena to buy two postcards in the harbor, from one of the tourist stands along the *riva*. "Pick nice pictures," he told her. "But make sure that the postcards are exactly the same size."

She chose a picture of the Devil's Stones and another of an old woman tending her goats. The woman's face was so wrinkled that the lines appeared like cuts in her face, but the wiry goats reminded Magdalena of the stuffed lamb her cousin had mentioned, a toy that Jadranka had inherited and would not relinquish, although it had lost both eyes.

Her grandfather studied the postcards and finally handed the goats to Magdalena. "Write a message to your cousin," he told her, touching the top of her head with his hand. "Tell her about the last time we went fishing."

She was happy with this idea. But when she finished describing the way her grandfather had let her navigate all the way back to Rosmarina, she looked up to find that he was writing his own message on the second postcard. In light, penciled strokes, he filled the entire card, and only after he read through his words did he look up.

"We'll send our own secret message," he said.

He found some glue in a kitchen drawer, dotted the substance around the edges of his postcard, and placed his granddaughter's neatly on top.

For a moment Magdalena was disappointed that the goats had been covered up, but then she realized that it was not the picture her grandfather wanted to hide, but his message. "How will they know?" she asked.

"They'll know," he told her. He tested the edge with his fingernail and seemed satisfied when the two cards stayed together. "Let's just hope that nobody else does."

Magdalena did not know who these letter openers were. They read other people's mail before sending it along, days or weeks later, and did not bother to cover up evidence of their trespass: a coffee ring or underlined word had been known to decorate the letter inside. She understood that her grandparents found such behavior shameful but that they saw no point in going to the police.

"They already know, Lena," her grandfather had tried to explain.

He warned her not to mention the postcards to anybody else, and she understood that it had something to do with politics, just like her cousin's departure from the island and the reason her uncle could not come back. Just like the neighbor whose son had been sentenced to hard labor because some anonymous snitch overheard him complaining to tourists on the beach about the way things were. But she did not stop to wonder if there would be any consequences to their secret message, even when her grandfather returned white-lipped from the port one evening.

"I hear your American niece rides a silver bicycle," a man he did not recognize had told him at a newspaper kiosk on the *riva*.

But he did not think that they had discovered the secret message. "If they had, we'd know it," she heard him tell her grandmother.

Magdalena knew that they had all been questioned following

her uncle's escape: her grandfather, her grandmother. The police had kept her mother for several nights.

"What did they ask her?" she wanted to know when she learned this detail.

But her grandfather claimed that her mother never spoke about it.

Months went by without a response from Katarina. When summer came, her grandfather told her glumly, "Best not to get our hopes up, Lena. It's possible that they just threw the postcard away."

Magdalena knew that he did not mean her cousin's family. She imagined the missive, carefully glued to conceal its true purpose, in a trash can somewhere. But she could not truly see it covered with cigarette ashes or somebody's half-eaten lunch, and so each time she ended by imagining it flying across the Atlantic Ocean, an arrow fired with such expert precision that it was certain to find its mark in America.

She saw her mother infrequently, awkward occasions that were like visits from a stranger, and her own father had drowned at the age of twenty-seven. And so she plunged down the only avenue of fantasy that was available to her. She imagined her uncle prying the postcards apart, and how he would see her grandfather's message and devise an equally ingenious method of response. All that summer Magdalena pictured what this might be: words written in invisible ink, a coded message, perhaps something as simple as a picture. She had asked Katarina to include a photograph in her next letter, and she imagined that it would show the two of them, perhaps riding bicycles together. She pushed back jealousy at this thought.

She knew that her uncle had fished often with her father, and that he had been her own godfather. She had seen the family photographs to prove it: Marin smiling in his suit, herself a tiny baby. She daydreamed about his return to the island, despite her grandfather's warning. Perhaps just for a visit, bringing American chocolates, going fishing with them and taking them for walks along the *riva,* the same way that some of her schoolmates' fathers did. She spent long moments studying the photograph in her grandmother's vitrine, and with time her uncle's face took on the dimensions of an actual, living person. She imagined that his skin was still the same nut brown, his arms as wiry as the ones that had pulled fishing nets from Rosmarina's waters.

She longed to ask her mother about him. But Ana Babić arrived for her weeklong visit to the island in an even worse mood than usual. "Look at those fingernails," she muttered within moments of disembarking from the ferry, grabbing one of Magdalena's hands, so that her daughter merely counted the hours until her departure again.

All that summer, when she was not fishing with her grandfather, Magdalena prowled the deserted hamlets below the Peak. The houses there had stood empty for years. The first waves of emigration had taken place before her grandfather's birth, and the descendants of the houses' former inhabitants had their own lives as storekeepers or secretaries in faraway places like Canada and Chile. But although her grandfather cautioned her periodically about crumbling walls and falling roof tiles, she moved among the ruins like a cat.

Hardly anyone lived beneath the Peak anymore, and Magdalena liked the loneliness of those stone houses. They were ideal for games of hide-and-seek, and she often took along Jadranka, who was four years younger. She liked to stand on the stone porches and look out towards the sea as Jadranka played behind her.

Her grandfather had once shown her the house where his own mother had been born, the stark stone building with its caved-in roof and the small carob tree that had sprouted between two slabs of stone. She liked running her hand across the hewn limestone, the occasional carving or Latin inscription like some magical braille.

Luka Morić often pined for the island of his youth, when more of the houses had been occupied and every plot of arable land provided an abundance of fruit and olives. But his granddaughter had no way of imagining it; the houses had been empty for as long as she could remember them, and besides, she liked the way the wind made strange moaning sounds in their rooms.

She got so far with fantasies of her uncle's arrival that she prepared a place for him on the Peak. The house she chose was her favorite. Its roof was still intact, and although the second floor had collapsed, it had a tiny balcony above the front door, a rare flourish in a section of the island where structures were built for durability. Its positioning made it impervious to the worst winds, and even on days when a *bura* blew—when climbing the hill was difficult and their grandfather believed she and Jadranka were playing with other village children—the house offered shelter.

They began by carrying out the rubble, each day adding to a growing pile. She improvised a broom by tying together several branches from the carob tree and, once, tried to light a fire in the hearth, but smoke poured into the room, forcing them outside until the small pile of tinder extinguished itself.

"The chimney must be blocked," she told Jadranka, feeling foolish.

Their grandparents were preoccupied that summer. The country's president had died two years before, and the island, like everywhere else, had been gripped by uncertainty. Their grandfather watched the news obsessively each night and pored over issues of *Free Dalmatia* as if they, too, carried some coded message about the future.

Although their grandmother chided them when they returned with torn and dirty clothing, their hair filled with grit from the crumbling house, she rarely asked where they had been. Once a week, she placed them side by side in a hot bath, rubbing their scalps with her strong fingers, toweling them dry afterwards with such vigor that it made their ears ring.

"Why are you and *Dida* sad?" Jadranka asked her once in the middle of these maneuvers, prompting the older woman to hug both girls, soaking wet, to her chest.

"We're not sad," she told them, lifting the younger girl onto the bath towel. "We're just old, your grandfather and me. And we've been disappointed by the world before."

Magdalena did not understand the nature of that disappointment, nor whether those words had anything to do with their uncle, or Comrade Tito, whom her grandmother regarded with distaste, but also a certain grudging respect. Or with something else entirely. But towards the end of the summer, a familiar blue envelope appeared in their postbox.

Dear Magdalena, her cousin had written. *I am sorry that it has ben so long since my last letter. I liked the postcards of Rosmarina, especially the woman with the goats.*

Magdalena felt her heart lurch, remembering that it had been covered by the postcard of the Devil's Stones.

You asked about my cat, Marvin. I have sad news. He wandered off some time ago, and he has never come home since. We don't know what happened to him, whether a car got him or if he found another home. It's been a long time now.

Magdalena stared at these words over her grandfather's shoulder. "I thought her cat's name was Lola," she said.

But she realized her mistake when her grandfather bent forward over the table like a man in physical pain: there was no cat named Marvin. Only an uncle who had disappeared somewhere down the rabbit hole of America.

A small white rectangle had fallen out of the envelope onto the kitchen table, and she picked it up to find a picture of her grinning cousin. Light brown hair was feathered back from a heart-shaped face, and she wore braces, but her eyes were small and hard. Piggy eyes, Magdalena decided suddenly, hating this cousin who had lost her uncle.

She ran from the house, not even waiting for her sister, who was playing in the courtyard and called after her. She ran so that her sandals slapped the street with whiplike sounds, and did not stop even when she reached the dirt road that ascended the Peak. The town fell away behind her, and she had the sensation, for a moment, that she was flying, her feet nothing but motion and dust. Evening was falling, and somewhere far below her a man called out a name that was not hers, nor her sister's. The sound made her run faster, upward through the fallow olive groves to where the abandoned houses sat upon the hill.

PART I

CHAPTER 1

Although it had been over sixty years since the occupation—and more than four thousand miles separated her from Rosmarina—*Nona* Vinka was convinced that the reprisal would take place that afternoon. A few unlucky souls would be rounded up in the village and taken to the Devil's Stones, just beyond Rosmarina's harbor. The distant crack of gunshots would break the hushed silence of the *riva,* and then those same rowboats would return without their cargo, the oarsmen unable to meet the eyes of the few who waited there. This was why she had ordered her American grandson to hide beneath her bed.

She sat above him, so tiny that the mattress did not sag beneath her weight and her feet barely touched the floor. She was crocheting something, a cream-colored length that grew steadily in her hands as Jadranka observed her from the doorway. On the television across the room, a woman with very white teeth was advertising something: a bar of American soap, perhaps, or breakfast cereal. But there was no sound, and the set seemed to function solely as a source of light. Its flickering caught the darting of the crochet hook as it passed in and out of the wool.

At six, Christopher was still willing to humor his grandmother in a way his older sister, Tabitha, would not. He had wedged himself obligingly beneath the bed and grinned at Jadranka from between *Nona* Vinka's slippered feet.

"Is it fascists or communists this time?" Jadranka asked him, noting that the older woman did not look up at these English words.

"Fascists," he told her, although he appeared uncertain. In recent months, his grandmother had regressed into a dialect so thick that he needed his adult cousin to translate. Nonetheless, he understood the insistence of her hands, the way she lifted the coverlet and motioned him into that hiding place, her voice entreating him to be silent.

Nona Vinka had lived in America since 1977. By all accounts, she used to speak English, something even Christopher's sister remembered. "Da veels on da bus go round and round," Tabitha would sometimes sing, but the blank expression on the older woman's face made it clear that she never understood this joke.

Jadranka wondered if the English words were simply gone, or trapped beneath sludge so thick that they only sometimes made it to the surface. "Apples," the older woman had surprised them all by saying last week, then proceeded to laugh uproariously at this word. But when Jadranka cut up an apple, removing the skin so that it did not get stuck in *Nona* Vinka's dentures, she merely looked perplexed.

She spent most of her time conversing with her dead sisters, unable to grasp that she and Luka were the last of their siblings to remain. And when Jadranka tried to explain that even her grandfather had suffered a stroke the year before, the older woman only nodded sagely. "Have you seen my brother?" she asked a moment later. "It's getting dark."

But while Luka lay insensate on Rosmarina, *Nona* Vinka had become an adroit time traveler. In one moment she was off to tend the goats, and in the next UDBA assassins were lying in wait for her husband in the bushes outside their house.

It always took Jadranka a moment to catch on to her role; sometimes she was one of Vinka's sisters, sometimes a childhood friend from the island. It was easier to play along, even as she was observed by those sharp, black eyes but never really seen.

But today it was clear that the older woman was more terrified than nostalgic, that she had averted her eyes from the figure lurking in the doorway. And so Jadranka walked slowly into the bedroom and sat beside her on the bed. "What are you making?" she asked softly in the island's dialect.

The crochet hook stopped in midair. "It's for the baby," Vinka said, holding up the rectangular length for Jadranka's inspection.

For this anonymous baby, she crocheted day and night. Blankets, booties, caps: she turned out more woolens than a factory, garments that filled brown paper bags and which her daughter donated to charity.

Jadranka knew nothing about crocheting—had not been patient enough to learn something as simple as sewing on a button, though her grandmother had attempted to teach her several times—but she admired her great-aunt's even stitching aloud. "That's very pretty," she told her.

The hook began to move again, and Jadranka watched it go in, then out. Beneath the bed, Christopher was so quiet that Jadranka suspected he had fallen asleep. She thought that she could feel his even breath on her ankles.

After a moment of silence, *Nona* Vinka shifted beside her on the bed. "Are they gone?" she whispered, her eyes once again avoiding the doorway.

Jadranka studied that empty space. "They left hours ago," she assured her.

Jadranka had arrived in New York in January, when the weather was so raw that her cousin immediately took her shopping for a new winter coat.

"I have a coat," Jadranka protested.

But Katarina only looked skeptically at the three-year-old pea-coat Jadranka had brought with her. "That will let the wind go right through you," she said, browsing the coat racks in Saks Fifth Avenue. "And the stuff they make over there is shitty quality."

She selected a down-filled coat that reached past Jadranka's knees, then tied the belt so tightly that it forced the breath from her lungs. When she turned Jadranka to face the store's mirror, the reflection's red hair was startling against the charcoal color of the coat. "You're not on a small island anymore," Katarina told her softly, resting her chin on the younger woman's shoulder.

Jadranka was tempted to point out that she had bought the pea-coat in Italy and that winters were cold even on Adriatic islands, but she had already realized that it was useless. In Katarina's mind they were all trapped in amber on Rosmarina, a place she knew as much from her parents' descriptions as from a single childhood trip in 1984.

The cousins had not seen each other in more than twenty years, although they continued to exchange letters. Jadranka and Magdalena had taken turns answering this older American cousin whose details of slumber parties and ice-skating classes were as remote to them as life on Mars.

Last year, it was that distant correspondent who boldly suggested that Jadranka come to America. *It will be good for everyone involved,* Katarina had written, their exchange of letters having outlasted communism. *You've always wanted to travel and this way the children can practice their Croatian which, I warn you, is terrible.*

This was not false modesty, Jadranka discovered upon arrival. Christopher and Tabitha paid no attention to tense or case. They drawled through vowels and swallowed the ends of all their sentences. It clearly bothered their mother, but their father was an American who understood next to nothing of his wife's native tongue, and so they had grown up primarily in English.

Jadranka did not point out that Katarina's Croatian was also rusty. Her family had emigrated before her fifth birthday, and today there was an antiquated quality to the way she spoke, her vocabulary trapped in the time warp of her parents' generation. *She speaks like someone's grandma,* Jadranka told her sister in a letter, feeling guilty as she wrote the words because it was clear that their cousin felt cheated of the island.

"It was easier for you and your sister," Katarina had told her, not long after her arrival. "At least you knew your places in the world."

But it was precisely because Jadranka was not sure of her place in the world that she had agreed to come. Most other women of twenty-seven—at least the ones she knew on Rosmarina—were wives and mothers. They cut recipes from the pages of magazines and were already making costumes for school pageants. While such domesticity left her cold, Jadranka could not escape the feeling that she was missing something. She did nothing more than drift from one job to the next, alternately typing letters or putting dresses on mannequins, sometimes on Rosmarina, but more frequently on the mainland, where she had grown accustomed to her anonymity. Most of her possessions—except for her paintings— could be packed into a few cardboard boxes, and she had never felt the slightest inclination to get married.

The problem, as she saw it, was that nobody had yet demonstrated a viable alternative for how to live. Her grandmother, though happy in her marriage of many decades, belonged to a generation as different from Jadranka's as the earth is from the sky. She lived only to cook and feed her flock. To mend. To clean. To tend her garden. By contrast, Jadranka's mother considered herself a modern woman. But she had been miserable since her second husband abandoned her, and she would sometimes inform Jadranka that a woman without a man was nothing. "What's wrong with you and your sister?" she would demand. "It's not natural to be alone."

Even Magdalena had settled down, in her own fashion. She had adopted a tight schoolteacher chignon and the crisp blouses that Jadranka considered evidence of her capitulation. She slept in the same whitewashed room on Rosmarina that the sisters had once shared, a room that Jadranka found so far removed from reality that it was like entering the set of a film being shot about their childhood.

"I don't know how your sister stays sane living there," Katarina had commented. "Of all people, I expected her to have larger ambitions."

This had annoyed Jadranka, for while she agreed in sentiment, she did not consider her American cousin equipped to understand Magdalena's choices. Katarina, who had married a rich man and whose maid vacuumed their home with a special machine as efficient as it was noiseless.

Katarina's ambitions, on the other hand, were on full display: in her understated designer clothing and expertly cut hair, in the collection of blue glass in her living room and the brocade chairs that, she had twice explained, were upholstered with silk from Assam silkworms, the best and most industrious in the world.

"You're more like me," she had told Jadranka drunkenly one night, at an opening in her gallery where amorphous sculptures copulated on various surfaces. "You understand that life is short."

The ephemeral nature of life had not been the reason for Jadranka's trip to America, however. Nor ambition, nor the limbo of home, although it was true that in the months before her departure she had started to feel like a fish that merely traveled the circumference of its bowl. It was the picture of the empty room that her cousin sent, the bait dangling at the end of Katarina's hook. No more than ten paces across, it had one window and a wooden floor whose scars Jadranka could make out even in the grainy photograph. It resembled nothing so much as a prison cell, but it took Jadranka's breath away.

It's empty, Katarina had written to her. *We've only ever used it for storage, but it would make a perfect studio. You'd have plenty of time to do your work. And I can help arrange the visa and pay for your ticket.*

When Jadranka relayed this information to Magdalena, her sister was surprised. "If that's what you want, we can find something on the island," she protested. "Why would you go all the way to America for that?"

Jadranka could already see the wheels in her sister's head turning, planning to empty one of the rooms at their fishing camp, perhaps, or to find her a room somewhere in the village. "No," she told her shortly.

Their cousin's Manhattan brownstone was large and beautifully furnished, with slate showers and a gigantic stainless steel refrigerator. Paintings by well-known New York artists hung on the walls, and everywhere were silky Persian rugs so large that if they were to rise like the carpet in the story of Aladdin, they would be capable of transporting multitudes. But it was the tiny third-floor studio that was Jadranka's favorite room, its rough wooden planks now spattered with paint. Blue dots like electric lights extended in a line, and she had tracked crimson footprints into all the room's corners like the scene of a crime. She went there whenever she could: when the children were in school or in summer camp, or after Katarina and her husband returned in the evenings. Each time she closed the door behind her, she experienced the same weightlessness at being alone.

Only someone who had spent a lifetime sharing rooms with other people would be capable of understanding it. Not Katarina, who had grown up an only child. Not Tabitha or Christopher, who slept in separate rooms and whose conjoined play area was outfitted with duplicates of everything: bookshelves, beanbags, art supplies so luxurious that they made Jadranka, a grown woman, envious.

Since Jadranka's birth, there had always been another person present as she drifted off to sleep: her sister, assorted boyfriends, roommates too numerous to count. Before coming to America, she had been staying with their mother in her one-room apartment in Split, an experiment Magdalena predicted would end in disaster.

A chain-smoker and world-class snorer, their mother snooped during Jadranka's absences, sometimes resurrecting items indignantly from the garbage. "There's nothing wrong with this," she would say, waving an old nail file or battered shoe when Jadranka returned. Her mother, who professed to find privacy a perplexing notion of the young but who—Jadranka had special reason to know—guarded her own secrets with the ferocity of an attack dog.

Best of all, Katarina had given her a key for the room, and the space was hers alone.

Katarina had her own studio on the house's first floor, although she seldom went there. She had shown it to Jadranka once: a large, airy room with floor-to-ceiling windows that let in radiant light. Chrome lamps hung from the ceiling, and there was a large table of dark wood whose surface was entirely unmarked. It looked, Jadranka had thought in awe, like something from the pages of a magazine.

Christopher was less fascinated with his mother's studio than with Jadranka's narrow, locked room. He thought that something mysterious transpired there, although she had explained about the painting. He did not understand why she could not draw with them at the special table that existed in their play area for just such a purpose. He liked when she sketched his portrait and thought that she must be doing more of the same in that locked room. "Why can't we watch?" he wanted to know, because he loved this magic trick of making figures rise from the page.

Nona Vinka thought the room was her mother's larder, that her father had locked it to keep his children out. "I'm so hungry," she told Jadranka in a plaintive voice when Jadranka emerged one night to find her great-aunt standing naked in the hallway. "Can't I have a piece of bread?"

Jadranka allowed herself to slip in and out of Vinka's world because she could not see the harm in it. Katarina, she had noticed, was more squeamish. "That was years ago, Mama," she would insist, only to have Vinka look at her as if she had just announced an invasion of talking locusts.

Jadranka did the same with Christopher, after all, alternately playing ogre, space alien, and princess. It was not such a stretch to play Vinka's mother, to smuggle her a crust of bread.

But tonight *Nona* Vinka was fully dressed and crocheting furiously. Christopher was fast asleep beneath the bed, just as Jadranka had suspected, and so she pulled him out and carried him to his own room. He protested for a moment but then dropped off again, his mouth half open. His bedroom resembled the clutter of a toy store, and she left him dreaming in the middle of stuffed bears and dolphins.

She had left the door to *Nona* Vinka's room ajar, and although she wanted nothing more than to go to her studio, she watched the flickering light from the television. No sound came from within, but she knew that she should at least close the door. That, otherwise, the old woman would sit there in rigid terror all night, believing the hallway filled with ghosts.

But this time when Jadranka stood in the doorway, *Nona* Vinka regarded her with a wan smile. "Hello, dear," she said. "I can't seem to find my cigarettes."

These lucid moments no longer surprised Jadranka. She had always thought of dementia as a permanent destination, but now she understood that her great-aunt made the occasional return flight.

Katarina did not like anyone to smoke inside the house—least of all her mother—but Jadranka did not have the heart to refuse her. She crossed the room to open *Nona* Vinka's window and lit one of her own. When she handed it over, careful that none of the ash landed in the bed, her aunt drew on it and smiled.

"And my spectacles?"

The glasses were on the bureau, folded neatly atop a Croatian Bible whose gold lettering was so faded that Jadranka could see the grain of the leather underneath. "Bring the album, as well," Vinka said as the younger woman picked them up.

Jadranka sighed. In the past few weeks, she had been working on a series of paintings about her childhood. All day they had been calling out to her like babies standing up in their cribs, demanding food.

But her great-aunt's voice quivered, and Jadranka realized that the older woman was lonely. In moments like these, she always wanted Jadranka to describe what the *riva* looked like today, or asked if one could still rest in the shade of the carob trees, halfway to the Peak. And so, sensing her yearning for this geography, Jadranka pulled the album from the bookshelf and sat beside her on the bed.

There were pictures of the Pittsburgh house where Katarina had grown up, with its aluminum siding and its straggling lawn, and of her First Communion. There were *tamburitza* troupes and church picnics, and the tailor shop that Katarina's father had opened, a modest business whose interior appeared gloomy in photographs, although he smiled from ear to ear.

But *Nona* Vinka was looking for pictures of the island. These photographs numbered far fewer, as the family had not been able to take many when they fled. There was the stone house on Rosmarina, and a feast day procession led by a somber priest Jadranka did not recognize. There were pictures of Vinka's siblings, and Jadranka felt her eyes burn unexpectedly at the sight of her own grandfather sitting in his boat, restored to health on paper, the sun directly overhead, so that there were no shadows on his face.

"My only brother, Luka," Vinka said with a smile, pointing to the photograph. "Just wait until you meet him."

Jadranka nodded. Her great-aunt was fading again. In five minutes the fascists would be back at the door and there would be another reprisal. Or UDBA's secret agents and their minions would fill the hallway.

"He takes all the beatings," Vinka whispered, her finger hovering above Luka's face. "He does it to protect the rest of us."

Jadranka swallowed. She wondered if this was what growing old meant for everyone: a variation of the same grotesque film, the scenes cobbled together from the bleakest moments of any given life. She found the idea unbearable.

Vinka had brighter moments, of course. Days when the olive trees were in bloom, and the afternoon of her wedding feast. But tonight she was on Rosmarina, and the Italian soldiers had eaten all the village cats. "Every last one," she insisted with the sudden tears of an adolescent girl, for she loved to stroke their silken fur. "They roast them with potatoes."

You're safely in America, Jadranka was tempted to tell her in a soothing voice. But she knew that *Nona* Vinka would only wave her impatiently away.

Jadranka had heard most of her great-aunt's stories before. Prisons and plots and they were fleeing, fleeing through the night, and little Katarina was weeping for the toys she had left behind. There was one doll, in particular, but Vinka would not let her bring it because Katarina already carried a stuffed bear, and they were pretending to leave for just the afternoon.

"Be a good, brave girl," Vinka told her, squeezing her hand. "Don't make a fuss."

Jadranka closed her eyes and thought of the studio's four walls, the empty canvases that awaited their baptisms of color. The last time Vinka had been like this she revealed that she had given birth to two dead children before Katarina. Tonight there were the Italian soldiers, and then, so faintly that Jadranka was not sure she had heard the words correctly, the red-haired baby.

The last was a new subject for her great-aunt, and Jadranka opened her eyes in surprise.

The red-haired baby, Vinka told her, moving her hand up to Jadranka's elbow. She shook it as if for emphasis, or as if the young woman beside her would deny it. This bastard child who unraveled the entire world.

CHAPTER 2

On the day that Magdalena learned of her sister's disappearance, lightning struck Rosmarina. Two water-bombing airplanes appeared in the sky as she was dismissing school, and her students raced to the classroom windows, shouting in excitement. She stood behind them and watched the planes approach like apocalyptic horsemen. It was clear that a wildfire had started on the remote western part of the island, but instead of rising in a vertical line, the smoke moved in billows across the sky. Even from that distance, Magdalena could tell that the fire was spreading.

She was not a superstitious woman. She did not, for instance, believe that dreaming of spoons brought good luck to the dreamer or that cracked glass foretold disaster. She was amused by the idea that women of childbearing age should sit along the straight edges of tables lest the corners render them infertile. But even she acknowledged that a warm southern wind could make men temporarily insane, or predicted the arrival of bad news, although in those moments she was not thinking of her sister.

The fires themselves started earlier every year, whether from lightning strikes or human mischief. Some claimed that global warming was behind their intensity, others that they were a sure sign of Armageddon. Magdalena knew that the village priest preached divine punishment, warning the island's residents to

mend their wicked ways. She knew this not because she herself attended his masses but because her grandmother relayed the information, uncertainly, neither convinced nor dismissing it as so much hocus-pocus, as Magdalena's grandfather used to do.

It was the wind that made all the difference, Luka Morić had always insisted. Not some higher power. Without the wind, a fire could be contained with little damage to houses or vineyards. But when it blew, whether from north or south, it carried sparks over fire roads and turned pines into towering matches.

The *bura* rushed coldly from the north, but the *jugo*—which blew today—came all the way from Africa. It climbed the rungs of people's ribs in shivers and caused nervous dogs to chew their tails so violently that they smeared the limestone blocks of Rosmarina's main square with blood.

It had been blowing on the day of her grandfather's stroke, as well, so that Magdalena would forever associate those two sights: the way he fell forward suddenly, grabbing the edge of the kitchen table, and the jagged surface of the sea.

She let the children go. At eight and nine, they were still too young to join the lines, but their fathers would be on call to remove underbrush or operate the fire trucks.

"Will it reach the town?" one of the boys, more nervous than the rest, had asked.

"No," Magdalena answered, aware that twenty pairs of eyes had turned in her direction. "The fire is miles away from here."

Now, looking out the window, she was not so sure. Smoke filled the sky in greasy plumes, and when she leaned forward to pull the windows closed, the smell of charred pine burned her throat.

From the school she walked home along the *riva,* where a few fishermen were tying up their boats. They had seen the smoke from the water, and one or two called out to her in greeting. She raised her hand in answer but did not stop. Her grandmother was at home alone with Luka, and Magdalena imagined her listening to the radio in the kitchen, hands shaking as she cut tomatoes for their dinner.

Along the strand all the cafés had tuned their radios to Rosmarina's only station. People milled about on the pavement, watching the smoking sky and listening to the news reports. "They're fighting the whole fire from the air," she heard someone say behind her.

It made sense, she knew. There were few roads on that part of the island, and it was clear from the airplanes' jerking that the wind was complicating their approach. When fires were especially bad, every able-bodied person on Rosmarina joined the lines, but today they could only watch the horizon uneasily and hope that the wind would not blow the fire towards the town.

When one of the airplanes passed overhead, she slowed. She watched it sweep low over the sea in front of them and rise, and was about to resume her walk home when a neighbor called out to her from his boat. "How's your grandfather?" he asked.

She started at this question. "No change," she told him.

The abruptness of her response seemed to distress him, and she noticed the man in the next boat stare down at his palm as if he did not want to meet her eyes. Luka's condition had been unchanged for months. But the men in front of her had fished the channels with her grandfather, so she softened her reply. "Only time will tell."

They nodded, as if relieved by this, as if a crack had been left in the inevitable and they could now all comfortably breathe. The one who had been studying his hand looked up. "And those children?" he asked with a shy smile. "Are they behaving themselves?"

His daughter was in her class, and she made herself smile back. "Most of the time," she told him. "Your Verica is, anyway."

He looked pleased at this answer, and so she turned and continued home. She did not need to look back to know that they were watching her walk away, or that by the time she reached the end of the *riva* they would be deep in conversation over the gunwales of their boats.

Magdalena knew that the island viewed her with a mixture of pity and respect. Few who attended university ever returned for more than holidays, and at thirty-one she was an oddity in a place where teenage girls tended to marry out of boredom.

It did not help that on Rosmarina there was no such thing as privacy, one house so near the next that a man could hear his neighbor's toilet flush. Grudges went back generations, and children were judged by things their parents had done, some of them years before their birth. Small wonder, Magdalena sometimes thought, that her sister preferred places where nobody knew her.

"It's been a long time since you had a boyfriend," one officious neighbor had pointed out to Magdalena only yesterday, sympathetic but disapproving, too, as if sensing something defiant in her spinsterhood. And because Magdalena had a knack for picking discreet lovers, no one, not even Jadranka, suspected her of those encounters.

Her men usually came from other islands or from the mainland, and she met them secretly in hotel rooms in Split or in apartments they borrowed from friends. Some were strangers, others old acquaintances whom she ran into, unexpectedly, when she was running errands—buying construction paper for the bulletin boards at school, or filling a prescription for her grandparents. Sometimes attraction bloomed in the time it took to exchange pleasantries.

She had planned to meet one of them this afternoon, an electrician from Korčula. She had thought about it all day: his large, uncanny hands, which could untangle the finest wires, the way he would meet her at his front door and carry her to his bed. The fact that there was not a single book in his entire apartment, a distinct advantage because it meant that their relationship would never progress beyond the physical.

She favored easygoing men like him who did not talk of love. She did not want to carry anyone's photograph in her wallet, or go on holidays with them, or meet their mothers. It was only rarely that someone became possessive or demanding, and in such circumstances she would end things immediately.

"She should never have let that Damir get away," the same neighbor had told Magdalena's grandmother, loudly enough for her to hear.

More than ten years had passed since Damir's departure, but the island was agreed on this fact. As a result, he was mentioned often in her presence, as if she were solely at fault for their parting. As if she had defied the natural order of things.

She and Damir had known each other all their lives, even sitting together in the same Rosmarina classroom where Magdalena now taught. But it was only when she was seventeen—the same year the country's independence war began—that Magdalena considered the quiet, older boy with the widow's peak, the one she had never heard brag of summertime conquests with foreign girls. The one whose father had occasionally fished the Devil's Stones with her father when they were young men.

For several years they had studied together in the capital, where an atmosphere of near calm prevailed after the first year of the war. They frequented student bars and walked hand in hand along Tkalčićeva Street, and Magdalena regularly sneaked him into the room she rented from a half-deaf spinster aunt. They lay naked on the bed's crocheted coverlet, plotting the life they would one day build on the island.

But he had been drafted into the military after finishing his degree in journalism, and she had not recognized the man who returned at war's end, the one who took her face in his hands one night and told her gently that they could have a good life on the mainland, but he would not be going back to Rosmarina.

And because Rosmarina was the only solid ground she'd ever stood on—a fact he knew, a fact that made his defection all the more difficult to bear—she had returned to the island alone.

He was a journalist today. He circumnavigated the globe while she traveled Rosmarina's circumference again and again. He learned French and Russian and English, and she prowled the abandoned hamlets of the island's interior, watching the moon rise in different parts of the sky.

Sometimes he returned to Rosmarina to visit his parents, but he would only wave at her from a passing car, or on the street. She always smiled tightly and waved back, but they did not stop to speak.

Her grandparents knew better than to mention him. But while Luka had never expressed concern at her solitary state, her grandmother had long despaired. "What will become of you, Lena, when we're gone?"

Magdalena could not help viewing her grandfather's stroke as the warning shot, and sometimes she saw herself wandering from room to room in an empty house.

"A baby," had been her grandmother's solution. "You ought to have a baby."

This had caused Magdalena to shout with laughter. Most men of her generation had either left the island, like Damir, or married. And as far as having a baby on her own, Rosmarina was a conservative place. She could just imagine how they would whisper in the harbor that the splinter did not fall far from the trunk.

It was true that she dressed severely for teaching: snow-white cotton blouses and dark slacks whose only distinguishing feature was the sharp creases left by her grandmother's iron. True, as well, that she pulled her hair back into a tight knot so that when her pupils saw her at other times, fishing or riding her scooter on the island's back roads, they often failed to recognize the woman with the long, dark hair. But she did this because she was the size of some of the school's eleven-year-old students and not, she insisted to Jadranka, as an act of capitulation.

She was a good teacher who prepared her lessons at the small, scarred table in her room where she had done her homework as a child. It was the same surface where, years before, her mother had kept cosmetic tubes and pots that dripped onto the wood, leaving a pattern that could not be deciphered from one generation to the next.

Within the school she had a reputation for being stern and a second sense for malingerers and the clandestine passing of notes. Unlike some of the older teachers, she never coerced her students physically. This was a result not of her size, as many people assumed, but of her belief that a child should never feel threatened. She despised bullies and became adept at separating boys in fights, holding each by the back of his shirt with a ferocity that belied her size.

She had been at the school for eight years, and some of her first pupils now fished or worked in the island's small quarry or in cafés along the *riva*. It was always a shock for Magdalena to run into these young men and women, who towered above her without exception, proof that time was passing but she herself was standing still.

The afternoon ferry to Korčula was already slipping out to sea when she left the port and climbed upward through the town, past stone houses whose roof tiles had lightened in the sun. The dwellings closer to the *riva* were occupied by islanders and cluttered with the evidence of life: laundry lines and dog food bowls, children's tricycles and fishing nets that had been left outside to dry. But the farther she went, the more frequently she passed empty houses. These were the ones that had been refurbished, with air-conditioning and the occasional picture window. The roof tiles were startling in their ruddy newness, but because the tourist season was only just starting, many of the windows were still shuttered. Only the houses on the Peak remained entirely deserted, though in recent years there had been talk of summer visitors buying up these, as well.

Ash began to fall as she climbed. It drifted lazily through open windows and over walls. She saw through several open courtyard doors that it was already landing in a fine layer on sheets and undershirts that had been hung to dry. It fell like snow, which had fallen rarely on the island in Magdalena's lifetime. Twice on her way up, she stopped to watch it fall, holding out her hand so that a few flakes landed on her palm.

When she reached her grandparents' house, she put her full weight against the gate and pushed so that it made a scraping sound. The courtyard and the kitchen were deserted, but she found her grandmother upstairs, asleep in a chair beside Luka's bed.

"*Nona,*" she whispered, prompting her grandmother's eyes to flutter. "I'll sit with him a little while."

"The fire," her grandmother said, immediately awake.

"They're using the planes to fight it."

Ružica sighed and rose stiffly. "A bad sign that they're starting this early," she pronounced, and Magdalena heard her careful steps as she descended the stairs. A short time later there was the sound of running water in the kitchen.

"Hello, old man," she greeted her grandfather, although she no longer expected him to respond. Since his stroke he had been like a leaf in a bathtub from which water was being slowly drained. He clung to the surface, just barely, even as he sank. Although her grandmother had claimed small improvements in the months since then—he swallowed black tea from a spoon one day, and another time, she swore, he winked at her—the doctors had said that recovery was impossible.

He would die soon, in the same room where he had first taken breath, an idea that comforted Magdalena and which she often repeated to herself. It was a plain, whitewashed room with a single window that overlooked the courtyard. Beyond it was the town and beyond that the sea. In his childhood, she knew, he had slept there with his siblings, and it was the room that he had shared for more than sixty years with his wife. It seemed to Magdalena that he slept more easily there than in the hospital, although she could not be sure that he was aware of his surroundings.

A neighbor had given them an old baby monitor, and on nights when Ružica was particularly tired, when she was afraid that she might not wake up in a moment of grave consequence, Magdalena plugged the receiver into the electrical outlet beside her bed. She turned the volume to high and slept with her grandfather's shallow breaths in her ear and, behind them, the nonsensical sleep talk of her grandmother. "Three yards of fabric," she would hear the older woman comment.

She had quickly realized that her grandmother woke many times each night to make sure that Luka had not slipped away from her in the darkness. Lying in her own room next door, Magdalena would hear the squeal of the mattress as Ružica sat up beside him to hold her open palm above his mouth, waiting for the reassurance of his breath. "Don't think you can leave me behind, old man," she had told him once, so fiercely that Magdalena did not know whether to smile or weep in the dark.

It was remarkable, in fact, what the monitor picked up: people calling to one another in the lane outside and the subsequent barking of village dogs; the house's creaks and groans, so human in their elocution that Magdalena awoke several times convinced that someone was wandering the rooms; even the faint sound of her own pacing on the nights she gave up on sleep, the muffled footfalls arriving with a slight delay.

Ružica spent much of the day at Luka's bedside, but Magdalena always relieved her after school. She talked to him aloud, not caring what people passing in the lane beyond the courtyard might think. She told him news from the port and about her plans to repair the shack at their fishing camp on the Devil's Stones. She repeated jokes that she heard on the waterfront, leaning close to his ear so that her grandmother would not hear the ruder punch lines.

But today was different. "There's a fire on the island," she told him.

A shadow moved across the features of his face, and Magdalena held her breath. But she was imagining things. Her grandfather looked the same as when she'd first walked into the room, the same as he always did. It was a trick of the light. In moments like those, a part of her always believed that his eyes were about to open, but in nine months it had not happened once.

For Jadranka, their grandfather was already gone, and she did not like this business of oxygen and artificial life.

"Why don't we electrocute him so that he dances?" she had muttered the first time she saw Luka, his skin almost the same color as his hair, both an unhealthy gray against the starched whiteness of the sheets. "Why don't we paint eyeballs on his lids, and carry him down to dinner?"

"Shh," Magdalena had told her, hugging her so fiercely that she felt her sister's tears run down her neck. "Don't let *Nona* hear you."

Jadranka found it maudlin when their grandmother spoke of his getting better. And she did not approve of the fact that Magdalena talked to him, or of the town's consensus that his suffering was all part of God's great plan.

"It's a great plan that He has," she finally told a distant cousin who had come to sit with their grandmother. "We should all be so lucky to be part of a plan like that."

Jadranka had never understood—or observed—the thousand customs required by island life: she could not bring herself to greet old women she knew would gossip about her once she had passed, and she did not make pilgrimages to the graveyard, nor to old and dying extended family members whom she had not been fond of before their afflictions. "It would be hypocritical," she said.

She openly derided the island's hospitality—the quantities of food and wine at celebrations—and grew irritated with the exaggerations in gift giving: an excess of gold charms for baptisms and birthdays. She did not want to be godmother to someone else's children. "I'm an atheist," she said, turning down one such request from a close family friend, an unforgivable refusal in many people's eyes.

"Your religious views are beside the point," their grandmother had told her in a burst of uncharacteristic irritation.

"Not to me, they're not," she had responded gently, leaving the matter there.

Jadranka had long ago lost the thread of island life, and while she did not despise it as their mother did, she was restless when she spent more than a few days on Rosmarina. Their grandfather's stroke had merely been the final straw.

Despite what his younger granddaughter believed, however, Luka was not in a state of darkness, nor of silence. The house's strange electricity reached him even past his shroud of sheets, although he could not untangle time. Wars separated by fifty years were fought simultaneously, and from where he lay, people took their first and last breaths in a single instant. Houses collapsed and were built again.

It had taken him eighty-three years to discover that a third, intermediate state existed between consciousness and sleep, between breathing and the grave. Though not fully awake, he was sensitive to his surroundings—the smell of his wife's iron pressed against a linen tablecloth, or the ferry's horn as it departed every morning at six. But while that sound might once have pierced his days, stringing them together like beads on an abacus, the weeks and months and years had since shaken themselves loose of that device and now lay in wild disarray on his bedsheets.

He neither knew nor cared which pair of pajamas he wore, nor what the newscasters said each evening during *Dnevnik*, although his wife turned up the volume so that the reports reached the room where he lay. He was no longer the man who had watched the news every night, slapping his hands against his knees or muttering his outrage at the shameless behavior of politicians.

When the disembodied voices floated in to Luka, they pulled themselves apart like tufts of cloud. He was aware of the distorted echoes but, if he considered them at all, assumed them to be announcements from a distant railway station.

Often he existed in a half-consciousness in which his wife could feed him with his eyes closed. She mixed vitamins and made teas from herbs that women brought her from the Peak. She massaged his legs and rubbed rosemary oil into his chest.

He overheard his wife's conversations with neighbors who brought news of island scandals to relieve her vigil. The information orbited his head—someone was pregnant, someone had beaten his wife, someone was drinking again. The possibility of reaching out a hand and separating the conversations was always there. He simply lacked the desire to do it.

He lived, overwhelmingly, in the random scattering of days and weeks. Sometimes he was a boy working in the vineyards. "Like this," his grandfather would tell him, clipping a bunch of grapes so purple they appeared black, and placing them gently in the basket. Other times, he was a young man, strong enough to lift a laughing sister in each arm. In his world, the dead came back to life and were as real to him as his wife, his granddaughters, or the neighbors. One day he looked at his grandfather and slapped his back. "And all this time you were hiding from me," he said to the old man, dead more than sixty years, who smiled his good-natured, toothless grin.

The only thing that concerned him in the present was the bedroom window. He wanted it open morning and evening so that he could hear the island beyond it. So that he could feel day breaking and closing up again by the degree of warmth and shadow that fell across his face and hands, though he was conscious neither of the fact that day actually broke nor that it closed up again. He listened for the sound of Magdalena's footsteps, but by the time she dropped into the chair beside him, he had disconnected the two events. Seasons stopped. And though he was sometimes warm, sometimes cold, he existed mainly in the cloudy water of his dying, which was of uniform temperature. Very occasionally he was aware of this, of the floating that he could not maintain forever but was frightened to give up. He would think of a baby in the weightless sea of its mother's womb and even smile slightly.

How strange, he would think, *that there should be exactly the same weightlessness at the end as there was in the beginning. I had forgotten it completely.*

Ružica was in the kitchen. She was humming something beneath her breath, a tune that Luka could just make out past the sound of running water. Something was burning on the stove, but she did not seem to notice.

Luka's mother was equally unconcerned by that strange smell—like bread that the oven turns to cinder, or *palenta* that blackens the bottom of a pot. She sat at the table shelling beans, and he was mesmerized by the quick motion of her hands, the pile of husks that grew steadily on one side. When she looked up and saw him, she smiled and told him to play outside. "The sun is shining," she told him.

In his floating state, his mother was alive and perpetually pregnant. There had been five surviving children, and dead babies too numerous to count. He was the first to enter the world, then his sister Vinka, then Zora and Zlatka together. His mother had told the story of the twins' birth many times: Zora appeared first, and then, unexpectedly, Zlatka followed behind. Just as in life. Then the baby, Iva.

"Only one son. And the rest daughters!" his father would complain.

But when Iva had appeared, his mother—so drenched in blood and sweat, so frail and old before her time—had looked at Luka with wide, frightened eyes. "I can't anymore," she told her eldest child.

That night when their father was drinking in the harbor, he and Vinka sawed their parents' wooden bed in half. They dragged the two halves apart and propped them on opposite sides of the room with blocks of wood. He had been seventeen at the time, still young enough to be frightened as he did it. But by the time his father returned, staggering up the stairs, he had been too intoxicated to notice that his bed was smaller.

"Where's your mother?" he muttered to Vinka, then fell asleep before hearing an answer.

In the morning he had awakened in a foul mood and, upon seeing the state of his bed, raged at his son. He threatened to throw him out on the street, to beat him senseless.

The recipient of his father's repeated thrashings, Luka curled his hands into fists and narrowed his eyes. He straightened so that he was looking down at his father.

In his sickbed, Luka drew himself up so that he was very tall.

There. It had happened again, and Magdalena straightened. She had been fighting sleep, but her eyes had opened just in time to see that shadow cross his face. She wondered if he sensed the commotion in the town. A short time ago there had been sirens, as if the fire were coming closer.

She took his hand and straightened its fingers between her own, but they curled up again immediately, and she worried that she was hurting him. The island nurse had explained that his muscles no longer engaged to protect his bones. His head, she had demonstrated, turning him, needed to be supported exactly like a baby's.

Magdalena placed his hand gently by his side and leaned forward so that her forehead touched the mattress.

He cared only that the window was open. When his wife closed the shutters at night, his mouth fell into a troubled line. Sometimes he was able to muster a low, almost inaudible moan. He reached very far down into his throat for the sound, and was spent by the effort.

During his weeks in the hospital in Split, he had grown to hate the air that never moved and the stale smell of the hospital corridors. He was acutely aware of the noise that went on without respite: the one squeaking wheel on the nurse's medication cart, the voices of visitors in the hallway, the breathing of the other men in his ward. When the doctor stood in front of his bed, flipping through the papers of his chart, the noise was excruciating.

On the mainland he felt that the thread that bound him to Rosmarina had been cut. In his semiconsciousness, he looked for the outline of the Peak at night, and the smell of the pine trees. Sometimes he carried the smell of ash in the cavities of his nose.

In the hospital he could not remember childhood or the war, could not remember his sisters or his parents' bed. He existed in a constant, thick fog, where he was no longer Luka Morić but a barely breathing corpse in a hospital bed. Even his wife, holding his hand in hers and shedding her tears onto his hospital gown, bore no relationship to the place she had left only a few days before.

On Rosmarina, he knew only that when his bedroom window was open, something came through it and connected him to the world again. He could see the wire-haired goats on the hill and the grapes growing heavy upon the vines. His mother crouched in an open field as on the day he had been born, her labor pains arriving so quickly that she barely had time to make it back to the house. At night wind tore through the olive trees, and he heard their dry, leathery leaves brushing against one another like the palms of old women.

Sometimes his son was restored at last to the island. Marin hunched in his boat beneath a black sky, just beyond the harbor, and watched the fishing lamp light up the water like a low, hovering star. Luka could feel the fish rising, swimming gleefully towards that light. His daughter braided her daughters' hair in the courtyard, first one and then the other, humming under her breath. This although Ana abandoned the island years ago, as his granddaughters had likewise abandoned their braids.

His heightened sensitivity to noise continued on Rosmarina, but erratically. Sometimes nothing could interrupt the low humming noise in his head, not Magdalena's footsteps, nor the way his wife searched her kitchen drawers frantically for a missing ladle. At other times he was conscious that his wife prayed beside his bed, and he could follow each word of her laments. He was uncomfortable in such moments, almost embarrassed, and wished that she would stop. He believed in many things—the laws of navigation, the way a *bura* wind was always followed by clean, bright air, the fact that spring would come for as long as the earth spun on its axis. But he no longer believed in God.

Sometimes he said their names, but they were so garbled that by the time they reached the air, they sounded like nothing more than ragged breath. Sometimes he realized that only Magdalena remained. Her troubled face hovered for a moment in front of him like a fishing lamp bending the dark water with light.

When the telephone rang in the kitchen, he could hear her rise from the chair beside his bed. He could not make out the words, but whatever she was saying, she was insistent. He opened his eyes, and the ceiling stretched above him, blue and cloudless. She sounded upset, as if she were on the verge of tears. *Something has happened,* he thought, frowning. His thoughts startled him because they seemed to arrive from nowhere. His lips struggled to produce words, but it was like wringing water from a dry cloth. *She must not learn of it,* he wanted to call out, even as he knew that the words would not translate to the air. *She must not,* he thought fiercely, already forgetting who she was, and what she must not do.

His dead sisters were filing down from the Peak. Their figures were recognizable despite the distance, and their voices carried across the afternoon. At the other end of the hall, Magdalena was not speaking at all, but singing, unaware of their approach. He wanted to tell her to boil water for their coffee, to set the table for their meal.

There was something unsettling about his granddaughter's song, but even as he attempted to understand the words, his sisters were singing along. It was a different song, now, the shift so fluid that he was unsure where the first stopped and the second began. From the window he watched them enter the courtyard, one by one, the skin of their young faces glowing smoothly in the fire of the sun.

It has been so many years, he thought, listening to them, *since I have heard that song.* It had been popular in his youth, but he could not remember its being sung in decades. It was like finding something he had not realized was missing. He could not even remember the name of the song, but his heart started painfully when he realized that Magdalena—a child again—was singing along. She looked up and smiled when she saw him at the upstairs window. She raised her hand in greeting.

*   *   *

She had been dreaming of birds. Thousands of them glided through the sky in slow formation, like her grandfather's stories of World War II bombers, and she was so intent on the strange sight that it took a moment to realize that she had fallen asleep.

But when the telephone rang a second time, she lifted her head from the mattress. She could hear her grandmother outside in the lane, talking to one of their neighbors. Her grandfather's hand was exactly where she had placed it, and she watched his chest for a moment, to be certain that it still rose.

Her head was still thick with sleep when she reached the kitchen. The birds had been heading north, she remembered, like the smoke clouds she had seen that afternoon. The kitchen smelled like fire, and for a moment she wondered if they were evacuating the town. It had only happened once in her lifetime, but she dreaded the idea; she did not know how she would get her grandfather down to the waterfront.

When she picked up the receiver there was a moment of silence on the other side. Those delays often preceded Jadranka's calls, which made the space between the sisters seem greater. She did not know if it was because of the geographical distance or satellites orbiting overhead, but even when she called Jadranka back at the numbers she provided—imagining her sister standing at a pay phone in the unfamiliar city—there were the same awkward delays in conversation, so that it felt to Magdalena that they had not talked properly in months.

"Jadranka," she said, by way of greeting. "There's a fire on the island."

But it was Katarina calling to tell her that Jadranka was gone.

CHAPTER 3

Three days had passed since Jadranka's disappearance in New York. Katarina's family had risen one morning to find the door to her room ajar and the narrow window cracked, as if she had turned into air and merely slipped out into the atmosphere. The children, Katarina told Magdalena, had crossed to it instinctively and searched the street below.

"They're upset," she added in a voice that managed to fuse concern with irritation. "They can't understand why she wouldn't say goodbye."

Jadranka had made her bed, leaving a quilt neatly folded across the foot. A few garments still hung in the closet, but the small suitcase was missing from beneath her bed.

They had searched the entire house for a note, unable to believe that Jadranka would leave without some form of explanation. Katarina had gone through the crumpled papers in the wastebasket in Jadranka's room and found a few receipts, gum wrappers, a ticket stub for a film Jadranka had seen with the children, but nothing to indicate her current whereabouts.

Three days, Magdalena thought with a sinking heart. Her sister could be anywhere by now.

*   *   *

Jadranka had disappeared before, though never from her sister. She liked to slip her skin periodically, a habit Magdalena only grudgingly accepted. "I get restless," Jadranka once explained. And Magdalena understood this to be true, her sister like an undomesticated cat that some well-meaning person longed to give a home. No matter how much milk you served it, no matter how soft its bed, it still chafed at confinement.

Jadranka had once made it as far as Italy, earning money by sweeping up hair cuttings in an Ancona salon. After several weeks she returned so thin that her ribs made furrows above her breasts. "I wasn't paid well enough to eat" was her only explanation.

An object in continuous motion, she returned from Rijeka several pounds heavier, but after Dubrovnik her hair was dyed black, and she was thin again. "Your beautiful hair," Magdalena said, picking up a length that was as dark as her own but with blue undertones.

"We match," Jadranka laughed, but by the next summer her dark red hair had grown out again, a shade so uncommon that people often stared and curious children grabbed for it in handfuls.

Jadranka was not so much irresponsible as a force of nature, difficult to predict and difficult to contain. As a child she used to place her hand over candles and hold it there for as long as she could stand it. Once, her hair caught fire. But instead of frightening her, the singed pieces that landed on the tablecloth made her laugh. She liked their strange patterns and the way they turned to black dust when she tried to pick them up.

"As long as you don't disappear from me," Magdalena had made her promise.

Katarina did not know where Jadranka could have gone. She was unsure if she had made any friends since her arrival, as she preferred to spend most days off in her studio or visiting the city's galleries.

"I made a list of what she should see," Katarina explained absentmindedly. Though the delivery of her words was innocuous enough, they made Magdalena's eyes narrow. *Professor Katarina,* Magdalena thought. *You always were a know-it-all.*

Magdalena felt the same flare of irritation whenever she read her cousin's letters: the detailed descriptions of the other woman's children and her house, her gallery and the holidays she took with her family to exotic locations, though never to Rosmarina. Magdalena's responses were always terse and controlled, with a minimum of description and little that bordered on the personal.

Magdalena had denied having an e-mail account, unwilling to face an in-box filled with her cousin's messages, so that they continued to write to each other the old-fashioned way, Katarina's parchment stationery now devoid of rainbows, while Magdalena always wrote back to her on the ragged pages she tore from a spiral notebook.

I feel I hardly know you anymore, Katarina had written when they were in their early twenties, an observation that Magdalena did not bother to address.

"She's really pretty good," Katarina conceded now, and Magdalena knew at once that she was referring to her sister's painting. "A little rough around the edges maybe, but there's a lot of promise there."

The words were clearly meant as a concession.

"That's nice to hear," Magdalena said, even as she thought: *Jadranka was better than you from the beginning.*

It was Magdalena who had driven Jadranka to the airport in January, the younger woman waiting on the *riva* when Magdalena arrived by ferry from Rosmarina. Clad in a coat and scarf, she had placed her suitcase beside her on the pavement, and expectation filled her face. Jadranka was happy, Magdalena realized as she drove their grandfather's Fiat out of the hull. She looked happier than she had in months.

"This way you don't even need to see Mama," Jadranka told her with a knowing look as they lifted the suitcase between them into the trunk, a job made more difficult by the wind.

Magdalena ignored her sister's comment but returned her quick embrace. "What's the plan?" she asked, because Jadranka's flight did not leave until the morning.

Something jumped in her eyes, a light that Magdalena recognized from her wilder youth. "Who needs a plan when the possibilities are endless?"

It was already late afternoon when they followed the coastal highway southward, through the urban sprawl of Split. They stopped for dinner at a roadside restaurant, Magdalena drinking a single glass of wine, Jadranka laughing as she polished off the first bottle and ordered a second.

Halfway through their meal, two American men sat down at the next table, and Jadranka struck up a conversation with them in broken English.

"Croatia is a beautiful country," one of them told her. They both wore hiking boots, and their faces were sunburnt.

"Yes," she agreed.

"Are you from here?" the other—a blond with very blue eyes—asked, prompting Jadranka to smile coyly.

"I am like you. The stranger."

Magdalena frowned at this, but her sister was already on a roll, inviting them to guess where she was from.

"Are you Polish?"

"No."

"Russian?"

"No."

"French?"

"Non!"

With her red hair, Jadranka did not look Croatian, and this was a favorite game of hers. It had amused Magdalena when they were teenagers, but now she found it tiresome, as if there were some made-up taxonomic system by which people believed all nations could be categorized. An Italian-shaped box for the Italians. A Chinese-shaped box for the Chinese. What would a Croatian-shaped box look like, she wondered? The bones of goats down one side, and grapevines down the other? She imagined it covered with an embroidered tablecloth, like the ones gypsies sold on Rosmarina's beaches.

"I am the Lapp," Jadranka told them finally.

This was a departure for her sister, but Magdalena only sighed.

The men looked surprised at this. "Lapp?" asked the blond. "Like from the Arctic?"

"Very good," she told him. "People often think is in Antarctica."

"Nobody lives in Antarctica," he told her.

"No," she agreed. "Only penguins."

The other man smiled. "Are you really a Lapp?"

"Yes," she said. "But tomorrow I go to America."

They looked at Magdalena as if for confirmation. Her English was better than Jadranka's. She had studied it in school, and it was one of the subjects she taught, but now she only attempted to catch the waitress's eye for their bill.

"How long will you be staying?" asked the blond.

As Magdalena studied her sister's face, Jadranka shrugged. Instead of answering, she spent the next five minutes regaling them with entertaining facts about the Lapps. It was clear to Magdalena that the vast majority of these were made up, ranging from the *uk-tuk* building that Lapps lived in to the nicknames they gave their reindeer.

"Akborg, she was my favorite," she told them. "Her name means *rosebud.*"

The blond's Adam's apple bobbed up and down. "Rosebud," he repeated in amusement. "I assumed it would be too cold for roses in the Arctic."

"For ordinary roses," she conceded. "But this is special, hardy type."

He grinned. "I think you're making fun of us."

"No," Jadranka insisted, though she herself was smiling broadly now. "Akborg bush. Official plant of Lappish nation."

When the waitress came over at last, Magdalena reached for the bill. But Jadranka pushed her hand playfully away. "Bad karma, big sister," she told her in Croatian, forgetting her audience, who had returned to their meal. "I'm the one going on the trip, so I'm the one who has to pay."

"By whose logic?"

"Mine," Jadranka insisted, and Magdalena could not help but smile at the decisive way she said this.

When they rose to leave, the blond man at the next table reached over to take Jadranka's hand. "What's your name?" he asked her.

She hesitated. "Jay."

Magdalena's eyebrows rose at this, but she said nothing.

"Like bluejay?"

"Yes," she told him. "Okay."

"I'm Peter. Do you and your friend want to join us for a drink?"

For a moment Magdalena was afraid that her sister would agree, but Jadranka shook her head.

He released her hand. "Okay, Bluejay Rosebud," he said. "Maybe I'll see you around in America."

"Maybe," she told him with a smile, though it was clear to Magdalena that she was already bored with this game.

✶   ✶   ✶

As night fell they had driven still farther southward, towards the mountains where the Magistrala crept upward and folded into serpentines. The road was cut into the mountainside, a thin ribbon of pavement between a sheer rock face and limestone cliffs that plunged hundreds of feet to the sea.

When they had gone some distance, they passed a sign that indicated an overlook.

"Stop here!" Jadranka ordered.

"It's freezing," Magdalena said even as she pulled over. "And it's nighttime."

Jadranka still cradled the second wine bottle from dinner in her lap, and when she got out of the car, she tucked it beneath her arm like an umbrella. For a moment Magdalena watched her sister walk backward in the headlights. She was smiling, and the wind blew with such force that it whipped her hair upward, as if Jadranka were no longer subject to the laws of gravity. She threw her head back and howled, a sound Magdalena could just make out above the wind.

She sighed and turned off the engine, watching for a few moments more before opening her car door. There was a dangerous quality about Jadranka tonight, like something preparing to explode.

But the cold outside nearly drove her back into the car. "You're crazy!" she shouted at her sister's retreating back.

Jadranka was right, however, for although the wind was punishing, the view was achingly clear. Along the coast in either direction, Magdalena could see the cold lights of several towns and, behind them, the black weight of the mountains. Island after island lay in front of her, their shorelines glowing like Christmas trees, and when she made out a soft light on the horizon, she wondered if it was Rosmarina.

"Come on!" her sister shouted, and Magdalena jogged towards the place where she was standing, at the very edge of the pavement. Jadranka stepped forward a little unsteadily so that Magdalena grabbed the back of her coat, not trusting the railing that separated them from the edge.

"No you don't," she said with a short laugh. "Unless you want to go to the hospital instead of America." She could not see the point below them where the waves broke upon the rocks, but she could hear the crash of water above the wind.

Jadranka appeared not to have heard her. "Look at the stars," she insisted happily. "How often do you see stars that bright?"

Her sister began to sway slightly, and Magdalena hid a smile. "All the time," she answered.

But Jadranka ignored this, too. "There's Sirius," she said so softly that Magdalena strained to hear her. "And Orion."

Magdalena looked up. "You haven't forgotten," she said.

Jadranka snorted. "How could I forget? The number of nights I spent in *Dida's* boat when all I wanted to do was sleep."

Magdalena's heart jumped painfully at this because she knew that while they drove around, their grandmother would be watching his face for signs of life.

Luka Morić had always hated the way the island hemorrhaged its population to the mainland. He regarded with melancholy the fact that in a decade or two, there might no longer be working fishermen on Rosmarina, nor enough hands to combat fires after the tourist season ended. Most of all, Magdalena knew, he hated the glass cabinet in the kitchen where his wife kept a shrine to family members who had died or emigrated.

Over the years, the cabinet's shelves had become filled with photographs as Luka's sisters had died one by one or, as in the case of Vinka, left for good. His only daughter wanted nothing to do with Rosmarina, and his only son had disappeared, sending no word even after the end of communism. This silence had prompted Magdalena's grandmother to add the pictures of saints to Marin Morić's shelf, a blessed rosary from some cousin who had visited the Vatican, and a medal of Saint Christopher.

Magdalena knew that their grandmother prayed in front of the cabinet when she thought no one was watching, but that before his stroke Luka could barely stand to look at it when passing through the kitchen. He had once confided to Magdalena that Marin's shelf too closely resembled a grave, and what other explanation could there be for her uncle's continued absence?

Due to her relative proximity in Split, their mother warranted only one corner of a shelf, together with assorted cousins and friends, and on rare visits to the island she regarded the cabinet with irony. "Our saint!" she would salute her brother a little bitterly, announcing her certainty that he had become prosperous abroad and merely discarded his links to the island like so much ballast.

The last time Jadranka had visited the island, she brought their grandmother a photograph of herself. "This way you can keep an eye on all of us together," she told her, already planning her escape.

Magdalena alone had caught the look of despair that crossed the older woman's face. "You shouldn't have said that," she chided Jadranka later.

They had driven for the rest of that January night, Jadranka remembering the way they used to ride Magdalena's scooter around the island as teenagers. In the first year of the war there had been blackouts, and Magdalena had taken the bulb out of the scooter's headlight, so that they had flown through the dark. "I'd look up at all those stars," Jadranka said in a dreamy voice, "and you'd be going so fast that they'd start shooting."

Magdalena remembered her sister's arms clasped around her waist and the way she would sometimes sing, the wind distorting her voice, her hair so long that it lashed Magdalena's cheeks like little sparks. They had not worn helmets in those days—nobody did—and they had traveled the roads so quickly that the tires barely made contact with the island.

"I remember," she told her. "It's a wonder we're alive to tell the tale."

At this, Jadranka turned to look out the passenger window. She studied something, some feature of the dark sea that was invisible to Magdalena's eyes.

"That's the problem," Jadranka told the window. "You remember too much."

Her words stung Magdalena. After all, it was Jadranka who had started these reminiscences. She gripped the steering wheel more tightly and concentrated on the road in front of them.

"Lena?"

But Magdalena refused to turn her head.

"I know you hate to talk about it—"

The tiny door that Magdalena had left open in the presence of her sister now slammed promptly shut.

"—but you've been alone for ten years. Not even widows wait this long."

They were climbing a hill, and the car heaved as Magdalena shifted into a lower gear.

"Not even Mama waited this long."

Silence.

"And I hate leaving you like this."

"You're not leaving me," Magdalena said, at last. "You're going. There's a difference." She shifted gears again, satisfied by the car's violent lurch.

"Because the truth is that I may not be coming back."

Magdalena looked sharply at her sister, remembering how she had ignored the American's question about how long she would stay. But Jadranka had turned to look out the window again. "Don't be dramatic," Magdalena told the back of her head. This time there were lights on the dark sea. A ferry, perhaps, or a night fisherman with a death wish. They flickered for a moment before disappearing into the black.

She told none of this to Katarina, who insisted that Jadranka had been happy, that she had put on a bit of weight, a vast improvement from the pale, skinny girl who had arrived in January, poorly equipped for the harsh New York winter with her paper-thin coat. She had gotten on well with the children, playing with Christopher in the park and standing for hours in the bathroom with Tabitha as she experimented with her mother's lipsticks and eye shadows.

She adored her studio, though she had only shown Katarina a little of her work, preferring to keep the rest under lock and key.

"Was it locked when she left?" Magdalena asked.

Katarina hesitated. "Yes. We had to break in because she took the key with her."

Magdalena considered this.

"We hoped it was a sign that she'd be back, but..."

Magdalena waited.

"I think someone had better break the news to your mother."

And so the next morning Magdalena took the ferry to the mainland. The fires had been extinguished during the night, but smoke still hung above some sections of the island. The wind had died, and there was something eerie about those unmoving clouds. Magdalena sat on deck and watched the island retreat, those gray patches of sky visible long after Rosmarina itself had disappeared.

When she arrived at their mother's apartment in Split several hours later, she found the shades still down and the air so still that a cold sweat broke out on her skin. In the kitchen a fly flew in drunken circles over three slices of stale bread, and she watched it make several revolutions while she waited for water to boil.

She had not visited their mother's apartment in all the time that Jadranka had been staying there, and retrieving the spare key from the ledge above the front door had left her fingertips black with dust. As she washed them at the kitchen sink, she was unable to tell whether the soft groans coming from the next room were human or made by her mother's mattress, and she scanned the kitchen quickly. There were no empty bottles on the kitchen counter, nor medication boxes in the trash, but she steeled herself nonetheless. With her mother, nothing was ever certain.

"I don't know what you expect to find here," Ana had said defensively the night before, when Magdalena telephoned to say that she was coming. "I'm not hiding your sister under the floorboards. I have no idea where she might have gone."

Now, Magdalena lingered in the kitchen, watching bubbles of water rise from the bottom of the pot, slowly at first, then faster and faster. She added powdered coffee and sugar, stirring them slowly, the spoon making a thick sound against the metal side. Removing it from the flame, she waited several minutes longer than necessary, staring at that inky circle as the grounds settled. But when she poured it into a cup and carried it into the next room, her mother saw through the gesture immediately. "Don't look at me like that." She eyed the cup with suspicion. "I told you already, I have no idea where she went."

Magdalena sat down on the other bed—Jadranka's old bed—which was covered with clothes and old magazines. She flipped through one so quickly that the pages sounded like cracks from a tiny whip. *How to tell if he's willing to commit,* proclaimed one headline. Another: *The look for spring is GLITTER.*

The single year that Magdalena and her sister had lived under their mother's roof had effectively ended all their fantasies of maternal affection. Ana Babić was not the gentle beauty of her wedding photograph but a nervous woman who ingested the contents of various blister packs. Nikola, her second husband, was not the good-natured father figure she had promised her daughters but a violent drunk who once broke Magdalena's hand by shoving her into a wall. The bone had failed to heal properly, and today there was a knot beneath the skin, which she rubbed in moments of distraction or worry.

Nikola had finally decamped while Magdalena was in her second year of university, Ana telephoning one evening with news of his departure. He had left her a letter, she said, although she never allowed anyone else to see it. He took almost nothing with him—most of his clothes remained hanging in the closet, and she let his razor sit so long on the lip of the bathroom sink that it permanently scarred the porcelain with rust.

"Good riddance," had been Magdalena's immediate response.

"You've always hated him," Ana responded acidly before hanging up.

Her mother could no longer afford her old apartment, and so she moved into a high-rise that was a carbon copy of the twelve that surrounded it. Magdalena disliked it, but she did not have the same sensation of panic every time she crossed its threshold. Inside there were no traces of Nikola, no closets where she had hidden, pushing her sister backward into the gentleness of hanging coats.

Now, her mother sat on the edge of the bed, her nightgown bunched around her hips. She looked at Magdalena unhappily, as if she had been dreaming something pleasant and found consciousness a disappointment. "I'll make up a place for you," she said, but made no move to stand.

Magdalena shook her head. "I'm not staying," she said, then rose to open the shades. It felt good to let light into the apartment, to open the window so that fresh air could dislodge the stale smell of cigarettes and cooking oil, but when she turned around, her mother was blinking angrily in the sunlight.

"*Nona* sent you figs," Magdalena said after a moment. "I left them on the kitchen counter."

Her mother did not acknowledge this gift, but she rose, finally, put on a pair of pink slippers that were turning gray around the toes, and walked into the kitchen, where Magdalena could hear her shuffling through papers. A moment later she returned with a postcard. "Here," she said, tossing it onto the table between the beds. "This is all I have."

Picking it up, Magdalena tried to picture her sister among the sunbathing women in a place called Concy Island. She turned the postcard over to discover that Jadranka had scrawled a quick note on the reverse. *Everything here is fine. I'll write more later.* The postmark was January, a few weeks after her departure.

"This is it?" she asked, but her mother only returned her stony look. *It's my younger daughter who takes after me,* Ana liked to tell people. *If things had been different, who knows how far I would have gotten?*

Back in the kitchen Magdalena threw away the old bread. On the counter an ashtray was overflowing, and she emptied that, as well. She had quit smoking several months before, and the sour smell now turned her stomach.

Above the trash can a calendar showed a picture of Our Lady of Sinj, her dark face gentle beneath her crown of gold. No one in their family was religious except for her grandmother, and Magdalena assumed that it was a gift from her. It was open to the new year, and someone had filled one of the squares with a perfect star in blue ink. Her sister's day of departure, Magdalena realized, because the blocks before it had each been marked by a deliberate slash, and she could see by the dust-covered surfaces and newspaper stacks that time in the apartment had ground to a halt on that day.

Her mother shuffled by in the hallway without a word, and a moment later Magdalena heard water running in the shower.

She took the calendar from the wall and sat down with it at the kitchen table. There were no marks on any of the other pages, and so she returned to January and the blue star. Above it, the Madonna's face had turned inscrutable, the soft curve of her lips mocking.

Because Ana refused to visit the island and because Magdalena went to extraordinary lengths to avoid her mother, they rarely discussed that lost year of her childhood. On the rare occasions that they saw one another, they argued about Rosmarina instead.

It had never been clear to Magdalena how someone who had taken her first breaths on the island could regard it with such disdain, but Ana only held up an impatient hand whenever her daughter began to talk of the sea, the silence at night, the sound of the cicadas. Magdalena liked to think that her words stabbed at some tender, hidden place, but her mother was always dismissive. "What use are those things to me?" she would ask.

For her part, Magdalena bristled at her mother's complaints about the island's scorching heat, its narrowness, its wine that could anesthetize a horse. "How," Ana demanded, "can you be satisfied with the smallness of that place?" With winters that were nothing but a killing season, with one small town on the entire island and no doctor to speak of? There was nothing, she railed, but stone houses and electricity that died daily and water that collected in cisterns so that there was never enough for the humans and the animals to drink and a proper bath besides, never stopping to listen to her daughter's protests that there had been water from the mainland since the late seventies.

"I left," Ana would tell anyone who asked, "because I knew that Rosmarina would destroy me as well."

It was conventional wisdom that islanders should marry people from other islands, but a marriage to someone from the mainland was sure to end in disaster. Magdalena's father was from Šibenik, a metropolis in comparison with Rosmarina. "Your father wasn't used to how quiet the winters were," Ana would say. "That's why he killed himself."

But Magdalena's grandfather grew apoplectic at this charge. "Your father drowned," he insisted. "And more than that we'll never know."

Since leaving for the mainland after Goran's death—which the local police ruled an accident—her mother had scorned anything that was from the island. Not for her the old wives' remedies, the herbs that could cure headaches or lessen arthritis, the lavender or rosemary oil that eased tension and shrank lesions. She embraced the city's noise and dirt. Her second husband, everyone readily told Magdalena, bore no resemblance to her first. And Nikola hated the island. "A backwater," he used to taunt Magdalena. "An inbred shithole."

"It's strange, I suppose," Magdalena's grandmother once told her. "There was a time when your mother loved Rosmarina, but she was a different person then. She was a good mother, too. She used to rock you and sing to you—"

"I don't believe it."

"It's true," her grandmother insisted. "But that was before."

Jadranka had not slipped anything into the books that she kept on a small shelf beside her bed. She had not even dog-eared pages to mark her place, though it was clear she had read each of them because their spines were cracked. Magdalena's eyes fell on *The Silk, the Shears*, a memoir by the poet Irena Vrkljan, which lay horizontally across several other books. Its positioning seemed somehow significant, and Magdalena opened it to read *The biographies of others. Splinters in our body.* She closed it abruptly and replaced it on the shelf.

Some of Jadranka's clothes still hung in the closet, and sweaters were folded in a plastic crate. Magdalena pulled a gauzy scarf from a hook on the closet door and wrapped it once around her own neck. It still smelled like her sister, a mixture of soap, peppermints, and cigarettes, although they had both

quit smoking together, making the pact on the night before
Jadranka's departure.

When she dragged a chair over to look on the upper shelves,
she found everything neatly organized, their mother's chaos not
having reached there yet. A few shoeboxes were stacked, one upon
another, and she took them down and sat on the floor, spreading
them out around her.

Inside were receipts and old pay stubs, batteries, and half-
empty tubes of makeup. There were photographs, pictures of
their grandfather in his boat and of the sisters as children. In one
shot they stood against a wall of the house, Magdalena—about
five—looking to the side, as if something had suddenly caught
her attention. But Jadranka, who appeared to be barely walking at the time, was laughing at the photographer, so that her
eyes were nearly shut in the baby fat of her cheeks. *Who could
have made her laugh like that?* Magdalena wondered. She could no
longer remember.

Down the hall, her mother turned off the shower, and a short
time later Magdalena heard the radio on top of the washing machine jump to life. There were a few moments of white noise as
she twirled the dial, passing through a weather report and a clas-
sical music station. She settled finally on the Beatles and began
singing along in broken English.

She had a good voice, and Magdalena listened for a moment,
softening slightly when she heard that in her mother's interpreta-
tion, Lucy was in a sky with lions.

Halfway through the year that she and Jadranka spent in Split, her
younger sister stopped speaking. It happened without warning.
One day she was chattering about the stray cats in the courtyard,
and the next she was absolutely silent.

"Say something," their mother had insisted on the first morning, kneeling before her seven-year-old daughter on the linoleum

of the kitchen floor, shaking Jadranka as if she could make the words fall out of her mouth like apples from a tree.

But Jadranka only stared at their mother as Nikola muttered in the background that he knew the surest way to restore her speech.

"Shut up!" their mother had told him for once. "Can't you see that the girl's upset?"

But Jadranka did not look upset. She returned to her breakfast of bread and butter and refused to meet anybody's eyes. Even later, when she and Magdalena were alone in their room, she refused to say a single word.

Don't worry, she wrote on a piece of paper as her sister watched. But when Magdalena insisted that she write more, Jadranka only crumpled it in her fist.

The silence continued for several weeks, their mother coaxing her to speak, Jadranka resolutely staring back as if she could not be certain as to the nature of these requests, Nikola raging in the background that it was clear the girl wanted nothing more than attention. Even one night when he hit her, the blow landing on the side of her face with such force that she crumpled to the floor, Jadranka refused to make a sound.

Their mother had been working an evening shift, and Magdalena lowered her head and charged him like a bull. But Nikola had swatted her away, stumbling to the kitchen in search of a bottle.

"It's okay," Magdalena promised her sister in a whisper when they were safely in their room, the door locked, lying face-to-face on the mattress. "I'm going to make him sorry."

But Jadranka only regarded her sister somberly and shook her head.

Children in the neighborhood began to call her names, but she ignored them. Teachers punished her, nonplussed by her willfulness. But still she maintained her obstinate silence. She was taken to see a doctor, an older man with snowy hair who could find nothing wrong with her. He sat her on his examining table and looked into her eyes. "Now, child," he told her sternly. "Explain this nonsense."

But Jadranka merely blinked at him.

"There's no physiological reason she isn't speaking," Magdalena overheard him explain to their mother. "This degree of stubbornness is rare in such a small child."

She drew incessantly. She sketched on napkins and scraps of paper. After school, she drew taunting children's faces. When Nikola went on benders, she drew pictures of the sisters flying high above the city or huddled together in a room with earthen walls.

"Like rabbits," Magdalena had said, because she knew they were Jadranka's favorite animal.

"No more drawing!" their mother had screamed, confiscating her pencils and scraps of paper, emptying the drawers in the desk that the girls shared. "No more drawing until you stop this!"

But Magdalena always managed to smuggle paper to her sister: the back of her math homework, a page torn from the end of a book, pieces of cardboard that she scavenged from the garbage. And in this way they developed a secret language. Slowly at first, Magdalena not always understanding the nature of her sister's drawings, Jadranka frustrated at not being understood.

"You could always open your mouth and say something," Magdalena would remind her.

But Jadranka's lips remained steadfastly shut until six months later when their mother admitted defeat and returned them to the island.

Today, Jadranka continued to sketch constantly. She drew on napkins and paper tablecloths. She carried a small sketchbook with her and always kept a larger one at home, and it puzzled Magdalena not to find any of them among her sister's things.

Ana had returned to the room and was standing in front of a

floor-length mirror, drying her hair with a towel. "I burned them when she left," she explained calmly. "I didn't want her coming back here."

The women regarded each other for a long moment through the reflection, and then it was her mother who broke the silence, her eyes sliding away from Magdalena's. "I wanted her to go. To be rid of us."

At first Magdalena did not believe her. She watched the rigid line of her mother's shoulders, a pose that managed to be both resigned and challenging.

"Why?" she asked after a stunned moment. "Why would you burn them?"

"I needed to be certain that she would stay away," Ana said, applying powder to the bridge of her nose. "That's what they did in the war. When they wanted to make sure nobody returned to the villages, they would burn them down and kill all the animals. They'd make sure there was no reason to come back."

Magdalena felt the old fury rise.

"She's making a new beginning—" Ana started to say.

Magdalena stopped only long enough in the kitchen to yank her purse from the back of a chair, upending it with a crash. But even as she plunged down the stairs, she could hear her mother calling after her, down the building's stairwell. "If you were smart, you'd leave, too," she was shouting.

CHAPTER 4

The courtyard gate creaks open, and for a brief moment Luka picks up the sounds of Rosmarina's port: women hawking their lavender oil from stands and the laughter of boys who are fishing from the pier. He thinks he can even hear one man slap another on the back and say something about the previous evening. But as he waits for a response, the gate slams as if the wind has blown it back on its hinges, or as if someone has leaned against it with all their weight.

He can hear a woman's steps through the courtyard, the way they falter outside the kitchen door. But when she enters the rooms below him, her voice is artificially bright. His daughter's voice, perhaps, or one of his granddaughters. He cannot be sure.

Ružica's response is low and worried. *Drowned,* he thinks she is saying.

He was six on the day a ferry from the mainland capsized. The sea was perfectly calm, a *bonaca* turning its surface into a single sheet of glass, but the ship had overturned regardless. By the time the alarm was raised in the town, most passengers had swum to the Devil's Stones or awaited rescue by hanging on to the ship's debris. But two women, both from Rosmarina, had not even known how to float.

He was on the *riva* when their bodies were brought in. He had slipped between adults who spoke in low, anxious voices and shaded their eyes to watch the horizon where the survivors treaded water, too far away to identify. When the fishing boat conveyed the drowned women to shore, a collective silence fell over the waterfront, and it was the boat's owner who noticed him standing where he meant to tie up. He shouted for the boy to move away, but it was too late, and all the way home Luka was pursued by the sight of the wet and twisted dresses at the bottom of the boat.

He could not fathom what it meant to drown, nor why women of his mother's generation considered swimming an indecent act, preferring the stifling drapery of their long skirts. He had been secretly teaching his sister Vinka to swim in deserted coves where they stripped down to their underwear and then allowed the sun to dry all evidence of this transgression.

The first rule of swimming, he had told her, was to stay afloat. He had demonstrated by lying back in the water, buoyed by the warm currents on the surface.

The first time he let go, she went under and came up coughing water, but the second time her hair spread out on the surface like the sudden blooming of a flower, and she smiled. "It's like flying," she told him happily as they walked home.

News of the drowned women reached his mother before he did. "What is it?" she asked frantically when he burst into the kitchen. She took his pale face in her hands. "What did you see?"

He wanted only to hide in some dark corner of the house, but instead she hurried him to the chapel that was halfway to the Peak, dragging him along so quickly that they were breathless when they reached its doors. They knelt before an oil painting of the Virgin Mary, and although his mother usually prayed quietly, on that day he could hear each word of her lamentations.

He reached out and grabbed a handful of her dark skirt.

Without pausing in her prayer, or even looking at him, she took his fist into her warm hand.

He discovered that his sister was a fearless diver, and together they explored the ledge that separated Rosmarina's shallows from the open sea. Beyond it was a sharp drop where the water turned inky and cold, and although their grandfather had warned him against going so far from shore, they returned there on dive after dive. Sometimes, holding hands, they allowed the currents to sweep them over so that they had to kick furiously until the ledge was beneath them once again and they could go back to taunting the open sea from safety.

He taught each of his sisters, then his children. He taught his granddaughters, one after the other. He wanted to teach his wife, but she was part of that modest generation and claimed that she did not wish to learn.

"What if something happens?" he wanted to know.

But she rarely left the island and was content with dry land. "What's going to happen?" she asked him in amusement, telling him that she was too old to learn new tricks and that he should concentrate his efforts on the young.

Both their children took to the water like fish, but Marin was more cautious than his younger sister, coaxing Ana to stay close to the shore. "If you drift out too far," he told her reasonably, "you'll get swept out into the Channel."

Luka had also warned his daughter not to go past the shelf, but the girl was stubborn, and one day he looked up to discover her floating far from the shore. He panicked because strange tides began where the seafloor dropped off, and he had seen sharks in the deep water.

It was the only time that Luka spanked her, dragging her from the water by her arm, her mouth open in shock. For the duration of the punishment she was silent, and it was Marin who pleaded with him. But he shook the boy off, and it was only when her brother stumbled and fell that she burst into tears.

Afterwards, shame overwhelmed Luka, and he took a crying child in each arm, wading back into the shallows with them. He looked down to see a thin, red ribbon in the water and realized that he had bloodied one of Marin's knees.

He could not stand the look of fear that was in their eyes.

The *jugo* has blown for several days. Warm and sallow, it stirs up the detritus of the sea and brings it into Rosmarina's shallows. The waves move in long rows from the south and crash against the shore like an assault by lines of endless infantry. In the morning, the rocks will be covered with seaweed and rotting pine branches, soda bottles and plastic bags.

His father's drinking was always especially bad during the *jugo*, so that from an early age Luka took it as a bad omen. None of the islanders are themselves when the wind blows. His wife becomes melancholy and his daughter uncharacteristically silent. Magdalena becomes irritable, and Jadranka grows angry over nothing at all. Those are always the days when motors refuse to start or glass breaks without reason.

But tonight the wind has brought an unsettling clarity, and it is like reaching the surface for a breath of air. He can neither move nor speak, but he watches his wife's still profile from the corner of his left eye. He cannot untangle one day from the next.

He did not like Ana's new boyfriend from Split. He did not like the man's eyes, his way of speaking, and he initially refused to relinquish his granddaughters to their mother's care. "Use your head for once," he told her angrily. "The girls are used to life here. Come back and make a life with them on the island."

But they were *her* daughters, she told him, and it was *her* right.

At seven Jadranka was too young to understand. She was a

girl who laughed easily and found her way into everything: her grandmother's pots and pans, the shed in the courtyard. Luka had caught her trying to uncover the cistern. "I only wanted to see what was underneath," she told him, sniffling, after he shouted at her.

Why does he prefer to use the silver line for fishing, she wanted to know, and not the white? Why are there figs at the beginning of summer and at the end of summer, but very few in the middle? Why do islands stay in one place and not move around like boats?

But she never wondered why she was leaving.

At least he could teach her to swim before she went. At least he could do that much.

Up to that point, she had refused to learn, and he thought he knew the reason. Two years earlier a child visiting from the mainland had drowned in Rosmarina's waters. While Magdalena took the news in stride, Jadranka developed an immediate fear of the sea, waking some nights to the belief that her hair had caught in something and was holding her underwater. She refused lessons the summer she turned five, then again at six, shivering in his arms, and would not relax her stranglehold around his neck when he insisted that she try. Both years his wife had told him, "Patience, Luka. She'll learn when she's ready."

The summer before his granddaughters' departure, he enlisted Magdalena's help, because Jadranka would follow her older sister anywhere, and they spent hours in the shallows. He showed Jadranka how to float, how to tread water, how to take a few strokes. He was trying to cheat time because her mother did not see the importance of this instruction.

"When we get to Split, they'll probably teach her in school," Ana said indifferently.

Magdalena floated on the other side, shouting words of encouragement. She showed her sister how to do handstands in the water, how to flip forward and backward. She was a motion of arms and legs, and the dark, slick hair of her head resembled a porpoise's skin.

Jadranka tried to spin but came up coughing water. It would be a while before she mastered the somersaults, Luka thought, but she was a proficient floater, and he was satisfied. He picked her up and held her so that her legs kicked above the surface and water poured from her in sheets.

The girls were inseparable. At night he could hear them whispering together in their room.

"You must continue looking out for one another now," he told them solemnly, as autumn drew near.

To this end he had told them stories of his own escapades with Vinka. Those tales were his granddaughters' favorites, so that they asked for them by name. Again and again he described sawing their parents' bed in half, their clandestine swimming lessons, the way they shared everything.

"Tell us again, *Dida*," they begged, "about the asps."

And so, for the hundredth time, he told them of the warning system that Vinka had devised, the way of hanging laundry a certain way. If a sheet was first on the line, he could come home, but if any article of clothing hung in that position, his father had been drinking and Luka needed to stay away.

"Two nights," he told his wide-eyed granddaughters. "For two nights we hid out on the Peak, afraid, because it was autumn and the asps come out in autumn. The nights were freezing cold but Vinka refused to leave me, and so we huddled together with the goats."

"What would have happened if you went home?" one or the other always asked.

"*Ajme*," he would tell them gravely. "I don't like to consider it."

For two nights Luka and Vinka had slept side by side beneath constellations so bright that brother and sister could see the features of the other's face. "I'll kill him one day," he had sworn, although he did not tell his granddaughters this part.

He readily narrated the fates of his other sisters: Zora, who died as a young woman in an accident on a foggy stretch of road; Zlatka, who passed away peacefully in her sleep as an old woman. And Iva, who died of cancer a year after Zlatka. But when talking about Vinka, he confined his stories to their childhood adventures.

He suspected that these tales were the reason the sisters disappeared from the house on the morning they were supposed to leave the island, missing the morning ferry and postponing their departure by a day.

Ana looked for them beneath beds and in the courtyard's shed. She searched all the cupboards and closets, and the expression on her face turned from bafflement to irritation. "I told Nikola we'd be back today," she kept repeating, looking at her father as if it were his fault, as if he had been the one to suggest they run away.

"They don't want to go," he finally told her. "Imagine what life in Split will look like after this?" He gestured towards the lane where cars seldom passed and to the waterfront where every shopkeeper and fisherman knew the girls by name.

It was Magdalena, he realized. Magdalena who had gone to bed last night with that betrayed expression on her face. "I don't want to go, *Dida*," she had whispered.

They discovered that the girls had taken their schoolbags, emptying paper and pens in a pile on the desk in their room. Ružica reported a short time later that bread and cheese had been pilfered from the pantry, along with a box of Jadranka's favorite biscuits. They had taken water, as well, and candles from the box on the washroom shelf, and secretly he marveled at Magdalena's resourcefulness.

He found them some hours later in a deserted house beneath

the Peak, Jadranka grinning at him happily from where she sat cross-legged on the floor, eating her biscuits in the midst of this adventure. But Magdalena backed away from him into a corner of the room.

"Come, child." He held his hand out to her, heavyhearted.

"No," she told him evenly.

Her refusal saddened him, not because it was insolent but because it would change nothing. A quick-witted girl, she had been as much his shadow as Jadranka was hers. Since she could walk, she had been fascinated by boats of every variety, missing no opportunity to accompany him when he went fishing. She could recite the names of fish, their feeding patterns, the likelihood of encountering them in shoals or in the deep.

"What will I do in Split?" she had asked him miserably.

At eleven, her contemporaries were already wearing makeup and simpering at boys, but other fishermen observed Magdalena's proficiency with nets and the lightning speed with which she could scale a fish. "She's worth her weight in gold," they told him. "So what if she's a girl?"

When they were at their fishing camp on the Devil's Stones, her sister occupied her time by weaving rosemary into wreaths or building small structures with rocks, entire colonies for a race of invisible, three-inch men. But Magdalena was at his side constantly, and years after his son's escape he poured his knowledge into this second eager vessel.

He was tempted to return and tell their mother that he had not found them, to allow her to return to Split alone, but he knew that this would only postpone the inevitable, and through the window he could see that night was already falling. "Come," he told her again. "You can do better than the life of a fisherman."

He had spoken halfheartedly of the better schools in Split, of the city's illustrious history. But she burst into tears at his words, and he only managed to lure her down with the promise of one more swimming lesson in the morning, Jadranka lying on the surface between them as if they alone could make her float.

Rosmarina had always existed, he told them in his stories, although he knew this could hardly be true. He was not an educated man, but he understood that land rose upward into mountains only to be scraped down again by wind and rain. Tundras melted and froze over, entire seas dried up into deserts. Still, he let them think that Rosmarina had existed since the dawn of time.

It was the farthest inhabited island from the mainland. The journey took five hours, but he could remember a time when Rosmarina was remoter still, before automobiles and daily ferry connections, when a trip to Split was like striking out into a different country. Now the mainland drew them ever closer, as if it had caught Rosmarina on a hook and was reeling it steadily in.

He was often returning from night fishing as the ferry slipped out of the harbor towards the open sea. He watched its illuminated bulk from his fishing boat, imagining the hull filled with the island's children, all lying head-to-toe in stacks like canned sardines. The problem, he thought, was that they had watched too much television and believed in softer lives in other places.

"As if we're bleeding to death, my Lena," he told his elder granddaughter on nights she accompanied him, the ferry lights spectral on her young face.

He himself went to Split on the same ferry several times a year. So, really, he knew the passengers did not lie head-to-toe in stacks like sardines. He made the trip when he needed to buy fishing equipment or when Ružica needed something for the house. She packed his lunch—a sandwich and some hardboiled eggs—and he drove his ancient Fiat onto the floating monster. Each time his wheels relinquished the stone pier of the island for the rumbling metal loading plank, he panicked and had to concentrate on keeping his hands on the steering wheel. The episodes had only worsened with age.

Sometimes he grew angry with himself. He asked himself, a little viciously, *What is it that you fear, stupid old man?* And the answer had not changed in twenty years or more. He saw it in the eyes that watched him from the rearview mirror: *I fear death away from the island.*

Part of him believed he might die on the boat, or in Split. He was afraid that the last thing he saw before he closed his eyes would be Rosmarina receding behind him, or, worse, the filthy water along Split's *riva* from where the island could not be seen even on the clearest days. In fact, he knew that it could not be seen from any point in the city because decades ago, returning from the Second World War, he and Vinka had climbed Marjan Mountain to see for themselves. Rosmarina was so far out to sea as to be wholly invisible, a state of affairs that pleased him when he was home and frightened him when he was not. In a recurring nightmare he'd had since the war, he was returning from the mainland in his own boat, but the island had vanished. He crossed the space where it should be, oriented himself using the other islands, and recrossed it. But the island had disappeared.

On the ferry journey back, he usually bought coffee. In good weather, he found a bench outside and watched the other islands slip by like pebbles through his fingers. First Brač and Šolta, then Hvar, then Vis and Lastovo on opposite sides in the distance. In summertime billowing sails dotted the sea, and he watched their graceful dips and turns. He looked around him, noting that there usually seemed to be fewer passengers on the return.

Rosmarina always appeared in the distance like a mirage, the Peak like a titan's head breaking the surface of the water. As they drew closer, he could make out the town and the abandoned olive groves on the terraces beneath the Peak. Like all neglected things, the trees had mutinied. Many had stopped producing fruit because they were not pruned, and because the weeds at their feet sucked all the moisture from the soil. Logically, he knew this, but he could not help thinking that the trees had stopped producing out of anger. Because there were no hands left to pick the olives.

These dark thoughts usually accompanied him on his drive home from the ferry landing. Inside the house, however, he always found warmth and the smell of soup, the girls doing their schoolwork at the kitchen table or helping Ružica slice cucumbers.

If Luka's dominion was water, then his wife's was air, and Ružica was teaching Magdalena to pray. She showed the girl how to place her palms together, to point her fingers to the sky, just as she had once shown their son and daughter.

"In the beginning was the sea," Magdalena told her grandmother confidently one evening as he was coming in.

Ružica laughed at this, looking over the girl's head at Luka, who was hanging his jacket behind the door.

"That's not how it goes," she told her, and showed her in the Bible. "In the beginning was the Word."

But each time Magdalena began, she got it wrong. "In the beginning was the sea," she said, so that Luka's heart expanded, exactly as wind filled a white sail. "And the sea was God."

CHAPTER 5

It was not easy to say goodbye to her grandfather's unconscious form, so still at dawn that Magdalena wondered if he had died in the night. But when she placed the flat of her palm on his chest, she could feel its incremental rise and fall.

She was leaving because there was still no word from her sister. No matter how abrupt her previous departures, Jadranka had always confided her movements to Magdalena, telephoning from a bus station or ferry terminal and leaving it to her older sister to break the news to their grandparents. "I'll always tell you," Jadranka had once assured her.

"So, I'm your keeper," Magdalena told her a little testily.

"Yes," Jadranka had responded automatically, with no trace of guile.

She had never vanished altogether, until now.

"Of course you should come," Katarina told her. "We know people in the State Department who can rush your visa. And I can send the money for your ticket."

But Magdalena declined the second part of this offer, uncomfortable with the idea of her cousin playing the generous benefactor.

School was in its final weeks, and an older friend—one of

Jadranka's former teachers, in fact—agreed to come out of retirement to teach Magdalena's remaining classes.

"Your sister has always moved to her own music" was all she
would say when told about the matter, her reticence so welcome,
her lack of questions such a departure from the prying of other
islanders, that Magdalena startled her with a small, fierce hug.

So she kissed her grandmother, who had wept silent tears since
making Magdalena's coffee that morning, and she shut the gate
on the quiet courtyard behind her. On her walk to the port, she
took in the dark stone houses and the occasional burst of purple
bougainvillea. Since her childhood, each leave-taking of Rosmarina had resembled the first one, so that something inside her
rebelled at going, even as her feet carried her towards the ferry
landing.

She had left everything in order behind her—her grandmother
had access to the funds in Magdalena's bank account, and she had
paid the newest crop of bills—but still she descended through the
village like a woman on the way to her place of execution. It was
as if a cord connected her to Rosmarina, and only for Jadranka did
she have the will to fight against it.

This attachment was both habit and biology.

In her childhood a researcher had studied the islanders' sense
of direction. It was a capability he explained in terms of the Inuit
in the far-off Arctic, who could find their way through blizzards.
"It's a rare genetic gift," he had explained to her grandfather.

Magdalena was the only girl involved in his study. She could remember being tested with blindfolds, her boat turned in so many
circles that it made her dizzy, and striking out on moonless nights.
The scientist had concluded that not everyone on the island possessed the skill—which he termed *innate nautical orientation*—but
she belonged squarely to the group that did. As an adult she had
looked up the study and found herself referred to simply by her
initials: M.B.

It was a pull, she could remember explaining to the scientist when pressed. Like a nail that is dragged across a table by a magnet.

The subject spent one year of childhood on the mainland, he had written in the study, *although this has not compromised her instincts.*

While Jadranka Babić's forays had taken her farther and farther from home, her older sister had never flown before the day she left for America, had certainly never stopped to consider the nature of sky she could not see from the ground. While people around her inspected the contents of their seat-back pockets or read newspapers and books, she stared through the window and searched for the plane's shadow on the runway. But the day was overcast, and she did not think that the ground registered the shape of their ascent.

She was a voracious reader, and so books had already introduced her to the winding alleyways of London and the high passes of the Himalayas. She had stood on the ramparts of barricaded Paris and moved along New York City's teeming streets.

Although she would not be parted from Rosmarina for long, she had always meant to visit other places, and had even saved her meager teacher's salary for this purpose. She envisioned returning from those destinations with postcards that she could tack to the bulletin boards of her Rosmarina classroom. The suitcase she checked at Split Airport had lurked in a corner of the attic since her student years, however. She had evicted a family of spiders nesting inside and taken a damp cloth to its exterior, but it still retained a musty odor.

She wore her teacher's clothes on the journey but left her hair loose. In the harsh fluorescence of the airplane's toilet, she regarded her reflection dispassionately: small and lithe, her dimensions had not changed appreciably in fifteen years, but tiny fault lines had started at the corners of her eyes. Her hair was still the same dark mass, but there were several long silver threads at the front that she had not considered pulling until that moment. In the end, she left them where they were and returned to her seat for the duration of the flight.

She had not seen Katarina in over twenty years, not since the summer her cousin had spent on the island. She still remembered her as the girl with the piggy eyes, although Jadranka had sent pictures of the family, and Magdalena knew that Katarina's face had lost its baby fat, that her hair—at one time mousy brown—was now the color of honey. *She's a big deal,* her sister had written. *Her gallery is always in the newspaper.*

The woman in the photographs looked younger than her age. She shared Magdalena's strong jawline and wore funky silver jewelry. Her smile for the camera was broad. *She has a chip on her shoulder about Rosmarina,* wrote Jadranka. *She got a little drunk one night and told me that the smartest people had been forced to leave the island. That the ones left were mostly gangsters and former Party hacks.*

This did not surprise Magdalena, who remembered that, after a year of exchanging postcards and letters, their cousin had arrived on Rosmarina at the age of twelve prepared to find nothing but informers—in the newspaper sellers on the *riva,* and the shopgirls in the market, even among their closest neighbors.

Sunlight struck the airplane's metal wing, and Magdalena closed her eyes. She imagined Jadranka sitting in a window seat, months earlier, and cloud cover as thick as today obliterating the sea beneath them.

She wondered if Jadranka had the Rosmarina gene. Or, for that matter, if Katarina did.

The American girl who had landed at Split Airport in the summer of 1984 was different from what Magdalena expected, despite the photographs they had exchanged. She was taller, for one thing, with breasts that already stretched the cotton of her T-shirt. Her braces—strange, torturous-looking devices—had been removed and perfect white teeth left in their place. But she was also softer around the middle, a detail her school pictures had hidden, and had an oily complexion that caused tiny white pimples to sprout in the creases of her nose. And while it was impossible for Magdalena to register all these details from the observation deck, watching with her grandfather as her cousin walked across the tarmac, she already sensed that Katarina's arrival meant trouble.

It might have been her age, and the fact that Katarina threatened to trump Magdalena's own status as eldest child in their household. Magdalena did not like to think about the years she could not remember, the ones when she had allegedly worshipped her older cousin. At least part of this resistance was territorial. Rosmarina was her island because, after all, the other girl's family had given it up. They had traded it for ten-speed bikes and colored stationery. In short, they had picked an easier life, and it only seemed fair that they should lose something in that transaction.

Luka had already explained that Katarina was coming alone because her parents would risk arrest by returning. But they wanted her to see the place where she was born and the family that had been denied her in America.

When Katarina emerged from customs, she was clutching a white leather purse. Her expression was uncertain, as if she expected someone to wrest it from her, or as if she were afraid she would be devoured in the crowds of the small airport.

"That's her," Luka told Magdalena, who was already taking the other girl's measure. "She looks exactly like her mother."

He called out in welcome and walked forward to embrace her.

There was something about his familiarity, about Katarina's smile of recognition and the arms she threw around his waist, that troubled Magdalena. This was *her* grandfather, she thought stubbornly from behind them, and for a moment she was afraid that Katarina might not leave at the end of the summer as she was supposed to. That she would stay with them forever.

Katarina had not been questioned about her parents at the airport. She seemed surprised by this fact, and Magdalena made a face in the backseat of her grandfather's car, wondering if her cousin had expected to end up in jail. It seemed a silly kind of fear to her when everyone knew that this only happened to adults.

They had not even opened her suitcase for an inspection, and for the entire ferry trip Katarina babbled about the things she had brought: chewing gum, vegetable peelers for Aunt Ružica, tape cassettes for Jadranka and Magdalena. She crowed as if she had succeeded in smuggling stolen jewels into the country.

"We have chewing gum," Magdalena told her, so that the other girl's face fell.

But her cousin's response a moment later was confident. "American chewing gum tastes better."

Jadranka had been running a low fever that morning, and so she was waiting for them on the island. But Magdalena already disliked the way her younger sister talked nonstop about their American cousin. "Will she have pompoms?" she had asked just this morning, having seen these somewhere on a television show.

Now, studying the way Katarina kept the white purse in her lap, winding the strap around her hand, Magdalena realized that her cousin was anxious. It was the first time she had ever been away from her parents, she explained, a revelation that drew understanding grunts from Luka but a stony silence from his granddaughter.

"I brought perfume for Cousin Ana," she told them.

"Magdalena's mother lives on the mainland," Luka told his niece. "But she'll come for a visit in a few weeks and you can give it to her then."

Katarina's bright eyes took in her cousin, who had turned to watch a ferry approaching from the opposite direction. Long after the conversation moved on to other subjects, Magdalena could

still feel the American girl studying her, considering this information she had been given.

Katarina's suitcase did indeed contain many marvels. There were
Hershey bars and dozens of packs of chewing gum, which she
shared generously with her younger cousins. There were white
lace bras and a bag of sanitary napkins, and several books in
English about a young red-haired woman who solved mysteries,
an idea that enchanted Jadranka so much that she demanded to be
told the plots to each of them. There was a Walkman, a rectangle
of black plastic that Magdalena secretly coveted. And there was a
box of colored pencils such as they had never seen, with a dozen
different shades for every color.

"I take art lessons after school," Katarina told them. "My
teacher says that I'm one of her best students."

At night, when the three girls shared a double bed, Katarina
spoke of Croatian picnics in Pittsburgh and the better-looking boys
who played soccer there. She performed in a folk-dancing troupe,
she told them, demonstrating some of the steps as Jadranka sat up in
bed and clapped her hands in time to imaginary music. An authen-
tic Croatian dance, Katarina insisted, although Magdalena stated her
suspicion that it had been made up by someone in America.

Her cousin could claim anything, she realized. Katarina's distance from home meant that she was no longer constrained by the
truth. Gems had been sewn onto the hem of her confirmation
dress, she told them, and she lived in a mansion.

"She's making it all up," Magdalena complained to her grandfather.

"Things, Lena," he only told her sadly. "Give her that one small
satisfaction."

Katarina hardly remembered her older cousin, Marin Morić ,but
she told Luka and Ružica what little she knew about their vanished son. Seated self-importantly at the kitchen table across from

them, she explained in a breathless voice that he had lived with them during their first year in America. He had taught her how to tie her shoelaces, but there had been no sign of him in the six years since then.

Magdalena eavesdropped on this conversation. Sitting in the kitchen doorway, she kept her back to where they sat and her bare feet in the sun. She studied a curious lizard that had darted between her legs and waited in the coolness of her shadow.

Marin and her father had fought, Katarina admitted, lowering her voice officiously, sending glances at Magdalena's back that the other girl could not see but sensed nonetheless. "It had something to do with Barren Island."

"Barren Island?" Luka asked sharply.

Magdalena continued to watch the lizard. He had gone completely still, but something pulsed in his throat. His heartbeat, perhaps. Or his breath. Behind her, Katarina repeated the words. *Barren Island.* Magdalena had never heard of it, but she could tell by her grandfather's voice that it upset him.

"And he hasn't contacted us in all the years since then." Katarina's voice was now adult in its indignation.

Magdalena rose at this and brushed off the seat of her shorts, then turned to find that her cousin was watching her.

"That's unlike him," her grandmother was saying in a bewildered voice.

Magdalena had never heard of Barren Island. She imagined it like a dead pine tree that had lost all its needles and was nothing but a brittle piece of timber.

"It's a terrible place," Katarina explained that night in the dark. "Not a thing grows there. There are only rocks as sharp as fangs and heat so terrible that people catch fire."

Magdalena snorted at this, even as her younger sister asked in a small voice: "They catch fire?"

"Just like paper" was their cousin's knowledgeable reply. "The hair goes first, and then the face. And there are dogs that will eat you if you don't do exactly what the prison guards say. And the guards—"

"How do you know?" Magdalena demanded. "Have you ever been there?"

"No," Katarina admitted in a satisfied voice, as if she had been anticipating this very question. "But your Uncle Marin was."

It could not be true. As far as Magdalena was concerned, it was just one more thing her cousin had made up. She had it under good authority that her uncle had been one of Rosmarina's best fishermen. He was not a criminal.

"I can't believe you've never heard of it," her cousin told her in wondering tones.

"You're making it up," Magdalena accused.

"Am not," Katarina told her. "Ask your grandfather."

But Magdalena could not bring herself to do this.

To Magdalena's relief, Katarina did not entirely take to life on Rosmarina. She liked to sunbathe on the rocks, but she feared the sharp black urchins in the shallows. She liked to accompany the family to their fishing camp on the Devil's Stones, but she did not care for fishing, or for boats. Instead she played with Jadranka or drew in her sketchbooks, pictures that Magdalena thought only marginally resembled their subjects. Or she listened to her Walkman, lying on a towel and looking up at the sky, occasionally singing aloud in English.

She liked to prowl around the Peak with Magdalena, but became easily spooked. Magdalena realized this one day when she hid from Katarina behind a crumbling stone wall, watching smugly as her cousin looked for her, the annoyance on her face turning quickly into fear.

"That's not funny," she said, pushing Magdalena when she jumped out to startle her.

Magdalena landed on her bottom in the dust, and Katarina did not speak to her for several hours. "Your sister is mean," she told Jadranka, who relayed this message to Magdalena.

"It's true," Jadranka added matter-of-factly to her sister. "You were mean."

Katarina claimed that the noise of Pittsburgh's city streets did not bother her, but the crowing of roosters did. She missed her friends at home and her bedroom. She griped about the island's dearth of television channels, brands of chocolate, jungle gyms.

In her comparisons, America always won out against Rosmarina, and she did not limit reporting this conclusion to her two cousins. One day in the port, she regaled a group of children with stories about cinemas that were as big as cities. "It's not like here," she said with a wrinkled nose, gesturing in the direction of the summer *kino.* "It's a real movie theater, not just a painted wall."

"You should go back, then," one of the older boys told her. "My father says this country knows what to do with *govno* like you."

"Shut up," Magdalena told him, surprised by the venom in her voice. "Everybody knows that your father's a drunk!"

The boy's face turned purple with rage. "Well, your mother——"

But Magdalena swung at him before he could get the word out. Although smaller, she had the advantage of surprise, and he held the side of his face in stupefaction as a circle of children formed. A woman from one of the nearby shops had been watching them. She hurried out and took both Magdalena and the boy by the ear, before the fight could go any further, and ordered them home.

That night in bed, Katarina was quieter than usual. "In America, you can say whatever you want," she informed them in a whisper. "It's not like here."

Magdalena could hear Jadranka's even breathing, and she pretended to be asleep, as well. But her cousin continued bitterly. "My father says this country is nothing but a giant prison."

Magdalena's mother made one trip to Rosmarina after Katarina's arrival, cooing over the perfume that the American girl presented. "That's very nice, little cousin," she said after spraying it on her wrist and sniffing appreciatively. "I imagine that America smells just like that."

This won a smile from Katarina, but Magdalena merely watched them from a careful distance.

Katarina found it strange that her cousins did not live with their mother, and she was fascinated that nobody ever spoke about their dead father.

"Do you remember him?" she asked Magdalena.

"A little."

"Even though you were only two?" she pressed with a doubtful smile, reminding Magdalena of a spider that sets a sticky trap.

The truth was that Magdalena knew very little about her father, and still less about his death. She knew that the man who had found her father's boat adrift had occasionally fished the Devil's Stones with him, and that he had returned to port that day to raise the alarm in the village that Goran Babić was gone.

She could not remember him opening the gate or walking rapidly through the courtyard, where she had been chasing lizards along the stone wall. But she thought she remembered being lifted into someone's arms while her mother screamed the word *dead* from inside the house, repeating it so many times that after the first moments it sounded more like the cries of an angry seagull than any human voice.

To this day, Pero Radić—the man who had delivered the news of her father's death—always made a point to stop and talk to her, to inquire after her mother and her grandparents' health. She knew that it was not affection that prompted his concern but the simple fact that he had been the one to find the empty boat with Rosmarina markings turning towards the channel. "A strange sight," she had heard him tell others.

Magdalena clung to snatches of information about her father the way other girls filled jewelry boxes with seed pearls and gold. She was more curious about him than Jadranka, who was born after his death.

"You look exactly like him," Katarina told her, having already scoured Ružica's photograph album for his picture, and even examined the pages of the family Bible where births and deaths were recorded. Her cousin's words swelled Magdalena with silent pride, although she refused to acknowledge them.

Jadranka was less fascinated by Katarina than she was fascinated by Katarina's enormous box of colored pencils. Before bedtime, she would sit at the table in the room the girls shared and pull them out, one by one.

"Look," she demanded of Magdalena, who could not see anything out of the ordinary in the blue-gray color that Jadranka waved in front of her, nor about the red. But her younger sister spent hours organizing them in careful piles, divisions of color that made little sense to anybody else.

"It's okay to look at them," Katarina told her. "Just be careful. They were expensive."

On the day she discovered their points dulled, she knew exactly where to find the culprit. "They're *mine,*" she told Jadranka, small lights flaring in her eyes.

Observing the way that her younger sister's lower lip trembled, Magdalena grabbed the box in one sudden movement and emptied it on their bed. She picked up one and snapped it in half, then picked up a second as if she meant to do the same.

Katarina only looked at her in shock before turning on her heel and running down the stairs. But when Jadranka dove for the broken pencil—a sunny shade of yellow—Magdalena was surprised to see that her sister was crying. She sat on the floor, trying to refit the two halves.

She looked up at Magdalena. "It was beautiful," she told her. "And now it's ruined."

Within half an hour, Luka Morić had remedied the situation. The pencils were Katarina's, and Jadranka was to leave them alone. But he found a box of colored chalk and gave this to his granddaughter instead.

He did not remember where the chalk had come from, but it bore the unmistakable scent of the mainland—a sharp and slightly chemical odor with no trace of mildew. On Rosmarina, damp inhabited every room. It softened bread and rendered paper as pliable as cloth, and like other island fishermen, Luka brought it ashore in his nets and sodden trouser cuffs. But the cardboard box was exotic in its stiffness, and Jadranka was immediately captivated by the crisp edges of the chalk inside.

He watched in satisfaction as she left a flurry of handprints on the stone walls of the house, likening the pastel sticks to a type of candy sold by Rosmarina's only shop. When she placed the chalk on her tongue, however, she observed with disappointment that the taste was not at all like the candies.

"That isn't for eating," he told her in amusement, selecting one of the pieces from the box and leading all three girls through the courtyard to the lane. The tarmac had lightened beneath the Adriatic sun, and he knelt before them to draw the rough outline of a boat, giving it a tall mast and triangular sail. He drew an island beside it, pleased when they immediately identified its crescent shape as Rosmarina.

"Now me!" Jadranka begged, so that he handed her a few pieces of chalk, then did the same with Magdalena and Katarina.

He watched as they set to work a short distance from each other, intent on their stick figures and lemon suns.

It was not long before Magdalena tired of this new game, however. She threw down the chalk and announced that she wanted to go for a walk. Katarina, still miffed, turned her back at this suggestion, and Jadranka was too intent on her drawing to even lift her face.

"Jadranka," Magdalena said, but her sister gave no indication that she had heard her name, and Luka studied the younger girl's expression of rapt concentration. This temporary deafness descended on Jadranka from time to time. Lost in a game or chore, she claimed not to hear when she was being called. Just a few weeks before, the house had been in a state of panic when Ružica discovered the cistern in the courtyard uncovered and Jadranka nowhere to be found. They had called for her and shone flashlights into the darkness of the well, relieved to see their unbroken reflections looking back from the bottom. A short time later Magdalena found her reading a picture book beneath the bed they shared, oblivious of the commotion.

Now Luka studied Jadranka's bowed head, the way her red hair fell forward to reveal the delicate swells of her vertebrae. There had always been something salamander-like about her long limbs, and the back of her thin neck looked in those moments uncannily like the decomposed lizards her sister sometimes produced from the garden, their spines like chain links of bone.

"Jadranka," he echoed, his voice soft, the way he would address a sleepwalker.

Her back was curved like a bow. Her hand made an arcing movement, but she gave no indication that she had heard him. Nor did she seem to sense Katarina, who had raised her head to stare at her younger cousin, nor Magdalena, who was approaching from behind. But as Luka watched, Magdalena faltered, eyes darkening at something on the pavement.

He thought that she must have seen a scorpion, and so he rushed towards them. The animal's venom would not kill a healthy adult but could sicken a child, and he had taught them to be wary of those small, dark bodies. The creatures ordinarily kept to the shade, but there seemed to be a greater number of them that year, emerging from beneath stones in the courtyard, on one occasion traversing the kitchen's whitewashed ceiling, so that his wife's shriek had brought him running.

"Where?" he barked at Magdalena, but she only pointed at the ground, where nothing moved except for Jadranka's arm. Looking for the telltale pincers and curved tail, he realized belatedly that it was Jadranka herself who had caused her sister's alarm, and he, too, stopped short, taking in the pictures that were flying fully formed from her hand: birds that lifted from the ground with wings in perfect proportion to their bodies, and fish that swam across pavement made to look like water.

Magdalena's expression had turned to one of wonder, as if witnessing an act of alchemy, but Luka felt uneasy as he took in his younger granddaughter's trancelike state. He crouched beside her, placing a hand softly on her shoulder. "Did your cousin teach you that, little one?" he asked, and it was only then that she looked up with a smile of recognition and shook her head.

Later, he watched her demonstrate this newfound ability for her sister, moving Magdalena's hand in her own as Katarina watched. He could tell by Magdalena's pleased expression that for those few seconds she was certain that she understood—that she believed it would be like riding a bicycle or tying a shoelace, a skill she had taught Jadranka just the year before. It was a code that needed only to be cracked, a secret language that practice might improve. But without her sister's guidance the code was impenetrable, and she invariably produced graceless stick figures and rhomboid houses. After a few attempts, she gave up and watched Jadranka draw the house behind them in startling detail, never once turning to study her subject.

By that afternoon a small crowd of neighborhood children and curious adults had gathered, and although Luka retreated to the house, he heard someone mention a musical prodigy who had composed an entire symphony by the time he was four. Through the kitchen's open windows, he thought he could also detect tones of envy and even of suspicion. A neighbor sniffed that her young son could solve complicated arithmetic problems and that this, surely, was more useful than drawing pictures that the rain would only wash away.

"That's good," he heard Katarina concede. "But it's my turn now."

In the weeks that followed, it became apparent that Magdalena possessed no artistic inclinations of her own. Rather than envying Jadranka's talent, however, she took it upon herself all that summer to scout suitable locations for her sister's drawings. Katarina was a halfhearted participant in these endeavors.

"I prefer pencil," she told her cousins. "Or paint."

Jadranka's drawings began to appear across the island, on the crumbling stucco of abandoned houses and in the dark tar of roads. "I saw Jadranka's pictures," islanders would tell Luka in awed tones on the waterfront, occasionally adding that his granddaughter was destined for fame and that the newspaper was sure to write an article about her.

Jadranka's drawing, though harmless at first glance, made her stand out still further. Over the course of that summer, the island adopted a subtle guardedness towards the six-year-old, as though she were something native but not quite right, like their half-Swiss neighbor, or like the boy up the lane who was Magdalena's age but crawled on all fours and could not speak.

"That girl's a strange one," Magdalena overheard on the *riva* one day, repeating this statement in confidence to her grandfather, certain that the woman had been talking about her sister.

"Why do people look at her like that?" Magdalena wanted to know.

"Like what?"

"Like she's from outer space."

"You're imagining it," he had told her carefully. "She's as much from the island as you or I."

It did not help, he thought, that Jadranka resembled nobody else on Rosmarina, not even the members of her immediate family. Her red hair stood out like a flame among all the blond and brown-haired children, making her look like she had indeed been delivered by aliens, or switched at birth in the Split hospital where she was born.

For his part, Luka could not understand Jadranka's need to leave drawings of birds and dancing figures in her wake. He believed that it was a game whose novelty would wear off, even as she wore the sticks of chalk into tiny pebbles.

On the afternoon Jadranka first drew pictures on the lane in front of their house, Magdalena embarked on a project of outlining things. She circled the cistern with blue and drew a white rectangle on the ground around Luka's car. She drew the lines, he thought, like defenses, and he watched her work feverishly to contain the entire house, pushing her way through the bracken that grew outside the kitchen window.

"Come and draw me," he heard her tell her sister, who left her pictures to trace an outline of Magdalena's legs and arms as Katarina looked on. When Jadranka was done, Magdalena instructed her to lie down in the same position. When she finished, the outline of her sister's body was contained entirely within her own.

Luka did not notice Katarina's repeated inspections of his wife's Bible, nor the way she became suddenly watchful in those days. Her boasts of early summer had ceased, and if anything, he thought that she and Magdalena had declared a truce, the cousins eating side by side in companionable silence and disappearing to remote corners of the island together when meals were done.

He did not realize that Katarina was biding her time for the ideal opportunity to reveal what she knew. But Magdalena sensed it. She felt something brewing within her American cousin. Each time Magdalena looked up, Katarina was watching with a little smile. Each time Jadranka drew something else—a playful monkey, a fishing boat—Katarina's silence became deeper.

"Your mom is pretty," she told Magdalena unexpectedly one day.

Her cousin shrugged. "I guess," she said.

"When she was here, all the men on the *riva* were looking at her."

Magdalena frowned, unsure what her cousin was getting at.

"I bet she's had a lot of boyfriends," Katarina added.

In truth, Magdalena did not know her mother very well, and had certainly never stopped to ponder her boyfriends.

"You're becoming a real little fisherman," Ana had told Magdalena on her visit earlier that summer, taking in her sunburnt nose and calloused hands with an expression that was more annoyed than playful.

It was clear that she found it easier to talk to Jadranka, who loved to have her hair brushed and decorated with barrettes.

"Your mother said that she'll never come back to Rosmarina," Katarina told Magdalena after she had left. "She likes it better in Split."

Magdalena shrugged her response, prompting a stare from Katarina.

"What a funny thing you are," she said, in her amused older-cousin voice. "I'd die if I couldn't live with my mother."

Magdalena understood that Katarina was lying in wait. She saw it every time the American girl observed Jadranka with her chalk. It was there—a naked jealousy that both satisfied and disturbed Magdalena—whenever their cousin considered those drawings that belonged at once to nobody and everybody, decorating roads one day only to be washed away in storms the next.

"Maybe you should draw on paper," Ružica had suggested to her younger granddaughter. "So you can keep the things you've done."

But it was clear that Jadranka was unconcerned with building such an archive. For her, the joy was in the making. And once that was done, she happily consigned her creations to the elements.

Katarina, on the other hand, was possessive of her sketchbook, her pencils, her position as older and wiser cousin. And so she began by picking at Jadranka's pictures, ever so slightly. This face was a little long, she offered in pleasant tones, or that cat looked more like a rabbit.

"I like rabbits," Jadranka told her enthusiastically, and then proceeded to draw an entire family of them on a large, flat rock beneath the Peak.

Katarina and Magdalena sat on a stone outcropping above her, swinging their legs over the side, watching the top of Jadranka's bent head.

"It's funny," Katarina told her unexpectedly. "Before you wrote back to me, we didn't know that Jadranka existed. We thought you were an only child."

Magdalena looked at her cousin in surprise.

Katarina lowered her voice. "It will be hard on her when she finds out. About her father, I mean."

"What about our father?" Magdalena asked automatically.

"Not *your* father," Katarina said, studying a fissure in the rock, a nervous smile playing around her mouth. "*Her* father."

Magdalena only looked at her blankly, but that night the two girls descended quietly to the kitchen, where Katarina showed her the dates in Ružica's Bible—Goran Babić's death, which was followed two years later by Jadranka's birth—her hand shaking slightly in the flashlight's glow.

"It's a mistake," Magdalena told her stubbornly, slamming the book shut. She took the flashlight from the other girl's hand and turned it off.

Katarina gave an exasperated sigh. "It takes nine months to make a baby," she told her younger cousin. "Everyone knows that."

Magdalena could sense the other girl watching her in the dark, waiting to see what she would do.

And so Magdalena rose wordlessly and returned to their bedroom, where she crawled into bed beside a sleeping Jadranka. Katarina appeared in the doorway, and again Magdalena could sense the other girl watching her, nervously this time. After a moment Katarina slipped quietly, almost contritely, into the other side of the bed.

The next morning when Katarina awoke, she discovered with some shock that she was pinned against the mattress, Magdalena's face mere inches above her own. The girls stared at each other for several seconds, Jadranka's voice rising from the courtyard as she said something to her grandmother.

"If you tell anyone," Magdalena said in a fierce whisper, "I'll make you sorry. Do you understand?"

Katarina nodded, her expression so stunned that a rush of satisfaction momentarily blinded Magdalena to what she now knew.

They did not speak of it again. In August, Katarina left Jadranka the box of colored pencils, the fractured yellow bound together with tape. Magdalena understood that this was a peace offering, but while Jadranka exulted over this bounty, Magdalena did not acknowledge it in any way.

On the day of Katarina's departure, the entire family accompanied her to Split Airport, Magdalena's mother showing up unexpectedly to give the girl some chocolates for her trip. Katarina hugged each of them in turn, but when she got to Magdalena, who allowed herself to be embraced for the benefit of the adults who were present, Katarina burst into tears.

"There, there," Ružica said, and placed an arm around each girl. "Don't worry. You're family. You'll see each other again."

PART II

CHAPTER 6

The first time the red-haired woman came into his restaurant, in May, she ordered a cup of coffee and a slice of cake, a chocolate and hazelnut concoction that his wife, Luz, had created when they first opened some years before. It was just past the lunchtime rush, and he was going over receipts at the bar, so he did not pay much attention to the young woman, who sat alone and stared at the rainy street. But when an enormous umbrella bobbed past outside—a shock of yellow in a colorless landscape—he looked up to discover that she was not watching its owner but studying him in the reflection.

"Lousy weather," he offered as their eyes met.

"Yes," she agreed without turning.

She rose a few moments later, half the cake still on her plate and a ten-dollar bill beside her empty cup. She did not meet his eyes again but hovered by the restaurant's entrance, watching the rain come down so heavily that the buildings on the other side of the street appeared deserted in their grayness.

"It should blow over in a few minutes," he told her back. "If you want to wait."

She gave no indication that she had heard him, and a moment later she was gone, her hair a red motion outside the same rain-spattered window where she had been sitting.

Hector, his headwaiter, looked up from the other end of the bar where he was folding napkins.

"I guess we scared her off," Marin told him with a chuckle.

She returned a week later.

"The little red bird is back," Hector told Marin, passing behind him in the kitchen. "And she's asking for *rožata*."

Marin straightened at this. "Okay," he said. "I'll bring it out."

Writing the word on the menu next to *flan* had been his idea, a caprice not altogether typical of him. But it was the food that he would forever associate with his mother's kitchen: the cool creaminess of the custard, the smoky sugar on top. "Just listen to the sound of that word," he had told his wife. There was something of dawn in *rožata,* of a Mediterranean sky climbing out of darkness. And Luz had sensed the word's importance to her husband, so that the dessert appeared on the menu under both its Spanish and Croatian names.

Only rarely did someone order it as *rožata,* however. So that it also served a different purpose, immediately identifying the patron as his countryman.

"I like to see them coming," he'd once told his wife in the dark days of the beginning, when such things had seemed a matter of survival because there were informers—and worse—even in America.

He imagined that they came armed with small notebooks in which they wrote down every detail, his life cracked open like the ribcage of a small, roasted animal. Over the years he had grown adept at recognizing them, and although he had not sensed their presence in years, he felt the same wariness whenever someone from his country appeared in the restaurant, the life he had left unrecognizable in the one he now led.

★　　★　　★

She was seated as before, watching traffic pass slowly in the street. Her red hair was gathered back from her face in an almost austere fashion, and a tiny fleck of gold sparkled at her nostril. It was not a typically Croatian face, although he wondered if he even knew what that was anymore. In his first years in America, he could identify his brethren at a distance of twenty feet. There was always a gaunt, careful look about them, and they wore the clothes that he, too, had worn upon arrival: the same pressed white shirts and dark slacks, the well-worn shoes, polished each morning before Mass, for jobs in factories and warehouses. In the 1970s, urban Americans did not polish their shoes like that. Only foreigners did.

But while it was still easy to identify his contemporaries—the middle-aged men and women who had never given up their gold or their Sunday best—youth perplexed him, and he would sooner have thought this young woman a Hungarian or a Swede.

"*Rožata,*" he told her, presenting the plate with a flourish. Then, in Croatian: "We don't get requests for this every day."

She studied him for a moment, smiling with an uncertainty that was at odds with the intensity of her gaze.

"It's my favorite," she told him in the familiar singsong of Split. Her voice was huskier than he had expected, and he placed a spoon beside her plate. A smoker, he thought, for this was another thing that often differentiated his countrymen from Americans, although this pattern, too, was changing.

"It's why I came in," she said, nodding at the plate. "It was a surprise to see it on the menu."

He looked at her in amusement. "It's why you came in the first time," he corrected, and for a moment she looked uneasy.

"Yes," she said. "The first time, although I ended up having cake."

"The cake is good, too," he told her. "My wife's recipe."

She nodded.

He held out a hand to her. "Marin Morris."

The dark centers of her pupils widened at this, like two tiny lungs filling with air, and he felt suddenly self-conscious, as if she were about to laugh at the ridiculousness of this name. Decades later and it still sat strangely upon his tongue. But it had been the suggestion of the judge who presided over his immigration case. *Forget all that,* the man had counseled him, and because Marin's country had spat him out with no more ceremony than an incinerator shows to ash, he had dropped Morić to become Morris.

But she did not laugh. If anything, she looked a little stricken.

"Jadranka," she told him. She looked down at her own hands, which lay clasped in her lap. Church hands, it occurred to him as she raised one to shake his, like the smooth skin of a plaster Madonna, a rosary clasped between them the only thing missing.

It was a strange thought for an agnostic. Besides, Marin chided himself in the same moment, there was nothing churchlike about the girl. She wore dark clothing that Luz would call *edgy,* and the nose ring gave her a slightly rakish appearance.

"Do you ever go back?" she asked him. "Home, I mean?"

The question caught him off guard. It seemed overly personal to him, and he had the same feeling as when a stranger addressed him with the familiar *ti,* a further bewildering characteristic of the younger generation of Croatians, whom he met only rarely, although she had been careful to use the polite *vi.* "Never," he told her.

Her nod was thoughtful. "I don't think I'll go back either," she said, and he felt something pull in his chest at the earnest way she said it.

"Surely it's not as bad as all that," he told her easily. "It isn't like before."

She looked down at her napkin, which she had started to fold into small squares. "No," she conceded after a moment. "Probably not."

A boyfriend, he thought then. Someone has broken her heart. Or she broke his. And as a result here she is, alone in America. He felt inexplicably sad for this young woman with the wide-set green eyes who slouched in her chair like a teenager. He resisted the temptation to sit down across from her, to warn her about the tricksters and cheats that populated this country, side by side with all the wondrous possibilities one always imagined before coming here.

"There are no jobs at home," she continued in a neutral voice, meeting his eyes again. "No prospects."

"It's hard here, too," he told her.

She nodded.

"Too many of our people come expecting that things will be easy—"

Her nostrils flared slightly, and he realized that she was irritated with this observation. "I never thought it would be easy," she told him.

She did not come in again for several weeks, an absence that troubled him, although he could not understand why. The girl was a stranger to him, after all. He did not know where she worked, though she had mentioned something about looking after a rich woman's children, and for all he knew she had returned home in the end, despite her brave words. He had seen it a hundred times: sooner or later, the teeth of home worked their way beneath your skin and carried you back the same way a wolf transports its cubs. It was only for a chosen few that return was impossible.

But it was uncanny how she had brought his nightmares back. He did not know if it was her Split accent or the orphaned air that surrounded her. She had not mentioned family or friends, and to his eyes she appeared as lonely as he had been some thirty years before her. If she died tomorrow, he wondered, would anyone mourn her?

His nightmares were the same as in the early days of escape, and after waking, he felt the same unease. The dreams revisited him every few years, always prompted by some trigger. He had once passed a woman on the street who so resembled his sister, Ana, that he called out to her by name, only realizing his mistake when she frowned and moved away from him. Another time he had opened an order of olive oil for the restaurant, the pungent smell of that crushed Spanish fruit so instantly familiar that it had forced him out of the kitchen for an entire hour.

Those dreams always took him back to prison, to the same cell and quarrying detail. There was the same inedible gruel, with its rotten vegetables and insect carcasses. The same rank smell of shuffling prisoners, all malnourished and blistering in the sun. "We knew we'd find you sooner or later," his interrogator always told him with a satisfied smile. A psychopath's smile, he'd since realized, like a deranged mother who sings her children to sleep beneath the peaceful surface of a bath.

Times had changed, of course. He'd had reason to be afraid in the beginning—even in America—and so he had lived carefully. But all that was over.

He did sometimes wonder what had become of his interrogators, and of several of the others. For years he had nursed a collection of revenge fantasies as brutal as they were unrealistic, always discarding them in the end. But he was not naive enough to believe them tucked safely away in jail for their misdeeds. Life shunned such symmetrical resolutions, and besides, those men were nameless, faceless. They were made of a slippery substance whose properties were unfathomable. He imagined that they lived quietly today, old men who read newspapers in the morning and puttered in their gardens.

Something about the girl took him back to that time, although he could not understand why. It was her guarded attitude, perhaps.

A certain hunted quality in her eyes. She was running from something, and he had not believed her explanation about the unemployment rate at home. Perhaps that was partly it, but in this day and age one did not draw a line through the possibility of return. There simply wasn't the need.

Perhaps this boyfriend was the jealous type, he thought. Perhaps she had needed to put an ocean between them, or perhaps she was in some other kind of trouble. He remembered that on both of her visits to his restaurant she had stared out at the sidewalk. Perhaps, he thought now, she had expected someone to appear.

He was familiar with that degree of watchfulness, and he chided himself for having missed it earlier. He who had seen danger everywhere in the first few years: in the small Italian town where they had languished for months in a refugee camp after their escape, little Katarina bitten mercilessly by the mosquitoes that swarmed whenever the lights went out, so that she picked at her bites until they bled and scarred.

He'd seen danger on buses, and in the vinyl booth of a New York diner. Unlike in films, their agents did not wear trench coats, nor did they have thin and furtive faces. They were the most ordinary of people, but they would occasionally make their presence felt by jostling him on the subway or nodding at him on the street.

When he had first started working as a waiter, a customer once wrote Marin's full name on the back of his bill and, beside it, the date of his departure from Rosmarina. "Do you remember what he looked like?" Marin asked the other waiters when he discovered it on the table, but none could remember a single detail about the man who had ordered the steak, well-done.

"Why, *Papi?*" one of his sons had asked tearfully when Marin reprimanded him for chattering to a neighbor about where he went to school, his parents' restaurant, the vacation they had taken to Miami the year before.

The city was a dangerous place, he insisted. But, really, it was his need for secrecy, that jagged border between what he confided to his wife late at night, whispering miserably as she rubbed his back, and the man who rose in the morning, teased his sons, and did his restaurant's books.

He knew that the secret police had infiltrated Croatian communities abroad, and he did not attend a single Mass in his own language until the end of communism. Unlike Vlaho, Katarina's father, he avoided Croatian centers, Croatian clubs, and Croatian gatherings. He had no interest in cultural festivals or concerts because he imagined those sly note-takers everywhere, recording who went where and attended which meeting. And, anyway, he did not like the narrowness of his countrymen abroad, the way they wore their exile like a badge of honor and barricaded themselves inside their communities.

"You've forgotten where you came from," Vlaho used to accuse him.

"And you're playing with fire," Marin would shoot back.

He had felt sorry for his aunt Vinka, who observed these exchanges with trembling lips. She had already started to take in sewing for a few extra dollars a week, her English limited exclusively to words like *baste* and *hem*. She would mend garments late at night, while Katarina slept. But Vlaho spent hours with like-minded friends who spoke of returning to Yugoslavia to mount armed insurrections. To Marin, these were delusions, fueled by too much wine and *rakija*.

Their final falling out had happened after one of those evenings. Vlaho had returned home in a combative mood. "They say I shouldn't trust you," he had told Marin, his eyes bright. "They say nobody who did time on Barren Island can be trusted."

Marin had gone still at this.

"That they only released the ones who agreed to be informers."

The accusation left Marin breathless, and by the next morning he had gone, leaving a little money for his aunt but no note, an exit that was an unmitigated relief to him at the time but a source of shame in subsequent years.

But while Vlaho's ardent nationalism left him cold, he could not stomach the other side of that equation, either, the one that painted Yugoslavia in the 1970s as something innocuous. In his first years in New York, he occasionally ran into people who had visited his country and spoke of the fact that its young people wore blue jeans and listened to American rock and roll. They referenced the Dalmatian Coast so casually that he felt something akin to physical pain.

"How could you leave such a beautiful place?" a woman at a party once asked him, then went on to describe its sunsets, its strong red wine, the leather belt she had bought at a colorful marketplace.

He had only nodded miserably, knowing there was no way to make people understand.

Yugoslavia seems so open, they told him. *Not like the Soviet Union.*

No, he had replied. *It is not like the Soviet Union.*

After his first attempts, he stopped explaining that there were political prisoners even in Yugoslavia. He certainly never mentioned Barren Island. He no longer spoke of the assassinations that took place abroad, of the men, women, and children who were asphyxiated or shot, who were stabbed when they went out jogging, or hung themselves, mysteriously, with no chair or table to assist their jumps. He had stopped speaking about those things because of the way people looked at him, puzzled, telling him that they had read some article about *communism with a human face.*

In America he had no affiliation with separatists or agitators, with émigré newspapers or independence movements, but still the audacity of those UDBA assassinations unnerved him. Until the end of the 1980s, they happened in Germany and England

and Canada. He thought they might be happening in the United States as well, and his strategy was never to allow any of his countrymen to get close to him.

Besides, it had been his father who insisted that he cut himself wholly loose. "If you write to us," Luka had said with tears in his eyes, "don't ever sign your name or send an address."

It would be the final humiliation, Marin knew, if his father were forced to pen a response filled with lies to his only son. *Everything is fine,* they had instructed others to write, the words like lures. *All has been forgiven.*

He had not felt the weight of these things for years, however. Not since the end of communism, not since the independence war he had followed from America, feeling neither threatened nor entirely unscathed. This was what so unnerved him about the girl: it was somehow ludicrous that she should inspire such a reaction in him, so long after all those things.

The restaurant was his life's work. He and his wife had built the business from nothing, so that when he approached it on the street, it seemed that his hands had felt the weight of every brick and that they alone had untangled vast networks of wires—as fine as silver thread—to deliver the light to its lamps.

In the beginning they had done the cooking themselves, hiring Luz's brother as maître d' and some of her cousins as waiters. His wife was a fine chef, overseeing bubbling vats of black beans and ovens filled with slow-roasting pork. The food had been squarely Cuban in the beginning, but over the years his own influence had begun to sneak in: grilled squid and Swiss chard, which was the nearest he came to *blitva.*

It was a neighborhood place, an early outpost on Park Slope's Fifth Avenue, long before the area's gentrification. The tables had checkered tablecloths and candles at dinnertime, and he knew many of his patrons by name. It was the type of place, he liked to think, where one would always feel comfortable. Reviewers had been kind, and the Zagat guide had, year after year, applauded the fusion of Caribbean and Mediterranean influences.

Mediterranean. He could live with that.

In New York, he was not even Marin but Mio. *Amor mío,* his wife had said somewhere near the beginning of things, teaching him Spanish words. *Amor mío.* It had started as a secret joke, but the nickname stuck.

Although Luz had been a child when her family fled Cuba, she still remembered taking shelter in her grandmother's house during a hurricane. "There was a mango tree in the courtyard," she told Marin. "They planted it when my father was a little boy, and my grandmother said that the day a storm pulled it up by the roots was the day we would all go flying from the face of the earth."

In exchange, he told her about the winds of the Adriatic.

"Is this a *bura?*" she asked him with a smile, one winter's day several months after they met in a community college business class, when the Atlantic wind tore bitterly down the New York streets, scattering coffee cups, newspapers, and dead leaves before them.

He had known then that they would marry because of the simple fact that she had remembered that word, foreign to her ears, and uttered only once in a description of his island.

"Would you go back if you could?" she asked in the days before their wedding.

"There's no going back," he said, to her visible relief.

They had two sons.

Perhaps that was it, he thought. A father's protectiveness. The girl had to have come from somewhere, after all. She could not have sprung to life from a clod of earth, and he imagined a father and mother waiting for her.

His own sons were nearly adults now. Twin boys who had grown into tall young men, one of whom studied economics, the other who loved stories of any kind.

They knew Cuba, although they had never set foot upon that island. They spoke Spanish fluently and had grown up in a large circle of cousins, aunts, and uncles that stretched from Florida to New England. Their mother had arrived with family photographs sewn into her dress, and before his death their grandfather had shown the boys books from his collection, with photographs of the village where he was born. Cuba was all around them. It was in the food they ate and the music they listened to, the jazz and rumba beats slipping beneath their door long past the hour they were supposed to be asleep.

Marin, on the other hand, had no photographs of Rosmarina to show them. He had only once found a picture book about the Adriatic in the local library, the deep blue sea like sapphires. There had been photographs of Vis and Mljet, of Korčula and Brač, but none of the island where he was born.

Still, he kept the book even when notices from the library arrived in the mail, even when a woman informed him over the telephone that another patron had requested it.

"I think I returned it," he lied, unable to part with it in the end. "But I am happy to reimburse you." After mailing them a check, he had torn out the small paper pocket from the book's last page, which detailed its history in other hands, and scraped the call number from its spine.

His sons had delighted in hearing stories about his childhood when they were young, and it bothered him that he had no pictures to show them. He told them about diving contests from high outcroppings of rock and about the time he and his father had caught a shark. They shuddered at this last story because those were the years after Mariel, when people floated to Florida in rubber boats or on rafts held together by floss. And they had both overheard their mother's family discussing the sharks that circled the people gliding to the United States.

The boys had wanted to see Rosmarina, land of peaceful olive groves and sardines whose bodies raced so quickly through the water that they left silver traces behind them. And of *klapa,* the soft and gentle songs their father sang when they had nightmares, but which they steadily outgrew as they hurtled bravely towards adulthood.

He had shown them the book's photographs of other islands, as well as Rosmarina's location on the map that hung in the room they shared. It was a tiny island like an escaping button from Italy's boot, in the very middle of the Adriatic Sea and half a world away from the zoo in Central Park, Circle Line cruises, and Nathan's hot dogs. As they grew older, however, Rosmarina became just one more storybook from childhood, like *Clifford the Big Red Dog* or *Goodnight Moon.* And while his sons might one day remember enough details of those stories to tell their own children, might even recall a few notes of those *klapa* songs, it pained him that they would not be able to describe the exact color of that water or the nature of that sky.

Over the years he had written to his family a handful of times. From Italy, then Germany. From Chicago, where they had stayed upon arrival in the United States but which they abandoned because Lake Michigan did not resemble the open sea to him, no matter what other immigrants said.

For the duration of the old regime, he did not sign the letters. Occasionally he would send his niece, Magdalena, a gift, a toy, once an Easter dress, though he had no idea of her size, or if the packages were ever delivered to his family. *I did not abandon you of my own free will,* he longed to tell her, but it was like sending letters into a void. He did not know if his parents were still living, if his sister had left, as she had always threatened. He did not know if there was anyone who bore the name Morić left on the island.

What could he say in letters that were by necessity vague? *I am well and I hope you are well.* How many times could he say it?

In the first few years of his exile, he imagined that their lives remained the same as when he left—that his father painted his boat every spring, and his mother still attended Mass. Magdalena remained a toddler, and his sister sat in her folding chair on the *riva,* extolling the virtues of rosemary oil to the tourists in halting German.

As the years went by, however, he could no longer be sure.

Little by little, he resigned himself to separation. It seemed to him that his life on the island was something another person had lived. It did not so much fade in his memory as sit behind glass, exactly as images appear on a television screen. Here he repairs the motor on his boat. Here he must dive down to loosen the anchor that has caught on some rocks. Here his mother hums as she bakes bread, and his sister tosses her head.

It was only when Croatia's independence war started in 1991 and effectively ended communism that he began to regard things a little differently. In the longest letter he had ever written, he told his parents of his wife and his two sons, of his restaurant and his life in New York. He gave them his address. *I am relieved by the news,* he wrote a little stiffly, *but am also afraid for your well-being.* He told them that he was planning to visit. *Once this madness ends, I will bring my sons to show them the place where I was born.*

He realized that the Croatian he had once written with ease now came out with wild inconsistencies. There were words he had to think about for a long time, and twice he crumpled the sheets of paper and began again. He included family photographs with this letter, stopping to look at his own face, rounder than it had been in his youth. His hair was half gray, and for a moment he was afraid of what they would think, looking at him. *He certainly grew fat in America,* he imagined his sister commenting with some disgust, *while we stayed here, waiting for him.*

He thought for a long time about the last paragraph, chewing the cap of his pen. *There has not been a day that I did not think of you.* He begged for their understanding, for their forgiveness. He begged forgiveness especially from his sister, although he did not put this into words.

He waited months for a response. He knew that the postal system would surely be affected by the war, and sometime after the first letter, he sent a nearly identical second. Over two years passed before that one was returned with a single handwritten word upon the envelope. *Deceased.*

It did not occur to him to question the truth of this. He was too consumed with the idea that his parents had died without ever hearing his voice again. It was like a sharp bit of flint embedded in the flesh near his heart, and it stabbed him each time he turned.

It was Luz who had suggested that they visit the island together. "The worst is not to know what happened," she told him, so reasonably that he nearly acquiesced. In 1997, two years after the last shell fell, he went so far as to consult a travel agent. The woman did not know much about Croatia—it was still an unusual destination for Americans in those days—but she promised to investigate the matter. A week later he sat in her office, a giant orange fish bumping against the sides of a gurgling fish tank, and looked through brochures for the Adriatic Sea.

Through a Slovenian travel agency, she had found a brochure that listed the Hotel Palace on Rosmarina. "It looks like it might be the only hotel on the island," she told him.

He looked numbly at photographs of the hotel's limestone facade, which he could remember from his childhood. His sister had worked there for a time, cleaning the rooms of tourists, and it had not changed at all since then: the awning was still dark blue, and café tables still sat on its stone terrace.

There were no people in the pictures, just photographs of simple bedrooms with dark blue draperies that could be rooms in any hotel, anywhere in the world.

He took the brochure home and reread the description of his island. *Come see the forested splendor of Rosmarina! Come swim in its crystal seas!*

It was the idea of returning as a tourist that he could not stomach. He feared finding another family in his family's house, one who would look at him suspiciously and tell him that there had not been Morićs on Rosmarina for years. The more he thought about it, the less likely he found the possibility that anything of his former life remained.

He knew other Croatians who had visited home. They spoke wistfully of selling their apartments and their businesses in the United States and returning, buying property perhaps, and recouping the lives that had been denied them. But he found these plans far-fetched and vaguely pathetic.

Most of all, he imagined stepping from the ferry onto the island's *riva,* greeted by blank faces and eyes that took in the American cut of his clothes. *Zimmer frei! Camere!* he could imagine the old women calling to the foreigners emerging from the ferry's dark belly. He remembered how they made a beeline for those passengers who exuded the unmistakable glow of the West, forsaking their countrymen for Germans or Swiss. He imagined their hopeful faces, the way they would tell him in English: *Rooms!*

Young men would be tying up their boats on the *riva,* just as he had done. He wondered then if his own eyes had ever passed over one of the island's returning sons, who had stood for a time in disappointment on the waterfront where nobody now knew him.

CHAPTER 7

She reappeared one day in June, an early summer heat wave bending the air above the pavement so that the city appeared like some rendering of a Martian landscape, the sky hazy and sunless. Although it was only nine in the morning, Marin was walking slowly, his shirt already damp with perspiration, cursing New York's humidity with every step.

After nearly thirty years he had yet to grow accustomed to the oppressiveness, to the dead weight of the city's heat. He did not mind winter's bitterness or the torrential rains of autumn, but there was something about summer that made him feel trapped.

He recognized her from a block away. She sat on the bus stop bench in front of the restaurant's entrance dressed in cutoffs and a T-shirt, and for a perplexed moment he took in the whiteness of her elbows and knees, the hair that hung lankly about her face.

He stopped at a distance, observing her. At first he thought she had fallen asleep, a backpack stationed between her feet, but then he realized that she was studying something on the pavement: a crack in the concrete or a slow-moving insect.

He did not know how long she had been waiting for him, or even if she was waiting for him at all. She might have planned to take a bus, her appearance in front of his restaurant a mere coincidence. But when a bus halted in front of her, she did not look up.

Even in profile he could see the hollows beneath her eyes, blue circles that made him think she had been sitting there since before dawn, biding her time on the plastic bench. When she looked up at last, she held his gaze for a long moment, and though a tiny voice inside his head whispered that it all spelled trouble, the larger part of him was already unlocking the door to the restaurant and inviting her inside. Seating her at the bar the way he used to seat his sons at the end of school days when they drank frothy *batidos* and swung their legs from the high stools. Assuring her that whatever the complication, she would see, these things had a way of turning out all right in the end.

She stood in the middle of the dining room as he made her a coffee behind the bar. He was aware of the way she studied the walls, her gaze lingering on the paintings by Cuban artists, some their patrons, some their friends. He repainted the walls—the aqua, the green, the blue—every year or two, whenever the city's grime and the smoke from their own kitchen conspired to dull the Caribbean lagoon they had created in the heart of Brooklyn.

"There's nothing from home," she told him.

He poured her coffee in a shallow white cup.

Her voice had been neutral, but there was a deflated look on her face. "I hadn't noticed that before."

She needed a job, and while he did not, strictly speaking, need another waitress, he did not have the heart to turn her away. His earlier self—the one who asked nothing of his countrymen and offered nothing in return, the one who sensed betrayal behind every word spoken in the ghost language he so rarely used—had disappeared. He imagined his own sons in some kind of trouble, so that there was a strange relief in showing kindness to this girl. The equation made sense to him today, the heat rising in the street

outside so that the people who passed the restaurant's windows resembled sleepwalkers.

"You're too soft," Luz said when he telephoned to tell her, although he sensed only minor reproach in her voice.

"I think she's all alone," he said in his basic Spanish, watching
as Jadranka cradled her coffee cup in both hands. The fine lines
at the corners of her eyes were visible for the first time today, like
the invisible-ink trick his wife had shown their boys with lemon
juice, the letters appearing beneath a lightbulb's heat.

She sipped methodically, shoulders hunched, eyes fixed on the
sign beside the cash register that read, *Occupancy by more than 125
persons is dangerous and unlawful.*

"What did you say her name was?" Luz asked him.

"Jadranka," he said.

She did not look up at this, her eyes fixed on the sign as if it
alone might save her.

"I don't know her last name," he added.

"Is she legal?"

Marin considered this. "I don't know."

Luz sighed. "I hope you know what you're doing," she said.
"Hector won't be pleased at having to train somebody new."

"No," he assented. "He won't."

There was a moment of silence. "But I suppose we all needed
to be trained in our time. Even Hector."

"Yes," he agreed, and smiled into the telephone.

She needed very little training in the end. She had worked as a
waitress in Split, and so she knew to serve from the right and to
clear from the left. She was as skilled at uncorking wine as she was
at deboning fish, and once dressed in the white apron that all their
staff wore, she was an unobtrusive presence in the restaurant. She
quietly refolded napkins and retrieved fallen forks in such a way
that conversations between customers never flagged.

"She's like a ghost," Hector told him towards the end of service on that first night, clearly meaning his words as a compliment.

Marin turned to watch her pour wine for one of the tables.

"—which is strange for a beautiful woman."

"Trust you to notice," he told Hector.

She had spent the afternoon studying the menu. It was not an extensive list, but in the space of a few hours, she had memorized its entire contents, and several times Marin eavesdropped as she described the pork *jus* or the *ropa vieja*. Only occasionally did she get tangled up in the Spanish words, or the English descriptions, and he was on hand to clarify things, hovering behind her like a mother hen.

"Leave us," Luz finally told him, taking the girl into the kitchen to sample the *ropa vieja*.

"*Pašticada*," Jadranka pronounced when she emerged, so that Marin laughed at the comparison.

"It's similar," he conceded.

All during that first evening, Marin studied her movements, pleased and yet somehow puzzled by her single-minded dedication to each task presented her. Gone was the slouching girl of their first meetings, the one who had told him with some annoyance that she had never expected things to be easy in America. The nose ring had been removed, and in its absence something else had shifted as well.

"Slow down," he had to tell her several times. "Take a sip of water."

But she only took breaks when he told her to, and only ate when he insisted, although a meal each shift had been part of their agreement.

Luz watched from the bar as the girl traversed the dining room. "She's a hard worker," she told him approvingly.

He placed an arm around his wife's shoulders, pleased that she had noticed. He sensed that Luz had left her observation unfinished. "But?" he prodded.

She did not answer right away, watching as Jadranka took drink orders from a table of four businessmen, her brow wrinkled with concentration.

"Her eyes, Mio," she said at last.

He frowned. "What about them?"

But his wife only shook her head and disappeared into the kitchen.

It took him a week to realize that she needed a place to sleep. He did not know where she had been going each night at closing, but one morning Hector discovered her in the bathroom, brushing her teeth at the sink.

"You can stay here for a little while," Marin told her, showing her the small office in the back, with its narrow, sagging couch.

"I'm sorry," she told him, unable to meet his eyes.

"Why are you sorry?" he asked her. "All beginnings are difficult. Mine was. My wife's. Hector's. Nobody is spared."

She said nothing to this.

"I lived from church donations in the beginning," he told her with a laugh. "We were so poor that my cousin received a bag of socks for her first Christmas present in America."

Jadranka looked up.

"She was five. Now, I ask you: what kind of gift is that for a little girl? But she needed socks, and that was what the charity could give us."

She considered this. "You were never tempted to just go back?"

She had asked something similar before, and he marveled for a split second at stubborn youth, at a generation for whom things appeared just that easy. "There was no going back. Going back meant jail, or worse."

She swallowed.

"But *you* could go back," he said, watching her carefully. "There's no reason you couldn't."

"There is," she said just as quickly, and something about the decisive way she said it made him believe her.

He worried about what it might mean, although he did not press her for an explanation. He continued to imagine a jealous boyfriend, someone who was lying in wait for her should she return. He had witnessed such incidents himself. In his youth one of their neighbors had beaten his wife with such regularity that his mother had secretly bought her a ferry ticket back to her parents on the mainland.

"She doesn't seem the type," Luz told him doubtfully. "Look at how she is with Hector."

His headwaiter—impervious to the charms of other women and, in truth, a bit of a snob—was now smitten with the young, red-haired woman. He watched her pass from dining room to kitchen, from bar to hostess station. His eyes followed her through the mirror behind the bar like the pining subject of a Cuban song.

Jadranka did not appear to notice when he trailed after her. She teased him, but subtly and without cruelty, which only made him redouble his efforts, one day leaving a red carnation in the pocket of the backpack she hung in the office. The busboys sniggered at this act, which might have remained anonymous had one of them not opened the door at that very moment.

All that evening the restaurant's staff was abuzz with the story that played out before them, watching both the lovelorn Hector, who appeared not to care that he had been found out, and the expressionless Jadranka. Each time the office door opened, the restaurant held its collective breath, but halfway through the evening, the same busboy reported, the flower had disappeared from the backpack's pocket and was no longer anywhere in evidence.

Until closing, it was clear that Hector awaited her reaction. He searched Jadranka's face. He followed her to the kitchen door, then nearly collided with her when she emerged with a tray of food. She smiled at him a little sympathetically, stepping around him in the next moment.

"The women from your country are a mystery," he told Marin in disappointment as he left that night.

She had few possessions, as far as Marin could tell: the backpack and a small suitcase that she kept zipped in the corner of the office. Luz had brought her a sleeping bag from home, and each morning it was neatly folded at the end of the couch.

"I've found a place to stay," she announced on the morning after Hector's flower.

"With a friend?" he asked.

"Something like that."

And although he was relieved—it was technically illegal for her to continue sleeping at the restaurant—the vagueness of her answer bothered him.

"Do you trust this friend?" he pressed.

She looked surprised at the question. "Yes," she told him. "Why shouldn't I?"

It was because she could not be running from politics that Marin cast her unknown hunter in the shape of a man. He was not conscious of his own chauvinism in this regard, and would have been alarmed to hear his theory characterized as paternalistic. His intentions were good, even if his vision was limited.

But her eyes widened when he asked her outright. "What makes you think I'm running from anything?" she asked him.

"It's as clear as the nose on your face," he told her.

She was folding white napkins into flowers, and for a moment her nimble hands slowed over the half blossom in front of her. "Well, it's certainly not a man."

"No?" he asked uncertainly.

"The day I run from any man is the day that gravity reverses itself."

He swallowed. "I'm glad."

Her eyes traveled to the family photograph that sat behind the bar, then back to the pile of folded napkins she had amassed to one side. "Your sons are lucky to have a father as protective as you," she told him. "Everyone should be so lucky."

He felt a sudden sharpness in his chest at her words. "You weren't?" he asked.

She shook her head. "But don't feel sorry for me. My sister nearly poisoned our stepfather. He's lucky he got out with his life."

A smile pulled at the corners of Jadranka's mouth, so that he did not know whether to believe her.

"It was her job to make his sandwiches for work, and she put rat poison in them."

"You're joking, surely."

"No."

He watched the top of her head, the way she matched up the corners of the linen, folding and rolling so that she reminded him of the women he had seen working in Caribbean cigar factories.

"What about your own father?" Marin asked. "Where was he in all of this?"

Her hands had regained their momentum, and now they made him think of a musician's, the long, tapered fingers making a stringed instrument sing. But she did not answer.

She was not a musician, but one day she showed Luz the sketchbook she carried in her backpack, the renderings of subway passengers and of nannies on benches in Central Park. There were pictures of the children she had taken care of. One, a little boy, looked out from the page with a near-radiant expression of adoration.

"What happened?" he overheard Luz ask. "Why did you leave?"

But Jadranka only mumbled something halfheartedly about wages.

There were also pictures of the restaurant. Of Marin standing behind the bar and talking to his customers, of Hector in his apron and Luz sampling something from the stove. There were pictures of the young men who worked in the kitchen, the delivery boys, the customers.

"These are good," Marin said, looking over his wife's shoulder. "Where did you learn to do that?"

But Jadranka only shrugged. "It's just a hobby," she told him.

"It should be more than a hobby," Luz told her, looking carefully at each of the pages. When she had reached the last, she asked, "Do you think you could draw something for us?"

Jadranka's expression was cautious.

"What do you call it?" Luz turned to her husband, then answered her own question with a snap of her fingers: "A commission."

Marin smiled inwardly at this suggestion, but Jadranka looked taken aback. "A picture of the restaurant?" she asked.

Luz waved her hand. "What do we need a picture of the restaurant for when we're standing right here?" She looked at her husband. "A picture of your country."

Marin shifted uncomfortably. "We can't ask her to—"

But Luz cut him off with a glare. "Haven't you been telling me for years that you don't have any pictures, *loco?* Haven't you been talking to me about the sea, the sky?"

Marin shrugged.

"A picture of your country," she told Jadranka, as if it were decided. As if she were placing their weekly order with the fishmonger. "Can you do that?"

Jadranka nodded.

He insisted on giving her money for the supplies.

"That's not the way a commission usually works," she told him.

"It does this time," he responded.

His wife had surprised him with her request, but he could see that she was pleased with the agreement. Jadranka would make some extra money, and Marin would receive something tangible from home.

"Not from home exactly," he corrected her. "She's from the mainland."

But Luz waved away this technicality. "You said she's from the coast."

"She is."

"Entonces?"

"It's a long coast."

Luz's eyes narrowed. "As long as your face?"

He smiled. "Longer."

He had assumed that Jadranka was from Split, but he did not tell his wife that her accent had lately begun to confound him. Slightly, at first. The occasional word he recognized from childhood sneaking in to replace its urban counterpart.

At first Marin thought he was imagining it. Then he considered the possibility that the language had undergone such a revolution in his absence that words specific to the islands had migrated north. He thought he even recognized inflections similar to Rosmarina's dialect but ultimately decided that he heard them because he wanted to hear them.

"You're not from Split," he told her one day when she was setting tables. "As they say in America, your mustache is slipping."

Jadranka's arm froze in midair, holding a fork.

"You sound more like a *bodul* to me."

"I'm a lot of things." She placed the fork carefully on the table.

"There's no shame in being from an island," he said. "I'm from Rosmarina myself."

She hesitated. "I'm from Čiovo."

This surprised him—the accent that peeked through the city veneer seemed too much a product of the southern islands—but he said nothing to this.

"I had no father," she added unexpectedly. "That was difficult on an island."

"It's difficult anywhere," he conceded. "But especially in a place where people remember everything."

"Do you remember everything?"

She had a knack for this, he had realized. For asking disarming questions with such ease that he always said more than he intended. "Yes," he admitted. "Everything."

It was true. His memory was singularly infallible, able to summon the smallest details. The smell of carob in the sun. The taste of island figs. The sound of the guards' boots in the corridors, and the way they would always come at night, with other prisoners who were anxious to do their bidding.

For three long years he had filled bags with gravel from the seafloor, standing up to his hips in water as the sun beat down without respite. He remembered how his skin had blistered and peeled from his face and arms in so many successive layers that it was a surprise to find that there was any skin left underneath at all.

Today, dark tumors continued to pepper his skin like something molting from the inside. It was his wife who insisted that he see a doctor, a man scarcely older than their sons, who clucked his tongue over the damage, mistakenly assuming that Marin had been a sun worshipper in his youth. Periodically he insisted on cutting those growths from Marin's face and hands.

Marin had a standing appointment every six months. Luz always insisted on coming into the examination room to point out the new and ominous additions to the map of her husband's body, holding his hand as they waited afterwards to pay the receptionist, because Marin found that he could not speak through any of it, could only stand as still and remote as a plaster figure.

But he showed the starfish on his arm to Jadranka, the one with the many arms and hazy borders. The one that had prompted Luz to make an earlier appointment, only rolling her eyes at Marin's protests that it was nothing.

"These are the memories our country gave me," he told her.

Aside from her accent, there were other things about Jadranka that unsettled him. There was the fact that she could not produce a passport, telling him that it had been retained by her former employers.

"That's illegal," he told her. "You've got to get it back."

But when he suggested paying them a visit together, she shied at this idea.

"You can pay me less," she told him nervously, after he had already agreed to pay her under the table because of her uncertain visa status.

He looked at her in shock. "I'm not going to pay you less," he told her. "But it isn't right for them to keep it."

Then there was the fact that she had searched the drawers of the desk in his office. He had found some papers disturbed, and although there was nothing of value in there—and certainly nothing incriminating—the idea of it troubled him.

"You're imagining it," Luz told him. "What could she possibly be looking for?"

He did not know, but he grew more reserved in Jadranka's presence. This stood in marked contrast to Luz, who was developing a soft spot for the girl. "She knows how to work, that one," she told him.

But it was when Jadranka began following him like a pale shadow that he understood her to be more than what she seemed.

At first he thought he was imagining it. He would see the reflection of her face in the window of a shop or passing car, but when he turned she was gone. He sensed her presence once or twice on the way to work, and on the way home. Once, when walking the dog in Prospect Park, he had been certain that she traveled the paths behind him. But when he telephoned the restaurant upon his return home—the dog pushing her wet nose into the palm of his hand—he was told that she had just finished her break.

"Do you want to speak to her?" Hector had asked.

But Marin had only muttered something about talking to her later and hung up the phone.

He sensed her surveillance for several weeks, but it was only one day in Saints Cyril and Methodius Church that she grew sloppy enough to give him proof.

Despite his lack of faith, he sometimes traveled into Manhattan to visit the Gothic Revival structure on Forty-first Street. He usually went during the week, when the church was nearly empty, when only the first few pews were occupied by a gang of black-clad women whose recitations of the rosary before Mass sounded like weeping, their hymns like wailing.

He always sat in the back.

He did not attend regularly and did not know the priests by name. If he happened to attend on a Sunday, he did not gather with the other men on the sidewalk, and he did not drink coffee in the hall behind the church. He did not speak to anyone, and if they had spoken to him, he was not certain how he would have responded. Only rarely did someone stand close enough to him to shake his hand during the Sign of Peace, and he never took Communion.

He told no one that he attended the occasional Mass. Not even his wife, who had attempted to nurture a certain religious devotion in their sons because she was Cuban of the old school and had never lost her God. She had suggested many times that they go as a family to Mass, but something always held him back.

"You go," he would tell her. "I have things to do."

He had stood in churches for his children's baptisms, their First Communions and confirmations. He acquiesced for funerals and weddings, but he could not agree to a standing date with God.

And it was not embarrassment that made him reticent on the subject, for his wife surely would have understood. He simply did not know how to explain it to her, the way his adult skepticism was the exact inverse of his childhood faith. He did not know how to enunciate the feeling that washed over him once, twice in a season. That longing for rote, familiar words, the songs from his childhood, the responses in his own language. The language that each year died slightly more in him, so that English words flew with greater ease into his speech than Croatian ones.

But in the church it was as he remembered. *My peace I have, my peace I leave you.* The way the women in front of him tapped their chests and murmured, "My sin, my sin, my enormous sin"—just as his mother had done—even as he wondered which sins old women like those could possibly commit. And even as he dismissed the mysteries he had long ago discarded, the grown men dressed up in baptismal dresses turning wine into blood.

It was more than language. It was the song, the voices that were one part melody and two parts tears. And in that church, as in the church of his childhood, the sound tapped at some hollow, secret place in him. It tapped and the door swung open, and the knowledge inside glided slowly out. It usually followed him onto the street afterwards, into the grayness that New York was never entirely without, irrespective of season. So different from the place he had known, an island that matched his heart's circumference perfectly.

But on the day he turned in his pew to discover Jadranka disappearing through the church's front doors, he attained a different form of knowledge. He took it as proof that her appearance in his restaurant was not a matter of chance, and he felt both embarrassment at having been so gullible, and fear.

He had heard stories about the secret police regrouping after the end of communism—of former UDBA operatives using dossiers for the purpose of blackmail, or even landing on their feet in the new government—but he had never taken them seriously. Now he was not so sure.

Her questions about his past and the deliberate vagueness of her own biography had long troubled him. Sitting in the pew, he built his case against her, not stopping to ponder the fact that she was too young to have had any hand in the old system or that most of the details were circumstantial.

When he rose, one of the women at the front of the church turned to stare in disapproval, but he paid her no mind. He hurried past the table of church circulars and the bulletin board where a hundred flyers flapped in his wake. He pulled open the door to the street. The sunlight outside blinded him for only a moment.

She was at the restaurant, standing across the bar from Hector. The two of them were so deep in conversation that they did not sense him passing the restaurant's windows. Nor did they hear him come in, their heads nearly touching above the bar. As Marin watched, Jadranka smiled and touched Hector's arm.

What had she been asking his headwaiter all these weeks, he wondered, and what sorts of things had he revealed? Hector had been with them for ten years, a distant cousin of Luz's who had started as a busboy. In his panic, Marin did not stop to consider how little Hector knew.

He wondered if she reported to someone else, or if she was planning to blackmail him with some tidbit of information. He imagined the front of his restaurant defaced with spray paint: *The owner of this establishment is a common criminal.*

"Leave us," he barked at Hector, who looked at him in shock because in ten years Marin had never raised his voice.

Jadranka went so pale that a birthmark below her right eye stood out in stark relief, but her face was devoid of all expression.

And it was this look that he recognized, this look that had haunted his dreams, prompting the realization that she was not the hunted but the hunter.

"I should have known you were one of them," he told her in a low, angry voice, ignoring Hector's worried expression as he hovered by the kitchen door. "I should have understood from all your questions."

She looked at him in shock. "Who do you think I am?"

"Not who," he corrected her. "What."

Her face fell.

"You want to hear it all?" he asked her.

She looked down at her hands, which were resting on the bar. Those hands had tricked him. They had even prompted his wife to ask her for a picture. The idea of it made hysterical laughter rise in his throat, but he pushed it back.

"You want to hear every last ugly detail?" he pushed.

She did not look up.

"Don't be timid. It's why you came, after all."

Still she did not lift her head. Her eyes were dry and her mouth did not tremble. No delicate flower, this one, he thought. Had anything she told him been real? Her name? The bit about the rat poison had seemed a stretch, but he had ingested her bastard status like a greedy fish swallows a hook.

"It's why you came!" he roared and struck the bar with his fist, so that the resulting tremor shook the liquor bottles behind her.

She looked up at last. She nodded.

CHAPTER 8

It was his father who had told him, "A flood begins with a single drop."

But even in 1969, when Marin returned from the far reaches of landlocked Macedonia for leave, he could not bring himself to tell Luka of the daily humiliations and the constant stupidities that compulsory military service entailed: the fleas, the stink of other men's feet, the pointless tasks. It was not that he minded the fellow conscripts in his barracks; they were all more or less all right. But when the commanding officers screamed that they would kick his soft Dalmatian ass, which did nothing but sit in the sun all day, drinking wine and chasing women, he felt a fury of which he had never known himself capable.

He had worked his entire life, he longed to shout back. He had fished from the time he was a boy, and his hands were covered with the scars and calluses to prove it.

His worst persecutor was his sergeant, a gaunt man from a town near Zadar. Because they were both from the Adriatic, Marin had expected a measure of sympathy. "I was once like you," the sergeant yelled instead. "All I cared about were my nets and my boat and my wine, but the Germans cared nothing for these."

When Marin protested that his father, too, had fought the Germans, the sergeant made him do push-ups until the muscles of his arms felt like they were on fire.

No matter how Marin completed his tasks, Sergeant Pavlović made him start over again. No matter how many times he remade his bed, pulling the rough blanket taut over the straw mattress beneath, the sergeant tore it off and threw it on the floor. No matter how often Marin had sentry duty, again and again the sergeant assigned this duty to him. He grew so exhausted from lack of sleep that several times he fell asleep during meals, his forehead resting against the greasy surface of the table as the men around him ate and burped, kicking him roughly awake at the sergeant's approach.

It did not seem right that the same territory had produced them both, that instead of feeling a kinship with him the sergeant lost no opportunity to ridicule his island accent or tell crude jokes about the region's indolence. During the daily hour of political education, Pavlović would read aloud to recruits from the morning newspaper, peppering his semiliterate orations with his own political musings. "Croatian nationalists want their own language, Morić," he would bark. "What do you think of that?"

Marin had little opinion on the matter. On Rosmarina, his aunt Vinka's husband had already attempted to stoke his national pride, citing hundreds of years in which their people had been under the yoke of others. He had tried to lend Marin books and invited him to secret political gatherings. "Where's your anger?" Vlaho had once asked in disgust. "Your dignity?"

But Marin cared nothing for politics or ethnic solidarity. Rosmarina's dialect would be equally unintelligible to someone from Belgrade or Zagreb, its way of life as foreign. He knew nothing of theaters and libraries, of traffic jams or victory squares, but he knew the coves that sardines favored and how best to press grapes into wine.

He did not have the energy to consider political movements, and the years of his mobilization stretched before him like an empty waste, bereft of light and warmth. The men in his barracks came from cities and mountains, from farmland and border towns, but most had never heard of Rosmarina.

He missed his mother's cooking, his sister's laughter, his father's counsel. Most of all he missed their touch: his father slapping his back and his mother's hands zipping up his jacket, believing even sunny days capable of conferring colds. Army life was pushing and shoving, a barely controlled violence as Pavlović shouted in his ear, misting it several times daily with his spittle.

After the first few weeks, he forged a friendship with the conscript who shared his bunk. "The sergeant is in love with you," the fair-haired Bosnian told Marin, laughing. "That's why he gives you so much attention. Perhaps you shouldn't play so hard to get."

Siniša made those first months bearable. When the sergeant left the barracks, he reduced him to a caricature, demonstrating his erratic gait and beetling eyebrows. "Morić," he would order. "Drop and give me fifty." He painted wild scenarios in which the sergeant wore women's stockings in his spare time and enjoyed being prodded with leather whips. "Have you seen the sergeant's wife?" he would say. "She could wither a man's balls with a single glance."

Like Marin, his bunk mate cared nothing for politics. "There's only one doctrine I subscribe to," he announced one day when the sergeant left the room during political instruction, "and it involves cold beer." Whenever the conscripts were allowed into town, he would demonstrate this by getting loudly drunk.

"What about the sergeant's daughter?" he asked Marin on one such evening. "A face like a doll's and tits like jelly-filled doughnuts." Several other conscripts at their table shot him warning looks, but the café was loud and filled with drinking men.

Marin only shook his head in amusement. The sergeant's daughter had a greasy face and the gait of a draft horse.

The object of Marin's affections was not that sallow girl, nor any one of the pictures his fellow recruits had shown him: an odd assortment of girls from home and well-thumbed pictures from pornographic magazines.

He had seen her only twice in the town. Once, through a bakery window when he was sent on some errand, and another time when she walked down the street in front of him, the wind lifting her skirt slightly so that he glimpsed the smooth skin on the back of her thighs for just a moment before she smoothed the fabric down again.

He did not know her name or who she was, though she seemed out of place in that small town. The girls of Bitolj, like the ones on Rosmarina, tried too hard to copy the pages of fashion magazines, resulting in overdone makeup and bouffant hairstyles. But this woman had an easy grace, and every time he was in town he found himself searching for her long brown hair, so silky that he was certain his hands would pass right through it.

With time he discovered that her name was Nada. She was from Zagreb and taught in the local school. She did not have the face of a doll, he decided with all the ardor of youth, but that of an angel.

He guessed that she was his senior by at least ten years, but he found that he could not stop thinking of her, of the way she moved, of the wind lifting the thin material of her skirt. He imagined the way it would feel in his hands, the pale smoothness of her thighs beneath.

One day when he was sent to do an errand in town, he went past the building where she held her classes. He had noticed the room before, the construction paper pictures visible from the street, but he had never seen her there, and he stopped to watch her distribute paper to the children inside. He stood there so long that he did not immediately register when she looked up and gave him an amused stare in return.

Two days later he ran into her on the street. "Do you have an interest in long division?" she asked him. "Perhaps you should join our class. You're just a little older than my students."

He felt himself flush, but before he could hurry away she wrote something on a piece of paper and pressed it into his hands. "Be a brave boy and come visit me sometime," she told him. "We can talk."

"T-talk?" he stuttered. But she only smiled, then walked away without looking back.

He did not know what to do about the paper, which he kept long after memorizing the address. He lay awake for several nights before falling into tormented dreams in which he undressed her, waking only to discover that he was pressing his erection into his sheets.

The following week he had an evening's leave, and after gathering his courage, he set off for the address on the far side of town. The building's front door was open, and he climbed slowly to the third floor, telling himself that he could leave at any time. On the landing outside her door, he hesitated, looking behind him, back down the dark stairway that was dimly lit by only a few working lightbulbs. Before he could decide what to do, however, she opened the door, a small spark of surprise in her violet eyes. He had not noticed their color before, always too shy to do more than glance nervously at her, but now he stood on the threshold, staring and feeling foolish. "I was about to ring," he said, thankful that he did not stutter.

"Come in," she said, taking his arm and leading him into a room where books covered every surface.

He could not seem to find his voice, and so he looked around him, taking in the worn couch and the scuffed parquet floor.

"God knows it's not much," she said with a laugh.

He was only nineteen and he had never been with a woman, though he had naturally said otherwise to the men in his barracks.

Now, all the easy words he had rehearsed on his slow march up the stairs deserted him.

"Undress," she told him.

He blinked hard at this unexpected order.

"If it makes you feel better, I'll undress too," she said gently.

Before he could respond, she undid the skirt at her waist and lifted her blouse over her head. She wore no slip or bra, and he stared at her flat stomach, at her small nipples, inexplicably darker than her lips—a correlation he had learned from listening to the conversations of other recruits. In a state of wonder and befuddlement, he allowed her to unbuckle his trousers, taking her hand as he stepped out of them. When she pulled off his shirt, he lifted his arms as a child would. She took one of his hands in hers and, smiling, placed it against her breast.

It was only in retrospect that he would understand that she had been as lonely as he was, though he would not remember how many months they continued to see each other. Time, he would come to understand, could contract or expand memory, so that events he remembered as consecutive actually occurred more than a month apart, and a single day could register, in retrospect, as endless.

He went to her apartment whenever he could pilfer a few moments from errands or make excuses to Siniša on the nights they were allowed into town. He made love to her on the couch, on each of the chairs, on the low, humming refrigerator in the kitchen.

"Why so happy these days, Morić?" Siniša asked with amusement. "You look like the fox that ate the chicken in one bite."

The hours with her took away the sting of army life and filled the long months of his recruitment with something other than homesickness. Even the sergeant became less harsh towards him, no longer singling him out for particularly unpleasant tasks, sometimes actually making small talk with him.

Then, one evening, Pavlović materialized beside him as he left the mess hall. "There are undesirable elements among us, Morić."

Marin faltered.

"Take your friend Siniša. His father was a provocateur who spent ten years in prison." He paused. "I bet you didn't know that."

Marin shook his head.

"You're a good soldier," the sergeant continued. "I know because I've been watching you. If he were to say anything suspicious, it would be your duty to talk to me about it."

Marin found his voice. "Suspicious?"

"Anything at all," the sergeant said. "I think we understand one another."

When he told Nada, she looked at him carefully. "He wants you to become an informer."

On Rosmarina there were at least a half-dozen known informers, and everyone was careful in their dealings with them. Marin had never considered their recruitment, the way they would have been approached as the sergeant had approached him, slapping his arm and speaking of duty. If anything, he had thought of them as born that way, their treachery an innate flaw of character.

"What a mess this country is," Nada told him late one afternoon as they lay naked on her couch. "When things could be so different."

"Why are you whispering?" he asked, and she lifted her head from his chest, telling him with a smile that one never knew who might be listening.

"Anything yet?" Pavlović asked the next day, looking at him with a guarded expression.

"Not a word," he replied.

"Good," Nada told him later, so that he basked in the warmth of her approval. "Let those bastards do their own dirty work."

★ ★ ★

He was aware of the stacks of books in her apartment, the way she would remove a volume from one towering pile, read a few passages, then leave it on top of another. Sometimes she would read lines of poetry aloud to him, always locating the book she wanted within seconds, as if she had mapped out the contents of those stacks.

He never stopped to study their titles, although she admitted that a few were banned. "There's an entire world inside those covers," she told him once, "if you'd only stop to enter."

But his world was one of fish and sea, and he had teased her that there was no room in it for poetry.

"But look how much poetry has to do with the sea!" she insisted. "Pages and pages of it. Your Rosmarina is more connected to the world than you'd like to think."

A constant stream of friends stayed in her apartment, so he could not always see her when he liked. Most were friendly enough, but he knew that some merely tolerated his presence, as if he were a child. A woman from Ljubljana had cornered her in the kitchen, the sheer astonishment in her voice carrying to the next room where he sat: "But he's a teenager, Nada!"

Another who came to visit with his wife found Marin's sudden appearance in his army uniform one evening highly amusing. "Tell me, young fisherman," he said, lifting his glass of wine as if Marin's response would determine whether he took a sip. "What is your opinion of Kant?"

Across the room, Marin saw his lover flush at these words. "Leave him alone, Šimun," she said in a warning voice, for although she had offered to lend Marin several of her books, he had always declined, fearing the mockery of the barracks.

He was aware, as well, that certain conversations were subverted in his presence, that when he came in, the words trailed off into discussions of films or reminiscences. He had once found Šimun pacing the living room in agitation as his wife and Nada looked on, trailing off when he caught sight of Marin in the doorway. "We were just discussing these awful Macedonian summers," he said, fanning himself with the newspaper in his hand as if to prove his point. "Must be hard for someone from the sea, to be in a place where the air never moves."

Marin nodded, although he knew the man had been reading from the newspaper only moments before. But by the time of his next visit, the newspaper was gone, and Nada told him that he was only imagining it.

Despite his suspicion that she was lying to him, it was still a shock to learn several weeks later that Šimun had been arrested.

"But—"

"Don't ask me any questions," Nada begged, and Marin sat beside her in stunned silence, picturing the slender man whose hands had been as white and delicate as a woman's. Šimun had told him that he had managed to avoid most of his own military service because of his weak lungs, and Marin could not imagine how he would survive jail or, worse, slave labor.

On the night that Nada did not answer the door to his knock, he waited in her hallway, thinking that she had gone to buy bread, or to visit a friend. But an hour went by and still she did not come.

I was here, waiting for you, he teased her in the note that he slipped beneath her door. *But I couldn't wait any longer because the sergeant will skin me alive if I'm not back by lights out.* He had signed it with his first name, leaving the doodle of a fishing boat beneath it.

She was not there the next day either, or the next. On the fourth day, he knocked on a neighbor's door, and an old woman opened it to peer into the hallway with a frightened expression.

"They took her," she whispered. "The police came and took her away."

He went through the rest of that week as if he were dreaming.

At every point that he could get away from the base, he returned to her apartment, but she was gone. When he walked past the neighbor's door, he thought he could feel the weight of the woman's stare through her keyhole.

The first time he was taken for interrogation, a man not much older than himself asked so many questions that he became dizzy. He tried to confuse Marin in his answers, doubling back to ask the same questions a dozen ways. He wanted to know the names of Marin's friends, whether he had attended any political meetings, what his links were to dissidents abroad. "What kind of shit have you gotten yourself into?" he asked finally, producing the note that Marin had pushed beneath Nada's door.

Marin took it with shaking hands. "It's mine," he admitted. "Of course it's mine."

She was a good comrade, he insisted, and had never talked against the government. "She's a teacher," he protested. "She has no interest in politics."

But the man only laughed in his face. "You're either a liar or extremely stupid," he told Marin.

Each time he was summoned for questioning, they kept him for hours, asking him the names of her friends, of others involved in her movement.

"Movement?" He had only frowned. "What movement?"

He waited another week before returning to her apartment. But this time a middle-aged woman answered the door. When he looked past her, the threadbare couch in the small room was the same, but her books were gone.

"Yes?" the woman asked him with a frown, the smell of cabbage soup filling the hallway in great, nauseating waves.

"Who is it?" a gruff male voice called from inside.

Backing away from the door, Marin only mumbled that he had confused their apartment with another.

*   *   *

He did the only thing he could think of doing: he went directly from her front door to the bus station. The first bus went to Sarajevo, and it took him another day to reach Rosmarina.

When he reached the courtyard of their house, he found his father sitting on the stone bench, mending nets. "You have to go back," Luka pleaded with him. "You're playing with fire."

The police were already looking for him and had come to their house that morning.

"Just one night," Marin begged. "I only want to spend one night on the island."

But they arrested him for desertion just before dawn.

He saw Šimun once more, on Barren Island. He nearly failed to recognize the strange, gaunt prisoner who stared at him on his first march to the gravel pits. It was only when the other man lifted his slender hands to his face that Marin connected the birdlike figure to Nada's friend.

"Do you have any news of her?" Marin whispered.

The other man's hair, clipped close to his scalp like every other prisoner, had turned completely gray, and the once sardonic mouth was a single, grim line. "I don't know anything," he responded tightly.

In that moment the world went black, and when Marin finally awoke, believing for a joyful moment that he was back on Rosmarina, a guard was throwing water in his face.

"You have lost the right to talk," this dark shadow informed him.

He did only the minimum to survive. He did not snitch, once spending two weeks in solitary confinement because he would not denounce another man. The floor where he slept was covered in an inch of water, and rats scurried over his face at night.

He never saw Šimun again, and he never saw Nada. Those three years were a progression of beatings and thirst, exhaustion, and hunger. In winter, water on the floor of his cell regularly froze, and in summer the harsh sun made the prisoners appear as if their skin had been peeled from their bodies.

Nor did his misfortunes end with his release. Instead they followed him back to the island, where his every errand was recorded, his every statement added to a file somewhere, on which he imagined the words MARIN MORIĆ, ENEMY OF THE STATE.

At home he was not prepared for the suspicion of their neighbors. Barren Island in those days was considered a prison like any other, filled with rapists and murderers. It was a well-known fact that those who made it out had likely paid for their freedom by informing on someone else. Or by agreeing to become an informer once home, listening to the conversations of friends, writing reports on the movements of neighbors.

It was useless to explain that he was none of these things. That he did not know why he had been released, the day coming so abruptly that he did not trust them even when he was given civilian clothes and told to change. He was so thin that the trousers hung from his hips and he needed to hitch them up, to the constant hilarity of the guards, whose eyes he refused to meet. It would be just like them to find some technicality to delay his freedom, to tell him in the end that it had all been a joke, to return him to his cell without ceremony.

You didn't imagine we'd let you go that easily, did you? he expected them to tell him.

Before boarding the small police boat to the mainland, he was taken once more for questioning. His interrogator told him in no uncertain terms that he was not to reveal a single detail about the years of his incarceration. Not the color of the prisoners' uniforms, not the names of those on his work details, names he did not know in any event because anything as intimate as a name had been stripped from them the moment they reached that island gulag.

"I could have you back here tomorrow," the man had told him.

So that even when he returned to Rosmarina he could feel those invisible strings tethering him like a marionette. Threatening to lift him from the island and return him to hell.

He tried to live quietly after his release, but still they summoned him for questioning. In 1974, the year after he returned to Rosmarina, Yugoslavia adopted a new constitution with greater protection for individual rights—except for anyone attempting to subvert the country's social order. Marin had no intention of subverting anything. But Barren Island marked him as an agitator forever.

The chief of police was a younger man from the mainland whose path Marin went to extraordinary lengths to avoid. There was something that reminded him of his sergeant, of that tough and brutish man who had enjoyed stripping conscripts naked during winter, although the policeman—Vico was his name—was in fact soft-spoken.

Sometimes when Marin was in the middle of some errand, or sitting in his boat on the *riva,* he would look up to see the man's cold eyes watching him.

Only his sister understood the depth of his despair. After his return it was Ana who noticed certain people listening more carefully in his presence. "I'll never let them take you back," she told him.

In another period her fierceness might have amused him. But he had come back to them a different man, his mother pressing her handkerchief to her eyes on the night of his return as much from shock, he realized, as from relief.

"You'll do nothing," he ordered his sister.

He had been her keeper from an early age, adoring the abundance of dark hair already on her baby's head, so unlike their distant cousins, who looked like old men as newborns, wrinkled and bald. Later, it was Marin whom she would allow to remove a splinter from her foot or the occasional needle from a sea urchin, a rare event, anyway, because he cleared a path for her whenever they went swimming.

A light burned more fiercely in Ana than burned in others, and she was fearless, so that their parents worried constantly that she would fall into the harbor or from a balcony, or that she would walk through the plate glass window of the ferry office, like the island's birds who could not identify that smooth surface and ended up in twitching heaps on the pavement outside.

She had been a heartless flirt throughout her youth, and so it had been a relief to their parents when she met her husband at the age of twenty. Marin had returned from Barren Island to find her already married, and pregnant with Magdalena. *Electricity needs to be grounded,* he would think, watching her with Goran, *lest it burn everything in its path.*

His brother-in-law was the only man, aside from his father, with whom he still fished, his former friends too frightened by the prospect of that association. The two spent long hours talking—though never about Marin's imprisonment—and taking turns with the engine. It was Goran who asked him to be godfather to their child, a tiny and delicate baby whose eyes grew from a deep sapphire blue to black. Goran asked apologetically, understanding that his brother-in-law risked inciting the regime's wrath by standing up with them in a church.

"We don't want to get you into more trouble," he told Marin.

For much of the ceremony, Marin held Magdalena in his arms, looking at her sleeping face, so peaceful that he missed several of the responses. Her innocence both frightened him and filled him with longing. He doubted that he himself would ever be capable of producing something so unspoiled.

★   ★   ★

If his sister's face grew longer after his return, he did not notice because her tongue was as sharp as it had always been. But he was aware when she and Goran began to argue sometime later, angry whispers that broke the confines of their bedroom and brushed uneasily through the rest of the house. If anything, he assumed them to be the growing pains of a young marriage, just as his mother claimed.

A pall descended over the entire house, and something about his brother-in-law also changed abruptly in those days. Goran no longer laughed as easily. He grew thin, Ružica wringing her hands when he claimed that he could eat no more than a few bites of food at a time, and she worried aloud that he had developed an ulcer. For the first time, he began drinking in the port, stumbling home in the early hours of the morning.

"Come on, man," Marin heard Luka tell him in the courtyard once, his voice heavy with dismay. "This is no way to live."

But if Goran responded, he did not hear.

To escape the house, Marin went often to the Devil's Stones. He had long planned to build a shelter at their fishing camp, and he began to spend several days at a stretch there, sleeping beneath the stars, thinking that a more expansive sky could surely exist nowhere else in the world. He had missed that sky. He had missed its blackness and the crisp edges of its stars, and he was relieved to find himself beneath it again.

He spent days drawing a simple two-room design, planning a window in each room and how he would rig a lamp from a generator. There would be no running water, but there was a cistern on a nearby hill, and he designed a small paved area in front for drying nets. His father and Goran both liked the idea and agreed to help him when they could.

His design was deliberately simple, and he liked the way the structure grew, slowly, to resemble what he had sketched on paper. For several years after his release, he worked on it whenever he was not fishing. All the materials had to be taken from Rosmarina, which in turn had to be brought from the mainland or building-supply stores on larger islands. He waited for the cinder blocks to come in on the ferry, and he cannibalized stone from derelict buildings across the island.

The night he put on a temporary roof of corrugated iron, however, a storm blew up from the sea. He heard it from his bed and imagined the wind peeling the roof back like a sardine tin, a fierce rain toppling the walls. The project had begun to obsess him, and while the storm raged for two days, he waited impatiently on Rosmarina, looking out towards the Devil's Stones, which were at times obliterated by rain.

On the third day he woke to a calm sea and set off anxiously to check the roof. "Whatever damage there is can be repaired," his father told him reasonably before he went, and although Marin nodded, there was a tightness in his throat. All the way to the Devil's Stones, he thought about what he might have done differently, which building materials he should have used instead. He had bought some of the cinder blocks cheaply, and now he fretted over their quality, imagining that they had dissolved in the rain like lumps of sugar.

It was on his approach to the hut that he heard the low groans. He was too relieved to see the walls standing and the roof intact to register what the sounds were at first. They grew louder as he neared, however, and he concluded that some teenagers had escaped the town to rut in privacy. He stopped uncertainly a few meters away, both amused and annoyed by this trespass.

But something about the woman's voice made the hairs on his arms stand up like tiny needles, and he approached the window cautiously, the way one would the edge of a precipice.

It had been years since he and his sister had swum naked together as children, but he recognized her bare, slick back at once. Vico was watching her with those lifeless eyes, the expression on his face somewhere between a smile and a grimace. He had wrapped her hair around his hand, pulling it so far back that her face was turned up, towards the ceiling.

In the first moment it was shame, not rage, that washed over Marin. He was ashamed for her, ashamed for himself that he had come upon her like this, that he was witness to her bare feet planted firmly on the floor, to the way she strained against her lover. He wanted to weep, and when he saw Vico take the same nipple into his mouth that she had regularly offered her infant daughter, he turned blindly from the window and fled.

A voice wailed in his head as he ran all the way back to his boat. *Not him,* it pleaded. *Not him. Not him.* It was only as the distance between them grew that he began to curse them both. They had tainted the thing he was building, and he was sorry that the wind and rain had not demolished it.

Later that day he saw Ana back on the *riva,* selling rosemary oil from the tourist stand where she worked, no hint of shame in her heart-shaped face.

"What's eating you, brother?" she asked, but he did not acknowledge her as he walked past.

He did not know how long it had been going on, nor whether his brother-in-law suspected. For weeks Marin brooded, so that his sister looked curiously at him, and his father commented that he had grown surly.

He watched Ana feed Magdalena and iron her husband's shirts, and she looked up anxiously whenever she felt the weight of his eyes. He even goaded her slightly until she finally cornered him one day in the courtyard, telling him to spit it out.

The ugly words flew out of him then. *Slut* and *whore* and *I know what you've been doing,* and she could only look at him stunned, her eyes filling with tears. At that moment Goran appeared at one of the windows, telling her in a strange voice that Magdalena had fallen and hurt herself. Vinka, who was visiting their mother, stood behind him, her eyes everywhere and nowhere at once.

He did not know how long Goran had been standing there, but his brother-in-law's ashen face and his aunt's open mouth made Marin think they had heard everything.

That night Goran went out alone to fish. Marin did not accompany him because he had agreed to patch an elderly cousin's roof in the morning, a chore that needed to be done before winter. And he feared the other man's questions.

The next day he and Luka hiked up to the cousin's house at dawn, carrying tiles on their backs. They stopped once, halfway, to slake their thirst and looked out across the bay, at the dots of boats below them, and he wondered which of those boats might be Goran's, for now was the time when he would be returning to port.

They spent all morning on the Peak, replacing cracked and decrepit tiles, launching them from the roof into the courtyard below so that they exploded on the stone in bursts of red clay. Afterwards his cousin fed them before they returned to town, a walk that was five times quicker than the ascent.

It was when they turned onto their lane that they heard wailing, both men breaking into a run when they realized that it was coming from their house. "Dead!" Ana was screaming inside, sitting on the kitchen floor and pulling at her black hair. "Dead!"

The fisherman who had found Goran's boat adrift and towed it back to the island was smoking nervously in the courtyard, and in a daze Marin returned to the port with him. He found the boat in its usual station, bobbing eerily at the end of its rope. He searched it as several people watched him from the *riva* with somber faces, and found two drops of dark blood on the gunwale. The sun had dried them to the consistency of thin rubber.

It was Vico who came to file the report. "Unlucky bastard," he said, taking one look at the blood.

The death was declared an accident, although a body was never found. Marin thought he knew better. *You drove him to it,* he wanted to tell his sister. *You killed him as surely as if you held a gun to his head.*

Ana took to her bed and did not eat. He avoided her, taking the tiny Magdalena with him when he went out, because she was nearly two now, and fascinated by boats of every size and shape. He had scrubbed those drops of blood away, the pigment more stubborn than he would have guessed, trailing red threads through the water he poured over the side.

He could not stand the way Magdalena's eyes scanned every room for her father, the way she looked for him behind doors, scrambling upstairs to check every corner of the house whenever they returned home. She was too young to understand that Goran Babić was not merely on an extended fishing trip and would not be coming home to play with her in the courtyard, to hide candies behind his ears, revealing them with flourishes that made her squeal with laughter.

He never spoke to his father or mother about what he had seen. When he could not avoid his sister, because it was a small house that had grown suddenly smaller as if the thing were deflating, its dimensions shrinking more every day, they barely spoke to each other.

When Ana started to get up again, she sat at the kitchen table and smoked cigarettes—a habit she had always hidden but now found pointless to conceal. She smoked cigarette after cigarette until Luka finally forced her into the courtyard, where she sat on the stone bench for days at a time, watching the grapevine that Goran and Luka had planted at Magdalena's birth. She watched it as if she could see it growing, never taking her eyes from it. The movement of her hands was mechanical as she brought the cigarette to her lips and inhaled, then lit the next.

"You have to pull yourself together," Marin overheard his mother saying. "You have a child."

Her only response had been silence, and the sound of smoke being drawn deep into her lungs. When she exhaled he imagined the thick clouds that blurred the features of her face.

Ana returned to her stand on the *riva,* to selling rosemary oil and wreaths. She worked without smiling, without really looking at the faces of tourists or at the girls at other stands. From the opposite end of the *riva,* Marin watched her mark prices on the tiny bottles and twist the still greenish-yellow stalks into bundles and hearts.

On the night he came home to find her weeping in the courtyard, it was so dark that he could barely make out the shining features of her face. Nor did he understand immediately what she was telling him, though it clearly had something to do with leaving the island.

"You can't," he told her, surprised by his sudden grief. "Where would you go?"

"No," she told him with a shake of her head. "It's you who has to leave."

At her words the moon came out from behind the clouds, and it was as if his sister's face changed in front of him, as if the bone and flesh retracted beneath her skin.

"What are you saying?" he demanded, although later he would realize that he had known the answer all along.

"They're arresting you tomorrow."

In the morning, his father left with him so that no one would be suspicious.

His aunt and uncle went, as well, having appeared in the middle of the night as if a second sense alerted them to his departure. He later learned that news of his impending arrest had already made it around the island.

"It's time to leave all this behind," Vlaho said, slapping his arm, and there was something about his glee that only increased Marin's desolation.

His aunt and uncle took their own boat, pretending that they were going to the Devil's Stones for a picnic. Katarina took only her stuffed bear.

Marin and his father made it look as if they carried nothing but their lunches. As he left their house for the last time, his mother wept, so that Magdalena watched her with a puzzled expression. His sister stood at an upstairs window, hidden by the wooden shutters. In the last moment in the courtyard, he looked up and saw her silhouette.

He left with money shoved into the waistband of his trousers, documents in the lunch bags, some food and water.

He dropped his father off on another island. Luka would catch a ferry to the mainland, then another back to Rosmarina, and Marin would rendezvous with his uncle and aunt so that the boats could cross to Italy together.

"The boat," Marin said miserably, because father and son owned it jointly.

It was Luka who had insisted that they take two vessels, believing that safety lay in numbers. But now he looked away, and Marin realized that he was crying.

"There will be other boats," Luka told his only son.

CHAPTER 9

Marin had left that boat—his last, as it turned out—on a dirty beach in Italy, surrendering immediately to the *carabinieri* with his aunt's family, who had come ashore alongside him. He did not know what became of it, whether it was given to some Italian fisherman, the Rosmarina markings painted over by a new owner, or left to rot where he had pulled it up.

Some nights in America he dreamed about it, the inverted hull sinking beneath empty bottles and old newspapers, decomposing as a human corpse might until there was nothing left but its sun-bleached wooden ribs.

Sometimes he dreamed of Vico. That the policeman watched as Marin and his wife made love, as they slept, as they pulled the boys into bed with them on Sunday mornings and warmed cold, bare toes against flannel and skin. In the dreams Marin always realized his presence belatedly, looking up in shock to see the derision in the other man's eyes.

He always sat in the chair across from the bed, where Luz had draped her dress, or where her stockings trailed on the floor. No matter how many times Marin moved the chair before sleep, dreaming would return it to its familiar station, and Vico would be sitting upon it easily.

Marin would awake to find the room empty except for his wife's slumbering form, the lights of the alarm clock making their bedspread green, the time always between one and two in the morning. The seventh hour of the day at home. The hour in which he was usually already on the sea.

Jadranka did not appear the next morning at the beginning of her shift, but this did not surprise him. She had not said a word to him after he finished, sitting in a silence so thick that, to his mind, it only confirmed her guilt.

"Vermin," he had told her. "Those people poison everything they touch."

In another time and place, he would have refused to reveal so much about his past, but the words had poured out of him. He had told her everything because with each detail he added, the confounding shame of exile grew less.

"It's they who should be ashamed," he had told her in an acid voice, looking at her meaningfully. "They should burn with it."

She had risen unsteadily then and untied the apron around her waist. She retreated to the office for her backpack and left without a backward glance. As she passed the window, her face glowed like a Halloween mask beneath the streetlights, but she kept her eyes straight ahead and did not cast even a sidelong glance into the restaurant's interior.

"Good riddance," he told his wife the next morning. But she only looked at him in shock.

"The bogeyman is dead," she told him. "You really believed that she could be a part of that?"

He said nothing.

"She wasn't even born when it happened!"

But he only shook his head stubbornly. His wife was an innocent, he thought, if she believed that they had merely ceased to exist. Communism might be dead—in Croatia, at least—but the people who had benefited from it would hardly have given up. No, he thought. They would have clawed to keep their positions, hanging on as he had seen rats do after floods, scrabbling at anything to stay afloat.

"Oh, Mio," she finally told him. "What have you done?"

He looked at her for a moment, upset that she should doubt his judgment. But she had spent most of her childhood in the United States and, as a result, knew the heartlessness of those systems primarily through the stories of others. He had thought she understood, but it was clear that she didn't, and in that moment he felt as lonely as the last member of a dying species.

"I survived," he answered her before retreating to his office.

Jadranka did not appear again, and for the next few days both his wife and Hector went around with a dejected air, refusing to meet his eyes. A pall hung over the restaurant, as if the dining room were filled with smoke, and even their customers seemed to notice it. Their conversations were less animated, and they did not tend to linger at the end of their meals.

"Where's that nice, red-haired girl?" one of their regulars asked, and Marin mumbled something about her having to return home.

In mid-July, two weeks after Jadranka's departure, he received a large, flat package at the restaurant. It was addressed to Marin Morić, wrapped in brown paper and tied with twine, and he knew without opening it that it was the painting she had promised them.

They had not yet started serving for the day, and he took it to his office, where he stared at the brown paper packaging. He considered placing it on the curb without opening it, letting the garbage collectors haul it away with the morning trash. He thought for a moment of the satisfying sound it would make as they fed it to the iron jaws of their truck.

But curiosity got the better of him, and he found a pair of scissors in the desk drawer to clip the twine. He peeled away the brown paper, careful not to tear it, staring as he did so at the familiar handwriting of the address. He had kept her order pad, which was filled with that looping script. He had pored over it as if the lists of appetizer samplers and glasses of wine might reveal something. Evidence, he had convinced himself when he could not bring himself to discard it.

The view was from the window of the bedroom he had shared with his sister when they were children, and he could make out the grapevine that his father and Goran had planted on the day of Magdalena's birth.

One of the busboys stuck his head into the office at that moment, but Marin waved him away, rising a moment later to lock the door.

He did not understand. A thousand explanations circled like flying birds. They made such a noise in his head that he sank again into the desk chair and rested his forehead against his palms.

Was she playing with him now? he wondered. Was it not sufficient that she had spied on him, ingratiating herself into their lives so that even he was tricked into feeling her absence?

She had clearly gained access to the Rosmarina house, and he marveled for a moment at the elaborate nature of this plan, at the energy that had gone into snaring such a little fish as himself. What on earth could they have been after? he wondered, not for the first time.

The painting was good. Even his untrained eye could see that. And it contained details that he had forgotten: the way the courtyard gate sagged slightly on its hinges, the vines that covered the walls, the giant flagstones that had been worn smooth.

Had she even painted it? Or was there a studio somewhere filled with artists in their employ? He imagined them hard at work, providing exiles like himself a momentary glimpse of the lost landscapes of their childhoods. Like crumbs of bread placed beneath the noses of starving men.

There was the bench where his sister liked to sit, drying her long, dark hair in the sunlight. There was the stone table where his mother shelled peas, and the place where his father's boat stood sentry in the winter. In different circumstances, he realized, he might have been grateful to the sender.

"Take over," he told Hector as he passed through the restaurant, the painting under his arm.

He returned home to find Luz sitting at their kitchen table, looking through old recipe books. She had not heard him enter the apartment and was intent on the pages in front of her, her finger moving from one line to the next. He had always loved his wife's single-mindedness, the tenacity that had kept their restaurant afloat through lean years when he might have given up, and he watched her for a moment before clearing his throat. He fought hard to adopt a neutral expression, but when she looked at him over the top of her reading glasses, she frowned slightly and rose from her chair.

Over the years of their marriage, it had always amazed him how she was able to decipher his mood, just as she did now, embracing him wordlessly so that he was tempted to linger in her arms the way their sons had done when they were small.

"What's wrong?" she asked, catching his chin in her palm.

He took her hand in his and studied its olive smoothness, then turned it over and examined its lines, a smattering of scars from handling hot pans and knives in the kitchen of their restaurant. He lifted it to his face again and kissed it.

Usually that hollow place inside him closed up, the door swinging shut as he left the hymns of his childhood behind in the Forty-first Street church. He was an expert at segregation, at keeping the various chambers of his heart walled off from one another, the same way that a single apartment building contained lives that never intersected. But for weeks now the door had refused to swing shut.

"I have something to show you," he told her, then led her back to the apartment's entrance, where he had left the painting leaning against a wall.

She did not understand what it was at first, staring at it with a confused expression.

"This is the house where I was born," he managed to tell her, so that she only stared at it in shock. She picked it up and walked with it into the living room, taking it over to the windows to look at it in the light.

"It's beautiful," she told him.

He nodded. "I don't understand it."

She studied every inch, drinking in the landscape. She had never before been able to attach an image to the things he had described, he realized. And he had never had tangible proof of them.

"There's a number," she told him suddenly.

He joined her at the window, frowning. He looked where she pointed, and it was true. In the left margin was a series of numbers that he had missed.

She read them aloud in her soft Spanish. "They must mean something."

He watched her copy the numbers onto a piece of paper and frown at them. She had a fondness for riddles and Sudoku puzzles. She would spend hours poring over them, whereas he never had the patience.

"It can't be a date," she said. "Perhaps it's a telephone number?"

He looked at the piece of paper. "Too long," he told her.

"Too long for a number in the United States," she conceded. "But it could be an international number."

He looked at it again. "I don't recognize the prefix."

"We can check on the Internet," she told him.

His wife was already fluent in that strange language of the younger generation, the one he had dismissed in the beginning as a fad, his sons speaking in confounding terms like *web* and *virtual* and *server*. It was she who monitored the restaurant's website, a useless expense, he had incorrectly predicted in the beginning.

They sat side by side at the computer in their sons' room, beneath a poster of Robert De Niro in *Raging Bull*. Luz's hands moved rapidly across the keyboard until she found what she was looking for.

"That's it," she told him. "Three-eight-five. That's the country code for Croatia."

He stared at the screen.

"Let's see if we can find an address," she said.

Ten minutes later he was staring at the address where he had grown up.

Luz sat beside him as he dialed the number. It rang several times before an older woman picked up. He tried to place her voice in the pantheon of neighbors and distant cousins who might have occupied their house after his parents' deaths. She was going a little deaf, he thought, because at first she could not understand him.

"You're mistaken," she said in a wavering voice before hanging up. "My son, Marin, left years ago."

He stared at the receiver in his hand, a recorded voice now telling him reprovingly that if he would like to make a call, he should hang up.

"Mio," Luz said in dismay, "why are you crying?"

But he could not bring himself to answer, his hand shaking so badly that Luz had to dial, reading the number from the pad of paper where she had written it, handing him the receiver.

"Mama," he said immediately the second time, a word that had not passed his lips in thirty years.

And when Ružica Morić heard his voice, when she heard those

two short syllables that were like the beating of a heart, she cried aloud then dropped the telephone against a hard surface—the floor, perhaps, or the kitchen table.

"Luka!" he heard her shouting in the background, above the swift movement of her feet.

PART III

CHAPTER 10

Jadranka's letters from America had described coffee shops that teemed even at three in the morning and dreadlocked artists who filled pavements with chalk drawings. She wrote about the musical buskers who performed on moving subway trains—mariachi bands, earnest folk musicians with beards and baby faces, a mournful accordionist—and Magdalena knew her sister well enough to picture Jadranka digging into her pocket for whatever loose change she could give them.

On her days off, Jadranka liked to wander the city, and she had spent one spring afternoon watching grizzled men play chess in Washington Square Park. She sketched the concentration on their faces and the hands that hovered birdlike above the pieces, and she included a few of these drawings in a letter to Magdalena. *This guy told me that the world is my oyster,* she had written beneath the sketch of a man whose broad smile revealed a missing tooth.

But to Magdalena the city brimmed more with pandemonium than opportunity, and from the moment she stepped outside the airport terminal, New York assaulted her with its noise, with its smell of gasoline, its chipped concrete and litter-covered streets. Traffic snarled, and a barely contained chaos rumbled upward from the subway tunnels, so that the pavement trembled beneath her feet.

Jadranka's letters had also contained lively accounts of her duties in their cousin's household. Each day, she dropped the children off at school—a place where limousines vied for position in the street—then picked them up again. In the afternoons she accompanied them to Central Park, where bench after bench of foreign nannies rocked babies to sleep. In the evenings, she helped Tabitha with her homework and made sure that Christopher brushed his teeth instead of merely running his toothbrush under the tap, an old trick with which she was well acquainted from her own childhood.

In her spare time, she had been helping Katarina prepare for an autumn exhibit at her gallery, though she had mentioned this only briefly in her letters.

"There's still so much left to do," Katarina explained to Magdalena as they looked through photographs on the evening of her arrival. It was a sentiment that hung in the air between them until Katarina suggested, a little too brightly, that Jadranka might yet return in time. "It's only June."

Katarina's outward appearance had changed dramatically since that summer on Rosmarina. The awkward, pudgy girl had been replaced by a slender woman who wore designer sunglasses and appeared on the society page of the *New York Times*. But the eyes that studied Magdalena were the same as she remembered, hungrily taking in every detail.

Looking through the photographs had been Katarina's idea, and Magdalena studied the way her sister played with the children in Central Park and at the family's beach house, in a place called Shelter Island. There were pictures from a gallery opening, Jadranka dressed in a green silk dress that still hung in her closet upstairs. It was a striking color that showed off the paleness of her shoulders, but Magdalena had the sensation that the smiling face she gazed upon—the one that resembled Jadranka in every way—was different from the one she remembered from a few short months before.

"She fit right in," Katarina was telling her. "People in the art world can be biting, but she bit right back, especially as her English got better. She's a quick study and there's nothing provincial about her."

Magdalena tensed.

"I didn't mean—" Katarina began in dismay.

"Don't worry about it."

But Katarina shook her head. "I used to be jealous of you and your sister, of the fact that you lived on the island when I had to live in Pittsburgh."

"That's not what you said that summer," Magdalena reminded her. "You kept telling us all the ways Pittsburgh was better."

Katarina snorted. "You've never seen Pittsburgh."

Magdalena shrugged, but her cousin placed a hand on her arm. "You have to forgive me, Lena," she said, squeezing it. "I said a lot of stupid things back then."

It was the closest they came to discussing what Katarina had revealed that summer so many years ago. In the next few days, she described how Jadranka had learned to make grilled-cheese sandwiches, how she had taught the children a new card game and a trick with vinegar and baking soda, but she did not return to the subject of Rosmarina.

The autumn exhibit Katarina had mentioned was three months away, and so Magdalena suspected that her cousin's frequent absences had as much to do with discomfort as with any pressing business. During her explanations of deliveries or lighting mishaps, Katarina's hands moved constantly. They worried at her hair or rubbed invisible spots on her sleeve.

"It's okay, Katica," Magdalena finally told her. "Jadranka is a grown woman. It isn't your fault that she ran off."

The nickname—which Magdalena's grandfather had used that summer—won a small smile from Katarina, but she continued to twist her wedding ring.

Magdalena had met Katarina's husband, Michael, only once. A dark-haired man who wore Clark Kent glasses, he had mixed her a gin and tonic on the afternoon of her arrival, and they had chatted in perfunctory English. But he traveled frequently for work, and Magdalena had not seen him in the days since.

In the end it was Jazmin, the housekeeper, who provided Magdalena with a map of the city, explaining that streets increased numerically from south to north, and avenues from east to west. A friendly, older woman from Bangladesh, she had fallen silent in the middle of these explanations. "I showed your sister, as well," she said almost apologetically.

According to Jazmin, Jadranka had fallen easily into the rhythm of the household, and Christopher and Tabitha, while a bit spoiled, were still a hundred times better behaved than the children in other families. Her previous employers, she confided, had a little girl of Christopher's age who would follow her around rooms she had already cleaned, intentionally dropping things behind her. "She emptied an entire carton of apple juice on the kitchen floor once, just after I finished mopping it," she said indignantly. "She thought it was funny."

Christopher was a sturdy and amiable boy who enjoyed digging in sandboxes and thrashing high weeds with sticks. He had begun almost immediately to call her *Lena,* following his mother's lead in a way that astounded her with its confidence.

Tabitha had an oily, moon-shaped face, reminiscent of her mother's at that age, and she wore baggy clothes to camouflage her growing breasts. The other girls at camp were mean, she told Magdalena, and her younger brother could do anything and not get into trouble for it.

It was clear to Magdalena that both children saw her as an

extension of her sister. Tabitha had immediately confessed to hating their mother's gallery, and Christopher insisted that Magdalena read to him in the evenings as Jadranka had done. "She left before we got to the end," he said, handing her a copy of *Charlotte's Web*.

Magdalena did not open it immediately. "Did she say anything before she left?" she asked.

But Jadranka had gone while he was sleeping, without even saying goodbye.

"She told me stories about a magic island," he added unexpectedly.

"Rosmarina?"

But he did not think it had a name.

It was only in Jadranka's letters that Magdalena recognized her sister. She had brought the entire half year's archive with her, clipping the letters together and printing out the e-mails.

It was through one of those missives that she had first learned of her ex-boyfriend's presence in New York. Jadranka's casual mention of him, months ago, almost prepared her for the way Damir's voice sprang to life on radios all across the island as he reported on some session of the United Nations or high-level meetings between heads of state.

I haven't seen him myself but I've heard that he's almost fully recovered, Jadranka informed her.

He had been wounded while reporting in Iraq the year before, his mother delivering this news on Rosmarina's waterfront. The two women rarely did more than exchange a few awkward words, but Magdalena's face must have betrayed her on that occasion, because the older woman tried immediately to comfort her. "He won't die, dear," she said, patting Magdalena's arm. "If that's what you're worried about."

For several years now, she had secretly followed news of his movements, from exhumations in Bosnia to bombings in Afghanistan. He would disappear from print for months, only to reappear in some distant and usually dangerous place. He was a common subject of island conversation because Rosmarina had never tired of hearing its native son on the radio.

Likewise, the global network of island gossip made it inevitable that he would learn of Jadranka's disappearance, and on the day before Magdalena's departure from Rosmarina, he had telephoned, his voice deep and unmistakable.

"They're saying that you plan to come look for her," he said.

"Who's saying?"

"Come on, Lena. Let me help you."

Her sister and Damir had always gotten along. One summer he had tutored her in mathematics. She amused him because every time he left her with equations to balance, he returned to find that she had left drawings in the margins instead.

But Jadranka had only mentioned him once in her letters. There was no indication that their paths had crossed in New York, and Magdalena convinced herself that curiosity had prompted his call. Perhaps he wanted to see for himself that she had remained in place for all these years, exactly as he had prophesied at their parting. Perhaps he wanted to congratulate himself on his lucky escape.

"I'll let you know" was all she would tell him before hanging up.

Katarina had already filed a missing-persons report at the local police precinct, but they had been dismissive. "Your cousin is an adult," they had told her. "She's free to come and go as she likes, for the duration of her visa."

And so Magdalena began searching blindly, armed with her sister's letters. She visited the places Jadranka had named—the coffee shops and parks, even showing her sister's picture to the chess players in Washington Square Park—but none of them recognized her, and though Magdalena looked for the man with the missing tooth, she did not think he was among them.

It was Katarina who suggested that she focus her search on Astoria and Long Island City, places where Jadranka's immigration status might not prevent her from finding temporary work. Large numbers of Croatians lived in those neighborhoods, where shops sold Vegeta seasoning, Podravka packaged soups, and Čokolino for babies' bottles. Katarina explained that she had little use for these old-country articles herself, but her mother sometimes pined for them.

"She has a sweet tooth," she added. "She'd sell her soul for a few Bajadera."

But it was unclear if *Nona* Vinka would even recognize those chocolates. Since Magdalena's arrival, the elderly woman had existed in only two states: sleep and exhaustion. She could not seem to keep her eyes open, and when she did manage to utter a few words, she had little grasp of where she was.

Her bedroom could not have helped in these matters of orientation. Unlike the rest of the house, its contents seemed to have been imported, item by item, from a Croatian island. Lace curtains hung at the window, and doilies covered every surface. A crucifix guarded the head of the bed, whose fuzzy acrylic blanket was identical to those that still graced many bedrooms on Rosmarina. A Bible rested atop a bureau, and Magdalena did not have to open its cover to know that the pages were well thumbed. She recognized some of the photographs that stood beside it as copies of the ones in her grandmother's vitrine.

"My mother has been homesick for thirty years" was Katarina's only explanation.

And it was homesickness that might have explained the section of western Queens to which Katarina directed her, for it was there that old men stopped and greeted each other in the street, an elaborate ritual of arm slapping that Magdalena had witnessed nowhere else in this American city. Restaurants served grilled fish and *palačinke,* and newsstands carried the same magazines whose stories of scandals and trysts Magdalena's grandmother read religiously at home.

It was like entering a place where two countries, separated by thousands of miles, oozed together. And while Magdalena's unease over her sister's disappearance only grew, she roamed this territory comfortably enough, saying her sister's name to grocers, to an electrician from whose rearview mirror a Split soccer team ornament swung, to an old man on the street who had sounded as if he might be from Rosmarina but, in the end, turned out to be from the nearby island of Vis. He looked so long and hard at the picture of Jadranka that Magdalena was certain that he recognized her. But he finally apologized that his sight was not what it had once been. "I'm sorry, child," he told her. "I've never seen your sister."

She repeated the name of the island. "Rosmarina," she told everyone who asked and some who did not. The elderly man had once visited there. Long ago, he told her, just after the Second World War, when conditions were very difficult.

"Which island did you say?" one of the waitresses in a Croatian soccer bar on Broadway asked, then wanted to know if it was near Kornati.

Magdalena shook her head. "Between Lastovo and Vis," she said, sketching them on a cocktail napkin.

"In the middle of nowhere" was the waitress's only reply.

She was sent on wild-goose chases by people who thought they might have heard about a red-haired Croatian girl living or working in such-and-such place, but when she rang the doorbells of houses and apartments, people looked at her suspiciously through the grilles of their doors. There were raspy voices through intercoms or shouts through open windows. Many were not Croatian, and she explained in careful English why she had come. Some thought it was a trick and threatened to call the police, but some of them agreed to look at the photograph.

Magdalena had studied English at university, but only now did she realize how fully her English was the English of schoolbooks, of professors who had enunciated every syllable. Her English had nothing to do with the cacophony that emerged from people's mouths, the slang, the half-eaten words, the way that one sentence ran into another. People in Queens spoke English as if they were shouting, or crying or laughing. There was the singsong of girls who giggled together on the subway and the slurring of drunks who stood on street corners with paper bags.

She further discovered that there was an entire nether language spoken by people who did not really speak English at all. Its hand gestures and grunts enabled her to trade mutual complaints about the heat with a woman who wore a head scarf, and to accept a handful of salted pistachios from an elderly man on the street.

"Subway?" she could ask a group of men milling around a gas station parking lot waiting for work. And they could point her in the right direction, holding up four fingers to show how many blocks she had to go.

But nobody had heard of her sister.

It bothered her that so few people knew of Rosmarina—even among New York's Croatian population—as though it were a mythical kingdom like Atlantis. It seemed to cast doubt on her sister's existence by association. As if one day Magdalena would pull out the photograph she carried for sentimental reasons—a shot of the sisters in a Split photo booth—only to discover a picture of herself, sitting alone.

For this reason she felt her spirits lift when she ran into the same elderly man from Vis a week later. "Rosmarina!" he hailed her on the pavement in front of a ninety-nine-cent store. "I was hoping I would see you again. Any luck finding your sister?"

"None," she told him.

He nodded gravely at this. "Might I make a suggestion?"

His words surprised her. "Please," she told him.

"It occurred to me a few days after I ran into you. You see, an old man like me hates to throw anything away. My children say that I'm a pack rat, but I consider myself more of a collector. You never know when you'll need something, Miss—?"

"Magdalena."

He smiled at this name, as if it reminded him of something pleasant. "Magdalena. And it occurred to me that your sister might have answered an ad in one of our local Croatian newspapers, if she was looking for employment. Or even placed one."

This idea had not occurred to her.

"I have copies of all of them, you see. Going back months."

She could just imagine it: towers of newsprint filled with stories about picnics and church bake sales, but she nodded anyway. Her sidewalk canvassing had certainly brought her no closer to finding her sister.

"I would be most obliged if you could show me," she told him.

He walked with a cane, and so their progress was slow. Several times people nodded at him, or greeted him with *Ej, profesore!*

"Professor?" she asked him.

"Of history," he told her, wheezing slightly. "But that was long ago."

Professor Barić was a widower and nearing eighty. He lived alone in a block of two-story homes that were identical except for their flourishes: one house had neoclassical railings, while a plaster Madonna holding an Italian flag guarded the narrow concrete garden of a second. A Greek flag hung in the window of a third.

"An international neighborhood," he told Magdalena with a smile.

There was a small, well-tended garden to one side of the front door, and inside, his rooms were filled with bookcases. Hard-backed tomes covered every surface, and a marble chess set occupied a low table in the living room, the whites and blacks regarding each other impassively across the board.

"Do you play?" he asked when he saw the direction of her gaze.

"I used to," she told him, brushing her fingertips over the ridged halo of a rook. "With my grandfather."

He nodded. "An excellent game. A teacher of strategy and life."

She had been quite good, in fact, occasionally beating Luka by the time she was thirteen, although now it occurred to her that he had let her win.

"You've just reminded me," the professor told her. "I promised a friend that we would play this afternoon."

"Do you play often?"

"As often as we can," he said, so that Magdalena pictured two old men sitting on opposite sides of the board, staring at it with the same concentration as the players in Washington Square Park, but with coffees and glasses of brandy.

"Now about those newspapers——"

She followed him into the kitchen, where papers stood in stacks on the counters and floor. His children were right in calling him a pack rat, she thought, taking in the rest of it: an assortment of third-class mail, pill bottles, and empty yogurt containers, washed and stacked neatly against the refrigerator. But the expression on his face was so pleased as he regarded the kitchen's contents that she told him, "It's lucky for me that you collect things, Professor."

"Please," he told her, pulling a chair out from the kitchen table. "Make yourself comfortable."

As he filled a pot with water for coffee, she pulled the nearest stack towards her. It was a weekly broadside, printed in New York, and she stifled a smile when she noticed that one of the articles on the first page was, indeed, about a church bake sale.

"The advertisements are in the back," he told her, looking up.

The classified section was not extensive, and there were ads for restaurants as far away as San Francisco, as well as descriptions of items for sale. *Brend new!* one of these proclaimed beside the picture of a lawn mower.

The employment listings were limited to a handful of advertisements placed by businesses looking for help: a restaurant, a florist, a travel agency in San Pedro, California. There were no advertisements placed by anybody looking for work, far less one that might have been her sister.

She refolded the pages.

"Take heart," he told her, looking around the kitchen at the issues still waiting to be searched.

The professor collected three different newspapers in addition to two church circulars and the newsletter of the Croatian Fraternal Union. The pages swam in front of Magdalena's eyes, with their digests of old-world news and new-world celebrations.

As she read, the professor hovered. The yogurt containers, she gathered, were for seedlings, because an open bag of soil stood beside them. She did not know what the pills were for, but she watched him read the label of one bottle, then sigh. "They're always making mistakes," he muttered, then went into the next room to telephone the pharmacy.

He returned after a few minutes with a sheepish smile. "Getting old is a terrible thing, Magdalena. It's only slightly better than the alternative."

In dozens of newspapers, Magdalena found a single advertisement that might pertain to her sister. It had been placed by a woman looking for a room to rent.

As Magdalena considered the details—*responsible, neat, non-*

smoker—she heard someone knock at the professor's front door. She looked at the clock above the sink, surprised to see that two hours had already elapsed. "Your chess partner," she said, rising. "I've taken up enough of your time."

"No, no," he told her. "There's no hurry."

But she capped her pen and picked up her purse. She was about to follow him to the front door when she heard it: the voice from the radio, but very near at hand.

She froze, straining to make out the professor's response, a low collection of words that sounded like the faint thrumming of a motor.

"But she's still here?"

The voice was unmistakably Damir's, and Magdalena felt a tightening in her chest, as if the house's oxygen supply had abruptly run out. Her eyes traveled to the kitchen door, whose rectangular window looked out onto a narrow garden. But when she grasped the doorknob, it did not give.

When she turned, Damir already filled the kitchen's other doorway.

It was the professor who spoke, appearing behind him in the hall. "Forgive my subterfuge," he told her. "But my young friend explained that you weren't likely to wait for him if you knew."

"Your chess partner," she said flatly.

"That's right," Damir told her with no hint of irony. "You came up during our last game."

Professor Barić cleared his throat a little anxiously. "One runs into so few people from Rosmarina, you see. And I really did think that it was worth looking through the newspapers."

She stared at Damir. His dark brown hair was shorter than she remembered. His body, too, was different, as if the substance that composed it had hardened like clay, making his shoulders more pronounced and deepening the grooves in his suntanned face. Beneath his smart clothing, she knew, there was an oval birthmark on his shoulder and a scar that ran down one knee. And there would be new marks, of unknown shape and location, although his newspaper had reported the shrapnel wounds from Iraq as *non—life threatening,* just as his mother had promised.

What did he see when he looked at her, she wondered?

But his face gave no indication of what he might be thinking.

CHAPTER 11

H is car stood in front of Professor Barić's house.
"I nearly missed you," he said, descending the front steps and turning to look up at her. He made his voice light. "You wanted to make a break for it."

It was more a statement of fact than an accusation. As she followed him down the steps, regarding him with equal caution, she was aware from the way the curtains trembled that the professor continued to watch them from his living room window. She nodded.

"What stopped you?"

"The door was locked."

He smiled at this. "Foiled," he told her softly and unlocked the car doors.

Going for a drive was his idea, and for the first few minutes they said nothing. They turned from Professor Barić's quiet street to one with a profusion of restaurants and fabric stores, throngs of people pushing past each other on the pavements and into the crosswalks.

"I saw your sister," Damir said as they waited at one of these. "That's why I wanted to see you."

Magdalena met his eyes in surprise. "When?" she demanded.

"A few weeks ago. She invited me to an exhibit at your cousin's gallery."

Jadranka had said nothing about this in her letters, and Magdalena felt herself sink into the leather of the passenger seat. "You didn't mention it when you telephoned," she told him with a frown.

"I wanted to see you," he told her again. He reached over to touch the back of her hand. "I really do want to help you, Lena. Can you believe that?"

Magdalena stared at his hand. When she did not answer, he returned it to the wheel.

"What did she say?"

"We talked about New York, mostly. She said she was happy here. She told me that she was painting again." He turned onto another street, this one with shops whose awnings were covered in Arabic. "And naturally you came up."

She did not doubt it. But there was something unsettling about knowing she had been discussed. She could just imagine it—*You know her, stubborn as a Rosmarina mule, a real island fixture these days*—and so she changed the subject, telling him evenly, "I don't understand her disappearing act. It's not like her."

"She's disappeared before," he pointed out.

"But never from me."

He was silent for a moment. "No," he acknowledged. "And in the beginning you disappeared together."

It was true. The first time, they had run away as children to avoid going to live with their mother in Split, a miscalculation that had only stoked their stepfather's rage. The second time had been later, during the war, and Magdalena knew that this was the disappearance he referred to.

"Jadranka was looking for her father," Magdalena told him.

"And you?"

She had been looking after Jadranka, who would not be convinced to abandon her harebrained plan, no matter how much Magdalena railed against it. "I'll tell *Dida*," she had threatened her sister in desperation, causing Jadranka to counter with her own threat: "Do it and I'll never speak to you again."

And although Jadranka had been only fourteen at the time, Magdalena did not doubt for a moment that she meant what she said.

"You didn't even tell me where you were going," Damir reminded her now.

"No," Magdalena conceded. The subterfuge had been difficult at the time, because that was the period of telling Damir everything. But she had known that Jadranka would go, with or without her. That if Magdalena raised the alarm, her sister would find a way of leaving the island and going in search of her father's shadow. Jadranka had been so utterly convinced that time, so certain that she knew precisely where to find him, that even today Magdalena remembered the ferocious way she said, "You're either with me or against me, Lena."

Damir sighed. "Who knows why she didn't tell you this time? People don't always make sense."

This, at least, was something they could agree upon, and as she turned to study his familiar profile, his eyelashes still as black and glossy as the spines of a sea urchin, she felt her resolve waver for the briefest moment.

She and Jadranka had made it all the way to a military hospital near the front line in Dubrovnik. They had come close to the war without actually stepping inside it. But wandering that hospital, Magdalena had seen all she needed to see of it: the beds of wounded crowding the hallways, the way some of the men—not much older than herself—had reached out their hands to touch the two sisters, as if wanting to make sure they were flesh and blood.

"What the hell are you doing here?" one, a complete stranger who was missing an arm, had demanded. He had looked from Jadranka to Magdalena, his eyes wild with panic. "I told you a thousand times to stay at home."

Two years after that, the draft notice had come for Damir, its blunt lettering returning her to that hospital where all the sheets were stained with blood. They had spent the hours after its arrival curled tightly together on his bed, and she still remembered the way he had promised her that it would change nothing, and that when he came back life would begin again. And she—fool of fools—had believed such a thing possible.

They had been lying to themselves. After his return from the war, they had driven around like this, in a borrowed car, Damir navigating the dark streets of Zagreb, Magdalena strapped into the passenger side, feeling for all the world like the seatbelt was the only thing pinning her to the earth.

I can't go back to Rosmarina, he had said, pulling over to the side of the road so that they could face each other.

For years afterwards, she believed that he had betrayed her. Of all people, he best understood what the island meant to her. He remembered her returning from that year in Split so quiet and thin that her former classmates had not recognized her, despite their teacher's insistence. *But you must remember, children. This is Magdalena.*

It was only since her grandfather's illness that she allowed herself to consider a different explanation for his departure: that the war had changed the course of his life the way an earthquake can crack a road and leave it pointing in a different direction. The way the year in Split had changed hers.

"I mean it, Lena," he told her now. "I want to help."

She studied the fine lines around his eyes, the scar that started at the base of his throat and disappeared under his shirt. It was shiny and red, and she had not noticed it at first. "I know you do," she told him softly.

A subway trestle loomed ahead of them, and Magdalena told him to drop her there. For a moment he looked as though he would object, but he pulled over.

"You never know," he said as he turned off the car's engine. "Your sister might decide to come back to see her work on exhibit."

Magdalena started at this. "What do you mean?"

He looked surprised. "Your cousin promised to put one of her paintings in a group show this summer. Didn't Jadranka tell you?"

She shook her head.

Neither her sister nor Katarina had breathed a word of it, and she frowned at the subway track above them, the way the entire apparatus now shook with the approach of a train.

He took her hand in his and squeezed it, and this time she did not pull away so quickly. "Maybe your sister wanted to surprise you."

"Maybe," she said.

Before she got out he gave her his card. It had been inside his breast pocket and was the same temperature as his hand. She slid it into the back pocket of her jeans without really looking at it, but all the way into Manhattan she was conscious of its warmth.

When Magdalena returned to her cousin's house, there was a note on the kitchen counter explaining that Katarina would be at her gallery all evening. Neither the children nor Jazmin were anywhere in evidence, and for a moment Magdalena stood in the foyer, listening to the barely audible whirring of a washing machine somewhere within the house. Where the washing machine was located, she had not discovered. Her dirty clothes disappeared as if carried away by phantom hands and only reappeared when they had been washed and folded.

The guest room where she slept was unlike her sister's, where the only furnishings were a mattress with a pine bed frame and a matching dresser. The curtains in Magdalena's room were a deep, burnished yellow, and the silk bedspread was edged with a border in the same color. There was a painting in black and white that

Magdalena had decided depicted either falling rain or the vertical lines of a bar code, and the rug rested on dark floorboards so shiny that she could see her reflection in their surface.

Ordinarily she took her shoes off on the bedroom's threshold, afraid of tracking the city's dirt across its floor, but today she turned and descended the stairs again.

She did not know what she was looking for, but as she wandered through the first-floor rooms, she was conscious of seeing things in a different light. She had already searched her sister's studio several times, surprised to see that Jadranka had not left even a single sketch behind. And so she read the titles of the books in the living room and pored through the extensive notes on a calendar that stood at attention on the kitchen counter. It was a thick book with pictures of paintings from the Museum of Modern Art, and she found a two-month-old entry for Tabitha's dental appointment in her sister's hand.

She did not know why Katarina had not mentioned her plans to exhibit Jadranka's work. The omission made her uneasy. Briefly she considered the possibility that it was an offer her cousin had retracted. But Jadranka's mention of it to Damir meant she was fairly sure it would happen.

Why, then, had she not mentioned it in any of her letters?

When Magdalena turned the handle to Michael's office, she was surprised to feel the door move beneath her hands. Her cousin's husband worked long hours for a firm in the financial district and when he was home spent most of his time here, with the door closed. He traveled on a weekly basis, jetting to places like Geneva and Singapore, and he was in one of those locations now, doing something—Katarina had intimated—that involved lengthy discussions and vast sums of money.

Magdalena could not tell if Michael's frequent absences made her cousin lonely. In pictures throughout the house, he and the children smiled from fishing trips and from atop snowcapped mountains, their faces rubbed raw with wind, their ski goggles reflecting other mountains. There were few shots of Katarina herself, and so Magdalena understood that her cousin had been the photographer in most of them. But there was something unsettling about the sheer number of pictures, as if Katarina were trying to take hold of each moment, to pin it like a butterfly in a shadow box.

"The children are easily bored," Katarina explained. "That's why when we go somewhere on vacation we have to pick a place with lots of activities for them." When Magdalena pointed out that they could come to Rosmarina, her cousin only mumbled something about its inaccessibility from the mainland.

Her eyes dropped to the documents on Michael's desk—agreements, fiscal projections, a clipping from the *Wall Street Journal* in which she saw his name. She contemplated opening the desk's drawers, but the cat, an alien-looking Siamese that had followed her into the office, was watching her from atop a bookcase with unblinking eyes and an expression that seemed to say, *I know what you're doing.*

"I don't even know what I'm doing, cat," she told him in soft Croatian, and decided against any further trespass.

The cat accompanied her when she left the study, weaving almost urgently around her ankles when she stopped outside her cousin's studio door. But while the doors to all the other rooms stood open, the studio was locked. And when she lowered her eye to the keyhole, she could make out nothing in the gloom.

A short time later the children returned, Christopher making the sound of an airplane and Tabitha telling Jazmin—who had been drafted into ferrying the children around since Jadranka's disappearance—about a computer game she wanted.

Jadranka's letters had prepared Magdalena for the children's packed schedule of art classes and playdates. They were as different from the children Magdalena taught as the earth is from the sky. On Rosmarina, children much younger than Christopher knew the tracks that led to the Peak. They spent hours outdoors, in bands that roamed the island. But Katarina's son and daughter had milky complexions, even in summer, and were as helpless as baby mice.

"*You* have to draw something," Christopher ordered Magdalena when she passed the open door of their playroom.

"Like what?"

He looked at his sister. "Like us."

"I don't really draw," she told him with a smile.

She was not used to being ordered about by children, but she missed the way her pupils filled her Rosmarina classroom with their laughter and shouts, disrupting the neat rows of desks and spilling into the aisles. And so she joined them at the table, making an attempt at the children's profiles, satisfied in the end that she had gotten the proportions of their faces. But when she presented the sketches, she saw immediately the guarded look that they exchanged.

"What's wrong?" she asked.

Tabitha shook her head.

"Can you keep a secret?" Christopher wanted to know.

"Of course."

He wore a sly expression when he went to one of the easels, as if knowing he was doing something for which he might be punished. Peeling back the empty sheets of paper, he removed one sheet from beneath and delivered it to her at the table.

Magdalena stared at the multiple studies of the children: Christopher in profile, Tabitha listening to her headphones, both of them sitting at the table where she now sat, working in rapt attention on some project.

"These aren't even the best ones," he told her.

"No?" she asked.

"Mom took those."

"Chris," Tabitha said in a warning voice.

"Why would she take them?" Magdalena asked.

"She said we couldn't have them anymore after Jadranka left."

Tabitha had returned to her own drawing, shading something a furious shade of red.

"Don't tell," Christopher told her. "Mom would get mad."

Magdalena frowned, "Why would she get mad?"

But Christopher only shrugged.

It took twenty minutes to pick the lock on her cousin's studio door. The children were still in their playroom, and Jazmin had mercifully disappeared to some distant corner of the house.

The metal cocktail stick that Magdalena found in a kitchen drawer broke immediately in the old-fashioned keyhole. Next, she tried a wire hanger. Picking locks had been a prized art among the children in her Split neighborhood, and while she had never been particularly good at it, she had once managed to lock her stepfather into his room with the bent tine of a fork.

When the lock gave, it made a soft clicking sound beneath the pressure of her fingers. A tight pain between her shoulder blades released simultaneously, as if she had been holding her breath and now, finally, could exhale.

Katarina had skipped this room when giving her the tour of the house, but even from the threshold Magdalena could see that the studio had been decorated as deliberately as the other rooms. The dark wood of the bookcases matched the large table that stood at the exact center of the room. Plain, almost industrial, lamps hung from the ceiling, and a square of blank canvas stood upon an easel.

The room was eerily neat, a realization that prompted Magdalena to another: unlike Jadranka's narrow studio, where the floor was spattered with paint, this one appeared barely used. Dust covered many surfaces, and when Magdalena moved forward to inspect the brushes, it was obvious that the majority had never touched paint. Katarina often spent time in here after returning from her gallery or when the children were asleep. But whatever her cousin did in the room, Magdalena now realized in surprise, seldom included painting.

The table had several drawers, and she opened one to find an assortment of bills and brochures. In the next, beneath some pads of blank paper, she found news clippings about Katarina's gallery opening from several years before. One reporter had been enthusiastic about *this welcome newcomer to the Chelsea gallery scene,* but another was more backhanded in his assessment: *With her Park Avenue looks and her husband's substantial resources, Mrs. Pennington is a former art student who has put away her hobby to turn dealer in the arts.*

It was the word *hobby* that made Magdalena hesitate. Mildly derisive, it was reminiscent of Katarina's telephone conversations about artists she considered mere dilettantes. "There's no courage there," she said of one exhibit in a rival gallery. "He might as well be painting wallpaper," she said of another.

But just as Magdalena began to feel sorry for her cousin, she found a sheaf of sketches in her sister's hand. They were in a leather-bound folder on a bookshelf, and while there was nothing remarkable about them—they were merely studies of the children, of Katarina and Michael, of church spires and trees in Central Park—they were badly creased and torn in places, as if they had been balled up and then smoothed out again.

As Magdalena prepared to leave the room, the sketches clutched against her chest like something she had rescued from drowning, she saw the canvas that leaned against the wall, nearly hidden by the open studio door.

It was a picture very like one that Jadranka might paint, a length of craggy Rosmarina shoreline viewed from underwater. It was the perspective that was familiar, Jadranka forever seeing things in a way nobody else would see them.

Magdalena did not understand much about art—she had only a rudimentary grasp of its history and movements—but she would recognize Jadranka's work anywhere, the use of color and the brushstrokes as familiar as her sister's voice. Which is why she knew that the painting she looked at now was not Jadranka's. It was not even a competent piece of mimicry.

Katarina had even copied Jadranka's way of signing, the thin red strokes of her name like the footprints of a wounded bird.

The address of Katarina's gallery was printed on her business cards, one of which Magdalena found in the kitchen. She let herself out of the house quietly, and for the duration of the subway ride south she thought about the copycat painting, her face a stormy reflection in the subway car's dark window. Katarina had always begrudged Jadranka her ability, she thought, and it was clear that while their cousin might run a gallery, she had fallen short of the illustrious artistic career she had predicted for herself the summer she was twelve.

She wondered if Katarina had copied Jadranka's work outright, or whether the imitation had been subconscious. But then she remembered those damaged pages from the folder. What had prevented Katarina from throwing them away, she wondered? Was it a guilty conscience, or had she intended to copy those as well?

Magdalena's anger propelled her through crowds of commuters, but when she emerged from the station in Chelsea, she felt momentarily disoriented. This happened whenever she came above-ground in Queens, too, and she stood for some moments in the early evening sunshine, blinking in confusion as other pedestrians hurried past.

Gallery K was nearby, in the middle of a block filled with other galleries. Magdalena slowed to look through the windows at the well-heeled men and women who stood inside them. A party was going on in the gallery next to Katarina's. The people who packed its interior were holding glasses of wine, their mouths moving with exaggerated fervor, like the chins of marionettes.

By contrast, her cousin's gallery was deserted. A long, white space, it was fronted by an enormous floor-to-ceiling window. Once through the heavy glass door, she studied the mishmash of paintings on the walls. The exhibit was titled *Tomorrow*, bringing together young artists who—a brochure explained—were on the "cusp of arrival." Magdalena did not have to look too hard to ascertain that her sister was not among them.

The gallery was empty, though she could not see past the point that it narrowed, like an hourglass, flanked on one side by a desk and on the other by a small seating area. "Katarina?" she called.

But the figure that rounded the corner was a man's. Dressed in a gray T-shirt and faded dark jeans, he stopped when he caught sight of Magdalena. "Judging by the expression on your face," he told her, "I'd hate to be Katarina."

He was about her age, with sandy hair, and although he was not smiling outright, his eyes were amused. He was clearly at ease in the empty gallery, and Magdalena looked past him for some sign of her cousin.

"She's on the phone," he added, then nodded towards the black couch. "Have a seat."

Magdalena took in the rich leather of the couch and a vase of flowers so brightly colored that she would have assumed them to be artificial if not for the almost overpowering musk that filled the air.

She shook her head. "I will look around," she told him stiffly.

To her surprise he followed her to the front of the gallery, and as she pretended to take in the paintings, she was aware that he was studying her profile.

"What do you think of them?" he asked, then immediately laughed at her uncomfortable expression. "Don't worry," he said. "I didn't paint any of them."

"You're a painter?" she asked.

"Yes."

She nodded. "My sister, too." She looked at the canvas in front of her, where a mouse's skeleton had been affixed to a painted maze. "And she's better than this."

"That wouldn't be too hard," he told her.

For a moment they studied the tiny skeleton together in silence.

"You're from Katherine's country," he observed.

"Yes."

But before he could say anything more, Katarina's voice called from the back of the gallery. "Theo?"

"My master's voice," he told Magdalena with the ghost of a smile.

Katarina's shoes made a clicking sound against the floor, but when she rounded the corner her broad smile vanished, and she stopped short at the sight of her cousin.

"We need to talk," Magdalena told her in Croatian.

Katarina's eyebrows shot up in surprise, but she recovered quickly. "You've met Theo," she replied in English.

Magdalena nodded.

"This is Magdalena—"

But before Katarina could say anything more, he whistled as if putting two and two together. "You're the one who made the poison sandwiches," he told her.

CHAPTER 12

Her stepfather had not actually eaten those sandwiches, a fact that she did not bother to point out to the stranger in the gallery, who regarded her with a certain presumptuous sympathy, as if Jadranka's tales gave him access to the inner workings of her mind.

She had found the box of rat poison beneath their mother's sink in Split, the white pellets that could be ground into powder and mixed with warm butter. Alone, the mixture was gritty and slightly bitter, but the taste could be masked when smeared on bread. Magdalena knew this because she had taken a bite herself, spitting it out after the first experimental morsel.

"Poison sandwiches?" Katarina echoed in confusion, waiting to be let in on the joke. Her eyes traveled from Magdalena's stony face to Theo's expectant one.

But in the ensuing silence the painter began to look unsure. "She mentioned what things were like with your stepfather," he said, so that Katarina's eyes widened.

The summer that Magdalena's mother began to see Nikola was the same that Katarina had spent on the island. Ana Babić had smiled mysteriously whenever mentioning her new *friend* in Split. He had a solid job with the railroad, she told them. And he was so strong that he had once piggybacked her home in the rain. But

Katarina had never met this pillar of chivalry, and she certainly knew nothing of the year her cousins had spent under his roof.

Theo cleared his throat. "It was very heroic, the way your sister described things. It even gave me the idea for a new piece."

Magdalena gave him a hard look. She had encountered this fascination with her past before. Some people nursed the vain notion that they could peel back the layers of her brain and expose the hidden things beneath, and Theo was watching her as if intending her to be flattered.

"Jadranka should paint those things," she told him. "They don't belong to anybody else."

When she and Katarina left the gallery, night had already fallen, and for the first time since arriving in America, she felt a wave of homesickness so great that she was tempted to lean her forehead against the glass window of her cousin's gallery. But Theo still stood inside, and although she avoided looking in his direction, she could tell that he was watching them.

In New York there was no such thing as true night. Buildings held light the same way that they trapped heat during the day, and the air had a bleached quality, like overexposed film.

She and Katarina got into the sedan that arrived within moments, as if equipped with sensors. But the street's unnatural glow penetrated the car's dark interior, and Magdalena could feel it lighting up the features of her face.

"You never told me that things were so bad in Split," Katarina told her quietly.

The driver—an unsmiling man who had opened the rear passenger door with surgical precision—started the engine, and Magdalena studied the back of his neck.

"No."

"What did he—"

"It doesn't matter."

Katarina stared at her. "But it explains so much."

Magdalena did not believe that it explained anything, and she did not like the expression of understanding on her cousin's face. "It's in the past," she said carefully.

"Your mother—"

"—did nothing."

They spent the rest of the journey home in silence.

Nikola's temper had been known throughout their building. As an eleven-year-old, Magdalena had felt that the apartment always darkened before his arrival, as if the sun fled behind clouds at his approach. Sometimes he arrived an hour before their mother, and that hour was always the worst. He would enumerate every mistake of that morning—the milk had been left out of the refrigerator, or she had dawdled in the bathroom. It was her task to make sandwiches for his lunch, and he always complained that there was too much ham, or not enough, or that she had sliced the bread too thickly.

Even on the days he returned in a better mood, she knew to lock herself and Jadranka into their room the minute he began searching for a drink. Their mother made halfhearted attempts at hiding his bottles at the backs of cupboards and in the vegetable drawer of the refrigerator, but she never poured them out. The first drink would make him quiet, the second surly. By the third he would pound the door so that it shook on its hinges. But on other days, they would find him already lying in wait when they got home.

It was only later that Magdalena realized with shame that their neighbors heard the punishments of that hour: the belt, the shoe, the palm of his rough hand.

Magdalena could not battle her mother's new husband physically, and so she developed subtler forms of warfare. When he returned to the apartment after drinking, she hid his wallet or his keys while he lay passed out on the sofa. Once, after he had cursed their grandfather—"He thinks he's better than anyone else," Nikola had slurred, "but you're all the same shit"—she took his shoes and threw them into the courtyard of the building.

Jadranka watched her wide-eyed as she did it.

"You came home barefoot," Magdalena told him the following morning when he woke up, her sister nodding in confirmation.

They tried to run away once but were caught at the Jadrolinija ferry landing, their mother shouting at Magdalena that she could not just go anywhere she pleased and had better stop teaching Jadranka her tricks. Nikola glowered at them from the idling car where he waited on the other side of the street, saying nothing when they got in the back.

"I don't know what to do with you anymore," her mother began to cry, turning around in the passenger seat as they drove. "I'm at my wit's end."

When they pulled up in front of their apartment building, her mother got out first, hauling Jadranka out of the backseat and slamming the door. Magdalena met her stepfather's eyes in the rearview mirror. "Just you wait," he told her.

For the next three days, Nikola tied her to her bed. The rope would not allow her to do more than stand beside the bed, and she was not permitted to wash. She ate her meals on the bed, slept in the clothes she had worn on the day of her escape, and used an old kitchen pot as her toilet.

"We should let her use the washroom, at least," her mother pleaded with Nikola, after she had emptied it the first time.

But he would not be swayed. "This is what they do to deserters," he told Magdalena.

During the day Jadranka was not allowed into the bedroom, but at night she would crawl into bed beside Magdalena, casting an arm around her sister and holding the rope in her small fist.

*   *   *

After those three days, Magdalena returned to school, to brushing her sister's hair, to making their stepfather's sandwiches, cutting them into triangles and wrapping them tightly in waxed paper. But something was changed. Some shift had taken place, so that when she regarded herself in the bathroom mirror, the face that peered back was no longer one she could claim with any certainty.

In the days that followed, she became increasingly quiet and withdrawn, Nikola observing this transformation with satisfaction. "You're learning," he said as her mother looked on with troubled eyes, watching the way she pushed the food listlessly around her plate.

She had not tried to feed Nikola the first poisoned sandwich, shoving it into the garbage instead. But two days later Jadranka told her tearfully that several cats had died in the courtyard. Instead of sunning themselves in patches of sunlight, she had found them in stiff piles.

Magdalena immediately understood that the sandwich was responsible. Horrified and triumphant, she returned to the box of poison repeatedly in subsequent days. Sometimes she would hold it in her hands, shaking it so that the contents danced. Once she extracted a single pellet and licked it with her tongue, spitting out a mouthful of cloudy saliva in the next moment. To this day, she could still remember its bitter, noxious taste.

She did not know how Jadranka discovered her plan, but for an entire week Magdalena had waited for Nikola to die, increasing the dosage by one pellet every evening, while her younger sister secretly remade the sandwiches. It was a fact she only discovered years later on an evening when Jadranka had drunk too much wine, confessing her sabotage through laughter and sobs.

It was the reason Jadranka had turned mute, all those years

ago. Her strategy promised less disastrous consequences than Magdalena's, and six months later—after Jadranka had been taken to countless specialists, one psychiatrist, and a *travar* who instructed her to drink a dark green concoction of herbs and grasses—their mother agreed to return both sisters to Rosmarina.

It was only as Katarina unlocked the house's front door that Magdalena remembered leaving her cousin's first-floor studio open. *Let her see,* she had thought, too angry at the time to cover up the evidence of her search.

Now she watched Katarina falter at the sight of the open door, peering worriedly up the stairs to the second floor as if she expected thieves to be lying in wait.

"You didn't tell me about Jadranka's drawings," Magdalena told her cousin's back, which went rigid in surprise. "In the folder on your bookcase?"

Katarina turned slowly. "Chris found them," she said. "In the trash can in Jadranka's stu—"

"And that's an interesting picture behind the door."

Katarina reddened.

"I didn't know you still painted."

"I don't," she said quietly. "Not really."

"It doesn't look like my sister's work," Magdalena pressed. "I mean, it does. But it *isn't* my sister's work."

Katarina stared at her. After a moment, she said, "You've always hated me."

"And you've always been jealous of Jadranka."

The two women regarded each other in silence. "Of course I'm fucking jealous," Katarina said finally. "Your sister has youth and talent on her side. Why wouldn't I be jealous?"

Magdalena turned away in disgust, but Katarina grabbed her arm. "I was jealous of both of you. You had the island, and everything that was familiar to you. What the hell did we have?"

Magdalena shook off her hand. "You told Jadranka that you were going to exhibit one of her paintings."

"I was." There was no hint of deception in Katarina's face, and a moment later she turned and went to her open studio door. "You want to see?" she demanded.

As Magdalena stood in the entrance to the room, Katarina went to the bookcase—the same one where Magdalena had found the crumpled drawings—and pulled a canvas from behind it.

"You should have looked a little harder," she told Magdalena, pushing it into the other woman's hands as she brushed past her in the doorway.

It was a self-portrait, the figure on the canvas clearly Jadranka. But the face had been repeatedly scored by a knife or a razor.

"And before you ask," Katarina told her, already climbing the stairs, "I had nothing to do with cutting it up."

"Who—"

"Who do you think?"

After their return to the island, Jadranka began again to draw obsessively. She had always been prolific, filling any scrap of paper she found with her pictures, but at the age of eight she entered a phase with her art that bordered on mania. Late into the night she would sit at the desk in the room the sisters shared, her pencil making a scratching sound against paper.

There was only one subject that interested Jadranka in those days, and she committed hundreds of renderings to paper.

The men, Magdalena began to call them.

Some were light haired, some dark. Some were stout, and others thin. Some resembled people they knew, but most were complete strangers, figments of her sister's imagination. But all had faces that were uniformly featureless, a strange fog stretching from forehead to chin.

"Give him eyes, at least," Magdalena had teased her once. "The poor guy must bump into things everywhere he goes."

And for the first time Jadranka became secretive, electing not to show her sister every drawing she completed.

Jadranka had always been a talkative girl, often striking up conversations with tourists in the port in fragmented English or German. But the summer after their return she seemed to seek them out, asking them about the places they came from and how they were enjoying Rosmarina.

Magdalena would never have suspected what she was doing if a schoolmate had not mentioned overhearing her one day. "Your sister is telling fibs," she told Magdalena, who bristled at the accusation.

"What do you mean?"

"I heard her tell some old lady that her father was captain of a Jadrolinija ship."

Magdalena stared at her schoolmate, a girl with whom she was neither friendly nor at odds.

"Just thought you ought to know."

The schoolmate was telling the truth, as it turned out, and in the next few days Magdalena eavesdropped on her sister as she chattered to several strangers. Once, her father was a stonecutter in the island's quarry. Another time, he was a teacher in the local school. In every telling, he was kind. He had a gentle voice and never raised his hand in anger. Magdalena did not know how Jadranka had discovered that Goran Babić was not her father, but it was obvious that she had gleaned this information somewhere, although she had never asked her older sister about it.

"What are you doing?" Magdalena demanded once, after hearing her sister describe the last film her father had completed, an action movie exactly like one they had seen in the summer *kino* the month before.

But although Jadranka's cheeks flushed, she did not attempt to explain herself. If anything, her tales grew more outlandish. And when the summer ended and the tourists disappeared, she began to try these tales out on other island children.

"What a liar you are," one older boy told her in disgust, "when everybody knows your father didn't want you."

Years later, when Jadranka applied to the Academy of Fine Arts in Zagreb, her portfolio contained a wider range of subject matter: charcoal portraits of her family, paintings of abandoned houses beneath the Peak, and the mist that shrouded Rosmarina's harbor on winter mornings. But here and there, Magdalena still found evidence of *the men*. Jadranka no longer left their faces blank, but they were always looking away, or turning, or studying something of interest on the ground.

Jadranka's pictures were not recreations of life. They did not depict every line of a wrinkled face, or translate every window or tree onto paper, but they were something closer to truth. She captured exactly the curve of their grandfather's shoulders when he sat in his boat, the one eyebrow their mother raised when she told Jadranka that only rich people's children studied art, and that it was all a matter of connections anyway.

During high school—as the war on the mainland dragged on endlessly—Jadranka had been the star pupil of an ill-tempered art teacher. A former professor living out his retirement on Rosmarina, the man gave the occasional art lesson in order to supplement his pension. He had struck fear into the hearts of his other pupils but refused to charge for Jadranka's lessons, going so far as to give her a key to his studio so that she might have a place to work.

One day he had come to see Luka, sitting awkwardly at the other man's kitchen table. "Your granddaughter has a gift," the art professor said. "Please don't let her waste away on Rosmarina."

Their grandfather had frowned at this. "The island isn't a jail."

The professor had looked thoughtful at these words. "No," he conceded. "But for someone like your granddaughter, it could easily become one."

Jadranka was accepted to the Academy the same year that the war ended, the same year Magdalena returned to the island without Damir, refusing to tell even her sister what had happened between them. But within months Jadranka had dropped out, reappearing on Rosmarina one day in the middle of her second term. It was too constricting, she told her sister. And the professors were too old and set in their ways. They prattled endlessly about solid foundations, assigning tiresome exercises and stamping out any hint of innovation. "They wanted me to crawl," she told Magdalena finally. "And I'm ready to run."

But if Jadranka had run in the years since then, it had been primarily in circles. To Zagreb or to Italy, then back to Rosmarina. To Split for several months, then back home again. She never struck Magdalena as unhappy. But she was restless if she stayed anywhere for very long.

Magdalena did not know what to make of her sister's self-portrait, the face so shredded that even the color of the skin was gone, and so she placed the canvas flat on the studio's table. But it looked like a body being prepared for burial there, so she changed her mind and propped it against one of the table legs, turning off the light, a faceless Jadranka watching her go.

When Magdalena climbed the steps to the second floor of Katarina's house, she stopped outside the children's half-closed playroom door. Christopher was telling his mother something another boy had done at camp, his voice high-pitched with excitement.

Magdalena wanted to believe that Katarina was lying. She could not imagine Jadranka attacking her own image like that—for all her restlessness, her sister had always been easygoing and slow to anger, and Magdalena had difficulty picturing this frenzied, knife-wielding version of her sister. But since her arrival in America,

Jadranka had grown less and less recognizable, and there was some-thing—some irrefutable seed of truth—in what Katarina had told her, though she had not bothered to explain her own copycat painting.

"Ma, nemoj," Katarina was telling Christopher now. "You don't say."

Whatever her frustrations with her art, Katarina was a good mother. She listened patiently to Christopher's tales and to Tabitha's woes. In their father's presence, she spoke to them in English, but when they were alone she used her rusted mother tongue, and Magdalena could see that Croatian functioned as a se-cret language between them.

The playroom was at the foot of the stairs to the third floor, and as Magdalena listened to their interchange, a sound on the stair-case made her look up to see *Nona* Vinka sitting on the top step. Since Magdalena's arrival, her great-aunt had been too unwell to leave her room, but now she gave a wan smile.

Magdalena considered knocking on the playroom door to alert her cousin, but she could hear that Tabitha was into her rendition of the day, and so Magdalena climbed the steps instead. "Do you want to go back to bed?" she asked softly in Croatian.

Vinka nodded and held out her hand, allowing herself to be guided back to her room like a child.

When Magdalena tucked the sheets around her, Vinka gave a contented sigh. "Have I shown you the album?" she wanted to know.

The question made Magdalena blink in surprise. Vinka had not managed a single coherent sentence in all the weeks that Mag-dalena had been in America, but now her eyes studied the younger woman's face.

She shook her head.

"It's on the bureau," Vinka said, motioning towards the wooden chest. "With my spectacles."

Magdalena looked at her uncertainly.

"Go on, child," she urged with a little smile.

Magdalena found the album beneath the Bible and returned with it, sitting beside Vinka on the bed.

"I like to think they're all here," Vinka said, patting the album's cover.

Magdalena nodded.

Vinka opened the album to the first page, to a picture of Luka and their other siblings. "Look how young we were," she told Magdalena in wonder, and the younger woman studied the unbent figures and their smooth, unwrinkled skin. The photograph must have been taken just after the Second World War, and instinct made her reach out and touch her grandfather's face.

"He's a good father, isn't he?" Vinka asked her.

Of course, thought Magdalena, withdrawing her hand. *She thinks I'm Ana.*

But Vinka was already flipping the album's pages. She seemed to be looking for one photograph in particular, but when she reached the end, she gave an agitated shake of her head and started again from the beginning.

"May I help?" Magdalena asked her.

"Nobody can help," said Vinka, leaning back against her pillow. "You should never have done it, girl."

Magdalena hesitated at this, unsure whom her aunt was seeing. "What?" she asked curiously. "What have I done?"

Vinka closed her eyes. "It was you who brought these things upon us."

Magdalena wanted to ask more, but her great-aunt's breathing became even, and so she slid the album from beneath Vinka's hands. She removed the spectacles from her face, folding them carefully.

When she looked up, Katarina was watching from the doorway

with an unhappy expression. "She fades in and out like that some-times," she told Magdalena quietly.

"She was showing me her photographs."

Katarina's eyes softened as they fell on the album. She nodded. "She says funny things sometimes, upsetting things."

Magdalena waited.

"She doesn't mean anything by them. But sometimes she'll tell you things you didn't know, things you wish she hadn't told you."

Magdalena waited, but if Katarina was going to say anything more, she thought better of it. "Come downstairs," she told Magdalena. "We need to finish what we started."

It was Jazmin's evening off, and Magdalena sat at the kitchen table as Katarina chopped vegetables at the counter, a glass of whiskey in front of both of them. The children were upstairs, and from time to time Magdalena could hear a television or the sounds of electronic death from Christopher's video games. The cat lay curled in her lap, purring, its tail moving in arcs as if trying to inscribe a message in the air.

Magdalena studied Katarina's bent head. Her cousin's hair was gathered in a loose ponytail, and she had washed off her makeup. Magdalena thought that she looked younger like this, like a softer version of the cousin she remembered from their childhood. But her eyes were red, as if she had been crying.

Magdalena steeled her heart against all of it: the smell of peppers frying in a cast-iron pan, the warmth of the cat, the way her cousin seemed to be searching for the right words, lifting her head several times as if she were about to say something but each time taking a swig of her drink instead.

"The painting of Rosmarina," Magdalena finally prompted.

"Mine," Katarina said, looking swiftly up. "But based on a con-versation I had with your sister."

Magdalena did not know what to say to this, and Katarina's gaze fell to the cutting board again. "I didn't copy one of her paintings, if that's what you were thinking."

It was exactly what Magdalena was thinking, but she refrained from saying it aloud.

"And I had every intention of putting that self-portrait in the show, but obviously I couldn't anymore."

"She damaged it before she left?"

"She did it the same night she left," Katarina corrected. "She must have. I found it cut up the next morning."

"But why?"

Again that look of discomfort. But Katarina shook her head. "I don't know."

For a long moment, nothing was said between them, Katarina's knife making a rhythmic chopping sound against the board.

"I'm sorry about the studio," Magdalena said, breaking the silence.

"Are you?"

Magdalena thought about this. "Yes. Though you should have shown me what Jadranka did to her painting from the start."

Katarina did not acknowledge this, continuing to slice the onion in her hand. After a moment she placed the knife beside the cutting board and turned around. "What happened in Split, Lena?"

The question caught Magdalena off guard, and she closed her eyes. When she opened them again, Katarina was still watching her face. "It's old history," she told her cousin. "It's done."

But Katarina, her hand still wet from the onion, reached over the table where Magdalena was sitting and grabbed her cousin's hand. When Magdalena went to pull away, Katarina held on with a surprising determination. She turned it palm down and studied the knot where the bones had fused improperly. "I wondered about this," she said. "You didn't have it that summer."

"No."

"Does it hurt?"

People seldom noticed it. Lovers did, occasionally, tracing that deformity in the dark. But on those occasions she usually made up something about a birth defect or a fishing accident.

Now, Magdalena studied the way the bone pushed her skin out like a small tent pole. "Sometimes," she admitted.

Katarina let go of her hand. "I don't know why your sister went," she said, standing so that the kitchen counter was at her back and folding her arms across her chest. "And I don't know why she would do that to her painting."

Magdalena nodded, but did not take her eyes from Katarina's face.

Her cousin was also watching her, and for a moment Magdalena had the sensation that they were engaged in a staring contest, like the summer they had spent together on the island, neither girl willing to admit defeat.

"You're not sure whether you believe me," Katarina told her.

Magdalena nodded again.

Both women were quiet as they ate dinner, and it was the children who filled up the silence with their stories of camp and a minor squabble about who deserved the last ice cream sandwich in the freezer. Magdalena excused herself early to go to bed, prompting an immediate protest from Christopher, who wanted her to read to him.

"Magdalena's had a long day," Katarina told him, neither child seeming to notice the way their mother suddenly used the formal version of her cousin's name.

"Sleep well," Katarina told her over the children's heads.

"You, too," responded Magdalena.

But every time she closed her eyes, she saw the shredded canvas where Jadranka's face had been.

★　　★　　★

In the morning she rose to find the house deserted. A note in the kitchen explained that Katarina had taken the children to visit a friend, and Magdalena stood barefoot and slightly hungover at the counter, surprised to see by the oven's clock that it was already past ten.

She did not feel like going to Queens. On her last trip there, she had begun to hang up flyers with her sister's picture, but she could not bear the idea of talking to any more strangers today. Briefly, she considered telephoning Damir. But she did not know what she would say to him, and so she took her time making coffee, drinking it as she stood at the kitchen window and looked into the small garden behind the house.

When she was done, she climbed the stairs, pulling the T-shirt she slept in over her head as she went. She padded into the guest bathroom, waited until the shower grew hot, then stepped in and lowered herself to a seated position, resting her chin on one knee.

Somewhere in the house a telephone began to ring, a sound she could barely make out above the shower. She closed her eyes and nearly fell asleep like that, her forehead resting on her knee, so that the water drummed against the back of her head. But eventually she pulled herself up, turning off the water and wrapping herself in a towel.

Downstairs, the telephone rang again, no doubt some art world critic or camp counselor. Six rings, and then it fell silent, voice mail picking up somewhere in the tangle of New York.

Magdalena dressed slowly and then brushed her hair, watching her pale face in the mirror. She did not know whether she should stay in her cousin's house or leave. And if she left, she did not know where she would go.

When she descended once more to the kitchen, the telephone began to ring a third time, insistently, the caller clearly not satisfied with leaving a message. It fell silent and then started up once more, the shrill noise like an alarm.

She picked it up on the fifth ring. "Hello?" she asked.

There was a brief pause on the other side, and then a man's voice told her, "I was hoping you would answer."

It was Katarina's painter, his voice more solemn than the day before.

"Are you there?" he asked.

"Of course."

"I'm sorry if I offended you."

But Magdalena ignored this. "What else did my sister tell you?" she asked him.

CHAPTER 13

That afternoon when Theo answered his front door, he wore a wrinkled T-shirt, and his hair stood up on end as if he had been sleeping. Several fingers of his right hand were stained dark blue, and a string of tattoos—black symbols that looked like something from a book of necromancy—covered the inside of his right forearm, a detail Magdalena had missed at the gallery the night before.

"Theo," she said a little testily, because she had been knocking for some time.

He had not been sleeping, he told her apologetically, but painting. "My studio is in the back," he said, running a hand through his hair as she followed him down a hallway to his living room. "I tend to lose track of time when I work."

A fan in one open window made the sections of a newspaper flutter on the scratched parquet floor. Papers covered other surfaces, pinned down by books and coffee mugs, their edges quivering, so that the room had the appearance of a staging area for birds preparing to take flight.

As he moved to clear a place for her on the sofa, she studied his wiry frame, the trousers that were slung low over his hips, the sleeves of his T-shirt revealing arms taut with muscle and sinew.

He was exactly her sister's type, she realized, wondering how she had missed it the night before. Jadranka had always been drawn to people who stood on the periphery of things. The ones who thumbed their noses at convention, who stayed up until dawn and only went to bed when the rest of the world rose for work.

She took in the tilting cushions of the couch and the blanket that hung over one armrest. She could easily imagine her sister sitting there, smoking weed, picking out shapes in the smoke that rose above her head the way she used to do with clouds. Down the hall a hastily made bed was visible through an open door, and Magdalena made note of the unlaced men's boots on the floor.

"Your sister gave me that one," he said, pointing out a canvas that sat on a bureau, atop two even stacks of books, and Magdalena was surprised to see herself: a nude sitting in a chair, face turned towards a source of light.

She remembered sitting for the sketches the previous winter, during her sister's last trip to Rosmarina. They had gone to the Devil's Stones despite the cold weather, and Magdalena had built a fire in the old-fashioned stove at their fishing camp.

To see the finished painting here unsettled her, though she quickly found her sternest teacher's voice. "You've seen her since she left my cousin's."

She did not know what made her so certain of this. Perhaps it was the jumble in Theo's living room, the proof of a creative mind turned inside out and so like every space that Jadranka had ever inhabited. Perhaps it was the painting, which perched atop the bureau like her sister's familiar.

He nodded. "She crashed here for a few nights when she left Katarina's. But I haven't seen her in weeks."

"You didn't tell our cousin."

A guilty expression flashed across his face. "Jay asked me not to."

Magdalena blinked at this. *Jay.* But she let it go for now.

⋆   ⋆   ⋆

Jadranka had knocked on his door in the middle of the night. She wore a hooded sweatshirt and dragged a small suitcase behind her. He had been sleeping, but even through the peephole—and the murky light of the hallway—he could see that she had been crying.

"I can't go back," was all that she would tell him.

She stayed with him for the next several days while she looked for work. She had found something—although she did not specify what—and on the fifth day he returned to the apartment to find that she had pushed his spare key under the door together with a note, which he handed to Magdalena now. *Thanks for everything. I'll be in touch soon.*

Theo had insisted on seeing Magdalena in person, away from Katarina's. This had made her hopeful. On the subway ride here she had allowed herself to imagine Jadranka waiting for her, apologetic, feeling a little foolish to have dropped from sight for so long. But now Magdalena felt as if she'd lost her bearings, as if some internal compass were spinning wildly, and she sat heavily upon the sofa.

"I don't know why I was so surprised to realize who you were last night," he told her. "Your sister said that you were close."

Magdalena gave a short laugh at this. "Yes," she said, scanning the apartment's walls: posters for exhibits and a few photographs. "You can see how close. I haven't heard from her in a month."

He shrugged at this. "She was upset."

"Why?"

"Something spooked her but I don't know what."

Magdalena frowned. "You don't know much, do you?"

Something changed in his eyes, a flicker of irritation or amusement. "I know that she was happy in New York."

Magdalena leaned her head back and closed her eyes. A moment later she felt the couch sag as he sat down beside her, and when she opened her eyes again, his earnest face loomed close to hers. His eyes were blue but his pupils were very dark, and the contrast was almost shocking at this close range. Magdalena considered them. "You and my sister—" she began.

When he understood what she was asking, he looked amused. "No," he told her. "We were friends."

"So she slept here?" She patted the couch between them.

"That's right."

She considered this.

"Surprised?"

"Yes."

"I'm flattered," he told her. "But I prefer men."

He was grinning now, and she flushed, feeling naive and provincial. To hide her discomfort, she looked around the living room with its odd assortment of furniture and mismatched cushions. She realized that he had probably accumulated most of these at stoop sales—a New York tradition that Jadranka had described enthusiastically in her letters, fascinated by the fluidity of American property ownership.

Although Katarina had introduced them, Theo and Jadranka kept their subsequent friendship to themselves. "We didn't want to hurt her feelings," Theo said by way of explanation. On Jadranka's days off, she would often visit and they would talk. He lent her books, and sometimes they went to see films together.

Once, she had taken him to a Croatian bar in Astoria. "She wanted to give me a taste of what life was like at home," he told Magdalena.

"What was it called?" Magdalena asked. "The bar?"

"Something like Club Darkness."

Magdalena had not come across it in any of her wanderings.

"It was strange," he said. "Intense."

He had observed the men in leather jackets at the bar, the

groups of young women in skimpy tops and makeup. The girls swayed to music imported from home and sent smoky-eyed glances at the men, who watched them over the tops of their glasses. The ones—Jadranka had explained—who hoped to go home with them, but who would be the first to call them whores in the morning.

"One guy looked like something out of a mob film," he told her. "He bought us a round of drinks. Apparently, he told her that she should stick to men from your country. To real men. When we left, she said, 'See? My people are as narrow as they are mean.'"

Magdalena bristled at this. "There are idiots everywhere," she said. "Even in America."

"Of course there are," Theo told her, surprised. "But New York is like a separate country. I told Jay that she should stay and go to art school, but she took off before I could convince her."

Magdalena digested this in silence, conscious that Theo was studying the skepticism on her face.

"Anyway, that isn't the reason I wanted to see you," he told her, abruptly rising from the couch and walking over to a laptop that sat charging on a windowsill. "I found something that might help you find her."

Last night, after returning from the gallery, he had looked through his computer's browsing history and discovered a single map search for an intersection in the Park Slope area of Brooklyn.

"I don't know why I didn't think of checking before," he said, refreshing the page for Magdalena now. "But it's the only thing she looked up the morning she left."

It took her half an hour to reach Park Slope on the subway, coming aboveground to a light drizzle. It was the first cool day since Magdalena's arrival, a relief after the hot hours she had spent searching Queens. The island had heat like the inside of an oven, but she had not been prepared for the humidity of New York.

She had rejected Theo's offer to go with her. At his front door, she had held out her hand, but he ignored it and leaned forward to kiss her cheek. "Good luck, Lena," he told her. "Tell your sister that I miss her."

Park Slope was quiet in the rain. On the way to the intersection of Fifth Avenue and Carroll Street, she passed an animal hospital, a bar, a few restaurants, and it was as she studied the interior of one of these—a Cuban restaurant with checkered tablecloths— that she caught sight of the red-haired figure walking on the other side of the street.

This had happened several times since she had arrived in New York. Magdalena would see her sister in women who rounded corners in front of her, and who rode by in buses. But none of them had turned into Jadranka, and now she followed the figure at a distance.

The woman walked quickly, a black umbrella in her hand. She headed south, then west on Ninth Street, Magdalena so intent on her careful pursuit that she no longer noticed the rain.

It was only when the figure ducked beneath an overpass, entering a subway station on the opposite side of the street, that Magdalena shouted her name aloud, people on the sidewalk turning to stare. But the woman did not hear her above the traffic, and Magdalena watched as she was swallowed by the station's dark mouth. A man on the corner tried to shove a piece of paper into her hands—an advertisement about English lessons or dry cleaning—but Magdalena's eyes did not stray from the subway entrance, and the green rectangle he released swooped to the pavement.

When the ground began to shake—a train arriving above them—she darted out into the intersection.

"No walk!" the man shouted behind her because she had not waited for the light to change, had not even noticed the car approaching from her left, which now swerved to avoid hitting her, the driver's angry honking no match for the swift beating of her heart.

Once on the other side of the street, she saw the woman's black umbrella ascending the steps on the left, and she followed quickly, nearly tripping at the top. A train was just pulling away from the opposite platform, ferrying passengers away in a kaleidoscope of purses and open mouths, shopping bags and shirtfronts. A child's face was pressed against one of the windows, but turned into a gray motion as the train disappeared down the track, a single sheet from a newspaper sliding along the platform in its wake.

The red-haired woman was waiting at the far end of the platform, her head turned, one foot over the yellow line as she peered down the track.

This was typical, Magdalena thought as she walked towards the figure. Jadranka never missed an opportunity to tempt fate.

But as she approached, the woman resembled her sister less and less, like an optical illusion in which one object is slowly replaced by another. Although the figure held herself as Jadranka often did, with her shoulders rolled slightly forward and her long, pale arms crossed, it was clear to Magdalena that she had made a mistake.

A train was coming. Magdalena could see it approaching, a length of moving gray in an overcast landscape, and she watched the woman step back from the platform's edge, then turn to look in her direction. Her face was rounder than Jadranka's, and there was no light of amusement in her eyes.

As the train pulled in, the two women stared at each other, Magdalena uncertainly, the stranger with an expression of warning, as if she had been conscious of Magdalena's scrutiny all along.

It was the stranger who looked away first, stepping inside the car, the doors closing behind her. The train began to creep forward again, and as she passed Magdalena, the woman raised her hand in a little wave. Her expression was bemused, but Magdalena dropped onto a scarred platform bench.

For a long time after the train disappeared, she stared down the rain-soaked track, remembering how the palm of the stranger's hand had left a momentary trace of white in the air behind her.

When she returned to the intersection of Fifth Avenue and Carroll Street, the sidewalks were deserted and rain was falling steadily. She stood for a while on one corner, taking in the awnings of restaurants and grocery stores and the dripping fire escapes of tenements. There was nothing remarkable about the intersection, and as she stood there she had the sensation that the buildings were drawing closer together, that they would never surrender her sister no matter how long Magdalena waited in the rain.

If Damir was surprised by her telephone call, his voice did not betray it. "I'll be there in thirty minutes," he told her, arriving in twenty to find her sheltering beneath some scaffolding, her clothing soaked and her hair plastered to her head.

She did not want to go back to Katarina's, and so she returned with him to Queens. They did not speak for the duration of the drive, but several times he reached over to take her hand, holding it tightly in his own, and she could not tell if it was her hand that shook, or his, or whether the trembling was from the engine and the uneven city streets.

His apartment was bare and startlingly clean and looked as if it had been recently painted. No pictures hung from the white walls, and there were only a few pieces of furniture in each room. The beige wall-to-wall carpet had been vacuumed into neat, horizontal stripes, and the kitchen looked as if it had never produced a meal.

Through an open doorway she saw that there were no bureaus or drawers in the bedroom, no table beside the bed. He had arranged his library in a row on the floor against one wall, and his shoes against another.

"Are you hungry?" he asked, handing her a towel from the bathroom.

She shook her head.

"Are you sure? I can make us some din—"

But she placed a hand over his mouth.

"Lena," he said against her fingers. "She'll turn up."

It came upon her without warning then: the face of the woman who was not Jadranka.

"Lena," Damir said again. He held the palm of her hand to his cheek.

She wanted in that moment to do as Jadranka had done, to slip loose from her life like a fish that breaks free of a hook. And so she led him into his bedroom, which was plainer than she had thought, the walls more austere, the beige coverlet bereft of any pattern.

There was an open package of almonds beside the bed, and she placed one experimentally on her tongue, as if it were a magic pill that could transport them to another dimension, away from New York, and away from Rosmarina. She offered him one, so that this was what he tasted of when he kissed her.

A low current passed from her legs to the muscles in her arms, more pronounced than in her youth, to the tip of her tongue, which had found a chip in one of Damir's teeth and probed gently at this new geography. In a moment, she thought, something inside her would contract so violently that it would pull them both under.

But after the undressing and the matching of curved and hollow parts, after the twisting and the joining of their bodies, after they lay side by side on his bed and looked at the ceiling, neither daring to look at the other, she felt the invisible fishing line growing back. Stretched taut, even from this distance.

*   *   *

The next morning she rose before dawn. He was still sleeping, facedown, one arm outstretched as if reaching for her in his sleep. Quietly, she gathered her still-damp clothes from the bedroom floor and dressed in the kitchen, the linoleum cool against the soles of her bare feet.

There was a writing tablet on the counter, and as she buttoned her shirt she read a few of his notes in the glow from the oven's clock. *Interview at UN, 3 p.m. Must replace tape recorder. Bread.*

She tore a sheet from beneath this one and stood looking at it for a long moment. But she could think of nothing to write, and so she folded the empty page and threw it in the garbage.

She let herself into Katarina's house quietly, climbing the stairs to Vinka's room in socked feet.

Magdalena had been a toddler when Katarina's family left Rosmarina, and so she could not connect the elderly woman who lived in the time capsule of her third-floor bedroom to the photographs in her album. And while it was true that Luka had spoken of his escapades with Vinka, she had been like a storybook character to his granddaughters, as remote and fantastical as America itself.

Katarina had already explained that emigration had been hardest on her mother. Her father had his political gatherings, his protests and his causes, but it was Vinka who stayed up half the night doing other people's mending as Katarina slept and Vlaho dozed on the couch.

She had given birth to Katarina late in life, at the age of forty-five, and she had been fifty at the time of their emigration to America. "That type of thing," Katarina had explained. "It's harder when you're older."

The forgetting had started eighteen months ago. At first Vinka forgot little things: the date or where she'd left her knitting. She would smile in embarrassment when it happened, telling Katarina,

Your mother has become a silly old woman. But within a few months she was misplacing ever more valuable things: money, a piece of jewelry.

It had been her custom to take daily walks in Central Park, and one day she got lost, wandering for hours until night fell. A policeman found her by the park's boathouse, trying to unchain a rowboat. "She wanted to go back to Rosmarina," Katarina told Magdalena. "She'd decided that life was better back there."

Because of her rapidly worsening dementia, *Nona* Vinka rarely remembered Pittsburgh anymore, even in lucid moments like the one Magdalena had witnessed the day before. She could not recall the names of families they had gone to church with, or any of the schools Katarina had attended. She merely looked confused at the mention of the tailor shop, although sometimes in dreams her hands moved as if she were sewing.

But she remembered everything about Rosmarina, and about her family's escape. Sometimes her eyes darted around the room, her hands poised as if to strike mosquitoes that had descended on their refugee camp room again.

She was wide awake and dressed when Magdalena pushed open her bedroom door. She sat on her bed crocheting, not bothering to look up. "I knew you'd be back," she told Magdalena in a level voice.

"What is it that I did?" Magdalena asked. "You said that I brought something upon us."

"You know," her great-aunt said, looking up in exasperation.

"Tell me."

"He killed himself because of you, because he couldn't stand the shame."

Magdalena's heart beat like an erratic drum. "Goran," she said, her father's name foreign on her tongue.

"Of course Goran. And with *him*. The chief of police and biggest UDBA agent on the island."

A radio alarm jumped to life somewhere in the house below them. It meant that Tabitha and Christopher would soon fill the air with their laughter and complaints, and Katarina would want to know where she had been all night.

But it was clear that *Nona* Vinka was only getting started. "And your poor daughter—"

She hesitated at this. "Magdalena?"

"No, the other one. You poisoned her life from the very start." *Nona* Vinka looked away, as if she could not stand to look at Magdalena anymore. "It's a sin," she muttered.

"What is?"

"To make a child share the blood of a man like that."

PART IV

CHAPTER 14

From his sickbed, Luka cannot identify the sound that comes after every roll of thunder, the one that goes *clack-clack-clack, clack-clack*. It is both metallic and wooden, like hail falling on a rooftop. But there is cause and effect between the thunder and that sound which perplexes him, each deafening roar followed immediately by *clack-clack,* and then by calm.

A child is shouting in the lane outside. Luka can hear the scraping of the boy's bicycle tires as he turns circles, the muffled sound of his sandal on the pavement as he steadies himself to make his revolutions tighter, the chain jumping from one gear to the next.

The sound reminds him of his mother's wooden knitting needles. Firecrackers. A game his sisters—sitting cross-legged in the courtyard—used to play with pebbles that they attempted to catch in a single hand.

His granddaughters demand to know how the story ends. They are no longer satisfied with the happy tales of his childhood, the adventures and escapades. He realizes that he cannot protect them from everything, but even so, there are things one does not tell children.

"Luka?" someone beside his bed leans forward so that the chair creaks. They press their fingers into his wrist, and he feels the echo of his heartbeat beneath this pressure, an erratic reverberation along the length of his entire arm: *clack-clack, clack-clack, clack-clack*.

His granddaughters must never learn of it, he wants to tell the sound.

It is 1942 and freezing rain pelts the forest, striking bark and bouncing from the wintry ground. It showers the coat he and Vinka huddle beneath, curled tightly together as if they share the same womb, and when they finally rise after the downpour, there are red welts where their hands held the edges of thick fabric.

They look so alike that in the mountains they are mistaken for twins, although Vinka is his junior by five years. She is also tiny by comparison, so that when she wears his trousers she must roll them at the cuff. But she shares his dark eyes and arched nose, and since they have cropped her brown hair—the lice too fiendish to be endured—she looks like his miniature double.

Clack-clack-clack, the crack of gunfire in the forest. *Clack,* the sound an axe makes when it splits wood.

Vinka had insisted on accompanying him into the war, but he had refused. "It isn't safe," he told her.

"Where is it safe?" she had wanted to know.

The danger is no longer their father, who is a shadow of his former self, but the Italians. They take a group of the town's young men to the Devil's Stones and mow them down with machine guns. He goes later to the site of that reprisal, the same place he has tied up his boat a thousand times. There are sharp chips in the pier's stone wall, and although an unknown hand has removed the bullet casings and washed away the blood, fragments of stone litter the ground. He crouches to pick up the sharp pieces, passing them from hand to hand: *clack-clack, clack-clack.*

It is sheer coincidence that prevents his inclusion in their number. The morning of the reprisal, his mother asks him to go up to the Peak and gather herbs for a cough that has plagued them all during the long winter. She gives strict instructions of where to look, which grasses to select, whether to cut them at the stalk or at the root. One of the herbs requires that he wait for the sun to dry all the moisture from its leaves, and it is while he is severing this very plant with his knife that he hears the reports from below.

Things look unchanged from his position on the Peak: woodsmoke rises lazily from several chimneys in the town, and the sea shimmers hundreds of feet below him, its surface fretted by a wind that has started in the middle of the previous night. Later he wonders if his mother had somehow prophesied the day's events. She usually sends her daughters on such tasks, but that morning insisted that he be the one to go on the errand. "It isn't safe," she told him, walking away from him abruptly, the matter settled, the rosary's wooden beads clicking in her pocket.

The place for women during wartime is at home, and he does not realize that Vinka intends to follow him in the next group of Partisan hopefuls who escape the island, the boats carrying only three or four people at a time, sliding quiet and dark into the nighttime waters. He does not realize that she has left a note for their sisters to read to their mother, and that by the time she finds him in Split nobody is able—or willing—to ensure her safe return to the island.

Other women have joined the guerrilla bands in the mountains, though at seventeen she is among the youngest. They show her how to fire a gun, how to conceal a knife. They tell her what happens to Partisan women who are caught, and her young face goes pale at the details of this torture.

"They'll never catch me," she tells him afterwards. "I'll kill myself first."

The words strike fear in Luka, and he will not allow their separation. At night he sleeps beside her, aware that even the other men in their unit—men he would lay down his life for under other circumstances—follow her with their eyes.

She is hungry for olive oil. Rancid pork fat and suet turn her stomach, and she is growing thin. He can see her cheekbones beginning to form triangles of shadow in her face. He is afraid that she will disappear before his eyes.

For his part, he longs for the smell of Dalmatian pine, its sap oozing in the sun. And for the sage, bay, and juniper that grow in the underbrush. It is his father's custom to infuse his grappa with those plants, and although Luka is no drinker, he imagines the way that sweet-smelling fire will burn a path down to his stomach.

It is his sense of smell that is most assaulted in the war. He does not mind the danger of living in the forest as much as he minds the unwashed bodies huddled together. Nothing is ever completely dry—not their coats or their socks—and everything festers with a whitish, human-smelling rot. Lice have the full run of their bodies, and he shaves his own head before helping Vinka crop her hair.

"It'll grow back," he tells her softly, running one hand through the uneven tufts, unable to look directly at the braid he holds in the other. But no sooner does he speak than she takes it from him and hurls it into the underbrush.

One day the political officer in their unit sees them praying before a meal. "Where is your God?" he asks them in amusement, waving at the trees, lifting his eyes to the sky. "How can you prove to me that he exists?"

"How can you prove to me that he doesn't?" Vinka asks evenly. "You keep your Marx, and I'll keep my God."

But the man does not smile at this. He tells them: "We are all brothers and sisters now, but I am telling you for your own good that a new day is coming."

Luka shakes his head dismissively. The new country will be all things that they envision, an end to plague and pestilence. He has lived a hungry life, and he looks forward to a time of plenty, a time of justice. The fight is pointless otherwise.

They dismiss this skinny man from a far-off city they have never heard of, aware as they do that he writes details in his little book. "There will be a time," he tells them.

In those days they see God everywhere, or what they assume to be God. In the songbirds that sing from the branches, but with different voices from the birds in Rosmarina's carob trees. In the creaking of timbers at night and the fires that they are allowed to build in caves, the wood never entirely dry, so that it crackles when exposed to the flame.

The clatter of horses' hooves, the sound of artillery, the quick boring of a bullet through bone: he will remember these things all his life. He remembers them now as he lies waiting in the anteroom of death.

Despite his best intentions, they are separated during heavy fighting. He thinks it is for the best and that she will be more protected at their base camp. And so he is farther up the lines when someone gets word to him that Vinka is ill.

"Typhus?" he demands fearfully, because the disease is tearing through their numbers, borne by the vermin that have permanently occupied their bodies. But they will not confirm this, nor will they meet his eyes.

He finds her curled in a tight ball beneath a tree, lying on her side. Another woman he does not recognize sits beside her, stroking her hair.

Vinka's forehead is cool to the touch, and so Luka runs his hands down her arms and legs, over her face. In his mind, he is looking for bullet holes, but when he rips her coat open he finds no blood. "You're fine," he insists, rebuttoning her coat clumsily with numb hands. "Fine."

But when he makes her stand, he sees that the cord that held up her trousers has been slit, and that there is blood on her legs.

"What happened?" he demands of the woman who holds Vinka up on the other side.

"What do you think?" she asks him. She is at least a decade older than him, with the thick skin and blunt speech of a peasant.

"Who?"

She shakes her head. "I found her like this."

"Who?" he demands of Vinka this time. He carries a knife in his boot, and he reaches for it now. "I'll kill him."

And perhaps for this reason, she refuses to say anything at all.

It is January and one of the key battles of the war is being fought, a German offensive that will end in failure, so that generations of Yugoslavia's children will sing of it in triumph. His own children will memorize its circumstances, the movements of divisions, the speeches of great men.

"Lice," he will tell them, because of all the details they are taught, this one is most commonly overlooked. "We were crawling with lice, at every moment of every day. That vermin even walked among us."

But in that moment he still thinks he can bring the lost thing back to Vinka's eyes, that he can avenge her, and so he hoists her over his shoulder. He makes it across the bridge with her, the Germans bombing with planes and the shrapnel tearing swaths through the canopy. On the safety of the far shore he lies all night beside her, holding her cold hand in his warm one. *Clack,* the sound of shovels in the distance, *clack,* the meeting of metal and stone.

Many years later, a semiconscious Luka lies in the dark, finally piecing together that the sound is the trembling of his closed bedroom door, the lightning strikes so close that they cause it to quiver on its hinges.

But the young Luka has no language for things such as this, and so he kisses his sister's hands and weeps on the papery skin of her face as she stares at the stars above them. She wears a pendant of the Virgin Mary, and at one point she removes it from her thin, white neck and he places that failed talisman between his chattering teeth.

★   ★   ★

For years after the war he is dogged by the smell of death, and he supposes that it is the same for Vinka, although she never speaks of it.

It rises suddenly as he passes the doors of dark and abandoned houses, or when he climbs upward through fallow olive groves. He will be working on the engine of his car, hands blackened, and it comes upon him without warning so that he freezes and quickly expels all the air from his lungs. Then he counts to thirty before breathing again. In this way, he manages again and again to elude it, though only for a time.

He is not a violent man, but he is prone to violent dreams: bright splashes of blood upon white walls and bones that give like wooden boards beneath his fists.

"Stop," a tiny voice orders him in the dream, and he sits back in surprise, only then noticing the man he has pinned to the ground and the rawness of his own knuckles.

He takes several shaky breaths, realizing that he has very nearly killed the man whose face he never recognizes, just like the faces he never saw from the Second World War, the ones he shot at in the forest just as they shot back at him in explosions of bark, as shrapnel dropped through the canopy of trees.

Sometimes the man is his enemy. Sometimes Vinka has agreed to point him out. But often it is a perfect stranger. And Luka looks at him in shock, taking in his swollen eyes and bloody mouth, feeling the burn of his own raw skin, and says in a choked voice, "I mistook you for another."

After the war ends and brother and sister return to Rosmarina, there are several plagues, in quick succession.

One year, a blight strikes the vineyards and half the vines die, shriveling beneath the sun like dead worms. In another, the sea is thick with jellyfish, their bodies gliding in eerie formations through the water like the airplanes he remembers from the war. In a third, a number of dogs in the village die of a mysterious ailment, including his bitch, Roki, who refuses to take food or water and slowly wastes away on the courtyard's stones, Magdalena slipping from her bed at night to lie alongside her, as if believing her body a shield that can keep death away. He refuses other dogs after that, even after the village has repopulated itself with new litters. He tells his wife and granddaughters that they must be content to play with the cats that appear in the courtyard from time to time.

There are plagues of tiny, black-winged insects, and his sister gives birth to two dead children in quick succession. There is contamination of the island's wells. Informers overrun the island, and both his son and Vinka disappear. There are political arrests and other wars.

In 1991, the island is under a naval blockade. Fishermen pace Rosmarina nervously, unused to so many consecutive days on land, and the island ferry sits uselessly in Split Harbor. After three days, fresh milk begins to sour, and after ten the shelves of the island's only stores are empty. "Surely they can't mean to starve us out," Ružica says with a worried face.

Even Luka, who never likes to leave the island, scans the horizon for the white shape of the ferry, which plows through the water as resolutely as a matron on her way to Mass. For months it does not appear, and they watch the news tensely as one town and then another on the mainland is bombarded and laid to waste. Sometimes, far above them, they see an airplane, black and birdlike, on its way to a bombing mission.

"I never thought I would live to see this again," he tells his wife.

Only a single bomb falls on Rosmarina for the duration of the war, landing just beneath the Peak and starting a brush fire that is brought quickly under control. Burnt fragments from the projectile are displayed on the *riva,* where youngsters clamor with a mixture of awe and fear to be allowed to hold one of the pieces of twisted metal.

Usually the ferry connects them to the world like a breathing tube. It brings food and engine parts, newspapers and mail, in its hull. At the beginning of the war it brought a handful of relatives who were fleeing the shelling on the mainland, women and children who arrived with piles of luggage and dazed, slightly embarrassed expressions.

"It's inhuman," he overhears a woman in the town say, because there is not a diaper to be had on the entire island, and she is forced to swaddle her child in dishrags.

When a shell falls on the ferry as it waits in Split Harbor, Rosmarina's residents watch in horror as it burns on their television screens, turning into smoke all the shampoos that promise to turn hair to silk and all the children's toys that are destined for a single shop on the island. Although the ferry's tanks are empty, a residue of petrol feeds the fumes, as does correspondence of every conceivable kind: love letters, tax letters, summonses to appear in court, letters with script that is pinched with worry. *Thank God, we are fine. But we are afraid for your well-being.*

During those months things unthinkable for generations begin to occur: babies are again born on the island instead of in hospitals on Korčula or Split, and funerals take place without the official paperwork.

When the naval blockade is lifted, newspapers sell out in the first hour they are delivered to the island kiosks. The ferrymen bring strange tales from the mainland: refugees have flooded Split and Zagreb, staying in hotels where they wash their laundry in sinks and set up camp stoves in the corners of rooms.

Because everything has changed, he wonders about the policeman, Vico. It has been years since he left the island, but *govno* like that always finds a way to float. He wonders if there will be political tribunals like there were at the end of the Second World War.

Those had been terrible show trials, the innocent hanging along-side the guilty. But the idea of justice—true justice—makes him giddy.

He even mentions this to Ružica, who surprises him for once with her bitterness.

"What does it matter, Luka? It won't bring any of them back."

He comes so close to killing the man that he sometimes dreams that he has beaten him flat, deflating him like an air mattress. Sometimes it is with his bare hands around his throat, other times it is with the pocketknife he always carries and uses for gutting fish. He feels the warmth of the man's blood and wakes to discover his hands sticky with perspiration. In the dreams he always looks down to discover that he is wearing the clothes he had worn as a young man in the mountains.

In the third year of the independence war, the kitchen sink overflows, and he makes a last-minute trip to Split to buy a new section of pipe. In the ferry café, two young men from Rosma-rina sit at the next table. They have recently begun their military service, and he finds that he cannot help but stare at their baby-smooth faces and their slender hands, which bring cigarette after cigarette to their suntanned faces. They have finished their basic training, and he listens for ten minutes to their bravado. When he rises and goes onto the deck, a punishing wind blows so that he shivers all the way to Split.

He is startled to realize that years ago, he and Vinka had been around the same age when they went into the mountains, and for the rest of the day he cannot stop thinking about the stiffness of the boys' camouflage, and their thin and girlish necks. He thinks about them as he visits the hardware store and selects the appro-priate length of pipe, and as he pays at the cash register, where a young woman in a blue smock wraps the pipe in paper.

He has not told his daughter that he is coming and, on a whim, takes a bus to her apartment so that they can drink a coffee together before the afternoon ferry returns him to the island.

It is not Ana he finds at home, however, but Nikola, who answers the door with a half-empty bottle in his hand. "Tell my daughter I was here," Luka says shortly, then turns to leave. He has not broken bread with the man since the year his granddaughters spent in Split.

He is surprised when Nikola protests his departure, following him unsteadily into the hallway. "Don't go—" he says, his voice strangely tremulous.

How close he comes to walking away, the sight of those two young men still weighing heavily on his mind. There had been something of Marin in them, as well, during the period of his own military service, and now Luka looks at Nikola in disgust.

"Our son had to leave," he had once howled to Ružica, "while that *kreten* can stay."

When Nikola retreats to the kitchen, Luka considers simply walking out and closing the door behind him. The man is so far gone he may not later realize that Luka has been there at all. But he hesitates too long, and Nikola reappears with a bottle of beer in his hand for Luka, who takes it unhappily and sits in one of his daughter's chairs.

"You must..." Nikola pauses so long that Luka thinks he has forgotten what he is about to say.

"Spit it out, man!"

"You must pay me..."

This half-finished imperative enrages Luka, who rises. For years he has avoided Nikola for his daughter's sake, but the farce has gone on too long. "Pay you?" He places the beer upon the table and picks his keys up from beside it. "For what?"

"...or else I'll..."

"You'll what?"

It is no secret that Luka blames his daughter. She who was so filled with promise, so beautiful that people stopped and stared at her in the street.

"Or else I'll tell everyone about Jadranka."

Luka stops. A coldness rises from his heels. It rises so that he feels the hackles of his flesh.

"...that UDBA agent's bastard..."

And he sees it suddenly—all of it—the way the sun comes over a mountain in a matter of seconds and floods the sea with light. His daughter, who would lay down her life for her brother, who would risk everything to keep him safe. He sees how long he has misjudged her, how long they have all misjudged her. "What are you saying to me?" Luka asks in a voice so quiet that the other man flinches.

"...see what that bitch Magdalena thinks of her sister then..."

Nikola is younger, but he is no match for Luka's sober rage. His fist, a piece of iron, makes blood pulse from the other man's mouth. It makes him howl. Nikola's teeth cut his hand, a gash that will grow infected in days to come, so that his wife must attend to it with antibiotic cream and plasters.

"What on earth happened, Luka?" Ružica will ask him.

But he will not speak of it to anyone. He will not describe the way that his own fist comes down, again and again, from a secret place inside him. It was different in the war because then it had always been from fear, but here there is a detachment that arrives after the anger breaks. He will not describe how he holds the man down—Nikola's face becoming Vico's, for though he has not put it together until today, it is painfully clear—and takes one of the pillows from the couch and holds it over his face until he is nearly dead.

"You'll go from here," he tells the man when he is done. "You'll disappear."

Nikola is breathing raggedly through a nose that is bent and teeth that are broken, because at some point Luka has picked up one of his daughter's figurines and smashed it into his face. He cannot remember doing it, but the proof lies on the carpet: a china ballerina cracked in half with blood at the base.

In the bathroom Luka cleans himself up. He takes off the shirt he wears on top of his undershirt and rolls it up and puts it in the garbage can. He washes his face and weeps into the sink, thinking of his daughter at five during their swimming lessons, how she tells him shrilly not to take away his hands, believing stubbornly that she can bend everyone in the world to her will. And how there is nothing she will not do for her brother.

Ružica turns him, humming under her breath. The nurse has shown her how to change the sheets, and though she is a slight woman, she has grown proficient at this task. He feels himself rocked onto one hip, and then onto the other. Her hands are so cool, so light, that he does not feel the shame of this maneuver.

His violence towards Nikola had stunned him because he never considered himself a violent man. *Stop,* the small voice in his head had pleaded, and he had stopped, just as his fist was poised to strike again.

"Alive," his wife is telling him in relief. "Just think of it, Luka. After all these years."

But his entire attention is on Jadranka. Her hair is spread upon the surface of the water, and each time she takes a breath, it sways gracefully, like red sea grass. He lowers his arms and sees her stretch. She opens her eyes and grins up at him.

"That's it," he tells her when she begins to float.

CHAPTER 15

It was love that made her burn Jadranka's sketchbooks, all those
months ago.

She used Nikola's grill, the low, iron mouth that had not tasted
flame in over ten years but which she could not bring herself to
abandon when moving to her new apartment. It sat in one corner
of her balcony, a dark and brooding presence that turned blacker
with every passing winter. The year before, when tiny, rodentlike
animals had used it for their nest, she did not have the heart to
dislodge them. Instead she brought them offerings of old bread
and apple peels, although they had since decamped with their off-
spring, leaving nothing behind but shredded paper and droppings.

She started with the sketchbooks beside her daughter's bed,
stacking them inside the grill. She was traditional enough to believe fire the exclusive domain of men, and her lack of expertise
meant that she spent several frustrated minutes trying to light them
from above, the matches merely charring the front cover of the
topmost book and scenting the air with phosphorus.

She had better luck when she opened the cover, lifting the first
few pages so that she could light them one by one. But although
the edges caught initially, the flames died within seconds.

It was going to take longer than she had envisioned, and so she
went to get a kitchen chair and her cigarettes. Passing through

the room she had shared with Jadranka, she stopped to study the drawings taped to the wall beside her daughter's bed. She had forgotten these: a scene from Split's *riva,* a picture of herself—unflattering, she thought, because her face managed to appear both swollen and wrinkled—and a portrait of her older daughter. Magdalena stared back at her now from the wall so accusingly that Ana's resolve cracked for the briefest of moments. "I'm doing it for her own good," she told those dark eyes.

It had been only half an hour since Jadranka walked away from their apartment building, pulling that suitcase whose wheels would tomorrow make contact with America. Ana had watched from the balcony as her daughter reached the intersection, then turned to wave before continuing down to the port. Long after she disappeared, Ana had watched the lights at the intersection turn red, then green, then red again, groups of people gathering and then dispersing in the very spot where Jadranka had stood, all of them on their way to somewhere. Including—at long last—her daughter.

Returning to the balcony, she sat down on the chair and lit a cigarette. It was cold even for January, and she pulled her housecoat together at the neck, looking out across the buildings. The sun had just started to drop, and soon there would be patches of pink sky between the buildings.

Briefly, she considered returning to the kitchen for the canister of butane that she used to refill her lighter. And for a drink. But she imagined this combination having disastrous consequences, and so she took a deep breath and removed the sketchbooks from the grill, placing them in a pile at her feet.

She tore a few pages from the top one, wadding them into balls. She lit these and watched with satisfaction as they burned, then added a few more to the pile. It took her hours, her Jadranka the most prolific of artists, but as it grew dark the task became easier; she could no longer see what she was burning: the faces of her parents, self-portraits, and—always and everywhere—Magdalena.

She developed a rhythm, careful after the first few batches to force them down with the rusted metal tongs that had hung from the grill, though even this could not prevent some of the smaller pieces from becoming airborne. They sparked and flickered around her on the balcony. A few landed on her housecoat, and it was only when she smelled the chemical odor of burning nylon that she looked down and saw the small, blackened holes.

Some must have floated farther out because at one point she heard her neighbor's balcony door open. "Hello?" a man's voice asked, unable to see past the concrete barriers between balconies. When she did not answer, he returned inside.

Her daughters were driving around tonight. Somewhere, out there, they were saying their goodbyes and, doubtless, complaining about her. But she didn't care. In the morning Jadranka would get on that airplane. Whatever happened tonight, Jadranka had promised that tomorrow she would leave.

She built a final tower with the pictures from the wall beside Jadranka's bed, and when they caught fire she did not bother to tamp them down. Instead she sat back and breathed. For the first time in years, it seemed, she breathed. And she watched those fiery pieces rise, their movements like miniature, combusting birds.

Seven months later, she followed in both her daughters' footsteps and packed her own suitcase for America, taking the shuttle bus from Split's *riva* to the airport alone.

She had always imagined airplane travel as something out of a 1960s film: Sophia Loren and Marcello Mastroianni jet-setting with their matching luggage and beautiful Italian clothes. Even as she waited in line at the airport, she continued to envision herself surrounded by pretty stewardesses and stylishly dressed passengers, eating a watercress salad from a china dish and washing it down with complimentary champagne.

Lying awake the night before, she had wondered what it would feel like to be weightless, to watch the slow progression of clouds and continents below her. She had expected a transformative event.

They were strange fantasies for such an unsentimental woman, but she had entertained them nonetheless. But as the plane took off, she found herself wedged between a small window and a middle-aged man whose lolling head threatened to land on her right shoulder. And so, in the end, she felt none of the weightlessness she would have liked.

Her disappointment did not last long before it turned to loathing for the stranger beside her, whose cheap suit and balding head shone with equal brightness in the plane's fluorescent light. He had displayed none of Marcello's grace, lumbering down the aisle behind her and taking his seat without so much as nodding in her direction, a slight she deemed especially unforgivable, since he had appropriated the armrest between them. As the plane rose higher, he listed still farther in her direction, as if she were a conveniently placed sofa cushion, as if she were his long-suffering wife.

At first she attempted to endure the heat from his hovering head, but when she caught a strong whiff of his odor—that particular smell of an unwashed scalp—she could tolerate her predicament no longer, and she brought her shoulder up, hard, to meet his left ear with a satisfying crack.

He straightened at once, giving a startled grunt. She could feel the way he studied her, shifting uneasily in his seat so that his girth was more evenly distributed between her and his neighbor on the other side, a young man in a suit who did not look up from his newspaper. For the remainder of the flight to Frankfurt, he held himself rigidly upright, stealing an occasional glance in her direction. But now it was her turn to ignore him, and she watched the wispy clouds beneath her, then the patchwork of green fields and mercury-colored lakes.

She wasn't a sofa cushion to be leaned on, she thought with sat-isfaction. She wasn't anybody's wife.

The plane from Frankfurt to America was larger but even more disappointing than the first, with several screaming children and a collection of tiny lavatories whose blue toilet water stopped mask-ing their stench within the first hour.

While the first leg of her journey had been filled with Croat-ians, the passengers around her now spoke German and English, and she leaned her head back against her seat and closed her eyes. It was a relief to follow none of the conversations, to lose her-self in meaningless thickets of sound. But just as she was drifting off she heard someone speaking her language, several rows behind her. A woman, complaining that her seat would not recline, and Ana opened her eyes as if she had been poked with a stick.

"I just want to get there," the voice was grumbling.

For her part, Ana was not at all sure that she agreed.

"What good is coming here going to do?" Magdalena had de-manded ungraciously when learning of her mother's trip.

"I know things" was all Ana would tell her, not entirely sur-prised by her daughter's acid response that she, too, knew things.

Jadranka's 4 a.m. telephone call had come weeks before, on the night of her disappearance. Good news seldom traveled in the dark, and so Ana nearly hadn't answered, expecting it to be her older daughter calling from Rosmarina and bearing news of Luka's death. She had expected that call for months, but still it shocked her, the telephone screaming at her in the early morning hours like a red-faced child.

But it had been Jadranka. "Is it true that *he* is my father?" she demanded from America.

She could have lied. Again. Years ago she had told Jadranka that her father was a Norwegian, an autumn visitor to the island who had carried about him an air of grace. A man with long, tapered fingers and eyes as green as sea glass, who had lifted her out of her widow's grief for a single night. This Sven. This Erik. This gentle Viking whose last name she had never caught. She had made him a violinist, a detail she knew her younger daughter would appreciate but which prompted Magdalena to stare at her with eyes like black nails.

But Jadranka was old enough to know. Old enough to eat her sack of salt.

Tell me, Jadranka had ordered. And so she told her.

She stopped short of revealing that she had seen Vico last year in Split. Almost three decades had passed, but there he was, walking as if he did not have a care in the world, looking into shop windows before finally pausing in front of a display of men's clothing.

God help her, she had followed him. She carried a metal nail file in her purse, and for a feverish moment she considered plunging it into his neck while he perused those ties and shirts.

She had not seen him since before Jadranka's birth, and for years after his departure nobody on Rosmarina spoke about him. If anything, she assumed that he had left the country at the beginning of the war, or finished in jail. But there he was, milling around as innocently as a bank clerk.

She had stood too close in the end. Her reflection appeared in the store window beside his, and their eyes met through the glass. He must have recognized her—or something about her—because he turned immediately and walked away.

A week later, he appeared at her apartment while Jadranka was out. Standing awkwardly in her living room, he explained that he had done some digging into her details, a statement that caused her to go momentarily breathless because it meant that he still had access to the information in her files.

"Don't tell me you're in *this* government, as well," she practically spat at him.

He did not answer, telling her simply that he knew Jadranka was his. He had never married and had no other children. "I have a right to know her," he insisted, his face so earnest that an outside observer might have believed them lovers, reuniting despite cruel fate.

"We," Ana told him, stabbing his chest with her finger. "We were never lovers."

"Regardless," he told her, "I have a right to know her."

No sooner did he leave her apartment than she embarked single-mindedly on the campaign of America, writing to Katarina with the suggestion of a babysitting arrangement. *Jadranka's pride would never allow her to ask you,* she had added, thereby winning Katarina's complicity. *But perhaps if you suggested it?*

As for Rosmarina's former chief of police and top UDBA agent, she allowed him to believe that she had acquiesced. "Wait," she implored him. "I need to prepare her first."

By his next visit, Jadranka was gone, and she had merely looked at him in triumph, this man who was now slighter than she, with gray skin and lips that time had thinned so that his mouth was like an incision in his face. It was unbearable to her that he had once been inside her body, a contagion—*stick with me and I'll keep your brother safe*—like some venereal disease that she now realized would be with her for life.

Holding Marin's freedom over her head had not been enough for him, however. For two nights after her brother's escape, they had kept her for questioning, this man her interrogator.

"Don't you know that I could squash you like a bug?" he had asked her.

There were prison camps for women, she knew, but she only shook her head dumbly. "I'm not my brother's keeper," she answered. "I have no idea where he went."

For months afterwards he had threatened to imprison her father. "It was stupid what he did, pretending to go fishing with your brother," Vico told her. "They'll send him away for years. They'll throw away the key."

She would go to extreme lengths to avoid him, but every time she went somewhere alone—to the Peak to visit her aunt, to the Devil's Stones—he would materialize, the most unwelcome of apparitions. His eventual transfer from the island and to points unknown had been the only thing that saved her.

"Tell me everything," Jadranka had demanded from America. "I deserve to know everything."

"There's nothing to tell."

"You can tell me why you did it," Jadranka wept.

But Ana could not bring herself to supply this missing puzzle piece. She knew her daughter's tendency to romanticize things, and she could imagine Jadranka casting her in the role of saint. "But you saved him," Jadranka would tell her. Better that her daughter think her the whore that everybody claimed she was.

"I'll find out," Jadranka threatened. "I'll ask *Nona*."

"She doesn't know."

"Who then?"

Ana hesitated. "Nobody."

"Liar."

"Nobody who wants anything to do with us," Ana said wearily. She could hear Jadranka digesting this information.

"I hate you," her daughter said a moment later, causing something inside Ana to snap, some final thread that had held her insides together the way butchers bind certain cuts of meat with string.

"Hate me, then," she had told her daughter before hanging up. "But don't you dare come back."

She did not think Jadranka capable of disappearing for long. Too much still bound her to her sister. During that year in Split they had spoken a secret language, so that when Jadranka turned mute it was Magdalena who answered for her, demanding drawing paper or declining vegetables.

As adults they had never gone more than a handful of days without speaking, as different as earth and sky but bound by some mysterious connection. So that when the telephone woke her again some weeks later, she answered it with relief. "Enough, Jadranka," she told the silence in a weary voice. "Your sister is out of her mind with worry."

But it was a man's voice, at once foreign and familiar. It was a voice she knew, and down the dark tunnel of history their last evening came back to her, brother and sister weeping in the darkness of their island Gethsemane.

"Jesus," she said to this unexpected ghost. "Jesus Christ."

He had telephoned Rosmarina first, he said, sounding almost apologetic, and their mother had given him her number.

For a moment Ana thought that it might be a trick, that the caller was only someone posing as her brother. Vico, perhaps, exacting some revenge. But then the voice began again. A voice that was older, yes, and cracking around the edges like dry leather, but irrefutably Marin's.

Her immediate response was not relief but nausea, and lying in her bed, she drew the covers up to her chin.

"I thought our parents were dead," he told her in wonder. "I didn't even know you had a second child."

She did not break the silence that stretched between them then, the one he rushed forward to fill, telling her that he had written at the beginning of the war, but one of his letters had been returned with that word on it, stark and terrible: *Deceased.*

Her hand on the telephone trembled uncontrollably now.

"Do you believe me?" he asked her, a note of desperation in his voice.

"Yes," she told him. "I do."

The letters had arrived together, two full years after their postmarks. She had intercepted them on her final visit to the island, during the same summer that Nikola had deserted her, chairs overturned in his wake. She had run into the postman on the *riva*. "Here," he told her, barely able to conceal his smirk as he handed her a bundle of mail. "You can save me the trip to your parents' house."

The entire island knew of her abandonment. She did not understand how the news had made it back so fast, but twice after exiting the ferry, old acquaintances had hailed her with scandalized expressions and gossip-hungry eyes. "Is it true about Nikola leaving you?" one had asked.

The postman was the final straw, with his gaze of ill-concealed amusement and his jaunty cap. So agitated was she by the way he kept looking back at her as he walked away that she almost failed to recognize the neat, forward-leaning slashes of her brother's penmanship on the envelopes.

She tore the first envelope open when she was a safe distance away. As she read, it became clear that her brother was enjoying an easy life, and each step towards her parents' house drummed in another of its details: the successful restaurant and the loving wife, the photographs of the two handsome boys who looked at their father with adoration. As she reached the courtyard gate, she buried the letters deep inside her purse.

"Sister?" Marin asked.

Months later, it had been she who wrote *Deceased* on one of the envelopes, disguising her penmanship by writing with her left hand. It was an act of cruelty, she knew, but she took for granted that he would write again. For months she prepared herself for their mother's telephone call, bearing news of his imminent arrival. When it did not come, she felt vindicated by how easily he had given up.

She hated him. She hated him, but she had been unable to throw away the first letter. She kept it in a bureau drawer, together with its envelope and photographs. In June, when Magdalena telephoned with her intention of searching Jadranka's things, she went to move it to a new hiding place, but it was gone. She emptied that drawer, and all the others. She called in sick to work and spent all night searching the apartment but never found it.

Throughout Magdalena's visit the next morning, she had held her breath. Every time the girl opened a box or inspected a drawer, she expected the accusing weight of those black eyes. *How could you do it?* she expected to hear her ask.

But it had been Jadranka, she realized now. Jadranka who had embraced her before leaving, Jadranka of the poker face, who had set off for America with her uncle's letter.

"Sister." Marin broke the silence with an agitated voice. "Please."

She felt the saved-up bile of years rise, and although she wept easily into the telephone's receiver, she could not speak. In the filmstrip that played before her eyes, she could scarcely believe how slowly—how senselessly—the decades since his departure had passed.

It was clear that he thought she might blame him for not recognizing Jadranka, for turning the girl away. But she understood what he didn't: that Jadranka had not found him by chance. And it was this subterfuge that rattled her, this proof that her daughter believed herself capable of controlling certain outcomes. Jadranka was more like her than she had realized, an idea that frightened her like no other.

She did not drink on the airplane. She did not accept the small bottle of wine that the stewardess handed out to other passengers, even when the woman sitting beside her whispered in encouraging English that it was free. Nor did she allow herself a cocktail from the tiny plastic bottles, miniatures of the ones in Frankfurt's duty-free. She did not do it because she knew that her older daughter would be waiting on the other side with her blood-hound's sense of smell.

Magdalena had not always been so hard. She had been a joyful child who adored boats and pomegranate seeds, who liked best when Ana sang to her as they lay together in their bed during the thickest heat of afternoon. Lullabies, mostly. Sometimes the Beatles or the Doors. *Try to set the night on fire,* she used to tell her firstborn's face.

Little more than five when Ana left the island, Magdalena became instantly poisoned by the whispering of others. Ana knew the things that were being said: that she was not satisfied with Rosmarina and considered herself too good for its tough life, its scorching heat, its songs of interminable crystal seas and singing crickets, its girls left waiting in windows for their sweethearts. That it was, in fact, she who lured away those sweethearts, creating green-eyed babies that islanders called *bastard* because they weren't inventive enough to come up with something new.

Nobody had suspected the blue-eyed policeman, and though Ana herself had caught wind of the wilder stories—Goran's best friend, an American sailor, a priest on the nearby island of Vis who was abruptly summoned back to the Vatican—she certainly did not bother to set anybody straight. The only people who might have guessed the truth were her brother and aunt. And they were gone.

She still remembered Magdalena's eyes at the table the morning she left the island. Knowing eyes, as if she understood that Ana would be gone for longer than the three months she claimed. And it was not fear of abandonment that shone there, or any fear at all, but suspicion, plain and simple. And so, halfway through feeding Jadranka, Ana handed the spoon to her mother, who took it with a troubled face and finished the job, making small noises of approval that Ana could never have mustered.

It was only later, when she stood on the ferry she had known her whole life, the ferry she had seen arrive and depart a thousand times but always for others, that she began to feel as though she could breathe. She was surrounded by German tourists who had spent a week on the island, their blond hair strange against their suntanned skin. They were talking and laughing and drinking beers even before the ferry pulled away. And they had already forgotten the island. The week of swimming and afternoon ice creams and mosquito bites was fading from their minds. Ana watched their faces and imagined the cities where they lived, where stately linden trees formed avenues of shade and the people were all well dressed and went to restaurants and the theater, things she had only seen in films.

She was so intent on imagining it, imagining how she would spend a few months in Split and then go to Germany or Switzerland or France, that she almost forgot them on the pier. Her mother holding Jadranka and showing her how to wave, shaking her fat hand back and forth, the little girl's attention already elsewhere, on a man selling popcorn to tourists perhaps, or on a seagull that sat on one of the boats. And Magdalena, stubbornly refusing to wave, those black eyes on the ferry, on her, so that Ana felt their burn all the way to Split and through every day that followed.

It was interminable, this trip. Even the stewardesses were beginning to look worn around the edges, despite their lacquered hair and artfully tied scarves. And when they reached New York at last, the plane was required to circle, the view from the window following the same endless pattern of ocean, land, and ocean.

Ana imagined Magdalena growing impatient in the airport below, looking at her wristwatch as if it were her mother's fault for being late. She wondered if her daughter would embrace her, if she would offer to take her bag. For the briefest of moments she allowed herself to imagine Magdalena linking arms with her.

But she knew how far-fetched this scenario was. She could not remember the last time Magdalena had touched her voluntarily.

That year in Split would always be between them, a juggernaut that could waken in seconds. She did not approve of these obsessions of the younger generation, this blaming of one's parents. It had been just one year—not a very good year, Ana could admit now—but just one year. She did not understand why they could not simply leave it behind them.

But her daughter carried that year within her like a cancer. "You didn't lift a finger to stop him," she had told her mother once, an accusation that left Ana indignant and a little light-headed.

"You turned out all right" had been her retort. "Stop crying about the past."

But Magdalena had only waved her hand in disgust.

That hand was the only impediment to Ana's forgetting. The left one with the knot, so that in every conversation with her daughter, in every interaction, sooner or later her eyes fell on that ridge of bone.

It was her fault, Ana knew. She had taken her to the doctor too late, after the bones had fused, and the man had looked at her sharply, though Magdalena said nothing. "She's so clumsy, my daughter," Ana had said. And, God help her, she had suggested that the doctor break it again.

But he would not hear of it. "Ridiculous," he told her. "The damage is done and she has the full use of her fingers."

Sometimes she had the feeling that her daughter taunted her with that hand. Even at rest, the furrow reproached her.

She felt their descent before it was announced, the captain's voice tired and—to her ears—unintelligible. America stretched below her, vast and strange. Both her daughters were down there. Her brother, too. But she felt no joy at the prospect of reuniting with any one of them.

She longed instead for the comforts of her tiny apartment: the bottles she had hidden throughout its rooms, a habit she continued although she now lived alone. She missed her bed, her tiny television. It was Saturday, and on Saturday nights she always watched the late-night mystery movie, wrapped up in her own bed with those flickering images.

When the plane drew at last to a halt and the doors opened, she waited for the other passengers to disembark first. She stared from the window at the flurry of activity on the tarmac: men dragging hoses and the baggage trolley that had pulled up alongside them. For some time she watched as suitcases were disgorged down a sliding ramp.

"Madame?" a voice beside her asked in mild annoyance. "We're here."

She turned to see one of the stewardesses looking down at her, and only a handful of stragglers in the aisles.

"Do you require assistance?"

Ana did not understand the question, but she shook her head, sensing that this was the reaction expected of her. She rose stiffly, clutching her purse to her chest.

"Ready?" the woman asked with the briefest of smiles, then stepped back to let her pass.

Ana did not understand this word, either, but she nodded because that was what the stewardess was doing, making a subtle up-and-down movement with her head as if she were trying to convince Ana of something.

She walked a little unsteadily towards the rectangle of light at the front of the plane, towards the captain and crew members bidding farewell to passengers who slipped like parachutists into the American beyond.

PART V

CHAPTER 16

Two days after leaving Marin's restaurant, Jadranka took a bus to Greenport and caught the ferry for Shelter Island. Because she was afraid of setting off the alarm in her cousin's weekend house, she decided to sleep in the greenhouse, an ornate structure of wrought iron and fogged glass that stood at the top of a slope behind the large Victorian. Woods covered most of the property, and Jadranka could remember wondering in April—during her only previous visit—if the trees had been felled to build the house, or if the forest had been planted afterwards for the pleasure of the inhabitants.

There was an outdoor tap for drinking water, and a wooden dock provided easy access to the ocean. Jadranka did not like the murky bottom with its slick seaweed, but day after day the July heat drove her to strip naked and float on the swells. If she closed her eyes, the rhythm was familiar. But if she did not rinse her hair with water from the tap immediately afterwards, a marshy odor followed her for the rest of the day.

According to Katarina, the greenhouse had been built in the late 1800s, a monument to another age when—Jadranka assumed—ladies attempted to outdo each other with their flower arrangements. It stayed cool at night but became unbearable when the sun rose, even if she propped the door open.

It had not been difficult to force the lock. Inside, she expected to find unused gardening tools or the remnants of old plants, but it was empty save for an ancient broom that she used to sweep the cobwebs away.

She slept on the dirt floor, on top of the sleeping bag Luz had given her to use in the restaurant. She had purchased food and candles before catching the ferry, the busybody at the cash register remarking brightly that Shelter Island was a wonderful destination for camping.

She did not need much: she slept when she was tired and dug into her arsenal of crackers and peanut butter when she was hungry. She had bought a bag of apples, and blackberries grew in the forest behind the house. The saltwater scoured her skin, and the soles of her feet thickened as morning after morning she left her shoes where she had kicked them off the first night.

For the first time in months she felt at ease. The house was separated from the road by a long and twisting drive, so if someone approached by car, she would hear them long before they turned the final curve and have plenty of time to reach the edge of the forest.

Sometimes when it was dark she could see lights from the neighboring property flickering through the trees. Occasionally, she would hear a car on the main road, or distant voices in the woods, but nobody approached the house.

She was not lonely. Not in the beginning, at least. If anything, it was a relief to be on her own. No Katarina with her unsolicited advice. No *Nona* Vinka and her secrets. No Marin with his disappointment.

After so many months in a city, she was preoccupied with the novelty of warm dirt and the clamor of birds that woke her at dawn. She had never seen fireflies before and spent her evenings mesmerized by the weaving and bobbing of their fat bodies, which always grew brighter in the moments before fading out. She thought that one day she might paint these things.

It was only once darkness fell that she found her circumstances difficult, lying alone in the dampness of the glass house. The wind would start, and the nearest tree tapped its branches against the panes of the roof. It was an uncanny sound, and night after night she dreamed of something outside, asking to be let in.

She blamed the dreams on her uncle's story about the policeman. She knew his name was Vico. Vico, the sadist. Also—and disastrously—her father. *Nona* Vinka's midnight revelation had been so unexpected that Jadranka had not even stopped to write a note to her cousin explaining that she was leaving.

Her mother had withheld this information for over twenty years, allowing Jadranka to believe—stupidly, she now thought—in a more auspicious version of her birth. On the night of their telephone conversation, Jadranka had not been able to see further than her mother's lies, but in the days since then she had begun to look at things differently.

"You were never supposed to know," Ana had nearly wailed. "Imagine what hell your life on Rosmarina would have been if everyone knew."

"So you were protecting me?" Jadranka demanded, the silence on the other side making her think for a moment that Ana had hung up.

"Is that so hard to believe?" a voice much smaller than her mother's had finally asked.

Their conversation made Jadranka feel a keen sadness now, and for the first time she regretted her own childish words. *I hate you.* She did not hate her mother, but while Jadranka had long ago accepted that she was not a child of love, to be the child of such a man was quite a different matter.

When Jadranka was eleven, a neighbor had mentioned that Pero Radić—one of the island's fishermen—had spent his whole youth in pursuit of Ana. He had brought her flowers, figs, and *girice,* their scales like delicate filigree. He had once serenaded her from the lane—to the amusement of all their neighbors—and brought her an ornate silver mirror with a pattern of flowers on the handle.

Ana had kept the mirror, giving it to Jadranka on one of her visits to the island. This was proof, Jadranka thought, that the mirror was somehow significant to her history, although her mother had made the gift in an offhand way, telling her that she had no need for it anymore.

It had been Pero Radić who found Goran Babić's boat on the day of his likely death and came to the courtyard with his hat crushed between his hands.

"He asked your mother to marry him a dozen times at least," the neighbor had told Jadranka, who was already coming to the conclusion that the lanky fisherman—who had never married—was her father.

And nobody could deny that he had taken a special interest in both Jadranka and her sister, giving them some of the stranger objects he dragged up in his nets: a piece of driftwood in the precise shape of a sleeping dog, a string of purple beads, a piece of incised pottery that Jadranka imagined had come from some ancient shipwreck on the seafloor.

Why, she reasoned, would he bother giving her these things if he were not her father?

In the second year of the independence war, when Jadranka was fourteen, he was on the front lines near Dubrovnik. One day in the port Jadranka overheard that he had been wounded badly.

"I have to find him," she told Magdalena that night, who looked at her as if she had grown a second head.

"Please," she begged her sister. "I need to talk to him before he dies."

Magdalena looked perplexed at this. "Why on earth do you think he's your father?"

"I just know that he is."

Reaching Dubrovnik in those days had been no small feat, with so many areas of the coast under attack. It had taken them nearly two days, through a combination of ferries, which now ran on abbreviated schedules, and hitchhiking down the coast as far as they could. On the last leg of their journey, they caught a ride with a young private around Magdalena's age who was on his way to pick up his boss, the colonel. "He's constantly on my case," he had confided in them as the sound of shelling grew louder in the distance. The private—not missing a beat—turned his music up to full volume. "Just think of the shelling like bass," he told them when both girls jumped at an explosion nearer than the rest. "It's one more part of the music."

He drove them to a military outpost, some distance north of Dubrovnik, where the older man in charge made them sit in his makeshift office, a classroom in a bombed-out school. "This is a war," he told both girls sternly. "What are you thinking by coming here?"

"My father is dying," Jadranka told him, and surprised herself by bursting into tears. "It may be my last chance to see him."

The man—Jadranka thought he had also been a colonel, though she could not remember much about him—had softened at this. After making a few calls on a scratchy handheld device, he told them that Pero Radić was in a hospital nearby.

"You have half an hour," he informed the girls. "And then you go back to where you came from."

Magdalena swore to him that it would be so, but Jadranka barely heard their conversation, so elated was she at the prospect of seeing her father. If he were conscious, she imagined, he would envelop her in his arms. If he were truly near death's door, she would hold a washcloth to his forehead the way she had seen in films.

Her elation lasted throughout the short jeep ride, the colonel himself driving them the four miles to the military hospital. He let them out in front. "Half an hour," he told them, looking uneasily at the building they were about to enter. "This isn't a place for little girls."

Magdalena gave him a withering look, but Jadranka was out of the car before it had even come to a halt, running into the hospital with her sister calling out behind her.

She found him on the second floor, in a room with at least a dozen other men. She found him as if she had been guided to him by sonar. He was sitting up, playing cards with another man who sat at the foot of his bed. He must have just won a round because he was smiling, but when he saw Jadranka, he only looked confused. "Who have you come to see?" he asked her. "I thought I was the only one from Rosmarina here."

When she explained that no, she was not here to visit anyone but him, that she had figured it all out and knew that he was her father, his eyes became as round as two plates. The man playing cards with him shot him an amused look, then beat a hasty retreat to his own bed at the other end of the room.

Jadranka had not cared. Nobody could keep her from her father. Not his friend the cardplayer, not the nurse who had caught sight of her and was now heading purposefully in her direction, not Magdalena, who was calling her name in the corridor. Not the war. And not her mother, who had withheld this most important information for all of Jadranka's life.

But the man in the bed clearly did not share her wild elation at their reunion, and for the first time Jadranka faltered. If anything, he looked a little uncomfortable, fumbling for his cigarettes after the initial shock of her appearance had passed. He would not meet her eyes, in marked contrast to the men in the beds on either side, who watched in rapt attention.

"Well?" she demanded.

But he only shook his head. "I'm sorry, *mala,*" he told her.

*   *   *

It was their mother who came to collect them, driving down the coast and through the checkpoints in her battered Yugo in record time.

"Get in the car!" she shouted when she saw them, the shelling that had been a low roar in the background growing ever louder, though several people had told the girls that it wouldn't reach the hospital, that the spot had been chosen for precisely that reason.

The colonel had washed his hands of both of them, leaving them on a bench on the hospital's ground floor with stern instructions not to move until their mother arrived. And it was there that Ana found them, Jadranka weeping quietly into her sister's lap, the hallway filled with beds of wounded.

"Are you out of your minds?" she demanded after they had traveled a safe distance north, destroyed buildings giving way to ones that were merely shuttered, two tourist seasons already—and countless lives—pissed away by the territorial pretensions of others.

It was during that drive, Jadranka had thought, that her mother told her the truth at last. A Norwegian. Lie upon lie, she now realized, had unspooled as her mother gripped the steering wheel and ordered Jadranka to put away these childish notions about finding her father because it would be like looking for a needle in a great Scandinavian haystack.

"He was a nice guy," Ana had told her finally. "And that's about all there is to know."

It surprised Jadranka, knowing what she now knew, that her mother had allowed her to live at all. An abortion would have meant a trip to the mainland under the scrutiny of others, but there were always other ways—secret practitioners on the island, recipes involving parsley and juniper. Jadranka was wise enough to understand that there had been methods for as long as there had been women.

And perhaps her mother had tried, after all. Perhaps she, Jadranka, was the result of some failed attempt. The daughter who was not meant to be, botched and unnatural. And perhaps she was the reason that their mother had left them both, all those years ago.

She had begun working for Marin with the notion that she would eventually tell him of her true identity. She would prove herself to him, show him that she was not afraid of hard work, that she was worthy of his affection in spite of who her father was. But it had all gone wrong in the end.

Most of all, she withheld the truth because of the suspicion that he might know more about her paternity, and she was afraid that she would never learn those things if he understood her to be his niece, opting to keep her in the fog of ignorance she'd been in all her life.

"And are you happier for knowing?" her mother had demanded during that same telephone conversation so many weeks ago, prompting Jadranka to reply that it had nothing at all to do with happiness.

She had brought most of the materials for Marin's commission to Shelter Island, hitchhiking from the ferry landing with the canvas under one arm. She spent the first week working in the shadow of the house, taking the canvas into the sunshine when she wanted to make sure that she was getting the colors right: the deep green of the vines, the gray limestone of the courtyard, the sea beyond her grandfather's gate, so deeply blue that it put to shame this murky ocean.

She painted the details simply but with a loving hand—the courtyard, the cracked plaster beneath the bedroom window, and the sheer lace curtains that her grandmother had hemmed with needle and thread. How many times had she and Magdalena stood on either side of the window with those curtains draped over their heads, as if preparing for their wedding days?

Adding her grandparents' telephone number had been an afterthought, but once she did it she realized that the intention had been there all along, from the moment she had stepped into Marin's Brooklyn restaurant.

"This much I can do for you," she muttered to herself, though even she did not know to whom she was speaking.

She walked into town to mail the canvas. After a week alone, it was strange to see people on the streets of Shelter Island Heights, shopping for antiques and licking ice cream cones. She felt at a great distance from them.

"No return address?" The clerk in the post office asked, regarding the painting, which she had packed in brown paper and twine.

"No," she told him.

"Anything hazardous, fragile, liquid?"

She hesitated, and his watery blue eyes searched her face.

She shook her head.

A collection of postcards stood by the post office's front door. As she paid postage for the canvas, she briefly considered writing to her sister.

Magdalena would be done with school by now. She would be painting their grandfather's boat and making repairs to the house, doing all the things she never had time for while she was teaching. Jadranka wondered whether their grandfather had finally slipped loose of this world, and for a terrible moment she pictured their grandmother draped in black. Most of all, though, she wondered what her sister knew.

For several years after her own discovery that she and Magdalena were half sisters, island children had made a game of guessing her father's identity. It was as if they sensed this knowledge the moment she herself attained it, and they had taunted her by naming all the island's drunks and village idiots. "Some German tourist!" they snickered within earshot. And their mother was a whore. *Kurva*. A word both soft and harsh, like an axe splitting wet wood.

Magdalena had bloodied a boy's nose once. Jadranka didn't remember precisely what he said, but she remembered the rage that surged through her sister's body as she bent and hoisted a rock.

Later, at home, Jadranka had crawled beneath the bed they shared. "Does it mean that we're not really sisters?" she asked between sobs.

"Of course it doesn't," Magdalena had responded, fiercely wedging herself next to Jadranka. "You can't listen to stupid people."

In the Shelter Island post office, Jadranka turned away from the selection of postcards. How would her sister answer that question, she wondered, if she knew that Jadranka's father was responsible for her own father's death?

She was at loose ends after mailing the painting. She was not ready to abandon the greenhouse and, anyway, did not know where to go next. She needed time to figure these things out, to figure herself out, as if her very anatomy had changed. She felt like an alien life-form who, despite years of thinking she is human, suddenly learns the opposite.

She was dimly aware that her hair had grown wild and that her lips were badly chapped. But she was glad that she did not own a compact and that the surface of the ocean was too rough to show her reflection. Otherwise she might have spent all of the second week staring at her face. She had always looked so different from Magdalena.

When the heart is heavy, the hands crave work. This had always been her grandmother's motto, and she followed it now, taking to the forest during daylight hours. There, she became an architect of sorts, building anything that took her fancy: a flimsy wooden bridge between stones, a pattern of green leaves on the dark earth. When she was a child, an island visitor—from Switzerland perhaps?—had shown her how to build fairy houses, tiny structures of stone and bark, and now she built an entire settlement around the twining roots of a massive oak. Rain would eventually demolish it, but she did not mind.

It was only at night that she missed her sister. She had never gone so long without hearing Magdalena's voice. Most of all, she missed her practicality, the way she rolled her eyes at old wives' tales and scoffed at dreams. If Magdalena were lying in the greenhouse, the tree branch that brushed the glass would be just a tree branch.

For Magdalena only two things were sacred: Rosmarina and Goran Babić. As a child, the mention of her dead father gave her a dreamy look. She hoped to grow tall like him, she had confided to Jadranka long ago, a desire that did not in the end translate into reality. She did not drink coffee for several years when she learned that he had avoided it.

During their time in Split, Magdalena once found a piece of paper with his handwriting among their mother's things. Goran Babić had been making a list of supplies he needed to buy for his boat, and his daughter took this list making as proof that he had not killed himself as they said on Rosmarina.

"See?" she told Jadranka triumphantly. "It isn't true."

The piece of paper was one of the last objects he had touched that she, too, could touch. Their mother had sold most of his things and given away anything that she judged of little value. When asked, Ana would say that she wanted to make a fresh start with Nikola, who did not like the idea of her dead husband's possessions lying about.

Magdalena carried the piece of paper around in her pocket for months. It grew soft as tissue, and the writing began to fade. That year for her birthday, Ana gave her a large, square locket, and she folded the paper tightly and placed it inside.

Just weeks later, after their foiled escape to Rosmarina, their mother ripped the locket from her neck. "Stop living in the past!" she had screamed, and flung it through the Split apartment window. It traveled five floors down to the courtyard, and Magdalena wailed as she tore down each flight of stairs, Jadranka at her heels. They spent hours searching but never found it among the broken glass and cigarette butts.

At the end of the second week, Jadranka ventured into town again, no longer satisfied with crackers and peanut butter. Her money was running out. She had less than two hundred dollars left—the remainder of her earnings from working in the restaurant—and that would not last much longer.

She spent some time walking the streets of Shelter Island Heights. Comparing the menus in several restaurants, she picked the least expensive, an Italian restaurant with scuffed wooden floors and plastic tablecloths.

She knew already what she wanted, and ordered a breaded chicken cutlet with a glass of water.

"That comes with potatoes or pasta," the waitress told her.

"Pasta," she said, hunger thrashing its tail in her stomach.

"And a side vegetable."

It was as the waitress reeled off the list of possibilities that Jadranka saw the man with the shaved head walk in, his sunglasses on top of his head, his shoulders straining the fabric of his black T-shirt. She knew that he was Croatian, although she could not place him in that moment.

The waitress was looking at her expectantly.

"Broccoli," Jadranka told her.

He owned the Croatian bar in Queens, she realized then. He had been rude to Theo, and a short time later Jadranka had made a flourish of leaving with her friend, letting the door slam shut behind them. But now Jadranka sank into her booth, pretending to study the paper placemat with interest. It had a map of Shelter Island on it, and she traced the shoreline with one absentminded finger.

He passed right by her table, and for a moment she thought that he would not notice her, but then she felt him stop. "I thought it was you, *mila*," he told her in Croatian. "Where's your friend?"

She looked up at him, feigning surprise. "Around," she told him with a small smile.

"May I join you?"

"Sure," she said after a split second of hesitation. "Why not?"

He slid into the booth across from her, smiling as though they were old friends. "What are you doing so far from home?"

She did not know if he meant from Croatia or from New York, and so she told him, "This and that."

"Mysterious lady" was his response.

"That's me."

For a moment they simply stared at each other across the table. Then he chuckled and picked up the menu that the waitress had brought over. "What are you drinking?" he asked, eyeing her glass.

"Water," she told him.

"Wine it is."

She had known plenty of men like him in Split. Macho men who were equal parts charm and swagger, they called her names like *ljepotica*—beauty—and *princeza*. They bore tattoos of sharks and leopards and spent their spare time in dark gyms lifting weights. Many worked regular jobs, but some aspired to gangster status. Jadranka was adept at dealing with either type, flirting with them in cafés but letting them down easy at the end of an evening. She had a talent for keeping things light, so that no matter how single-mindedly they pursued her, she always parted with them on friendly terms. *Little sister,* she had been called more than once, and the truth was that she had a soft spot for their streetwise wit.

"None for me," she told him when the waitress brought a bottle of wine over, but he was already motioning for another glass.

"Jadranka," he told her, and she was surprised that he remembered her name.

"Yes."

"You've forgotten my name."

She smiled in spite of herself. When she didn't answer, he held out his hand across the table. "Darko," he said. "It's a pleasure to meet you."

"We met before," she reminded him.

"Doesn't count," he told her, pouring a healthy portion of wine into both glasses.

"Why not?"

"I didn't impress you that time."

He wasn't particularly impressive this time, but she was lonely. And she was tired of sleeping on the ground and she wanted a shower, so she let him pour her a second glass, and then a third, all the while allowing him to imagine that he was the one seducing her.

"Are you still working for your cousin?"

She had forgotten telling him that detail.

"No."

"You ought to come work for me," he told her.

"My waitressing days are behind me."

He shook his head. "I have other businesses."

But she did not want to hear about these other businesses, and so she proposed a toast. "To America," she said, lifting her glass.

He was staying at an inn near the beach, only a short distance away. At one point on the walk there, he picked her up and hoisted her across his shoulder, and she knew by his steadiness that neither of them was as drunk as they pretended. His room had a crocheted bedspread and an old-fashioned soaking bathtub. It seemed an odd choice for him, but then Shelter Island seemed an odd choice to begin with. She could sooner picture him in the Hamptons or Atlantic City.

"I was supposed to come with a woman," he admitted, pinning her back against the railing on his balcony and kissing her neck. "But we had a disagreement."

She laughed at this. Even as he turned her and slid his hands beneath her shirt, she was laughing, looking at the way the ocean was the same inky black as home.

He stopped kissing her. "What's so funny?" he demanded, and there was the slightest edge in his voice. It made her shiver lightly, but it also made her nipples stand at attention.

"Look," she told him, pulling off her shirt to show him, not caring if anyone else could see her.

"Ludjakinjo," he told her softly. "Crazy woman."

She pushed him into the room, towards the bed. And when he turned she was amused to see the tattoo of a lion on his back.

The bed was too soft, and she awoke in the middle of the night, unsure at first where she was. The stranger beside her was snoring softly, and the clock radio beside him read 3:27 a.m. On Rosmarina, she thought, her grandmother would have long ago unpacked the vegetables from her market basket.

She was quiet as she slipped out of bed and closed the bathroom door behind her. In the shower she leaned her forehead against the tile, half afraid that Darko would awake and join her. He had already served his purpose—or, rather, he hadn't, because she had been too wound up to come, release skittering away from her like dry leaves carried by the wind—and she had little interest in seeing him again.

Come home, she imagined her sister telling her.

But it was not that easy. It would never be that easy again. And she could not ask Magdalena to save her this time.

We're sisters, Magdalena would insist. *It changes nothing.*

Jadranka wanted to believe this. *I'm still what I always was,* she had tried to tell her uncle. But he only held up an angry hand to stop her, muttering that he knew all there was to know about her kind.

Her kind.

When she returned to the room, she was relieved to see that Darko lay in the same position in the bed. She dressed and as she opened the door to the hallway, shoes in her hand, he stirred very slightly. But then he merely rolled over and faced the wall, half a lion roaring at her as she went.

CHAPTER 17

It was the postmark that gave Jadranka away, the canvas for their uncle arriving with the words *Shelter Island* on the upper right-hand corner of the wrapping. A surprising misstep, thought Magdalena, who hoped it meant that Jadranka wanted finally to be found.

Her sister had been to the island during the children's Easter holiday. She had played hide-and-seek with them in the woods behind Katarina's house and dangled her feet from the dock into the still-frigid waters of the Atlantic Ocean. But despite Katarina's descriptions of sandy beaches and golf courses, Magdalena pictured her sister amid the pine forests and white stone of Rosmarina every time she heard the island's name.

"Što znaći *Shelter?*" their mother wanted to know.

"It means…" Katarina fumbled for the word.

"*Sklonište,*" Magdalena said. "Refuge."

Ana looked startled at this.

Mother and daughter had barely spoken since Ana's arrival the day before. Magdalena had chosen to wait at the airport alone, pacing nervously as if death itself waited on the other side of those automatic doors. She did not know what to make of the news that her uncle had been in contact with her sister, and her mother did not elaborate.

"You're thinner" had been the first words out of Ana's mouth as she took in the dark circles beneath Magdalena's eyes and the bony shoulders that held no promise of an embrace.

But Magdalena only stared at her. "I know who Jadranka's father is," she said, causing the skin around her mother's lips to whiten.

"Who told—?"

"*Nona* Vinka."

Her mother said nothing to this, and they spent the taxi ride to Katarina's in silence.

Magdalena could not remember Rosmarina's former chief of police. He had left the island at some point in the 1970s, though even today islanders lowered their voices when mentioning him. *Evil,* Luka had told his granddaughters once, so that the man haunted their dreams like a bogeyman. *Some people poison everything they touch.*

They left for Shelter Island the next morning, Magdalena convinced that if they waited any longer, Jadranka would disappear again. For the duration of the two-hour journey to Greenport, Katarina made a valiant attempt at small talk with Ana, who only responded in grunts, while Magdalena pretended to sleep in the backseat.

Shelter Island was different than she had imagined it. Instead of white stone, grassy hills and narrow arms of land cleaved the water like a swimmer. And while it was true that evergreens filled the forests, they were outnumbered by oak and ash.

There was no sign of Jadranka in Katarina's large Victorian house, and so the next morning they went to file a report at the island police station. They photocopied Jadranka's picture, leaving flyers on bulletin boards in the library and in grocery stores. They tramped through the woods behind Katarina's house, where an occasional silver birch stood like a pale, naked girl among widows. The dark glass panels of an ancient greenhouse observed their comings and goings, but when Magdalena started up the slope to investigate the structure, Katarina told her that it had been locked for years, and the children thought it haunted.

Unlike in New York, where nobody had recognized her sister, they ran across several people who seemed to remember the young red-haired woman. One man claimed to have sat next to her in a bar just the week before; another said that he often saw her bicycling the roads around Dering Harbor. The island librarian was certain that it was Jadranka who brought a little, dark-haired girl to children's story hour every Thursday at three o'clock. But although the next day was Thursday and Magdalena waited at the library for her sister, neither Jadranka nor the dark-haired girl appeared.

Each evening they returned to the house, where Katarina watched television with Ana. Magdalena preferred to sit outside on the dock, letting her legs trail through the water. The wood was weathered and soft, and she imagined her sister sitting there at Easter, the same slats beneath her. On a whim she inspected every inch of its surface, looking for a place where her sister might have inscribed something. Once, she thought she found the curved line of a J but could not ultimately coax other letters from that rough surface.

It took her four days to declare defeat. "She's not here," she told Katarina.

"No," her cousin said. "I don't think she is."

On the return ferry ride, Katarina suggested showing Jadranka's photograph to the young men who guided cars onto the deck, something Magdalena had not tried on the way over.

"She left the island a few days ago," one of them told her. "She bummed a cigarette from me. But I couldn't let her smoke it until Greenport."

"Do you remember which day?"

"Wednesday," he told her unequivocally. "Last boat of the night."

Her mother was watching her through the windshield of Katarina's car, carefully, as if Magdalena were some hazard of the road that she hoped to avoid. But Magdalena's thoughts were elsewhere, and her legs felt unsteady as she walked towards the car.

It was Jadranka who claimed to understand their mother. "She's had a hard life," she would insist. But Magdalena always dismissed this line of reasoning, and she certainly didn't trust Ana's latest claims of sobriety, nor her impromptu arrival in New York with stories about her long-lost brother.

"He thought that your grandparents were dead," Ana said, as if that explained everything.

"Why on earth would he think that?"

The three women had returned from Shelter Island and were sitting in Katarina's living room, drinking coffee.

Ana only shrugged, but the hand that brought the cup to her mouth shook badly, and for the briefest moment Magdalena felt sorry for her mother.

"He won't recognize me," she said, when she returned the cup to its coaster on the coffee table. "He won't recognize this old woman."

"I'm sure he'll recognize you, Cousin Ana," Katarina protested. "You're brother and sister, after all."

But Magdalena thought that her mother might have a point. *Living like you did hasn't helped,* she nearly told her, because the consequences were writ large in the red veins of Ana Babić's face. But she caught herself before the words flew out.

Jadranka's room was exactly as she had left it on the day of her departure, and neither Katarina nor Magdalena had stripped the bed. Once or twice, Magdalena had even fallen asleep there, burying her face in her sister's pillow.

"I could put your mother in there," Katarina had suggested halfheartedly to Magdalena, who in turn gave her mother the choice. But Ana Babić took one look at the sweatshirt at the foot of Jadranka's bed and the loose change on the windowsill and shook her head.

"I'll sleep with you," she told her older daughter.

The night of their return from Shelter Island, lying in the darkness of the guest room, Magdalena realized that her mother was crying beside her in the bed. She was tempted to reach over and take her hand, to offer some words of comfort. But she imagined Ana snatching her hand away and turning over. Telling her that she did not understand.

Mother and daughter were due at Marin's the next morning, but when Magdalena woke it was still dark, and she could tell by her mother's breathing that she was also awake.

"Did you manage to sleep?" she forced herself to ask.

"Not really."

Downstairs in the kitchen, Ana drank coffee silently, her eyes red and swollen.

Magdalena wet a dish towel at the sink. "Lean back," she ordered, surprised when her mother complied wordlessly, allowing Magdalena to drape it across her eyes.

Her mother had been different since arriving in America. Gone was the combative woman who argued over every minuscule fact. It was as if the blood had been drained from her, as if she were a pale imitation of the mother Magdalena had left in Split more than two months before, the one who derided her eldest's profession by calling her *Our Lady of Snotty Noses*.

At first Magdalena had suspected tranquilizers, searching her mother's suitcase and handbag one evening on Shelter Island while

Ana snored on the bed. But she had only turned up an old army photograph of Marin. *For my little sister,* he had written on the back.

Now, Magdalena studied the face draped in the damp, white cloth. Her mother was right. It was a different face than Marin Morić would remember, and for a moment Magdalena imagined peeling the dish towel back to reveal the Ana Babić of early 1970s photographs, brows arched in amusement above dark eyes.

When she lifted the towel, however, her mother's face was less swollen but otherwise unchanged. Her eyes did not even focus on her but on some point behind Magdalena's head.

For my little sister, Magdalena thought, remembering stories she had heard of Marin Morić carrying his sister everywhere on his back.

"Not long now," Magdalena said, intending her words to be comforting.

But Ana Babić did not look cheered.

Two hours later they stood together outside his door. It was steely gray with two locks and a peephole at whose center shone a pinprick of light. Ana had arranged the visit by telephone, but now both mother and daughter hesitated, neither lifting a hand to knock.

Magdalena had only visited Brooklyn once, on the day she followed the red-haired stranger into the subway station a few blocks from here. The neat brownstones of her uncle's neighborhood were unexplored territory, as were the cafés and restaurants crowding its avenues. The pavements were smooth, and there were few of the weeds that grew in Damir's neighborhood, fewer ninety-nine-cent stores. No plaster Madonnas or flags.

When the door swung open—as if someone had sensed their silent presence in the hallway—her mother gave a little cry. But

Magdalena did not recognize the man who stood on the other side.

She knew that in the days after her father's death she had accompanied Marin every time he left the house, with its black sheet in the window and its somber stream of visitors. Those excursions, she was told, were the beginning of her obsession with boats. They would wander the *riva* as he held her hand or travel in the boat whose outboard motor sang *tuk-tuk-tuk* all the way to the Devil's Stones. It was her uncle, Luka once corrected her, not he, who had first allowed her to steer, placing his hand over hers on the shuddering tiller.

Magdalena could no longer remember which shadows of her childhood had been cast by her father, which by her uncle. She was only familiar with photographs, so that her father was a man perpetually on his wedding day and Marin Morić did not age past twenty-six.

But the man before her was older, much older.

He said nothing before embracing both Magdalena and her mother, drawing them towards him at the same time so that their hands brushed, each woman's face buried in a different shoulder. His embrace was so crushing that for a moment Magdalena could not breathe.

"Lena," he told her thickly.

The parquet of the apartment's entrance was scuffed and the leather couch in its living room smooth with age. Magazines and newspapers lay on many surfaces, and a diagonal crack in the window behind the couch made the building on the other side of the street appear as if it had split in two.

To fill up the silence, her uncle's wife, who had appeared behind him with a cheerful smile, explained in English that they had intended to replace the pane of glass for years. "But we have two sons, you know, and no sooner was something fixed than it got broken again."

Her name was Luz, Marin explained in careful Croatian, a name that meant *light* in Spanish. She kissed both of them in turn, Ana turning awkwardly to offer her cheek, her eyes so bleak that the back of Magdalena's throat began to burn.

She could not understand her mother's joylessness. Here, at last, was her reunion with her only brother. And while it was true that Ana had long regarded his defection with bitterness—commenting frequently on the way he had abandoned his family—Magdalena could not make sense of the almost anxious way she regarded him now.

For his part, Marin kept removing his glasses to wipe his eyes. "Those bastards," he said, explaining to Magdalena about his returned letter, the way his parents had been slain with a single word. "Can you fathom the cruelty behind such an act?"

She couldn't, although it went some distance to explaining his silence of decades.

But her mother sat primly on the couch, her purse on her knees as if she did not mean to linger. "You should have tried harder," she said in a quiet voice. "And I . . ."

Marin waited.

"I should have understood."

Marin opened his mouth as if to speak, but Ana cut him off.

"We should have left things differently, you and I. But there wasn't time."

"No," he agreed sadly. "There wasn't time."

Magdalena could not follow their conversation, and Luz, it was clear, did not understand Croatian, although her eyes did not leave her husband's face.

But neither sibling chose to clarify the situation for them, or to describe their last meeting in the darkness of the Rosmarina courtyard. Ana did not tell them of the way she had said to Marin in a whisper: "I made myself into a whore for you, so that he would leave you alone." And Marin did not describe the dead weight of his sister's eyes, unbearable even in the dark.

"Don't let it be for nothing," Ana had finally begged, and instead of responding, Marin had been sick. The vomit struck the flagstones of the courtyard like hail.

Now, each remembered the way she had cupped his forehead with her hand, just as their mother had done in their childhood whenever they were sick. The skin of her palm was so cool that he had pressed it more firmly to his brow. And when he had stopped heaving, he lowered it to cover his eyes.

It was Marin who broke the silence that stretched between them in his New York apartment. "You look well," he told his sister.

"Liar."

"You're alive," he said. "You survived."

Ana closed her eyes and nodded. "That's more than we can say for others."

When Luz went to make coffee, Magdalena volunteered to help her, relieved to escape the living room. She followed her uncle's wife into a kitchen where cookbooks lined the windowsills, and the refrigerator was covered with postcards and an abundance of notes.

"That's how we communicate when we spend different shifts at the restaurant," Luz said from behind her. "Your uncle and me. And then we never have the heart to take them down."

Studying the scraps of brightly colored paper with their details of telephone numbers and shopping lists, Magdalena's eyes stung, witness to all those hearts and crosses, those doodles and asides. *Let's go to a movie this weekend,* suggested one message in bold print. *You need a new winter coat,* a feminine cursive responded.

When Magdalena turned, the other woman fell silent at her expression. "Oh, my dear," she said, misunderstanding. She came around the counter and took both of her hands. "We had no idea who your sister was."

Magdalena only nodded.

On one kitchen wall were dozens of horizontal markings that rose at least a foot above Magdalena's head: a yardstick that clearly measured her cousins' heights.

Luz followed her gaze.

"They're tall," Magdalena said lamely.

"Yes," their mother agreed, handing her a picture frame from the counter.

Magdalena stared at the handsome boys who shared their mother's olive skin, but with faces so like their father's that they looked like one man aging within a single frame. She saw something of Luka in them, as well, and she felt her eyes burn a second time.

"What are their names?"

"José and Adriano," Luz told her. "You'll meet them. Both you and your sister."

When Magdalena returned to the living room, carrying the coffee tray, her mother and Marin were sitting side by side on the couch. He had draped an arm around her shoulders and was telling her something in a low voice. She was nodding, her purse surrendered to the floor beside her feet.

They did not sense Magdalena's approach, and for a moment she watched them, surprised to see her mother in such close proximity to anyone. But although Ana's face had lost its pinched quality, there was still something careful about the way she held herself, as if she suspected her brother was an impostor.

"The letters—" Magdalena heard her say in a choked voice, breaking off when a floorboard creaked beneath her daughter's foot.

"Lena," Marin hailed her, for the second time using the familiar form of her name. When she did not respond, he studied her more closely. "You don't remember me at all, do you?"

"Only bits and pieces," she admitted.

"He thought your sister was UDBA," Ana broke in. "He thought she'd been sent to blackmail him."

Marin looked ashamed. "She had so many questions and she didn't tell me who she was, you see."

"There's no more UDBA," Magdalena said with a frown. "It was dissolved years ago."

Marin swallowed. "I didn't even know she existed."

Luz had come into the room behind Magdalena, and while she could not have understood the exact details of the conversation, she clearly gathered that they were talking about Jadranka.

"Show her, Mio," she told him in English.

Marin led her down a short hallway and opened the door to his sons' room. There were posters on the wall, a stereo with a collection of CDs that went from floor to ceiling, and a framed shadow box with an autographed Mets jersey. But Magdalena immediately spotted the canvas that leaned against a closet door.

He lifted it. "This is the room where I slept as a child."

Magdalena nodded. It was her room today, though she did not say so to her uncle.

He pointed at the grapevine. "Your father and your grandfather planted that the day you were born."

"My father is dead," she told him.

"I know."

"—and my grandfather is dying."

Although he nodded, this last comment clearly pained him, and they spent a long, awkward moment staring at the painting, neither looking at the other.

"I'm sorry," she told him.

But Marin surprised her by handing her the canvas. He lowered the blinds at the windows and closed the bedroom door. "Look up," he told her when he had turned off the ceiling lamp.

Still holding the canvas, she took in the glow-in-the-dark stickers that covered the entire ceiling. Like real stars, they were brightest when viewed obliquely, and she studied the carefully mapped configurations in which Orion hunted and Canis Major stalked the dark sky. Directly above her, Andromeda raised her arm.

"*Dida* told me that she was chained to a rock," she told him, studying the arm with its glowing shackle. "And that Perseus saved her from the sea monster."

"Yes," he told her softly. "He taught me that, as well."

"—but I didn't like the idea and so I used to insist that she was holding something."

She was conscious of her uncle studying the faintly glowing circles. "What is she holding?"

"I used to think that the star was a knife, and not a chain."

There was a moment of silence as he took this in.

That's not how the story goes, little one, her grandfather had told her in amusement when she insisted that it was Andromeda who defended both the warrior and the winged horse, marking her territory in that patch of northern sky. But from that day forward, it was thus in all the stories Luka told her.

Her mother wept only once, as they were saying goodbye. She clung to her brother as if another thirty years were about to separate them, although they had already made plans to see each other again. Magdalena did not hear Marin's words of comfort, but whatever they were, they seemed to calm her mother.

"It's not his fault," Ana said when they reached the street.

"What isn't?"

"He thought they were dead."

"Yes," Magdalena said. "I know."

But Ana's mouth had resumed its familiar hard line. "You and your sister, you know nothing."

Magdalena studied the mascara that blackened her mother's eyes and decided to let this go. They did not speak for the duration of the subway ride back to Katarina's, their morning truce effectively ended.

Marin did not know where Jadranka might have gone after Shelter Island. Towards the end of her time at the restaurant, she had found a place to stay. *With friends,* she told him, although he later discovered that she had spent a week sleeping on his headwaiter's couch, disappearing from his apartment without a trace on the same night she had left the restaurant for the last time.

From what Magdalena could tell, Jadranka had made only one true friend, and he had not heard from her since June.

"Still not a peep," Theo confirmed when she telephoned to ask him. "Although I remembered the name of that place she took me. Club Darko."

It did not sound familiar to Magdalena. "And you're sure it was in Queens?"

"Sure as sure can be."

Damir had never heard of the club either. "I can call around," he told her in the darkness of his bedroom that evening, his hand tracing circles on her bare hip.

She had left her mother with the vague excuse of running errands and caught the train to Queens. When she rang his apartment's buzzer, his voice had betrayed neither elation over her appearance nor irritation that he had not heard from her in nearly two weeks. Still, Magdalena was surprised to find herself here again. Nothing about their situations had changed, after all, and whatever his next destination, she knew that it would not be Rosmarina. But she was weak, and although she berated herself soundly for her weakness, it had not once occurred to her during the subway ride here to turn around.

"She took her friend there months ago," she pointed out. "She probably never went back."

"Probably not," he told her reasonably, but the next morning she watched from his bed as he stood at the kitchen counter and telephoned a colleague at a local newspaper.

"Ever heard of it?" he asked, meeting Magdalena's eyes through the open bedroom door. There was a long silence, and then he hung up the telephone.

"No luck," she guessed when he returned to the bed.

"On the contrary." He opened his hand to reveal a yellow scrap of paper. "Club Darko. It's on Steinway Street."

Magdalena looked skeptically at the line of numbers in his palm.

"You're famous," he said, handing it to her. "At least in the Croatian sections of Queens."

"What do you mean?"

"Your flyers," he told her. "Apparently everyone is talking about a dark-haired *Rosmarinka* who's looking for her red-headed sister."

She snorted. "It sounds like a fairy tale. Snow White and Rose Red."

He smiled at this, but a moment later he was asleep again, his arm thrown across her chest. She waited until his breathing deepened before extricating herself and padding to the kitchen, where she stared at the yellow scrap of paper.

Jadranka had always loved fairy tales, with their stories of curses and enchantments. It had been their mother who bought them the book of Grimms' stories, a German edition with gold edges. It was an uncharacteristic gift and—considering that they did not speak German—a largely useless one. But Magdalena could still remember the vividly rendered illustrations, so different from the washed-out colors of the country's socialist presses. And the way Jadranka had made up stories to fit those pictures.

CHAPTER 18

When Jadranka boarded the ferry in Shelter Island, the lights on the other side beckoned her like a runway. She could go anywhere from here, she realized. More importantly, she could be anything. But her bravado ebbed in the five minutes it took to cross, and she disembarked to a line of cars that slipped, one by one, into the night.

She had not seen Darko again, had avoided Shelter Island Heights for several days after their encounter. He had seemed harmless enough, despite his shaved head and his crooked boxer's nose. Despite even the fact that his place of business was an unmarked storefront on Steinway Street full of male patrons who looked just like him with their thick necks and gold chains, their swagger, their nicknames like *Zmaj*—Dragon, she had translated for Theo while snickering into her beer—and Lucky.

The truth was that he had offered to help her, producing a business card from his wallet. "I can give you a job."

"What makes you think I need a job?" she asked, and he lifted one of her hands, the nails ragged from her art projects in the woods.

"A girl like you shouldn't be doing manual labor," he told her.

"Waitressing *is* manual labor."

"Who said anything about waitressing?"

She had not taken him seriously, but now, as she sat on the curb at the ferry landing, the next bus to New York an hour away, she began to look at things differently. She had little money left and nothing to lose. Going back to her cousin's was an unattractive option. Going back to Rosmarina was unthinkable.

She called Darko three hours later from a Port Authority pay phone. "Your offer of employment?" she asked him. "Does it still stand?"

There was a moment of silence on the other end, but he recovered too quickly for her to change her mind. "For you, *mila?*" he told her. "Anything."

Waiting in front of the bus station, she considered turning around and walking back into the arrivals hall, which teemed with people at three in the morning. She could catch a bus northward. She could try Boston next. Or, better yet, some seaside town where no one cared about green cards in the middle of a tourist season. But though she could picture it in her mind—a mixture of Shelter Island and a romantic comedy she had once seen about a New England bed-and-breakfast—she did not know the name of a single place that met these requirements.

She missed his approach. She had been scanning the street, assuming he would pull up in an SUV with tinted windows, or a Mercedes-Benz. But he came from inside the station behind her.

"Ciao, *mačko,*" he hailed her. "You disappeared on me."

Her talent for smiling easily came in handy now. "Family business."

She allowed him to take her backpack, and for the first time since calling him, it occurred to her that she was making a mistake. But he seemed innocuous enough. "Let's roll," he said, and so she followed him up Eighth Avenue.

If he was angry about the way she had left, he did not let on. But neither did he make any further reference to that night.

The New Jersey property had come to him in a business deal, and he only needed her to live there, to maintain a presence and wave at the neighbors. "You're perfect," he told her. "You can be my nice cousin from the Old Country."

She was surprised to realize that he wanted to take her there tonight, his car parked two blocks away from the bus station. "What's the hurry?" she asked him.

"No hurry," he told her. "We could always go back to my place."

But Jadranka responded vaguely about not wanting to stay too long in the city.

"Avoiding someone?" he asked her.

You, she thought. "Lots of people."

It was still dark when they arrived, but Jadranka could tell that the house—at the end of a cul-de-sac—was nearly derelict. The porch sagged in the middle and light blue paint peeled from wooden clapboards in the headlights of Darko's car.

"You're not afraid of ghosts, are you?" he asked in a low voice, then laughed.

"Just mice," she said, though this was not really true.

"No mice," he promised.

She stared at the house. "Why don't you rent it out?"

"I need to fix it up first."

Two men ran a tool-and-die business out of the basement. They didn't have permits for the machinery, and so the business was not strictly legal. But there was a separate basement entrance, behind the house, and so she was unlikely to see much of them.

Something about the way he said this made Jadranka hesitate.

"And you stay away from the basement," he told her, turning off his headlights so that she could no longer see the house. "Don't go distracting them with that pretty face."

★   ★   ★

Inside, the house's windowsills were covered with dust. It was as large as Katarina's Shelter Island house, but whereas each door-knob in that structure had been oiled, each pane of glass pristine, this house had clearly sat empty for years.

Darko's footsteps echoed loudly in the empty rooms. In the kitchen there was a refrigerator, but a sepia-colored gap stretched between cupboards where a stove had once stood. Not a problem, Jadranka thought, looking at it, because the house was stifling and she would be staying only as long as it took to plot her next move.

She followed him to the second floor, where a tiny room contained an oscillating fan and a single mattress.

"I crash here sometimes," Darko told her. "But it's yours now."

She looked dubiously at the naked mattress.

"Unless you want some company?"

When Jadranka did not answer, he only laughed. "Don't worry, *mila,*" he told her. "We're business associates now." He reached into his wallet for a hundred-dollar bill. "There are stores at the end of the street. Buy what you need, and I'll be back in a week."

She looked at the crisp bill in her hand. Together with what she had, she could make it even farther than Boston. But she was aware of the way Darko watched her, and so she nodded and tucked it into the pocket of her jeans.

A claw-footed bathtub stood in the bathroom. It was discolored with age, but the water that ran from the tap was clear and cold, and after she heard Darko drive away, she turned off the light and sat beneath the steady stream. She did not have soap or a towel, and afterwards she walked naked from room to room in her shoes, allowing the dark, warm air to dry her.

She slept heavily until the next morning, when she heard a man's voice below the window.

"Kreten," he was telling someone in Croatian. "You can't do it that way."

The tool-and-die guys, she guessed, although the only thing she could see in the driveway was a battered van, its rear doors open towards the house.

She dressed in the clothes she had worn the night before, making a mental note of how to spend Darko's hundred-dollar bill. She would conserve as much as she could. He had promised her the same amount in a week, and she had already started thinking of it as her escape fund.

When she walked onto the front porch ten minutes later, a light-haired man around her age sat there eating a doughnut. Bone thin, he did not look up, but when she went to walk past him, he startled.

He held up a hand in greeting, and it came to her suddenly that he was deaf.

She raised a hand as well, but he went back to his doughnut, and so she walked down the steps just in time to run into another, older man, more like Darko in build.

"Hello," she told him, blinking.

She would have identified them as Croatian from a mile away. She could tell by their track suits, by the way the second man wore his hair, clipped so tightly to the scalp that it took a moment to realize how far his hairline had receded.

He nodded at her but did not respond, climbing the steps to kick the thinner man's boot lightly with his own. "Time to go back to work," he said.

When they passed, the Darko look-alike gave Jadranka a measured look. It traveled from her hips to her neck before coming to settle somewhere beneath her collarbone. *My tits don't usually make eye contact,* she was tempted to tell him, but something held her back, and a moment later they both disappeared around the side of the house.

* * *

The shopping area was a strip mall, about a mile away. There was a small supermarket and a ninety-nine-cent store, and in addition to food she bought a hand towel, soap, and some twine. Darko had said to make the house look inhabited, and when she got back she stretched a length of the twine tightly between two half-dead trees.

He had told her to wave at the neighbors, as well, but she had seen nobody on the walk to and from the strip mall, and his house was almost invisible to its neighbors, set back from the street and surrounded with trees and overgrown bushes. Behind the property line, which he had pointed out to her with a flashlight the night before, were woods even thicker than the ones that surrounded Katarina's house on Shelter Island. They gave Jadranka the impression that the property bordered an abyss.

"Don't go wandering around back there," he had warned her, citing poison ivy and snakes.

In the kitchen, she unpacked milk, bread, and peanut butter, a substance she was growing heartily sick of. She had washed her clothes under the tap at Shelter Island, and she was wearing her last clean T-shirt, so she emptied the contents of her backpack into the tub, rubbing each item with soap and wringing it out.

She heard low voices outside, and the slamming of a car door. When she rose and looked through the window, the two men from the workshop were driving away.

She did not think she could spare money for pencils and a sketchbook, and so she spent the first few days sitting on the porch's front step, swatting mosquitoes and listening to occasional noises from the basement. The two men did not speak to each other, and when she did hear something, it was usually the stouter one cursing.

It surprised her that their basement machinery made no noise, and that some days they did not come to the house at all. She preferred the solitude of those days, and by the end of the first week, she bought a package of crayons at the ninety-nine-cent store, returning to the house to find that Darko had come and gone, leaving her another hundred together with a note that read: *Don't spend it all in one place. Back next week.*

She had already decided that she would leave then, after the next hundred dollars. This would bring her savings to over four hundred, enough to get far away from here. She would try Maine next—the name of that state coming to her one night as she was drifting off—which she remembered was as far north as she could go.

But until then she needed something to occupy her time.

The walls inside the house were all a uniform whitish gray, the paint worn so thin in places that she could see the plasterwork underneath. They were not ideal as canvases, but she was bored, and so she started upstairs in the master bedroom, across the hall from where she slept. To amuse herself, she drew windows onto a second room, one with flowering plants and lace curtains at the windows. A black dog lay curled on the bed, and a woman sat in a rocking chair, her back towards the windows, a bowl of figs on the table beside her.

As a child, Jadranka had been fascinated by houses, by the way one room led to another, all of them fitting neatly together. She defied these conventions in her sleep, however, and dreamed frequently about rooms that changed shape even as she entered them. Often the dreams were about her grandfather's house, so that the structure she had known for all her life—and whose every hiding place she had explored—became like a magician's box in her sleep, unfolding from the inside to reveal new stairways that led to unknown floors and entire wings that had been waiting patiently for her to discover them.

The dreams had their genesis in the bedroom she had shared with Magdalena, which Luka had repainted one summer long ago. Removing a section of rotten plaster, he had been surprised to find a block of chiseled limestone identical to the house's external walls. It looked like the edge of an old fireplace, but as he gouged more plaster away, the graceful stone outline of a Renaissance window emerged, albeit filled with rubble.

"Just look at this," he had told his granddaughters in awe, inviting them to touch the column that bisected it. "Your ancestors carved this and fitted it. They probably didn't know how to write or read, but look at what they did know."

Necessity or ignorance had prompted their grandchildren's grandchildren to reuse fragments of their sculptures and columns in more modern building projects, to fill in windows and doorways that were no longer of practical use. Throughout the town were new houses that had been built atop existing bases, and columns that had been placed on their sides in gardens to separate tomato plants from spinach. Sealed windows sometimes began at ankle height, and doors hovered several feet above the ground.

Jadranka had begged Luka not to plaster over the window again, and in the end he had even removed some of the rubble, making a small recess into which she could fit as a child.

The wall had clearly once been the outside of a house, and she used to lie in bed, imagining the flowering vines that wrapped around the column hundreds of years ago, snaking up from a garden that, today, was the kitchen. Imagining clandestine lovers who whispered to each other through that space, sealed for a period longer than the span of any person's life.

In New Jersey, she frequently pictured that window, and the soft light that had once glowed from the room behind it, where nothing but a wall now stood. A room that was lost entirely in her present circumstances.

She picked one of the rooms on the first floor for her next project, an olive grove that stretched from wall to wall. She added the figures of children between the trunks of trees, wearing the crayons down into nubs of wax.

Darko had left her with a pack of Marlboro Reds on the first night, though he had told her not to smoke them inside the house, an edict she had been ignoring by leaning out of the bathroom window upstairs and flushing the butts down the toilet. Only one cigarette remained, and when she finished the last of the figures, she went out on the porch to smoke it, sitting down on the front step just as the stockier man from the basement—whom she had nicknamed "Rottweiler" in her mind—came around the side of the house.

He reached her in a few steps, snatching the cigarette from her lips and stomping it out. "Are you fucking crazy?" he asked her.

She stared at him.

"You can't smoke here."

Jadranka looked around her at the sagging porch, and the weeds that had driven up between some of the slats like tiny yellow knives. There was nothing remotely flammable, and she frowned. "Why the hell not?" she asked him.

"We use chemicals in the basement," he hissed. "One spark and we'll all go up in smoke."

"For tool and die?"

Something moved in his throat. "Of course for tool and die."

"Okay," she told him easily. "Now I know."

But he only turned on his heel, muttering something about the stupidity of women.

She should have left then. She should have walked calmly away, pretending to make another foray to the strip mall. She had already asked directions to the bus depot and knew that buses departed for points north every hour.

Instead she waited until the two men left for the day, watching their van from the second floor until it disappeared.

There was a locked door in the kitchen that obviously led to the basement. It had an old-fashioned keyhole, but she could tell by looking at the gap between the door and frame that the lock was not engaged, prompting her to conclude that the door was padlocked from the other side.

It was a strange precaution for a tool-and-die business, even one run illegally out of a basement. *Walk away,* said the same voice that had been speaking to her for days. *Just pack your things and go.*

She had not ventured behind the house since her arrival, but now she observed that the basement door used by the two men was reinforced steel. She was about to give up and return to the house when she saw it: a small rectangular window at ankle height, almost hidden in the weeds.

Before she could think better of it, she dropped to her stomach and pushed the window inward. She understood that the house—and Darko—were trouble, but she was curious to see what happened in the basement. She suspected that it was used to store stolen property, and anyway, she had always had a talent for extricating herself from difficult situations. If Rottweiler appeared on the scene, she was capable of thinking up some excuse.

The window was barely wide enough for her shoulders. She slid through it up to her waist, bracing herself against the inside wall with her hands so that she felt like the figurehead of a ship, allowing her eyes to adjust to the gloom. When they did, she was able to make out a long table with a jumble of vials and beakers. Rather than flat-screen televisions and piles of jewelry, there were large drums and a profusion of plastic vats. She had been wrong about the stolen property, but whatever went on in the basement had nothing to do with tools, either.

She assumed that the workshop was for drugs or explosives, and she cursed her own stupidity. She would need to leave tonight, after all. She had enough for a bus ticket to Maine and a few meals. Darko could go fuck himself as far as she was concerned. But as she pulled herself back, her elbow caught the open window, sending a shock wave of pain down her arm and leaving a star-shaped fracture in the glass.

"You're bleeding," a familiar voice said from behind her.

She went completely still, but he had already wrapped a hand around her ankle and was dragging her back so roughly that both elbows scraped the ground. He did not give her a chance to respond but turned her neatly over with his foot.

The sun was behind him, and she blinked.

"What am I going to do with you, *mila?*" Darko asked her.

He took her to the room where she had been sleeping, propelling her up the stairs so quickly that she twice lost her footing. He stared only for a moment at the picture of a sailboat on the landing.

"It's nothing to do with me," she told him when he pointed at the mattress, then pushed her when she did not sit.

He sat on the windowsill across from her, arms crossed. "Why did you have to complicate things?" he asked in a voice so reasonable that only now did she begin to feel afraid. "Haven't I been fair with you?"

She nodded. "More than fair."

"Why then?"

She swallowed. In English, she told him nervously, "Curiosity killed the cat?"

He rose at this. "Stupid cat," he told her, almost gently. But there was nothing gentle about the way he pulled her to her feet again, propelling her towards the open window so that for a moment she thought that he was going to throw her out.

"Look at that drop."

She took in the two and a half stories that separated them from the ground.

"There's no way out of this room," he told her. "Try it and I'll bury you in the garden."

A part of her was tempted to laugh. The threat sounded like something from a film about the Russian mob, but when she looked at his face, she found no hint of make-believe.

"If that happens, there's no chance of your sister finding you."

For a moment, Jadranka forgot to breathe. "I don't have a sister."

But he only smiled at this bluff. "She's looking for you. She even came into my bar yesterday."

"My sister is in Croatia."

"Your sister is in New York."

When he saw Jadranka's expression, he gave a bark of laughter. "Don't worry, *mila*. She's not my type. Too skinny and I don't like irritable women—"

Jadranka closed her eyes.

"On the other hand, it wouldn't hurt her to learn a little respect."

"Respect," Jadranka echoed, remembering that word being wielded like a club.

When he closed the door behind him, turning a key in the lock, she sat down hard and faced the windowsill.

Outside, it was growing dark, but from the bedroom window she watched him walk to his car, where he sat for a time with the engine running. He was talking to somebody on his telephone, and as she watched he struck the steering wheel with his open palm. Her elbows burned, and she could feel the stickiness of blood, but she did not take her eyes off that car. If he turned off the engine and walked back towards the house, she knew that she could kiss this life goodbye.

But five minutes later he tossed the telephone onto the seat beside him and drove off.

She had never mentioned a sister to Darko. She was too careful and, in fact, had made up a different family name, inventing an entire history to go with it. But the description—*skinny* and *irritable*—was unmistakable, and for the first few minutes after his departure, she sat on the floor shaking.

Magdalena's face came to her, white and furious, hatcher of plans and purveyor of rat poison. Of course she had come to America. Of course she had. And so Jadranka dragged herself to her feet again, imagining that dark head nodding.

The door did not budge, even when she kicked it, and so she returned to the window, to that drop which took her breath away, damning herself that she had been too cheap to do more than buy a single sheet for the mattress. Two sheets might have delivered her halfway to the ground, but one sheet would do almost nothing.

The overhang of the front porch was more than five feet away, and she could not imagine completing the Tarzan-like maneuver necessary to reach it. But when she felt around beneath the window, her hands brushed a thick cable or cord affixed to the side of the house. Staples would never support her weight, she knew, but when she leaned forward, she could feel a solid metal bracket. Two feet below that one, she could just make out a second.

She threw her backpack out the window first, watching as it landed in a thorny bush below her, then wrapped the sheet around herself to protect her bare arms. Darko had taken her shoes, but once on the windowsill she flipped onto her stomach and felt gingerly for the bracket with her sock-covered foot. When she at last made painful contact with the metal, she lowered her other foot, finding the next and letting go of the windowsill with one hand. She hung there for a moment, easing her weight slowly onto the brackets and grasping the cord with a shaking hand.

It was as she reached the third bracket that she felt herself peel away from the wall. She fell for most of the first floor, landing in the bush with the cord still clenched in her hands. The sheet did little to protect her from the thorns, and she crawled away from the house on hands and knees, panting.

The house behind her was dark, and it came to her that for once she could not simply walk away, as had been her plan. Not when Darko knew about her sister. She imagined Magdalena coming here. Magdalena who would not give up, who would instead follow her trail like a bloodhound. She imagined Darko intercepting her at the front door, inviting her to come inside, all smiles and false promises. She had misjudged the situation badly, she now realized.

The house's front door was unlocked, a fact that suggested he would be back soon. But it took only a moment to find an empty glass bottle in the kitchen. Days ago, she had found the rusted tin of Sterno beneath the sink, and she carried these outside again with the leftover twine.

She was still wrapped in the sheet. It billowed behind her like a rogue winding cloth, but she cast it off and seized it in both hands. The fabric would not give, no matter how her knuckles burned, but when she used her teeth she was able to tear off a piece with a satisfying sound.

She hung the larger section on the washing line and, after a moment of deliberation, took off her shirt, which she hung beside it.

Her hands trembled as she used a stick to empty the Sterno onto the smaller scrap of sheet, smearing it on the cloth as best she could without her hands, then stuffing it into the bottle. The can had only been a quarter full, and she decided that it was the most pitiful Molotov cocktail that had ever been made. She carried a plastic lighter in her pocket, and now she flicked it nervously, careful to keep the flame away from the cloth.

Behind the house, she nudged the same small window with her foot, the broken pane of glass shining as it swung inward.

She would have to throw it close to the table, a problem because she could no longer make out anything inside. As she lowered herself to her knees, she half expected to hear Darko's voice again, to feel his hands around her neck this time, and so she felt something approaching joy when the cloth caught in a burst of blue flame.

She threw it in the general direction of the table, watching its arc light up the beakers, vats, and vials. She had aimed well, and it rolled along the table until stopping beside a container that trailed a piece of rubber tubing. She did not really expect it to work, but the voice inside her head said *Run,* and by the time the bottle shattered she had nearly reached the wood.

The explosion was deafening. At first she thought that Darko had found her, that he had thrown his entire weight against her. It was black and feral, this thing at her back. She could feel its teeth in her neck, and all she could do was cover her face with her arms just before crashing into one of the trees.

The impact stunned her, and she landed on the ground face up. Before losing consciousness, she thought she saw his face above her. Nikola's, perhaps. Or even her father's, and she wondered if this had been the face her mother watched as she, Jadranka, had come into being.

He placed a boot in the center of her chest and smiled in the dancing light of the fire.

CHAPTER 19

The explosion made the morning newscast in New York City. Katarina was watching the television with half an eye as she buttered toast, and Jazmin readied the children for summer camp in the next room. Ana was asleep upstairs, but Magdalena had not yet stumbled in from wherever she had been spending her nights, a mystery Katarina had so far resisted the urge to ask about.

The volume was turned low, and so she did not hear the newscaster describe the suspected meth lab, nor did she see the man with the shaved head being led out of a Queens apartment building in the early morning hours, turning his face—spectral in the camera light—into the shadow of a squad car. Had she been listening, it might have registered that his name was Croatian, but he meant nothing to her and she would not have recognized his face.

It was Jazmin who saw the wreckage of the house, the charred debris spread across the property as if the grass itself had combusted, beams of wood still smoldering as news helicopters circled overhead. Passing through the kitchen on the trail of a stray shoe, she clucked her tongue at the screen and then exited again, prompting Katarina to look up in time to see a sooty sheet and T-shirt hanging from a laundry line. And while the cameras returned in the next instant to the newscaster's face, Katarina lowered her knife to the counter as if the blood supply to her hand had run out.

Jadranka was fond of that T-shirt and wore it often. She had designed the stylized picture of waves for a friend who ran a Split tattoo parlor, and the friend had been so pleased that he had repaid her by putting it on a shirt. The blue tones were startling against Jadranka's pale skin, and it was one of the first items that Magdalena had looked for in her closet upstairs, taking its absence as further proof—Katarina knew—that her sister would not be back.

Downstairs, the front door opened and closed, Magdalena's footsteps echoing on the stairs. By the time she entered the kitchen, Katarina had turned the television's volume up, despite the fact that a Labrador puppy was now advertising the softness of toilet paper.

"Good morning," Magdalena said stiffly behind her.

But Katarina could not face her in light of this thing beginning to take shape.

"Sit down," she said instead of turning. "And listen."

The police had questioned Darko briefly in New York City before remanding him to New Jersey. Moments after hanging up the telephone with her local precinct, Katarina was navigating her car towards the Lincoln Tunnel, Magdalena staring intently at the slow-moving Buick in front of them as if she hoped to vaporize it through sheer will.

"All this fuss over a shirt," Ana muttered from the back. "That probably isn't even hers."

"It's hers," Magdalena told her, but did not turn around.

For the past hour the details of the newscast had been going through Magdalena's head: *Suspected illegal activity . . . neighbors evacuated . . . fire department on the scene.* But at no point had there been any mention of a red-haired woman, and she clung to this fact.

She had no doubt that it was the same Darko who owned the bar on Steinway Street, which she had called only two days before. The woman who answered in Croatian claimed never to have heard of Jadranka.

Something about the exchange had struck Magdalena as strange at the time. Perhaps it was the way the woman covered the mouthpiece of the telephone, not entirely muffling the annoyed male response in the background. Or perhaps it was the woman's voice, as artificially bright as a halogen bulb in winter: *Sorry, but we've never heard of your sister.*

That couldn't be right. According to Damir, every Croatian in Queens knew of Jadranka the red-haired *Rosmarinka,* who had disappeared somewhere among the tenements and subway tunnels of America.

Magdalena and Damir had gone to the bar that night, standing for a few minutes on the pavement outside as music pulsed in raw waves each time the door swung open. Inside, a black light had made shirts and teeth glow like a haunted house. In many ways it resembled a discotheque from home, something she had not set foot in since her twenties. But there was a manic undercurrent to Club Darko that made Magdalena scan the women's made-up faces uneasily, relieved that her sister was not among them.

"Where's Darko?" Damir had shouted to get the attention of a passing waitress.

In the moment before she turned to point him out, Magdalena saw the man standing at the end of the bar, studying his mobile phone. He was easily three times her size, with the flattened nose of a prizefighter. *Please don't let that be him,* she had thought as the waitress gestured in his direction.

She did not so much walk towards him as launch herself in his direction, Damir at her heels. "Wait—" he was telling her.

But the shaved head was already lifting at her approach.

"I'm looking for my sister," she said, raising her voice above the music. "Jadranka Babić."

He shrugged and turned away. "No idea."

It was the way he spoke without looking at her that had made her suspicious. "Are you sure?" she shouted, prompting a few of the men at the bar to look uneasily in her direction. "She came here a few months ago."

"A lot of people come here. Why would I remember any of them?" He continued to scroll through his telephone. When she did not move, he lifted his head at last. "Do you have a picture?"

She fumbled in her purse for the photograph she carried, aware of his amusement as he watched her. When he took it, he whistled long and low. "Not bad," he told her, handing it back. "I bet a girl like that gets up to all sorts of things. Are you sure she wants to be found?"

Magdalena felt her eyes narrow. *"Majmune,"* she told him. "I'm surprised your knuckles don't drag on the ground."

"Majmune?" he asked, the amused look still on his face. He pushed himself off the bar to his full height, and it was then that she saw the metal butt, half hidden by his jacket.

She stared at it.

"Time to leave," he said to Damir.

Ordinarily, Magdalena could sniff out danger the same way that a dog picked up the scent of blood. It was the only gift that Nikola had given her: this second sense, this ability to detect the savagery in others. It was enough for her to have a conversation with somebody or to lock eyes with them on the street. A single moment could tell her everything she needed to know. But still, the gun surprised her.

She allowed Damir to propel her towards the exit, but when they reached the street, she shook him off. An alley ran alongside the bar, and she made for this, for the shadow at the far end. She braced herself against a wall just as he caught up with her.

"Lena—" he said, but she was already bent over at the waist, the music from inside vibrating against her hand.

The explosion had taken place in Basking Ridge, New Jersey, but Darko and two other men were being held at a police station in neighboring Morristown. When Magdalena arrived with Katarina and Ana, a detective led them to a small, windowless room. Short and broad shouldered, with a helmet of graying hair, the detective reminded Magdalena of the older Scandinavian visitors who descended upon Rosmarina in the off-season. She took their statement with the same single-mindedness those women exhibited when hiking up the Peak in matching anoraks.

"When was the last time you heard from your sister?"

"Nearly two months ago."

The detective wrote this down, then excused herself, returning a short time later with a plastic bag.

It was Ana who began to moan, a sound that made the hair on Magdalena's arms rise. Belatedly she understood that her mother believed a piece of Jadranka to be inside the bag. "Shut up," she told her in fierce Croatian, angry that their mother would give up so easily.

She recognized the T-shirt at once, despite the sooty perforations in the cloth. They looked like cigarette burns, but the detective hastened to explain that the holes had been caused by debris from the house's explosion.

"It was pure chance that the laundry line didn't burn in the fire," she told Magdalena. "The force of the explosion traveled up, and in the opposite direction."

She tapped her pencil against a photograph of the property, the first in a stack. Blackened ground extended from the charred wreckage of the house all the way to a line of trees. Magdalena studied it before passing it to her mother and cousin.

Ana looked at the photographs mechanically, shaking her head at each one, but when she got to the single photograph of the laundry line—the T-shirt hanging beside a sheet—she stared at it.

"What is it?" Katarina asked.

Ana did not respond, studying the image as if she half-expected Jadranka to emerge in order to reclaim the T-shirt once again.

The detective had been watching them during this interchange, and Magdalena addressed her in English, pointing at the design of blue waves in the plastic bag. "This is my sister's."

The detective's pen made a scratching sound as she added this detail—officially—to her report.

Katarina straightened. "Have you found a body?"

Magdalena glared at her, but the detective shook her head. She picked up an aerial shot of the wooded property. "Along the periphery of the fire are things we can recognize. These were thrown out during the explosion. But the center . . ."

Magdalena looked at the charred black hole on the photo beneath her finger.

"We're running tests now."

"But?" Magdalena prompted her.

"The suspect has already admitted that a young woman matching your sister's description was staying in the house, in an upstairs room."

Magdalena felt a sudden pain beneath her navel. It was like something clawing at her from the inside, and she was only dimly aware of the way that Katarina raised a hand to cover her face.

"What did she say?" her mother muttered in Croatian, continuing to stare at the photograph of the laundry line. When Katarina translated the words, Ana's mouth tightened, but she did not look up.

The detective cleared her throat. Something else about her struck Magdalena as familiar, and for the first time as an adult, she saw very clearly the day when Pero Radić had come to inform them that her father was dead, the fisherman's face wearing the same expression of pity and discomfort.

"I'm sorry," the woman was saying. "But the fire reached such high temperatures that there may not be anything left to find."

It would end like this, Magdalena thought. A dead end. A wall. A canvas so blank that it could render one blind. She would return to Rosmarina empty-handed, and her sister would be nothing more than a cautionary tale that island mothers told their children.

There would be no more sketches. No more long red hairs, which Jadranka left behind her on every visit to the island, not knowing that Magdalena often rescued them from the bathroom floor, holding them in the light of the window before letting them float into the courtyard, believing that her sister would return for as long as there was a part of her on Rosmarina.

Outside the police station, she leaned against Katarina's car and closed her eyes.

She felt hands on her arms, and for a moment she allowed herself to be pulled forward into her mother's embrace—something she had not permitted for years, decades perhaps—before pushing her away. "I'm fine," she mumbled.

It was her mother who insisted on seeing the property.

"Cousin Ana," Katarina said softly. "I don't think there's anything to see."

"I don't care," Ana retorted. "I still want to see."

And so they drove there in silence, behind a school bus that stopped every few blocks, a stream of children pouring from its doors. More children—Magdalena thought—than could surely fit inside. And at every stop, groups of mothers waited for them. Mothers in shorts and T-shirts. Mothers with strollers. Mothers with ponytails, chatting to one another in the shade of oak trees.

The property was at the end of a dead-end street and had been cordoned off by yellow police tape. The fire had been extinguished during the early morning hours, and the three women sat silently in the car, looking at the gap between the trees in front of them. A blackened chimney was all that remained, and off to one side, the laundry line was bizarrely white where the sheet and T-shirt had hung.

"Strange that there aren't any police cars," Katarina muttered.

There was nobody, in fact, the evacuated houses dark and ghostly on either side, the air so still that no leaf or blade of grass moved.

Ana was the first to exit the car. She walked resolutely towards the police cordon, then stopped. She placed a hand on the yellow tape that was tied around the trunks of trees as if debating whether to snap it in two. Magdalena and Katarina did not move, and a moment later Ana returned, an intent look on her face. She walked to Magdalena's side and opened the door.

"Come," she told her elder daughter.

Magdalena ignored her.

"Come, I said."

Magdalena wanted only to leave, to put as much distance between herself and that length of burnt ground, but Ana's face was determined, and so she allowed her mother to pull her from the passenger seat.

"I don't think you're supposed to—" Katarina began, but then fell silent.

Her mother led her to the tape, then lifted it so that Magdalena could pass beneath. For a few moments, Ana paced back and forth inside the tape's perimeter, nose lifted to the air, as her daughter watched.

"She's dead, Mama."

It had been a long time since Magdalena had called her mother by that name, and she did not know what made her use it now, but it caused Ana to turn slowly and approach Magdalena, who steeled herself for another embrace.

Instead her mother took Magdalena by the arms and shook her. "The photograph," she said.

Magdalena frowned. "What are you talking about?"

"Think, girl."

"You've lost your mind," she said, throwing off her mother's hands.

But Ana had spied the laundry line. She approached it carefully, then pulled as if testing its tautness. *"Think,"* she repeated, more insistently this time, and turned.

Magdalena only looked at her blankly.

"Your grandfather's stories."

Katarina was still sitting in the car. Through the windshield, the cousins' eyes locked, and Magdalena shrugged.

"When things were all right, when it was safe for your grandfather to come home, his sister always placed the sheet first, closest to the house."

"The sheet wasn't first."

"Of course not," her mother snapped in exasperation. "Your sister was trying to warn you."

"Me?"

"Of danger."

Her mother had finally lost it, Magdalena thought in that moment.

"Which means that she had time."

"For what?"

But Ana did not answer, making a beeline for the trees at the back of the property.

Magdalena watched her go. She wanted only to return to her cousin's car, to fall asleep and wake up to find that she was back on Rosmarina. But when she looked in Katarina's direction, a squad car was approaching with silent, flashing lights.

Katarina had seen it, too. She got out of the car and closed the door, turning to look at her cousin. "Go," she mouthed.

Magdalena's mother was surprisingly quick. For a middle-aged woman who had lived three decades in a city of stone and concrete, she navigated the uneven ground with remarkable agility.

"For Christ's sake, slow down," Magdalena told her, following the back that disappeared every few seconds only to reappear, the cheap yellow material of her blouse—doubtless purchased from one of the stalls in Split's marketplace—bobbing like a flashlight.

But her mother ignored her.

Magdalena's anger built as they went deeper into the woods. It was their mother's fault that they were here. Her fault that Jadranka was dead.

At this final realization, she stopped. "It's because of you!" she shouted at her mother's back.

Ana slowed for only a moment.

"All of this happened because of you."

She moved out of sight again, and for a moment Magdalena thought she had not heard, but then a retort came floating back: "Poor Magdalena. Always crying about the past."

In that moment, Magdalena wanted to abandon her mother to the spiders and mosquitoes, to the vines that hung from the trees like nooses, and the burrs that had already lodged themselves in her socks. But they had come far enough that she was unsure of the direction back.

"My father killed himself because of you!" she shouted at the underbrush.

Something rustled in front of her, but it was only a squirrel, and Magdalena dropped onto the decomposing trunk of a fallen tree. She bent forward and pressed her forehead into the heels of her hands.

Her mother's return was more laborious, and Magdalena did not look up even when two feet in flat cork sandals appeared in front of hers, the stockings around the ankles shredded and flecked with blood.

Ana's voice, when it came, was more tired than angry. "Look here, girl, you think I went with him by choice?"

Magdalena lifted her head in shock. "What?"

But Ana had already turned. "None of your business," she said, over her shoulder.

Magdalena started after her. But her foot caught on something—a root or a vine—and she landed in bracken with thorns so sharp that she cried out in spite of herself.

When Ana retraced her steps a second time, she stood above her daughter for a long moment, the woods so dark that Magdalena could barely see the features of her face.

"I'm caught," she told her mother miserably, bucking so that the bracken shook.

In the end it was mainly her hair that pinned her to the ground, caught in the brambles of that bush, and both women were silent as Ana untangled it.

"You never said anything," Magdalena accused her, still lying on the ground.

But Ana put a finger to her daughter's lips, a gesture that made Magdalena feel unexpectedly like weeping.

"Why didn't you?"

Her mother lowered her head, and instinctively Magdalena lifted her face as she had once done long ago at bedtime. Before Split. Before Jadranka, perhaps. But her mother did not kiss her forehead. She took each of Magdalena's ears in her hands, not painfully, but not gently either. "Some things," she said, "belong only to the people who lived them."

Magdalena thought that they must be miles from the road now. Miles from Katarina's car and the quick talking that her cousin must be doing to explain why she was parked at the scene of a crime. Or perhaps they were not far away at all. Magdalena had lost all sense of direction, following her mother silently for the last five minutes, so that she was not sure if they had walked a straight path or in circles.

Several times Magdalena thought that she saw things in the wood: a symmetrical scattering of stones or leaves that formed a pattern on the surfaces of large rocks. But each time she investigated these configurations, she decided that nature had left them there by chance.

Fairy houses, she remembered suddenly. Her sister had built fairy houses as a child, taught by a German-speaking summer visitor who had shown her how to build the tiny structures with stones and sticks. He had been accompanied by his two children. Little girls, Magdalena seemed to remember. Jadranka had spent the afternoon with them, continuing to construct the houses for years afterwards, decorating their pitched roofs with bougainvillea blossoms, pinecones, and sea glass.

Once, as a joke, Magdalena had brought her the bleached spines of a long-dead sea urchin. "You can build a booby trap to keep intruders out," she had teased her sister. But Jadranka declined, telling her sister in utter seriousness that she did not wish to booby-trap anybody.

There it was again, and Magdalena stopped. This time a pile of stones in the shape of a long and winding snake.

Up ahead, Ana had also slowed. She was wheezing softly, and Magdalena was about to suggest turning back—not for the first time—when her mother stopped. "Look," she ordered, staring at something on the ground.

But now Magdalena saw only ferns and leaves and rotting branches.

Her mother dropped stiffly to her knees, crawling forward a few feet. "Look," she ordered again, so that Magdalena knelt as well, the damp earth soaking the fabric of her jeans.

It was when Magdalena followed the line of her mother's arm that she saw it, the long sticks heaped in an orderly pile. They

were all approximately the same length and beyond them was another pile. And another.

She sat back. The sticks were as straight as arrows, each with a
sharpened point.

"It's her," Ana said.

They heard her before they saw her, the scraping of stone
against wood like something burrowing through dry ground.

Magdalena was on her feet in an instant. Ahead in a clearing,
a woman lowered her rock. She looked as if she were building a
raft in preparation for a flood. Her back was white, her bra soaked
through with sweat and blood. But even in the shadows Magdalena recognized her.

"Jadranka."

The figure picked up another stick, as if she had not heard her
name. "Is he coming?" she asked.

Magdalena covered the ground quickly, pulling her sister to her
feet. She placed a hand on Jadranka's cheek, which was hot to the
touch and smeared with dirt. Looking down, Magdalena saw that
her sister was shoeless, and that she still held a stick in one hand
like a spear.

"What are you doing?" Magdalena asked softly, aware that Jadranka's hair was matted with blood.

At this question her sister dropped the spear. "Getting ready,"
she said, as though it should have been obvious.

"For what?"

"For when he comes back."

"He isn't coming back," Magdalena told her. "And you're
bleeding."

"Am I?"

Jadranka's eyes glittered like a madwoman's, and Magdalena realized then that she was feverish. "We need to find a hospital," she
said.

Magdalena was several inches shorter, but when Jadranka did

not respond, she pulled her younger sister forward until her face was buried in Magdalena's neck, her eyes watering at the burnt and metallic smell of Jadranka's hair. When she lifted an uncertain hand to Jadranka's head, she realized that the back was singed all the way to the scalp and that the blood came from a cut in her scalp. "We need—" she began again, but Jadranka cut her off.

"You're sure he's gone?"

Magdalena was suddenly afraid to speak, uncertain what it was that her sister was asking. In her mind she was already guiding Jadranka through the woods, her sister's body like a flame.

And so it was their mother who responded. "They're all gone, *mila*."

PART VI

CHAPTER 20

Luka is getting ready to walk out, to shed this body that has become a cage. They will have to burn the sheets, he thinks with some regret. They were a part of his wife's dowry and, in their day, as white as the flakes he had once seen fall during a freak snowstorm upon the sea. But he is certain that his body has discolored them, that it has left an oblong shadow in the shape of a man.

There are a great many footsteps in the house now. They tramp up and down the stairs, and he thinks that he can even hear them up on the roof. They shuffle through the courtyard beneath his window, and in the lane beyond the wall. The gate opens and closes, and he can tell that the latch is rusting because of the scraping sound it makes.

He knows that it is the salt air that corrodes everything. It eats away at bolts and paper clips, the metal parts of engines and the undercarriages of cars.

His daughter had owned a fancy silver mirror once. He remembers that the rust had risen in furrows behind the glass, and that each day she looked in it there was less of her.

What he knows: his son has returned and weeps in the chair beside his bed. He speaks strangely, as if he has forgotten how, but the timbre of his voice is the same.

His daughter worries at her necklace in the corner of the room, where the longest shadows stretch. She twists it until the thing snaps and its beads scatter across the floor.

Lena searches the floor on her hands and knees, retrieving the tiny pieces of perforated glass. She drops them into a tarnished metal dustpan so that each one makes a sound like a fat raindrop hitting a sturdy leaf. She misses a few but comments that she will search for them another time.

He knows by the way her voice tightens that this will happen on a day when he is already gone, but he also knows that they will never find all the beads. That they have slid so far between the wooden floorboards that they will remain there for as long as the house is standing, and he smiles very faintly at this thought. Somewhere, centuries from this day, perhaps, a child will discover one of the beads and roll it around his mouth with his tongue.

He knows that his wife sits at her kitchen table below him. That while she is relieved to have them all surrounding her, she also longs for those days of quiet when she heard only his breathing in the house, when she thought that he could continue like this for as long as they both were living and that when the appointed hour came, she would crawl into the bed as well and walk out with him.

Rosmarina, he longs to tell her despite her devoutness. *It is my final destination.*

The island has a history that stretches back through centuries of settlers and marauders, centuries of people who, like him, have been blessed by chance. Its residents' bloodlines are so mixed that untangling them would be as impossible as it is pointless. In addition to the happy unions that propagate the human race, he wonders now how many rapes and murders, how many kidnappings, illicit trysts, and unhappy couplings have gone into the making of any one person.

But the island is constant. It existed before the name by which it is now known. There have been Greek names, Illyrian names, names that existed before man became conceited enough to record his own history. Those names are lost in the present. The bays that he has navigated have seen generations of fishermen and sailors, naval battles and deaths at sea. And the bays will remain, he thinks, long after he is gone.

Days collide and the sea becomes the air. There are fish swimming through his room, and the smell of paint rises from the courtyard beneath his window.

He knows that it is Lena, that the others will leave again and she alone will stay. She has whispered something else in his ear, and he imagines that she is carrying a little girl, dark and strong, who will learn to fish the channel between Rosmarina and its neighbors like her mother. Perhaps it is the grandchild of this girl's grandchild who will one day find the bead, but he knows that these things are by no means predetermined.

He imagines that Marin stands behind Magdalena in the courtyard, that he is watching her prepare the boat, at last, for the sea. He imagines her small hands sanding the wood and applying the varnish, just as he has shown her.

His daughter sits on the stone bench, smoking and watching them. She refuses to sing, a little wearily, and tells them that she doesn't bother to remember any of the old songs anymore. Her brother tells her that this would be a mean trick: to forget exactly the things she chooses.

And it is Magdalena who begins to sing, her voice out of tune and missing some of the notes altogether, so that her mother laughs and tells her that it's a good thing she likes her job because she should not hope for a career in music. And so Ana gives in at last.

It is an old song that she sings. It was popular in his youth, but he cannot remember it being sung in years, decades perhaps. It is like finding something he has not realized is missing.

When she has finished, his wife's voice calls out that it is time for dinner, and he hears them filing into the house below him, and their voices disappear from the garden the same way that stars fade one by one at dawn.

He picks the same track he has walked a thousand times, the one that leads upward through the town and to the olive groves beneath the Peak. When he arrives, the light is thin and he must feel his way from trunk to trunk. He finds the sturdiest among them, and as he buries his face at its base, he hears his sisters laughing from the ground.

EPILOGUE

Five years later

His aunt has sent him a picture of his name. In a letter that ac-
companies the flat cardboard envelope, she explains that it is
an exercise she has done for school, and she is glad he does not
have a name with many letters.

From the *L* she has made a drawing of Rosmarina's lighthouse,
a length of the *riva* at its feet. *U* is the hull of a boat that plies a
very blue sea. For *K* she has chosen an overhang of rock on the
Peak, with small olive trees that cling to the slopes of the letter. *A*
is the boy's great-grandmother, and although the figure is clad in
black from her skirt to the kerchief that holds back her hair, her
cheeks are a soft pink, and the boy recognizes her at once.

Magdalena hangs the picture over the bed in his room. She is
aware that he watches it until he falls asleep, especially the figure
of a small boy that her sister has drawn just above it, who lies on
his stomach and holds a pencil as if he has just finished drawing
those letters himself.

"It's me," he tells her in excitement, pointing at the figure's
familiar head of dark hair, the shirt that is identical to a photograph she had sent her sister some weeks before with the message
He's getting so big that you'll hardly recognize him.

The boy has a vague picture of his aunt because she has visited the island only a few times since his birth. He remembers her red hair and recognizes her photograph, the one where his mother stands beside her and the two women have linked their arms and are smiling into the camera. He opens each envelope with anticipation, never sure what he will find inside, and the drawings arrive so regularly that they paper the walls of his room.

It is not like his father, who is often gone to places with names he cannot pronounce. Places like Kandahar and Havana and Durban that sound as if they come from storybooks. His father has given him a map, and when he is at home the two of them sit together at the kitchen table—Magdalena watching them with a smile over the assignments she is grading—and place little pins in all those distant places. The map had frightened him at first because when his father showed him Rosmarina, it was so small that it appeared like a speck of dust in all that vastness.

He has been to Split several times with his mother, a ferry ride so long that their passage seems to take days, although his mother shows him the elapsing hours on her watch, the big hand that moves quickly and the small hand that hardly seems to move at all. But the distance on the map is tiny, so that when his father shows him the places he goes on his trips, Luka is under the impression that it takes his father weeks to get there, then weeks to get back.

He recognizes his father's voice because he hears it regularly on his mother's radio. He is aware even at the age of four that it is much more serious than the voice he hears through the telephone each Friday. He has also heard his aunt's voice because she sometimes calls from New York, a city that is marked on the map with a special red pin. His aunt is studying art there, and his mother explains that students do not have much money and therefore cannot make many telephone calls to Rosmarina.

His cousins José and Adriano live in New York, as well. He likes them because whenever they visit Rosmarina with their parents, they teach him the Spanish names for things, words he forgets between visits but which his uncle Marin explains have planted themselves in his mind like seedlings.

This summer his mother is teaching him to swim, and every afternoon they walk to a shallow cove where she slides from the rocks first, making sure that there are no urchins in the way. He is a brave boy, but he is frightened of those black creatures with their ruffling spines, and he is glad each time she holds her arms out to him so that she can lift him away from the rocks where they may be hiding.

She will not buy him inflatable water wings like the tourist children often wear. "No, Luka," she has explained. "You're an islander, and that means you must learn to really swim."

But he likes the idea of those bright plastic doughnuts that keep other children afloat and watches jealously as they kick their feet and swim as far from shore as the grown-ups. They do not have to worry about their heads dipping beneath the surface and swallowing salty water that burns their noses.

"What if all the air goes out of them?" his mother asks him reasonably. She points to the distance, where the Devil's Stones loom. "What if you get out there and you don't know how to swim?"

He had not thought of this and concedes that this would be a problem, and besides, he likes their lessons. He lies back in the water, stretching out his arms and legs. For him, swimming is coolness and the sun that is always warm upon his face. He likes his mother's cheerful green bathing suit and the long, wet hair that she usually pins back. He likes that even when she removes her hands, insisting that he must learn to do it on his own, they are always somewhere there below him.

ACKNOWLEDGMENTS

I am indebted to the National Endowment for the Arts, Yaddo, the Bellagio Center, Künstlerhaus Schloss Wiepersdorf, and George Mason University. To Asya Muchnick, whose suggestions were so astute that they often took my breath away. To Elise Capron, who believed though the road was long. To Ethan Nosowsky and David Groff, who gave invaluable advice on early drafts. To my friends Maria Mayo, Laura Sims, Jennie Page, Nina Herzog, Mei Ng, and Meeghan Truelove, whose readings helped lift numerous fogs. To my mother, whose thoughtful comments helped shape this book. To my father, who gave me the sea. And to my husband, who ate each sack of salt with me so that I would not have to eat a single one of them alone.

ABOUT THE AUTHOR

Courtney Angela Brkic is the author of *Stillness: And Other Stories,* named a 2003 Best Book by the *Chicago Tribune,* a Notable Book by the *New York Times,* and a Barnes & Noble Discover pick. Her memoir *The Stone Fields* was short-listed for the Freedom of Expression Award by the Index on Censorship. Brkic has been the recipient of a Whiting Writers' Award and a fellowship from the National Endowment for the Arts. She teaches in the MFA program at George Mason University and lives outside Washington, DC.